Idiopathy

Idiopathy

SAM BYERS

FARRAR, STRAUS AND GIROUX

NEW YORK

Farrar, Straus and Giroux
175 Varick Street, New York 10014

Originally published in 2013 by Fourth Estate, Great Britain
Published in the United States in 2013 by Farrar, Straus and Giroux
First American paperback edition, 2014

Parts of this book originally appeared, in slightly different form, as "Some Other
Katherine" in issue 119 of *Granta*.

The Library of Congress has cataloged the hardcover edition as follows:
Byers, Sam, 1979–
    Idiopathy / Sam Byers. — First American edition.
      pages   cm
    ISBN 978-0-86547-764-3 (alk. paper)
    I. Title.

  PS3602.Y33 135 2013
  813'.6—dc23

                                        2012048026

        Paperback ISBN: 978-0-86547-812-1

Our books may be purchased in bulk for promotional, educational, or business use.
Please contact your local bookseller or the Macmillan Corporate and Premium Sales
Department at 1-800-221-7945, extension 5442, or by e-mail at
MacmillanSpecialMarkets@macmillan.com.

www.fsgbooks.com
www.twitter.com/fsgbooks • www.facebook.com/fsgbooks

idiopathy | ˌɪdɪˈɒpəθi

noun

A disease or condition which arises spontaneously
or for which the cause is unknown.

ORIGIN late 17th cent.: from modern Latin *idiopathia*,
from Greek *idiopatheia*, from
idios 'own, private' + -*patheia* 'suffering'.

Ubi pus, ibi evacua.

Comparatively recently, during a family function about which Katherine's mother had used the term *three-line whip*, but which Katherine's sister had nevertheless somehow avoided, Katherine's mother had shown a table of attendant relatives the photographs she kept in her purse. The relatives were largely of the aged kind, and their reliable delight in photos was a phenomenon Katherine had long been at a loss to understand. As far as she was concerned, ninety per cent of photographs (and relatives) looked the same. One grinning child was much like the next; one wedding was indistinguishable from another; and given that the majority of her family tended to holiday in depressingly predictable places, the resultant snaps of their trips abroad were fairly uniform too. So while the other relatives – Aunt Joan and Uncle Dick and their oddly wraith-like daughter, Isabel, plus two or three generic wrinklies who Katherine dimly remembered but with whom she had little interest in getting re-acquainted – cooed and hummed at the photos the way one might at a particularly appetising and well-arranged dessert, Katherine remained quiet and shuttled her eyes, as she so often did on these occasions, between the face of her mother and that of her watch, neither of which offered any reassurance that the event would soon be over.

Katherine's mother's purse, unlike the hands that held it, was smooth and new; recently purchased, Katherine happened to know, at Liberty, where Katherine's mother regularly stepped outside her means.

'What a lovely purse,' said some removed cousin or other, clearly aware that any accessory Katherine's mother produced in public had to elicit at least one compliment or else find itself summarily relegated to one of the sacks of abandoned acquisitions that she deposited with alarming regularity at the local charity shop. It struck Katherine that if the relatives had only shown a similar sense of duty when it came to the men in her mother's life, her mother might be living in quite different circumstances.

'Isn't it *darling*?' said Katherine's mother, true to form. 'Liberty. An absolute snip. Couldn't resist.'

The photos were remarkably well preserved considering that Katherine's mother treated the majority of objects as if they were indestructible and then later, peering forlornly at their defunct remains, bemoaned the essentially shoddy nature of modern craftsmanship.

'Look at these,' said Katherine's mother, referring to the photographs in exactly the same tone of voice as she'd used when discussing the purse. 'Aren't these just lovely?'

She passed round the first picture – a passport-sized black-and-white of Katherine's sister Hazel clasping a flaccid teddy. With its rolling eyes and lack of muscle tone, the little creature looked like it had been drugged, lending Hazel (in Katherine's eyes at least) the appearance of some sinister prepubescent abductor.

'The teddy was called Bloot,' said Katherine's mother as the photo went from hand to hand, 'although God knows why. It went all floppy like that after she was sick on it and we had to run it through the wash. There wasn't a thing that girl owned that she wasn't at some point sick on. Honestly, the constitution of a delicate bird.'

'Such a shame she couldn't be here today,' someone said.

'Oh, I know,' said Katherine's mother. 'But she doesn't have a moment to herself these days. She just works and works. And what with all this terrible cow business . . .'

Heads nodded in agreement, and although Katherine couldn't be sure, and would later convince herself she'd imagined it, she thought for a moment that more than one pair of eyes flicked her way in the reflex judgement typical of any family gathering: attendance was closely related to employment. People were grateful if you came, but then also assumed that your job was neither important nor demanding, since all the relatives with important and demanding jobs were much too busy to attend more than once a year, at which time they were greeted like knights returning from the Crusades and actively encouraged to leave throughout the day lest anything unduly interfere with their work. Katherine's sister had revelled in this role for several years now, and it irked Katherine that the less Hazel showed up, the more saintly and over-worked she became in everyone's minds, while the more Katherine put in appearances and made an effort to be attentive to the family, the more she was regarded as having wasted her life. It was, admittedly, slightly different on this occasion, given that half the roads were now closed on account of the cows. Everyone that had made it seemed grimly proud, as if they'd traversed a war zone. Katherine couldn't have cared less about the cattle, but she was enjoying the momentary respect her attendance seemed to have inspired.

The second photo was not produced until the first had completed its circuit. It was of Katherine's father, dressed in a waxed jacket and posing awkwardly with a shotgun.

'There's Nick,' said Katherine's mother. 'He didn't hit a thing, of course, but he enjoyed playing the part. He had all the kit, needless to say, but that was Nick. Strong on planning, poor in execution. I took that picture myself.'

She paused pointedly before passing it round, encouraging a few nods of sympathy from the aunts and uncles. Katherine's mother had, for as long as Katherine could remember, reliably played the sympathy card when discussing the man who had fathered her children, lingered a couple of years, and then decamped for Greece with a woman he'd met at the doctor's surgery while waiting to have his cholesterol levels checked. Katherine received two cards a year from her father, for Christmas and her birthday, with a third bonus card if she achieved anything noteworthy. He'd called her just once, soppy-drunk and clearly in the grip of a debilitating mid-life crisis, and told her always to beware of growing up to be like either of her parents.

The photograph circled the table and was followed, with precision timing, by a colour snapshot of Homer, the family dog, who, never the most intelligent of animals, had leapt to his death chasing a tennis ball over a series of felled trees, impaling himself on a shattered branch and leaving Katherine, who had thrown the ball, to explain to her mother why her precious mongrel was not only dead but in fact still needed to be prised from his branch, while her daughter remained inexplicably unharmed and unforgivably dry-eyed.

The next and, as it turned out, final photograph, was of Daniel, Christmas hat tipsily askew, raising a glass from his regal position behind a large roast turkey.

'Ahh,' said Katherine's mother. 'There's Daniel, look. Such a darling. Did you ever meet Daniel? Oh, of course, he came to that thing a few years ago. Such a charmer. I just adored him. Poor Katherine. He's the one that got away, isn't he, dear?'

'Not really,' said Katherine. 'No.'

'Still a rough subject,' said Katherine's mother, smiling at Katherine in a maternal fashion – something she only ever did in public. 'Daniel's doing ever so well these days, of course, unlike some, who shall remain nameless.' Her gaze, morphing like the liquid figures of a digital clock, became sterner. 'So easy to get *stuck*, isn't it?'

She slid the last picture back into the folds of her purse, snapped the clasp, and returned the purse to her handbag, leaving everyone to look once, briefly, at Katherine, and then gaze uncomfortably at the tabletop, silent until the welcome arrival of coffee, at which point Katherine politely excused herself in order to go to the bathroom and tear a toilet roll in half.

K atherine didn't like to think of herself as sad. It had a defeatist ring about it. It lacked the pizzazz of, say, rage or mania. But she had to admit that these days she was waking up sad a lot more often than she was waking up happy. What she didn't admit, and what she would never admit, was that this had anything whatsoever to do with Daniel.

It wasn't every morning, the sadness, although it was, it had to be said, more mornings than would have been ideal. Weekends were worst; workdays varied. The weather was largely inconsequential.

Time in front of the mirror didn't help. She got ready in a rush, then adjusted incrementally later. She hadn't been eating well. Things were happening to her skin that she didn't like. Her gums bled onto the toothbrush. It struck her that she was becoming ugly at a grossly inopportune time. Breakfast was frequently skipped in favour of something unhealthy midway through her working morning. She couldn't leave the house without a minimum of three cups of coffee inside her. Recently, she'd started smoking again. It helped cut the gloom. She felt generally breathless but coughed only on a particularly bad day. At some point during the course of her morning, any morning, she would have to schedule time for nausea.

For the past two years, Katherine, having moved from London to Norwich by mistake, had been the facilities manager at a local telecommunications company. Her job had nothing to do with telecommunications, but centred instead on the finer points of workplace management. She was paid, she liked to say, to be an obsessive compulsive. She monitored chairs for ongoing ergonomic acceptability and suitable height in relation to desks and workstations, which she checked in turn to ensure compliance with both company guidelines and national standards for safe and healthy working environments. She performed weekly fire alarm checks and logged the results. Each morning she inspected the building for general standards of hygiene, presentation and safety. She fired at least one cleaner per month. She was widely resented and almost constantly berated. People phoned or messaged at least every hour. Their chairs, their desks, the air conditioning, the coffee-maker, the water cooler, the fluorescent strip lighting – nothing was ever to their liking. The numerous changes Katherine was obliged to implement in order to keep step with current health and safety legislation made her the public advocate of widely bemoaned alterations. Smokers had to walk further from the building. Breaks had to be re-negotiated. Her job allowed no flexibility, meaning that she frequently came off as humourless and rigid. The better she was at her job, the more people hated her. By general consensus, Katherine was very good at her job.

Aside from the basic majority of colleagues who couldn't stand her, there also existed a splinter group comprising the men who wanted to fuck her. Katherine thought of them as contested territory. Some of them wanted to fuck her because they liked her, and some of them wanted to fuck her because they hated her. This suited Katherine reasonably well. Sometimes she fucked men because she felt good about herself, and sometimes she fucked them because she hated herself. The trick was to find the right man for the moment, because fucking a man who hated you during a rare moment of quite liking yourself was counter-productive, and fucking a man who was sort of in love with you at the peak of your self-hatred was nauseating.

To date, Katherine had fucked three men in her office, one of whom, Keith, she was still fucking on a semi-regular basis. The other two, Brian and Mike, had faded ingloriously into the middle distance, lost amidst the M&S suits and male-pattern baldness. Brian had been first. She'd broken her no-office rule for Brian and, with hindsight, he hadn't been anywhere near worth it. She'd broken her married-man rule too, and the rule about men with kids. She resented this because it seemed, in her mind and, she imagined, in the minds of others, to afford Brian a sense of history he in no way deserved. The reality was, at the time Katherine had made a conscious and not entirely irrational decision to jettison so many of the rules by which she had up to that point lived her life, Brian had happened to be in the immediate vicinity, and had happened, moreover, to be a living exemplar of several of those rules. Hence the sex, which took place quite suddenly one Tuesday afternoon after he drove her home, continued through to the following month, and then ended when Katherine began wondering if some of her rules had in actual fact been pretty sensible. Brian was fifty-something (another rule, now that she thought about it), fat, and in the midst of an epic crisis. He drove a yellow Jaguar and had a son called Chicane. They never finished with each other or anything so tiresome. Katherine simply ceased to acknowledge his existence and the message was quietly, perhaps even gratefully, received.

Mike was, on the outside at least, different. He was Katherine's age (thirty, although there was room for adjustment depending on her mood), single, and surprisingly good in bed. Even more surprisingly, Katherine found him to be capable of several almost full-length conversations when the mood took him. Their affair (it wasn't really an affair, but Katherine liked to define it as such because it added value to the experience and because she'd not long previously fucked Brian and was hoping, in a secret, never-to-be-admitted way, that she might be in a *phase* of having affairs, which would of course completely legitimise her sleeping with Mike) lasted almost two months. It ended when Mike found out that Katherine had slept with Brian. Much to Katherine's irritation, Mike turned out to be in possession of what he proudly called *a moral compass*. Katherine was not impressed. As far as she was concerned, morals were what dense people clung to in lieu of a personality. She told Mike as much after he tried to annex the high ground over the whole adultery issue. He ignored her. He couldn't respect her, he said. Katherine would always remember him walking away from the drinks cooler, shaking his head and muttering softly, *Poor Chicane . . . poor, poor Chicane.* She felt grimly vindicated. Mike didn't have any morals. He just had a bruised male ego and an inability to express himself.

All this, of course, had been a while ago, and there had been other, non-office-based men floating around during the same time period. Nothing had gone well. Katherine had started waking up sad a lot more often. The thing with her skin had started. She'd gained weight, then lost it, then lost a little more. Sleep was becoming increasingly difficult. Once, during a stretch of annual leave she'd taken purely to use up her quota and which she'd spent wearing a cereal-caked dressing gown and staring slack-faced at Nazis on the History Channel, she'd swallowed a fistful of pills and curled up in bed waiting to die, only to wake up five hours later in a puddle of vomit, many of the pills still whole in the mess. She had words with herself. She got dressed the next day and did her makeup and went into the city and collided with Keith, who suggested coffee, then food, then violent, bruising sex in his garage, her stomach pressed against the hot, ticking metal of his car bonnet.

'I remember once . . .' said Keith, lying back against the car afterwards, Katherine beside him, both of them smoking and waiting for the pain to subside. 'What was I . . . Fuck it, it's gone.'

There were days when it all seemed sordid and doomed; days which, oddly, Katherine romanticised more than the days of hope. There was something doomed about Keith generally, she thought, and she liked it. He was forty-one (because, she thought, once you'd broken a rule, it was no longer really a rule, and so couldn't be said to have been broken a second time); thin on top and thick round the middle. At work he wore crumpled linen and skinny ties. In the evenings he favoured faded black denims and battered Converse. He liked songs about blood and blackness: guitar-driven thrash-outs that made him screw up his face and clench his teeth like a man battling a bowel obstruction. He had pale, slightly waxy skin and grey eyes with a white ring around the iris. Katherine had read somewhere that this had medical implications but she couldn't remember what they were and so chose not to mention it. She liked the idea that Keith was defective; that he might be dying. She liked the fact that he was open about what he called his *heroin years*. She even liked the way he hurt her in bed: the sprained shoulder, the deep gouge on her left thigh. Keith was different in what Katherine saw as complementary ways. He would never love her, would probably never love anyone or anything, and Katherine admired this about him. He seemed beyond the concerns that threatened daily (yes, daily by now) to swallow her whole. By definition, of course, this also placed him beyond her, but she liked that too.

She didn't live in London. There were mornings when she had to stare forcefully into the mirror and repeat this to herself like a mantra. On a good morning she could just about say the name of her actual location, but it was hard. She and Daniel had moved here together, ostensibly for his job. There were unspoken implications regarding the pitter-patter of little feet. But announcements were not forthcoming, and then they broke up, and then London looked like it would be lonely, and now she was stuck.

Her mother rang with reliable frequency. Always a practical woman, Katherine's mother felt the best way to voice her concerns about Katherine's well-being was to be direct at all times. This seemed to involve repeatedly asking Katherine if she was OK, which of course had the effect of making Katherine feel a long way from OK.

'Are you eating enough?' her mother would say bluntly. 'Are you eating healthy foods?'

'Yes,' Katherine would say, midway through a doughnut. 'This morning I had porridge for breakfast, and for lunch I had a baked potato with tuna fish. For dinner I'm going to have grilled chicken breast.'

'Are you being facetious? Because it's unattractive you know. And not entirely mature.'

'I'm being honest. Is that mature?'

'That depends entirely,' said her mother, 'on what you're being honest about.'

She met with Keith only on selected evenings. They fucked and drank and rarely spoke, which suited Katherine. He bought her a vibrator as a present: gift-wrapped, with a heart-shaped tag that read 'Think of me'. She donated it, tag and all, to her local charity shop on her way to work, buried at the bottom of a carrier bag filled with musty paperbacks and a selection of Daniel's shirts she'd found amidst her archived clothes. She never saw it for sale, and wondered often what had become of it. She liked to think one of the elderly volunteers had taken it home and subjected herself to an experience so revelatory as to border on the mystical.

'Keith,' she said one evening, deliberately loudly, in a crowded restaurant she'd selected precisely because she knew it would be crowded when she asked the question. 'How many people are you fucking right now?'

'Including you?'

'Excluding me.'

'Three,' he said calmly. 'You?'

'Four,' she lied.

Is it Daniel?' her mother asked during one of her interminable phone calls. 'Because I understand, you know, I really do.'

'It's not Daniel, Mother.'

'He sent me a birthday card last week. He always sends me Christmas and birthday cards. Isn't that nice?'

'It's not nice,' said Katherine. 'It's anally retentive. He sends you cards because you're on his list. It's basically an automated response. It never occurs to him to change anything.'

'Does he send you cards?'

'No.'

She hated the idea that she might be the sort of person who had mummy issues. She was, or so she liked to think, much too alternative and free a person to find herself constrained by an unimaginative inability to slough off all those childhood hurts. That said, she wasn't entirely above the occasional girlish fantasy of dying and yet somehow still being able to watch her own funeral, where her mother would, she hoped, hurl herself, weeping like a Mafia wife, onto her coffin. As a child, Katherine had almost always imagined her death to be the result of suicide. Now, older as she was, and so much more aware of the utter lack of romanticism in killing herself, she imagined instead that some tragic external event would be responsible for her passing; something sudden and only just within the realm of possibility, such as being struck by lightning or pancaked by tumbling furniture.

One could, Katherine was aware, come to all sorts of dim GCSE-level psychological conclusions about her mother, her father etc. etc. Needless to say, Katherine drew none of these conclusions for herself and was so resistant to their application that few people tried to draw them for her. Daniel, of course, being Daniel, had been one of those few, and it had caused such an almighty argument, which snowballed from an exchange of words into an exchange of crockery, that he had never dared go near the subject again unless, as was sometimes the case, he quite consciously wished to start an argument. He had once, in a display so petulant and pathetic that Katherine had merely stood aside and laughed, flounced around the lounge in what he clearly thought was an excellent impression of Katherine – all pouty lips and flappy hands – saying in a put-on baby voice that forever afterwards severely limited his sexual appeal in Katherine's eyes, *My mummy doesn't love me.* This was, of course, towards the end of their relationship, and while not exactly a contributing factor in the split, certainly didn't work in his favour.

The truth, if there was such a thing, was that Katherine rather admired her mother. Daniel, clearly proud of himself at coming up with the metaphor, had likened this to Stockholm Syndrome. There was, Katherine would be the first to admit, an atomic element of truth in this, but it was also, or so she maintained, a rather gross misunderstanding of the sort of relationship she and her mother had enjoyed (yes, enjoyed) over three decades of mud-slinging, belittling, mocking and general one-upmanship. Katherine's mother was, plainly, so utterly dysfunctional that it was a wonder she even managed to wash her armpits and find something to eat of a morning. But far from concealing this, or feeling any sense of shame about it, she advertised it, as if it were the very thing that set her apart from everyone else. Which, of course, it was. Katherine had seen her mother in almost every degrading situation in which it was possible for a mother to find herself in the presence of her daughter: drunk on Pernod at ungodly hours of the day; sprawled naked in Katherine's bed having inexplicably led her latest conquest there instead of to the master bedroom; dumped in public by Julio, her swarthy squeeze of indeterminate Mediterranean origin. It was so predictable as to be banal. But oddly, Katherine felt rather proud to have come from such stock, and the whole picture reassured her that having children didn't have to be the end of unpredictability. After all, she and her sister had both turned out reasonably OK, and her mother had maintained a verve and sense of daring usually reserved for women with zero in the way of offspring. It seemed, Katherine thought, a reasonable compromise. Indeed, she *had* to think this; there was no other choice. Opinionated as Katherine was, and as quick as she might have been to charge into the realm of near-total judgement and dismissal of others who failed to meet her own, admittedly rather warped sense of the world, she was not a hypocrite, and would not allow herself, no matter what her inward feelings of predictable pain might be, to castigate her mother for enjoying a lifestyle and attitude Katherine herself aspired to. Whatever effect her mother's waywardness had had on Katherine, Katherine still had to judge her not as her mother, but as a woman, and this was convenient in that it simultaneously reinforced Katherine's beliefs about all manner of subjects (motherhood, womanhood, men, relationships, and so on and so on) but also allowed her to completely ignore so many other issues which would, if she actually thought about them, cause not only inconvenience but probably also considerable pain.

The problem, though, was Daniel, and all the things that changed with his arrival. Katherine had managed, through stubbornness and evasiveness and distraction, to stave off introducing him to her mother for almost a year, and when she did, her worst fears were realised. Katherine's mother, for all her flippant pronouncements about men and the ever-growing list of things for which they were no good, actually approved of Daniel in a way she hadn't even hinted at when Katherine had introduced her to previous boyfriends. After a suitably dull dinner, during which all concerned did their best not to stray from the middle of the conversational road, Katherine had seen Daniel out to his car and returned to find her mother smiling happily, her glass of wine unexpectedly untouched beside her, her cigarette not even lit, filled with nothing but praise for the man whom Katherine had been so convinced she would hate. Not that there was, on the surface, much to hate about Daniel. He was personable and polite and oddly charming in a quiet, slightly under-confident way. It was just that Katherine had assumed, given the weight of previous evidence, that her mother would by her nature disapprove of anyone so sensible, so reliable, so (or so she'd thought at the time) *normal*. And from the moment Katherine's mother pronounced Daniel the best thing ever to have happened to Katherine, everything that had felt so certain seemed to fall apart in Katherine's hands, and there was already, so early on, a creeping sense that she and Daniel were doomed and, as a result, so were she and her mother. Because as she listened to her mother talk that evening – sober and calm and sensible in a way Katherine was sure she had never been before – Katherine realised that the things she admired about her mother were not, as her mother was so adept at convincing those around her, things her mother admired about herself. Her individualism, her rugged isolation, her mistreatment of the men in her life, were only, it seemed, worn as badges of honour because it was better than wearing them as the things they really were: flaws, injuries, failings. The telling remark was when she told Katherine that this was what she'd always wanted for her – a good man, a stable relationship, a happy home life. In that instant, Katherine could feel it all evaporating, rising ceiling-ward with the smoke from her mother's cigarette, which she had waited for the duration of the conversation to light.

During the evenings she wasn't with Keith, which were numerous given that Keith had three other fucks to squeeze into his week, Katherine read and watched the news. She rarely watched anything else on television. Like much of Katherine's life, what she read and what she watched were governed by her sense of types of people: types she wanted to be versus types she couldn't stand. She didn't want to be the sort of woman who watched soaps and weepie movies. She wanted to be the sort of woman who watched the news and read the Booker list. She imagined herself at parties, despite the fact she never went to parties, being asked her opinion on world affairs and modern literature.

Confronted with such topical discussions, however, she found herself adrift and exposed. It wasn't that she didn't know what was happening, or that she didn't, in some distant and largely hypothetical way, care: it was simply that she felt unable to muster appropriate levels of distress. Once this fact became clear, it seemed to spread its tentacles into the rest of her life in such a way as to make her question, not for the first time, exactly how human she could lay claim to being. Watching the news was, essentially, watching life, and the manner of her watching unnerved her. She thought of it as a certain lack of connection, a phrase, coincidentally, that she often used about men with whom she hadn't gotten along. Others saw it as coldness, a phrase men Katherine hadn't gotten along with often used to describe her. *Unmoved* was a word that came up a lot, both in Katherine's head and in other people's descriptions of her. *Emotionally hard to impress*, was the way she preferred to think about it. Just as declarations of love were not enough to stir the same in her, so footage of, say, starving Haitians was not enough, in and of itself, to cause the kind of damp-eyed distress that seemed so automatic in others. Swollen, malnourished bellies; kids with flies in their eyes; mothers cooking biscuits made of earth. It was faintly revolting. Sometimes, when in a particularly quarrelsome mood, Katherine asked people exactly what the relevance was. For some reason, people tended to find this question offensive. They cited vague humanitarian criteria. The word *children* came up a lot, as if simply saying it explained everything.

Kath, Keith wrote in an email from an undisclosed location where he was holidaying with an un-named and un-gendered companion to whom he was almost certainly not related. *I miss you bad. I don't think I can live without you. Love me?*

Keith, Katherine wrote back. *I will never live with anyone who can't live without me. Grow up. PS: who the fuck are you on holiday with?*

Something had to be done. She was stagnating. For all she knew, she might already be dead. She needed a decisive act, she told herself, something that would galvanise her. She decided to quit her job. The fear of not having a job would force her to find a job.

She ambushed her manager while he was unpacking a sandwich.

'However did my wife manage to stop the mayonnaise soaking into the bread?' he said. 'Do you know? Is it a womanly secret? She doesn't return my calls anymore.'

'I quit,' said Katherine.

'Again?' said her manager.

'This time I mean it.'

'OK,' he said, tossing his limp excuse for a sandwich back in the box. 'What do you want?'

'Nothing. I want to quit.'

'I can't give you another pay rise. People will start to think you're sleeping with me.'

'I don't want a pay rise,' said Katherine, who found it difficult to believe anyone would think he was sleeping with anyone. 'I'm handing in my notice.'

'Two days' extra holiday.'

'No. One month's notice.'

'OK.' He held up his hands in defeat. 'One month. Hey, you know, that would mean there was no longer a conflict of interest in terms of us . . .'

She closed the door behind her as she left.

F uck me like you're a child,' said Keith, back from holiday and
fucking her in a way that reminded her of an animal in a veteri-
nary collar – as if she were something to be shaken off, a constraint
out of which he needed to reverse. 'Fuck me like you're scared
of me.'

It proved to be too much of an imaginative leap. She fucked him
like she pitied him and then told him afterwards he was pathetic.

'You're right,' said Keith. 'You're so right. Next time fuck me like I'm
pathetic.'

M aybe you should join a group of some kind,' her mother said.
'That's how you meet people. You've got to get out there.'

'By "people" do you mean "men"?'

'Well who wants to meet women?'

S he told herself that what she couldn't feel in life she could at least
feel watching the news. Emotion was like exercise, she thought.
You didn't want to do it but it was good for you. You had to push
yourself.

She told herself she would be moved by the very next story that
came along. She would really try, she thought. She'd look so closely at
the flies in that little kid's eyes. She'd picture them on her own face.
She'd conjure the heat and the dust and the stink of rotting goat. She'd
imagine how that pissy, cholera-riddled water would taste as it
edged its way down her dry little throat and pooled malignantly in
her horribly distended belly. How awful to have a belly like that!
How awful that must feel! It was wretched, she thought, a

wretched existence, and she knew, now that she'd given it such close consideration, that the second she saw one of those poor, poor children, she'd erupt into hot sweet tears, just like any other normal human being. She'd cry so much it would more than make up for all those other times when she didn't cry, when she just stared, dead-faced, at the wall of suffering . . . God, how she'd cry . . . if people could see her . . .

Then the news cut to talk of the virus, with grim-voiced narration over montages of men in boiler suits and face masks fork-lifting cattle onto smoking pyres, and Katherine sobbed like a baby and then ran to the bathroom to purge, the vomit hitting her fingers before she could pull them free; second-hand coffee and chunks of doughy matter spraying the bowl and turning her tears to nothing more than a gag reflex.

Where did you go on holiday?' she asked Keith mid-fuck, having suddenly (but with careful premeditation) kicked him off her at his most vulnerable moment, sending him sprawling to the floor with only his hard-on to break his fall.

'Jesus . . . fuck, I think you . . . what?'

'Your holiday,' she said, lying back on the bed and eyeing him coldly. 'Where did you go?'

'Tenerife,' he said, inspecting his rapidly shrinking cock for permanent damage. 'Do we have to talk about it now?'

'No, we don't have to talk about it now,' she said calmly. 'If you like I can just get dressed and go and we don't have to speak about it ever again.'

'I don't understand why this is suddenly such a pressing issue that you have to . . .'

'Who did you go with?'

'Oh, I see.'

'You see?'

'Yeah, I see. I see what this is all about. You're jealous.'

'I'm not jealous. I just want to know. Who did you go with?'

'Is it possible to break a dick? I've heard it is. I've heard they can snap.'

'Was it someone from work?'

'I'm going to have to go to work with my dick in a sling, you fucking . . .'

'They'd never find a sling small enough. Was she blonde or brunette?'

'Blonde,' he said miserably. 'Her name's Janice. Are you going to make me stop seeing her?'

Katherine was repulsed.

'What do you mean *make you*?' she snapped. 'How could I *make you*?'

'I don't know I just . . .'

'How come she gets to go on holiday? That's what I want to know. How come she gets to go on holiday while I have to make do with intermittent screwing in your shabby little flat?'

'We can go on holiday,' said Keith. 'If that's what you want.'

'Is that what you want?'

'Well . . . I mean, yeah, of course, but . . .'

'Because I'm not sure now. I'm not sure I'd want to go with you. I'm not sure I could bear it.'

This was in fact true. The more Katherine thought about it, the more going on holiday with Keith sounded like an awful idea. All those inane conversations in sunnily bland surroundings. His sweat-shined love handles; his shrivelled ball bag in Speedos.

'Why not?' said Keith. 'What's wrong with me?'

'You want a list?' she said.

He called her two days later and begged, offering a last-minute booking. No one at work would think anything of it, he said. They'd stagger their days a little. Katherine agreed, victorious and relieved.

'Where are we going?' she asked.

'Malta,' he said. 'God I'm fucking haemorrhaging money.'

In Malta, everything was clearer and more muddled at the same time. They fell into an easy routine of lazing, drinking and eating, then fucking and sleeping, which after the drinking became somewhat indistinguishable. For Katherine, everything seemed to pass not so much in a blur as in snippets. Here she was sitting alone on the balcony, staring out across the bay at the huddled, stone-cut splendour of Valetta, feeling both calm and deliciously lonely. Here she was by the pool, either drifting with her thoughts or squinting through one eye at the array of flesh around her. Brown flesh, reddened flesh; German and English and Italian flesh, all pressed together and sizzling under the sun. It was erotic and vile at the same time – the only kind of eroticism she seemed to experience these days. Here she was at dinner with Keith, exchanging heavy clods of conversation so deadening she was tempted, at times, to cause physical injury, either to him or to herself, just to have something distinctive to discuss. He said things like, *It's hot*, and then followed that statement seconds later with a clarification (*It's really hot*) and then, after a bit of thought, some further exposition (*It's so hot I feel like I'm melting in my seat*) until finally his thought processes reached their natural conclusion and he ended with a sort of ruminative coda (*So hot . . .*).

He'd turned an odd colour, Katherine noted: a deep leathery tan with a thin cherry varnish. This was partly to do with the dedication

Keith applied to his sunbathing. He lay in the heat with the gritty focus of a man making a long-distance drive. He took scheduled breaks. On the beach, by the pool, he was a ridiculous sight. There was, Katherine speculated, no possible way of concealing his Englishness, or any English person's Englishness for that matter. You could spot them immediately – pasty white; muffin-bellied; Rorschached with quasi-Celtic tattoos.

Not that Katherine was immune of course. She had, though she was loath to admit it, a worryingly English physique. What was it about going abroad, she wondered, that threw all your shortcomings into howling relief? Why did every other race seem so at home while the English remained determined to be uncomfortable? The differences, she thought, were physical. The English were always experiencing some sense of bodily shame. Men covered it with bravado, but for women it was harder. In the afternoons, by the pool, it was a parade of bikinis, of washboard stomachs and plunging cleavages. Keith had a way of angling his sunglasses away but then sliding his eyes in their direction, thinking Katherine couldn't see the whites through his Wayfarers. He lay in the sun for hours, simmering and staring at other women's tits, and then, back at the hotel, sticky with sweat and Ambre Solaire, he fucked her while she was still in her bikini, the images of those other women running across his eyes so clearly that she could almost see them, like figures in a zoetrope. Not that she saw his eyes much when they fucked. Keith had two favoured sexual positions: from behind or getting a blow job. If he could have found a way of fucking the back of her head he'd have been in hog's heaven. It saddened her that the fantasy was so depressingly clear: the sun, the hotel room, the way he pawed at her bikini just enough to get past it without ever actually removing it. Keith was reframing the experience as a holiday fling: the indulgence of all his sex-in-the-sun imaginings.

'Why don't we fuck in the morning?' she asked. 'Why don't we fuck at night? Why do we always have to fuck straight after we've been at the pool?'

'The sun revs my engine,' was how Keith put it, but Katherine knew better; knew he needed at least four hours of unadulterated pool-side porn before he could crank up the necessary desire for a screw. He also needed a few beers – more and more, it seemed. Katherine had a theory for this trend, developed while watching Keith's lizardly eyes dart from one bikini to the next. Keith's libido, she decided, was based on strangeness. This was true of most men, of course, but for Keith it was particularly true. He had an in-built urge to fuck people he didn't know – anonymous, foreign, mysterious people with whom he would need to exchange only a few ham-fisted pleasantries. In the beginning, he'd been rapacious to the point of aggression. Now he was cursory, distracted, frequently drunk and usually all-too-clearly thinking of someone else. At first, Katherine had been concerned that Keith was thinking of a specific someone else – that there might be one particular bronzed beauty by the pool who had caught his eye for longer than the others. After a while she realised he wasn't thinking of anyone else at all, or specifically, he wasn't imagining he was actually fucking someone who wasn't Katherine, he was simply imagining that Katherine wasn't Katherine. That's what mattered, that's what got his engine going. Keith's withdrawal from anything that could have been termed a shared reality between them was precisely because that reality, or any reality for that matter, was profoundly un-erotic to him. He didn't want to fuck Katherine, he wanted to fuck a stranger who looked like Katherine.

Under the pretence of checking her email, she used the hotel's criminally expensive internet access to google Daniel – a habit she'd quickly fallen into after he'd unfriended her on Facebook and thus forced her to employ more creativity in her virtual stalking. A few well-practised clicks and there he was: smiling and well-groomed and just the right side of smug, beaming out at her from his staff picture on the website of a biological research facility somewhere in Norfolk, where, apparently, he was the public face of research his biography described as groundbreaking. There were even one or two YouTube clips of him at press conferences, talking about sustainable development and secure food sources. She had no idea how this had happened: he'd somehow edged out of the drabness of office life and into a position both admirable and faintly glamorous. It was predictable, really, and she could picture him being good at it, but it still gave her something of a jolt. She imagined him at work – Daniel and his Jesus complex – surrounded by chrome and glass and Petri dishes. It was his natural environment, she thought – icy and microscopic. Sometimes, when they were together, she'd called him the Vulcan. She'd meant it as a term of endearment but it had cut a little close to the bone. Now here he was: sartorially, facially and interpersonally sharpened; every inch the beatific boffin.

She wondered if he thought about her and, if he did, what he thought. Perhaps she might even have passed him in the street and not realised. Perhaps he'd seen her and turned away. She wondered if he talked about her, if his new partner, whoever she might be, knew about her and had an opinion. Maybe they laughed about her, late at night after a glass of wine. Or maybe Daniel stayed quiet. Maybe he'd erased her completely. He was capable of it. Indeed, she'd seen him do it. Just a few short months after their friend Nathan had disappeared, Daniel had stopped talking about him almost entirely.

Out of habit, she googled Nathan too. There was, as always, a long-cold trail in the chat rooms. Coded locations for parties. Discussions of the night before. Substance inventories. Casualty lists. Difficult, she thought, to reconcile all that with the Nathan she knew: the Nathan who sat up with her late into the night after Daniel had invariably exceeded his limits and blacked out in the bedroom.

She trawled for anything with a recent date, but got nothing. Wherever he'd gone, she thought, he was doing a good job of not being found.

Unable to bear another unbroken afternoon of Keith's silent sunbathing, and keen to at least keep up the pretence that they were holidaying as a couple, Katherine coaxed him into the pool with her. She climbed awkwardly down the steps and stood bobbing in the shallow end. Keith entered the water with a graceless dive and then churned a path towards her through the overcrowded, heavily chlorinated stewpot of cooling, pinkening flesh. When he arrived beside her and stood, unnervingly breathless after a two-metre crawl, a long shoelace of snot swung from his left nostril. Making a face, Katherine reached out quickly and tugged it away, washing it from her hand in the blue water and watching it drift towards the filter like some sort of primordial sea life – ribboned and faintly green and seemingly possessed of mind. When she looked up again, Keith was eyeing her with undisguised repulsion. He didn't say anything, didn't comment in any way, but his face stayed with Katherine. In a way, the expression stayed with him, too, as if all of their interaction from that point on was sullied by the imprint of his phlegm upon her hand. Even as she stood there, bobbing slightly in the heat of Keith's gaze, Katherine knew that something had died between them, and that whatever that something was, and whatever the exact form of its passing, it was primarily sexual in nature. It wasn't the snot itself that threw him, she thought, or the surface-level disgust he experienced at the thought of her pulling matter from deep within his sinuses, it was the humanity of it – the horrible glimpse of Katherine as a base being in contact with the base being inside him.

Sometimes, when Keith drifted off during the late afternoon, when the sun was low and the streets were quiet, Katherine went walking alone. Across the bay, through the field of sails and masts, Valetta seemed to keep watch over its neighbours – timeless and tight-hewn and closely carved; more like a nest created by giant rock-eating insects than an actual city.

Occasionally, rarely, she had an ice cream. She was eating less these days, and when she did her guilt was pathological. She had a sense of ruining herself, of making everything worse by eating. She wanted to be light and loose – free not just in life but also, if possible, at a near-molecular level. Food had begun to feel like baggage: a taking-on of matter which then had to be processed and displaced using energy her body didn't have. She thought of Daniel and his efficiency: his clean, unfettered approach to everything that came his way; how she'd envied it; how she envied it still. Daniel always seemed to be shedding, she thought, always seemed to be growing lighter. How ironic that he now spent his time tinkering with the food chain while she simply consumed and expanded. She needed to be more streamlined. In her body; in her very being. She imagined herself passing through the world like an arrow, straight and deadly and keen.

She felt, she noticed, infinitely lighter without Keith. Keith was a burden. He was something to be carried when what she wanted was to be carried herself. How liberating it was to walk alone, to think alone, to have one set of decisions to make, to consider only her own inner drives and needs. But contrast that, she thought, with the awful burden of singledom and spinsterhood. What a chore, what a daily struggle it was, to be alone, to spend every day wondering if this was the day, if this man was *the* man, if your solitude was a fault of the world or a fault of your makeup.

She closed her eyes and listened to the creak of the yachts as they rocked in the harbour; the soft chatter of foreign voices along the promenade. She and Daniel had never holidayed. At first, they were too busy; later, they'd kidded themselves they were saving – the oldest excuse for failing to live – when really they were just terrified of being alone together.

Now there was a burden, she thought: loving someone; being loved. Dreams of houses. All that crap about forever. The conversation about kids that never quite happens. And what a weight to *be* loved, too; to know that another person had invested their future happiness in your weak self. The walking on eggshells; the daily effort not to hurt, and when you did, as of course you always would, all that effort was erased, the memory of all that you'd done to spare them pain simply obliterated by pain itself. Christ, the thought of going through it all again, all that love stuff . . .

A man disturbed her in the toilet as she was pulling up her bikini bottoms, then blushed claret and bolted. When Katherine told Keith she saw a pilot light ignite in his eyes. He told her to go back to the toilet and leave the door open. He followed her in and fucked her against the sink without removing her bikini, each of them looking themselves in the eye in the steaming mirror, Katherine all too aware of what had stirred Keith's libido: the fantasy of her as a nameless stranger, disturbed in the toilet, fucked without introduction. She could be anyone, she thought, watching Keith's reddening face in the mirror. Anyone at all and he wouldn't care.

Fuck you, she mouthed into the mirror. He didn't see. He'd closed his eyes as he came, imagining, no doubt, some other time and place entirely, some other fuck, some other Katherine.

B ack at home, after a wordless flight and a relieved parting at the airport, Katherine discovered she was pregnant. Her period was a week overdue. She'd put it down to the strains of the holiday, but pissed on a plastic stick to put her mind at rest. The stick promised total confidence. Nothing in her life had ever given her less. At the sight of the little blue bar in the stick's predictive window, she threw up. Then she went out and bought five more sticks of differing brands, all of which promised relief, reassurance, an end to doubt. She was not relieved. Reassurance was not forthcoming. She was riddled with doubt. She called Keith and said she needed some space. He gave it, of course, and save for a cursory text thanking her for a great time, he made no effort at contact. She was glad and disappointed. She had three days left of her leave and spent them pacing her flat and smoking. She googled Daniel again and stared at his picture. She called her mother and told her she was fine. She washed down takeaway pizza with cut-price wine and watched confessional television. She thought about the pills again and decided it was simply too pathetic, too predictable, and would allow her mother to wring far too much sympathy out of family events. On day three her phone rang. She let it go to voicemail in case it was Keith. It wasn't.

'It's me.' A pause. 'I mean, it's Nathan. I, um, I'm sorry to hear about, you know, about you and Daniel. I . . . You two really had something, you know? Anyway, I've, ah, I've been away, and now I'm back, and I'd love to see you. Both of you. Do you have Daniel's number? Anyway, give me a call sometime. It'd be great to, ah . . .' Another pause. 'I thought I could do this, but I'm not sure I can.'

She sat by the phone for almost half an hour – picking it up, putting it down. She thought about erasing the message and pretending she'd never heard it. Her hands were shaking. She found her phone book and dialled. To her relief, she got his answering machine. She kept it brief.

'Daniel. It's Katherine. Nathan called. He's back. We need to talk about what we're going to do. Call me.'

She pictured him at the other end: playing the message twice to be sure; closing his eyes to think. He would call, she was sure of it, but not until he knew what he wanted to say.

Daniel was in bed when he got Katherine's message. He had been there for three days, suffering from a crippling bout of what Angelica had diagnosed, rather unsympathetically, as Dan-Flu.

Daniel had always been stoically healthy. Recently, however, he had developed an odd relationship with illness. He spent quite protracted periods of time believing he was becoming unwell.

'I think I'm coming down with something,' he'd say, making vague gestures at his throat or nose, his presentation largely asymptomatic. 'I've got a funny . . . you know . . . like a sort of . . .'

'Like a sort of hypochondria?' Angelica would inevitably say. 'Like a sort of deluded-type feeling?'

'No. Like a *sensation*, a sort of *sensation* in my throat. I think there's something going round.'

On the verge of succumbing as he so often claimed to be, it was surprising how infrequently Daniel tipped the scales into observable disease. His relationship with illness was flirtatious; only a particularly attractive ailment could tempt him into bed. When it did, he reacted with all the high-flown sense of occasion one might expect from a man who was constantly yearning-and-putting-off.

'No, no,' he'd say, huffing another fistful of snot into a tissue and tossing the resultant goopy wad onto the heap of others he kept as a quantitative record of his malaise, 'it's definitely not a cold. Because my stomach feels weird and that suggests to me that it's more . . .'

He wondered what had become of him. In all the time he'd been with Katherine he'd been ill once, twice at most, and even then with great reluctance. He'd prided himself on his resilience. At his previous place of work he'd kept a copy of Field Marshal Montgomery's famous sign on his desk: *I'm 99% Fit, Are You?* Odd, really, given how generally diseased his entire relationship with Katherine had been. Perhaps, he thought, you never really shut disease out; merely shunted it into new areas of your life.

On this occasion, Daniel had succumbed to something that wasn't quite flu, since it was accompanied by a level of fatigue and lower back pain that were not, in Daniel's conception of flu, a normal part of the experience. Responding with his usual immediacy as soon as it became clear this was going to be a genuine bout of ill health, he'd taken to his bed and remained there for close to seventy-two hours, getting up only sporadically for such necessities as toast, orange juice and trips to the toilet. By day three he was in a satisfying funk. The bed reeked; he was greasy and unshaven; his dressing gown had become a grim second skin.

Disappointingly, despite these heavily vaunted external indicators, Daniel also seemed to be showing every sign of recovery, and the thought was beginning to occur to him that the thing might have run its course, and that he should probably start thinking about getting up and making himself halfway human again before Angelica got genuinely impatient and frustrated rather than just teasingly so. Given that he and Angelica had invited friends round for dinner (or, more accurately, Angelica had invited *her* friends round for dinner), he was under a certain degree of pressure to recover, and much as he resented this, it seemed preferable to an evening spent listening to their echoing laughter downstairs.

Daniel liked being ill. He regarded it as luxurious, almost decadent. He spent so much of his life being organised and well presented that he had come to regard illness as one of the few times he had permission to let himself go. He drank only occasionally, and although he had experimented with drugs in the past, largely supervised by Nathan, whose capacity for illegal intake was boundless and troubling and, to Daniel, faintly seductive, he had never really been the type to develop any regular habits of chemical relaxation. Indeed, the only time he was ever particularly tempted was when Angelica, as she often did, announced that she didn't need drugs to have a good time, prompting Daniel to wonder if he might need drugs to have a good time around people who didn't need drugs to have a good time.

His convalescence had not, however, gone according to plan, and it was this precise sense of missed opportunity that now led him to resent his forced return to the land of the well. One of the great things about being ill, or so he'd always thought, was that it was one of the few times he could justifiably escape interaction. He liked to take to his bed, turn off the phone, and lie prone for as long as it took to feel human. This time, however, Angelica had been home for the first two days, and much as he respected her offers of hugs and food and 'company', none of them were really what he wanted. This morning she had gone out, and he had looked forward to spending at least a small portion of his alone-time masturbating to the collection of low-grade pornography he kept in a locked file marked 'work' on his laptop. His aim was predominantly medicinal. Daniel took scant pleasure in masturbation these days, but had become concerned about the quality of his sperm, as if his increasingly staid existence might be directly affecting the efficiency and productivity of his testes. He imagined the little beasts in their gloopy pool, wet-brained and lame, swim-limping around in impotent circles. Was it possible to have depressed sperm? If so, how could you tell? When he finished he made sure to study the mess on the tissue, the bedspread, the old T-shirt, for signs of dubious consistency or colouration. It always looked much the same, but recently he could have sworn that it had lost some of its sheen.

As if aware of his intentions, however, Angelica had placed the cat on the bed before she left (her cat: Giggles, a vast, slovenly sand-bag of a beast, with matted fur and a gammy eye). Mistaking his dancing fist under the bedcover for some form of prey, Giggles had taken to leaping on Daniel's genitals every three or four strokes, rendering him, after about ten futile minutes, incapable of anything even approaching pleasure, so terrified was he that, if he did achieve orgasm, it would be forever linked in his mind to the feeling of an obese cat pogoing around on his penis, thus possibly triggering some sort of latent and horribly embarrassing fetish.

A frustrating day, then, made all the more disturbing by the sight, about twenty minutes after Angelica returned home, of his mobile phone vibrating and Katherine's name scrolling gently across the screen.

If it is possible to miss someone while simultaneously hoping you never have to see them again, then this is how Daniel felt about Katherine. He'd softened over time, of course, and in the end nostalgia had just about won out over revulsion, but it was touch and go. A kind of tender nausea, was how he thought of it; a wistful horror.

He listened to her message twice, sitting on the edge of the bed, half out of his dressing gown. He felt ragged and poorly put together. He lacked, suddenly, the energy and willingness to get up and change.

Angelica called from downstairs, her voice like full beams through fog, 'Daniel? Are you coming? It's ready, baby. But you've got to be *honest*, OK?'

He played the message again, trying to read Katherine's voice, flat-toned, business-like – her voice for *getting things done*. Was that a flutter he could detect? A tension? Did it fall a little at the end? Did her message seem hurried, as if she just wanted to get through it? As always with Katherine, he hoped for more than he received, and the fact that he still, after all this time of learning to know better, hoped at all, was itself a source of both irritation and sadness.

'I'm coming,' he said, his voice hoarse, his sinuses ballooning under the pressure of speech. It sounded like he'd said, 'I'b cubbig.'

He wondered if he should call her right away. Perhaps, he thought, he should leave it a few days, or call at the weekend, when he was more likely to find her at home, and when he was more likely to be able to hold a sensible conversation.

He fingered the tassels on the edge of the bedspread – one of those airbrushed cosmic designs that cram the infinite expanse of the planetary realm into the domestic confines of a mass-produced double bed. It was laughable, really. So much was laughable. In the corner of the bedroom was a large canvas where Angelica had expressed herself through the medium of Infant Art – capital I, capital A. One of her therapists had told her to paint with the innocence of a child. Angelica had finger-painted a sun and blue sky, except that her thumb had smudged the acrylic so that the sun's rays turned green at the tips. It was endearing and awful. He listened to the message a final time and found he could read even less into it than before.

'Honey? I said it's ready. Are you coming down? They're going to be here any minute and I'd really love it if you could . . .'

'I said I'm coming.'

He remembered Nathan the last time he'd seen him, standing under the summer stars in a forest clearing, naked from the waist up, standing perfectly still while a throbbing press of dancers ululated around him. He'd seemed somehow beyond it all, beyond time. Where *had* he been the past year and a half?

Daniel found some jeans on the end of the bed and half-heartedly pushed his feet through the legs. He wanted to get back into bed and sleep. He wondered if he should tell Angelica about the message and then realised, with a little drop somewhere in his small intestine, that he wasn't really wondering at all, merely pretending to himself that he was wondering. This was something he was capable of. He could go through the motions of decency in order to soften the inevitable indecency at the end. Whatever your moral fibre, as Katherine had always been fond of explaining, convenience trumped ethical resolve every time. Why else would God have invented remorse?

'What are you doing up there?'

'Nothing, honey, I'm just . . .' He swept his thumb across the screen of his phone, clearing a moist print. 'Just changing, that's all.'

Downstairs, he found Angelica swaddled in oven gloves, bearing aloft a glass baking dish filled with what looked like lentil cement.

'Who was that on the phone?' she said, standing in the doorway between the kitchen and the dining room, lit from behind by the halogen bulbs that spotlit the worktops, her face in shadow, her hair oddly aflame at the edges. She was holding up the food like it was some sort of offering, as if they'd have to kneel to eat it. She looked happy and precarious. He told himself she might drop the dish if he was honest.

'No one,' he said. 'Wrong number.'

Angelica had been holding something delicate, he thought – it would have been incautious to tell her. But then, Daniel considered all disclosure incautious, and as long as he'd known her, there had never been a time when Angelica, metaphorically speaking, wasn't bearing something delicate, something she was holding out to him like a fragile sacrifice, and even when she wasn't, there had never been a time when Daniel had struggled to imagine she was. And anyway, there was always something going round and Daniel was always coming down with something, or always feeling that next week he'd be less tired, less resentful, stronger, happier. But he never was. There was never, in so many ways, a good time.

When Daniel was six years old, his father took him to the office for the morning. There was, his father explained, no choice. Daniel had been up all night with an earache and couldn't go to school. Daniel's mother was away visiting her sister. Would he rather stay home alone?

It was a manipulative question. Daniel, at around the age of four, had developed a morbid fear of solitude. He woke in the night screaming, convinced he'd been abandoned or that his parents had died in their sleep. Later, some years after the trip to the office, when his mother announced, with what appeared at the time to be no warning at all, that she was leaving to go and live with a man she'd known exactly four months and two weeks (this could be calculated because the man in question was a friend of a friend and Daniel had been with his mother when she was first introduced to him, and years later could look back and diagnose the flutter in her voice and the suddenly odd tone not just of her speech but seemingly of her whole stance and way of being), Daniel would wake in the night even more often, his heart hurling itself against the bony bars of its cage, convinced he was alone. Through his life this dream would morph into different scenes and settings, but it would always be characterised by a sense of loss that would, over time, infect his daily sense of being and inform his reactions to seemingly mundane events.

It had already been an odd few days. Daniel was unused to spending protracted periods of time alone with his father, who was usually either working late or working at home. He was older than the other parents Daniel knew, and so seemed more adult than even an average adult. There was that little bit less youth in him, and so Daniel's understanding of him was that fraction more shallow. He had the beginnings of grey, but was a fit and active man who extolled the virtues of sport and good food, leading the young Daniel to anticipate that the four days they were to spend together (Daniel had no siblings. As his mother had once put it, last chances tend not to come in pairs) would be dull at best and possibly, at worst, quasi-military. As it turned out, he was wrong. Left to his own devices, Daniel's father revealed himself to be a surprisingly relaxed and friendly companion. For the time Daniel's mother was away, he didn't work at home, but instead passed the time with Daniel, watching television and teaching him to play chess. He cooked: curries, a shepherd's pie and, on the last night, fish and chips. Daniel would, through the years, regularly look back on these few days he'd spent in his father's company. Before his mother left, he regarded them simply as a sort of holiday, a private island in the wide, blank expanse of his relationship with his father. After her departure, however, they took on a darker tint, and the idea formed in Daniel's head that these days had been so pleasant not because his father was making an effort, but because he was happy, and had been able to relax to a degree that, for whatever reason, had become impossible in the company of Daniel's mother, giving Daniel, unconsciously at the time, more consciously later, a sense of pain at the idea of curtailed masculinity; of domesticity as a vacuum of individuality. They were alone again after she left, of course, but it was different then. Daniel was older and entering the phase of his life where he sought distance, not comfort, from his parents. In the years that followed, he had cause not only to regret the manner in which the time after his mother's departure had played out, but also to become firmer in his opinion that youth was overrated, characterised as it was by selfishness and awkwardness and a fascination with trivia. Of course, this meant in turn that, just as those later days with his father became tinged, in retrospect, with regret, so those brief days at the age of six when his father seemed to be all things at once – parent, friend and work-mate – became so much more important than they'd seemed at the time, imbued with a perfection and wider meaning to which they could never live up and which nothing could match or surpass, and at their shiny core was that day in the office, the beginning of Daniel's working life, and his only glimpse of his father as a man in his own right.

This was '85 – the boom years. Already a little too old by then to be at the bleeding edge of financial gain (Daniel's father was a strong and loyal worker, but lacked the killer instinct and moral flexibility required to shift what his colleagues referred to as 'major units' in the city), Daniel's father occupied a contented middle-management position in a small sales firm specialising in property deals. It was the beginning of what Daniel would later come to think of as MacGuffin jobs, or jobs in which the supposed thrust of the company or the realm in which they traded had little impact on the work of whole teams of employees who worked at deeper, more hypothetical levels. It was the detachment of work from product, of production from physical activity, and Daniel's father was the perfect example in that, when asked, he described himself as working in property, and indeed had a job title with the word property in it, but in fact had no recourse whatsoever to go near any property or even any deals relating to property. Daniel's father worked in an analytical department charged with the task of crunching whatever numbers had been deemed important by the upper echelons. He studied trends, was the upshot, and designed graphs that helped other people understand those trends. As Daniel's father regularly complained, most people didn't do numbers, so if you could get the numbers into a picture you were winning. Daniel's mother described the job as 'boring', the implication being that a boring job was perfect for a boring man, and although Daniel's father clearly saw it differently, he never said as much, choosing instead to shrug his shoulders in an each-to-their-own sort of way and imply, as he would later express it to Daniel when they'd waited over an hour to see a consultant, that boredom was in the brain of the beholder.

Within a few days of spending the morning at work with his father, Daniel had completely forgotten the subject of that morning's meeting. What he remembered were the details – the objects that had made the experience real, and the way the whole place felt so much more liberated than he had been led to believe. Up to this point, all he'd seen of his father's working life was the dapper, buttoned-down man who left promptly each morning carrying a smart black briefcase. It turned out, however, that Daniel's father dressed for the journey, not for the destination, and the moment he stepped into the wide, open-spaced third-floor office with its high, thick windows and carpeted, double-glazed hush that only served to further offset the beeps and trills of the machines, he stripped off his jacket, loosened his tie, rolled up his sleeves and made a cup of tea. The briefcase went under his desk, which was infinitely more untidy than Daniel had expected, and was not seen again until Daniel's father had re-dressed for the drive home. There were personalised mugs and name plates on the desks, and huge, boxy computers with green text on black screens that seemed, at the time, to be a new world of technological advancement, spitting chains of numbers onto reams of punched paper that went on for yards. There was stationery – not just pens and pencils but bottles of Tipp-Ex and Sellotape in special dispensers and electric pencil sharpeners and fat black clips holding stacks of pale green printouts. People had photographs in little stands on their desks. Every desk was an island, unlike at school where you just sat anywhere because everywhere was the same. It was a first-name place. Everyone talked idly not just about work but about anything, about football and the traffic and tax. Daniel's father was a different man. He was relaxed and respected. People came to him with sheaves of paper and he scribbled on them with a fat blue pen and said things like 'well done' or 'nice job'. In the meeting, there was a flip chart and more pens and a series of graphs that everyone agreed were 'good but not great' and which Daniel's father later confided, while driving home, had been 'pretty awful' but apparently everyone was keen to keep a good spin on things. Daniel's earache faded. They gave him things to do – papers to carry. His father called him his personal assistant and introduced him to people as his new employee. The office smelled of Savlon and sweat and coffee. Everyone had a place and a function. You couldn't be left out because you had a job to do, a role, and everything worked because everyone worked to make it work, and on the drive home when Daniel told his father he wanted to work in an office, Daniel's father's smile was the sort of glimpse of themselves people give you maybe once or twice in their life, and it struck Daniel, not then but later, that the whole morning had been Daniel's father smiling at him, and every office after that morning, no matter how blank or fractious or grim, was a part of that smile, and a part of Daniel, even then, seemed to know that this was going to be a difficult thing to explain and so kept quiet until a rain-drenched morning roughly twenty-four years later when he let himself into his father's house and found the old man at the dining table, surrounded by all the old objects, sorting scraps of magazine into bundles clamped with bulldog clips and scribbling across their faces with a marker before ordering the sheaves into stacks and keeping some sort of list on the back of an envelope that turned out to be a letter from Daniel's mother from before they were married. His father looked up with that same jovial smile and said he was terribly sorry but he was just absolutely snowed under today what with this audit and could they possibly re-schedule for tomorrow and he realised, Daniel did, the awful importance of work in our chains of being; the need for it, the yearning for it when it's gone, and the way all those rhythms and patterns of production hang so much deeper inside us than so many other facets which, when faced with the choice between remembering and forgetting, would seem to be so much more important. His father was going to forget who his son was. He was going to forget that day in the office and the hours Daniel had spent as his assistant, and was going to become unaware even of the time they were spending together now, and the ways in which Daniel was once again playing at being his aide. All his love and hopes and achievements and the shitty fears and prejudices that made him who he was were going to die, but the details of the office – the reams of paper and the left-to-right flow of in-tray and out-tray and the fucking bulldog clips – would all be remembered, stored in pockets of muscle and nerve until the day he died, and after that Daniel found the office a seriously difficult place to be, not only because there was something about it that now seemed toxic, but because he was no longer sure he could fill what had become a cavernous conceptual space. With his father still present, Daniel had been his father's boy at the office, living up to something, becoming something. With his father now absent (not dementia, the specialist had said, but a cerebrovascular accident, a fender-bender somewhere in the looping, semi-liquid curls of his brain), Daniel was once again the little boy trapped in little boy–hood, paddling around in his father's outsized shoes and billowing jacket, picking up the phone and holding a profoundly important conversation with the dial tone. He woke in the night and felt forgotten. He lay beside Angelica and felt only the confines of their intimacy. She couldn't sleep without touching him, it seemed, and he couldn't sleep when he was touched. He waited until she started snoring and then slid his hand from hers or rolled out from under her embrace. She stalked him across the bed – rolling this way and that; finding his arm and pulling it over her shoulders with a deep-breathed *Mmmmm* that spoke of both contentment and gentle reproach. But he needed to dream alone, and the very fact of her contact seemed to interrupt a circuit somewhere in his mind and served, if not to wake him, then at least to bring his dreams to a saddening and premature closure, so that he awoke, always, to a sense of incompleteness – the disappointment of started dreams.

He adjusted his body clock to optimise his respite. He had, on several carefully spaced evenings, gone to bed before Angelica and then feigned sleep when she followed him. He liked to vary the presentation. One night he was simply asleep, another he gave the appearance of having drifted off with a book on his chest. He'd pictured, as he carefully positioned himself on his back with the book spread over his chest, Angelica smiling to herself as she reached out and removed the book and then turned out the light before sliding into the bed beside him. In reality, though, she had simply ignored him, and Daniel had found himself trapped beneath the book, unsure if he should pretend to wake and make himself more comfortable or simply maintain the lie and remain as he was. He'd chosen the latter, spending half the night pinned and tense and unable either to sleep or to roll over.

He had, for a time, experimented with rising early and doing his dreaming while awake, staring out at the suburban dawn with its little tiles of domestic light, watching the gathering mosaic of parted curtains and illuminated rooms as the street followed him into the day. But Angelica, alert to his movements even through her ear plugs and eye-mask, had attuned herself to his sleep cycles and begun following him downstairs after mere minutes of blissful solitude, sitting beside him as he sipped his coffee and strained for small talk. She strained with him, of course, or even for him at times. *Tell me something*, she'd say, folding her legs beneath her on the sofa and tucking her dressing gown over her feet. *What are you thinking?* He didn't know, couldn't say. She had a way of reaching out and gently tapping his temple – *What's going on in there?* The more she pursued, the more he fled. Morning after grey morning, they sat side by side in resigned silence, each frowning slightly, shaping words they never said, until eventually she smiled and sighed and said, *Isn't it great that we can just sit together quietly like this?*

So he left for work early, arriving at The Centre long before he needed to be there. He liked to walk the labs before the nine o'clock influx, pacing the brushed-glass workstations and aluminium fittings; listening to the way the instruments hummed and ticked in isolation. When there was no one else there, you could feel the laboratories breathe. He never touched anything. Much like the rest of Daniel's life, you could have dusted for his prints and found barely a whorled smudge. He simply liked the feel of the place, the energy. Four wide rooms of quiet research and gently scrolling diagnostics, lit with the faintest tint of green. At the back was a heated bio-dome that housed a perfectly engineered cornfield. He liked to make his way through the clinical hush and then stand at the edge of the field, squinting until the clear walls and ceilings dimmed from his peripheral vision and there was nothing left but the gold expanse of the crop. In the winter, it was especially comforting, and he enjoyed the oddness of stripping off his overcoat and standing for a moment in the middle of a perfectly false summer's day, the smell of the field wafting up at him like the very essence of summers gone by, sheltered from the rain as it lashed the arched glass roof and made a marbled, swimming mess of the sky.

Daniel was conjoined with Angelica the way two melting candles might form a single, shapeless mass of wax. She believed in a degree of closeness and intimacy that was almost mystical. She wanted them to overlap, to meld. The difficulty was that Daniel had done too good a job of painting himself in her colours. Ventriloquism had always been a knack of his. On a good day, he could even do the faces to match. He found the easiest disguise was blandness – the disguise of having no face at all. Angelica didn't know, or could briefly sense but then optimistically disregard, the discreet territories of himself he kept in reserve. He told her he loved her. He did love her. She loved him. It was awful. Love, with all its formless cushioning and puffed-up protection, had inflated between them like an air bag in a car crash. She looked into his eyes while they made love and he imagined himself in a narrow tunnel with the weight of a river rushing above him. He would never leave her. He lived in fear of her leaving him.

Angelica was a year younger than Daniel, and several years behind in terms of her professional development, largely because she had invested large acreages of her life into what she thought of as her personal development. She'd travelled. She'd explored. She'd *spent time* in a number of places yet appeared, when it came down to it, to have *been* nowhere. Travellers always talked that way, Daniel noticed. It was designed to give the impression of nomadic flux, of freedom – a concept Angelica and her friends seemed to hold dear. To Daniel, it was an odd sort of liberty, as though their very pursuit of a limitless, weightless existence somehow constrained and burdened them. For him, freedom had always seemed more static, more solidly hewn. It was freedom from fear; the relief of no longer having to search – for a job, a partner, a house. Not for him the Goan sands and full-moon raves and Hare Krishna platitudes. Better the yearly bonus, the sense of completion that accompanied genuine quantifiable achievement.

Or so he'd always thought, and tried to think still, now, as he felt himself trapped and terrified of being free.

Daniel had met Angelica, slightly predictably but with an air of what-the-hell, in a bar, on a sleety festive Thursday, at a time when he'd composed in his mind such a long and compelling list of things he didn't want in a woman that he could be attracted only to their absence. Naturally, Angelica had her good qualities, but it was the things she lacked that drew him to her. She was the anti-Katherine. She wasn't harsh or abrasive. She didn't shout, she wasn't difficult to be around and, critically, Daniel could not imagine her defecating. After Katherine, who had a sort of rolling-news approach to the workings of her body; who detailed her bowel movements over break-fast; who followed him into the bathroom while he was brushing his teeth and studied her sanitary pad like it was the morning headlines, Daniel had forsworn the vulgar physicality of women he slept with, and so gauged each woman he met against the ease with which he could imagine her shitting or menstruating. Throughout his first conversation with Angelica, then, as they stood uncomfortably close in the press of damp bar-hoppers and shouted into each other's ears over the clatter, Daniel had tried and happily failed to demolish her beauty in his mind. His attraction to her was complex; reverse-reactive. It wasn't that he fancied her, it was that he couldn't imagine himself not fancying her.

Their conversation had flowed with their drinks: pleasantries over cut-price pints; intimacies over marked-up cocktails, and again Angelica had revealed herself to be everything Katherine was not in that she not only had a sense of the wider world but actually at times expressed opinions on how it could be improved. One of Katherine's most frequent complaints about Daniel was that he was little more than an idealistic middle-class liberal with a conveniently vague grasp of reality. Part of what made Daniel so angry about this remark was that it was true, and like any liberal he wanted less to change the world than simply to be around people who wanted the world to be different in all the same ways. What a thrill, then, to hear Angelica voicing her opinions on global responsibility, rising sea levels, and whatever was going on with the cattle. It wasn't that it was love, it was simply that it was closer to Daniel's idea of love than anything that had come along before.

They'd spent their dating days doing good. It was a bad time for beef, even then. Up and down the country, cattle were trancing out. Farmers were finding lone members of the herd at the edges of fields staring blank and unblinking into the middle distance, starving and dehydrating to death. Experts were at a loss. The term Bovine Idiopathic Entrancement, far from a diagnosis, was coined as an admission of ignorance. Daniel and Angelica had hounded McDonald's. On two occasions they'd taken to the streets, handing out poorly printed leaflets that spoke of the evil behind convenience. They felt they were kicking the Golden Arches while they were down. At some point, the environment had become the new Third World. Convenience was out. You had to work for your food. Anything fast was suspicious. Ease was both corrupted and corrupting.

Awful, then, that they, as a couple, were so convenient, so easy. People bought McDonald's because they knew what they were getting. Daniel stayed with Angelica for much the same reason. She was as she'd been advertised. She did what it said on her wrapper.

For Angelica, her daily life and sense of global concern were inextricably linked. There was always room for improvement, for growth. She regarded herself (and, unfortunately, Daniel and their relationship) as something to be worked on, a project with no definable goal or conclusion. *That's something I've been doing a lot of work on recently,* she'd say. *I know I need to work on that.* She read deeply and voraciously on the subject of her own shortcomings. She didn't talk, she *expressed*. She didn't think, she *explored*. Indeed, she appeared to have reached the conclusion that thinking itself was chancy, and possibly a symptom of some deep-seated syndrome or flaw or maladjustment that needed to be explored.

'Do I think too much?' she'd ask, midway through some minor domestic task. 'Like, I feel like I'm thinking all the time, and sometimes that's really good? But other times it's really bad. Like it's really paralysing, just *thinking* about stuff all the time.'

Daniel wasn't sure it was possible to think too much. He often found his private thoughts considerably more interesting than day-to-day events, to the point where he sometimes resented day-to-day events for interfering with his thoughts, an issue which Angelica had raised on more than one occasion, and on which he'd begrudgingly agreed he might need to work.

'I need to be more spontaneous,' she'd say. 'We both do. Let's be really spontaneous this weekend. Let's agree we're going to do something totally unplanned and nuts.'

She'd said this twice. The first time they'd spent much of Saturday debating activities that might be suitably nuts, and then deciding all of them were rather predictable, at which point they'd gone shopping. The second time they'd agreed not to debate anything and each ended up making completely separate and un-discussed plans, over which they then argued for the rest of the weekend.

Their sex life was, naturally, the most symptomatic area of all. It was constantly in a state of redress. Like some grossly over-ambitious architectural project, it always seemed to be propped up with scaffolding and obstinately deviating from plans. Intimacy was an issue. Intimacy and spontaneity and the balance of the two. Sometimes, for example, Angelica got it into her head that she wanted to tantrically merge for hours on end, seeking some semi-mystical state of union she'd read about in a second-hand book. At other times, she felt the whole dimming-the-lights-and-dousing-the-room-with-incense *planning* of the thing made it all rather moribund and predictable, at which point she just wanted to screw and be done with it. The difficulty was that Daniel never knew, so to speak, if he was coming or going, meaning he tended to get the timing wrong and find himself accused of having either intimacy issues or some sort of problem with spontaneity and passion. As far as his personal preferences went, suffice to say his heart pretty much sank whenever he saw Angelica fumbling for a joss stick.

High-minded though they were, frugality seemed always to escape them. The things they owned seemed to breed. Domesticity, it transpired, came down to a collection of products and a desire to continually augment those products until everything was just so, which of course it never could be, because what, then, would there be to work on? Objects broke, ran out, needed cleaning (which necessitated the use of further, more specialised products). Lacking children as they did, Daniel and Angelica needed something to tend to or they risked falling into the kind of vapid complacency they both professed to fear but also secretly craved. The rough, cluttered, faintly shabby look perfected by several of their friends wasn't an option. They needed all the same stuff as normal people. Multi-surface sprays that fizzed on contact; moisturisers that toned and lifted and lightly tanned; shampoos that thickened and added shine. Daniel and Angelica dreamed of a better world but still baulked at the smell of each other's shit, necessitating a variety of lavender-based infusions and, when merely masking the odour wouldn't suffice, a reserve artillery of heavy chemistry that promised nothing short of a bacterial Armageddon. They had stuff for everything. There was a sense of carefully applied science. Their juicer was powerful enough to wring nectar from a breeze-block; their bedding gave off scents designed to stimulate sleep. Their vitamin regimen was rigorous and complex. Daniel hadn't smoked in months. Each morning before work, after an invigorating ylang-ylang-infused shower and a breakfast of carefully selected nutritionally balanced cereals, he threw carrots and apples and oddly shaped multi-ethnic fruits he couldn't name into the gaping maw of his juicer and knocked back 250 ml of pure unadulterated well-being. Like so much in his life, it was healthily vile, but the sourness was sweetened by virtue: you could boast about it; it made you a better person.

All their friends were couples. Angelica had been in a long-term relationship (her phrase) and her ex had treated her so badly that she'd taken all their friends with her when they split. Daniel had few friends of his own. Her friends were their friends now. At weekends they took it in turns to play host. One couple cooked, the other brought wine. A sense of competition lurked amidst the camaraderie. The plurals were barbed. *And we just had such a great time in New York, did you guys go anywhere this year?* Or even the supposed simplicity of *How are you two?* Couldn't one be up and one be down?

The most common visitors were Sebastian and Plum, who were visiting this particular evening. Plum was Plum's given name. She had those kinds of parents. Her sister was called Nasturtium. Sebastian, rather ironically, was not Sebastian's given name at all but simply a name he happened to prefer to what he'd actually been christened: Walter. Sebastian, much to his chagrin, had those kinds of parents. He'd been baptised and, for a while, home schooled, but had shaken it all loose at the age of eighteen by running away to Goa, where he'd undergone a tie-dyed transformation and returned as Sebastian Freud. His parents were outraged, but Sebastian was *past* parents. He was past a lot of things. Like Angelica, he'd *worked through* a lot of stuff. He was narcissistically altruistic. He bragged about his selflessness. His soliloquies were two parts arrogance to one part suggestive condescension. He thought Daniel was repressed. Daniel thought he was a prick. They'd tolerated each other during the days of doing good, which Daniel now thought of slightly more clear-sightedly as the days of impressing Angelica, but in the six months following Daniel's acceptance of a position at the Jenssen-Meyer Centre, which Sebastian happened to be targeting with one of his protests, their ability to pretend to get along had, to say the least, waned.

Daniel was, broadly speaking, honest about his work in The Centre's PR department, and honest about the work in which The Centre was engaged. What he was not quite honest about was how he had got the job and the moral flexibility he was encouraged to enjoy now that he had it.

Operating in the field of biochemical crop research, the Jenssen-Meyer Centre was run by two of the eighties' more notable radical humanist biologists: Lens Jenssen and Colin Meyer. Their credentials when it came to life in the trenches of the nascent environmental movement were, as Daniel had grown adept at pointing out, pretty unimpeachable. Given their background, and the fact that the aim of their work was the creation of a sustainable food source, Jenssen and Meyer were understandably upset to find themselves the target of exactly the sort of protest they probably would have been part of twenty years ago, and so, when it came to selecting someone to manage their public statements, were keen to select someone who had what they slightly euphemistically called an *understanding* of the dreadlocked crusties currently frightening investors by touting banners in the car park. Daniel, who by that stage felt he had, if he was honest, done enough not only to impress Angelica but also to slough off the slash-and-burn anti-ideology of Katherine's world-view, and who was beginning, much as he'd enjoyed what he would later think of as his gap-months, to tire of Angelica's idealism and to miss the sense of professional advancement that had formed the bedrock of his life to date, saw an opportunity to balance one half of his life against the other, and so was excited to find himself shortlisted, which went some way to explaining the zeal with which he interviewed.

Jenssen and Meyer were seen as elitist, he told them. Their image had become secretive; self-satisfied. Their shared background in radical biochemistry; their once-alternative lifestyle which they'd always worn as a badge of pride, wasn't actually cause for admiration at all. The hippies, far from seeing Jenssen and Meyer as kindred spirits made good, saw them as sell-outs. To them, all engagement with the powers-that-be was suspicious. Hippies didn't want to achieve anything, Daniel said. They wanted to sit in rented halls and recapitulate old arguments, all the while comforting themselves with the notion that their inability to change anything was simply because society was tilted against them. This meant that Jenssen and Meyer had, in the eyes of the demonstrators outside their building, committed a kind of double sin. Not only had they sold out, they'd also accidentally demonstrated that selling out worked, and for that, Daniel said, the hippies were never going to forgive them. He understood that it might have been a point of personal pride to win over people they thought should have been their friends in the first place, but the truth was it was time to make new friends. Rather than selling the ideological integrity of their research to the alternative set, he suggested, they needed to sell the respectability of their research to the respectable set, because at the moment they were falling between two ideologically opposed stools and doing a grand job of pleasing neither. Just as the demonstrators used Jenssen and Meyer's background as proof they had no loyalty to firm ideals, so the more conservative amongst the research communities used it as evidence of their potential flakiness. In the end, no one cared about the hippies and what they thought. If Jenssen and Meyer wanted to succeed, Daniel said, building to a crescendo, it was time for a clean break. Fuck the hippies.

From here, naturally, he pointed to his well-documented background in the corporate sphere as well as his less-documented background in the hippie sphere and suggested that if they found anyone with a more perfect balance of the particular elements that this role would require someone to juggle they should let him know. They offered him the job on the spot. He sold it to Angelica as a way of genuinely making a difference, and to her credit she'd given him the benefit of the doubt. Sebastian, on the other hand, had not only failed to stop demonstrating but, probably out of sheer spite, had stepped up his efforts, meaning that the façade of friendship they maintained for Angelica's benefit was now thinner than ever. Nonetheless, every weekend Daniel had to smile his way through dinner, the phrase *fuck the hippies* sticking rather uncomfortably in his throat.

The evenings were all much of a muchness, and Daniel found them tolerable only in that they spared him having to spend another evening bonding with Angelica. Angelica always cooked – something lumpy and hearty and altogether heinous – and Sebastian and Plum always brought wine – something dry and unusual with impeccable political credentials.

Tonight was, naturally, no different. They arrived late enough to demonstrate their casual disregard for bourgeois punctuality yet not so late as to relinquish the right to get angry if anyone was ever overly behind schedule for one of their own gatherings. Plum was wearing a dress she'd fashioned herself from a collection of period cushion covers sourced, as she explained, from an amazing little charity shop they'd found while holidaying in Brighton. Sebastian was wearing brown boots with heels that were borderline Cuban, stonewashed jeans and a jacket with a Nehru collar. His long hair was tied back in a way that made it look like his smile was caused by tension across his scalp and face.

'Ange,' said Sebastian, kissing Angelica on the lips (cheek-kissing was repressed, everyone seemed to agree, and reserved only for uncomfortable or false situations). 'Great to see you. God, you look fabulous. Doesn't she look fabulous, Daniel?'

'Of course,' said Daniel as Plum kissed him on the cheek. 'As do you, Plum.'

'Barium irrigation,' she said, reaching over to embrace Angelica while Sebastian waved awkwardly at Daniel across the hugging women. 'I feel like superwoman.'

'It's amazing how much crap you can hold in your colon,' said Angelica.

They seated themselves at the dining table, where Angelica had lit candles. The stereo was playing something Brazilian. Angelica went off to gather the meal.

'Can I do anything, hon?' called Daniel.

'No,' she called back, much to his disappointment. 'Just stay and entertain, darling.'

Sebastian smiled. 'You don't mind me telling Ange how fabulous she looks, do you?'

'Of course not,' said Daniel. 'How are you, anyway?'

'Wonderful,' said Plum.

'Lots happening,' said Sebastian.

'That's great,' said Daniel.

'And how about you?' said Sebastian, flashing his teeth. 'How's life in the lab?'

'I don't work in the labs,' Daniel replied, for perhaps the hundredth time.

'Oh yes, I always forget. You don't research, you just proselytise the research.'

'Oh leave him alone, Seb,' said Plum.

'I'm just ribbing him a bit. You don't mind, do you, Dan?'

Daniel did mind, and also disliked having his name abbreviated, but commented on neither transgression, since to do so would ruin the atmosphere. Angelica set great store by atmosphere, and woe betide anyone who was caught jeopardising it.

'Well I think proselytising's a bit strong,' said Daniel. 'It's more a sort of educational capacity, really.'

'You're the minister of propaganda then,' said Sebastian.

'Not really, no.'

Like many in his circle, Sebastian determinedly equated anything he didn't like with fascism.

'You've seen the headlines, I assume?' said Sebastian. 'God, what am I saying? You probably wrote the headlines.'

'Which headlines are we talking about?'

'You know, the ones about The Centre.'

'Oh, those,' said Daniel. 'Yes, we're not sure where those are coming from, actually.'

'I assume you're about to tell me they're untrue.'

'Well I wasn't actually, but since you mention it, yes, they're totally false.'

'Spoken like a true believer.'

'Believing's got nothing to do with it. The Centre is researching a sustainable crop source. Whatever's going on with the cows is completely unrelated.'

'But what if they've been eating modified crops? What if this is a glimpse of us in the future?'

'If you think cows eat crops then you're incredibly naïve. More to the point, if it's true that this is a virus that's capable of jumping the species barrier, which everyone seems to think it is, then that would rule out the food source as the infecting agent.'

'Not really,' smiled Sebastian, who hated being called naïve to the exact same degree as he loved labelling others as such. 'It could be picked up in the food source, then passed to humans when they eat infected meat.'

'Yes, but that only brings us back to the question of the food source. Don't you remember Mad Cow? Cows eat mushed-up cows for breakfast, lunch and dinner.'

'You know,' said Sebastian, his lip curling. 'You should work in PR.'

'And you should spend your life picketing stuff you don't understand,' snapped Daniel. 'Saw you out there the other day. You looked dreadfully cold.'

'Warm in your office, was it?'

'Yes thanks.'

'Long way from that car park now, aren't you?'

At this, Daniel simply laughed, even if it was only to mask his grimace.

'We're not onto this already, are we?' said Angelica, carrying through the lentil thing and rolling her eyes. 'I mean for God's sake, boys, let it go.'

Sebastian spread his hands in a smug, blameless way. Daniel did the same in an equally smug, though slightly less blameless way.

The conversation moved on. Plum and Sebastian talked about Brighton. They always talked about places as if the people to whom they were speaking could never possibly have been there. Daniel had been to Brighton, but didn't say anything. He'd already flirted with a spell in the doghouse during his exchange with Sebastian. He was usually, he thought, better at managing these occasions. Perhaps it was Katherine's call, the stirring up of all those unpleasant memories and sensations. Perhaps it was the flu. Either way, he felt decidedly sharp-edged. Katherine would have said this was his true self. As far as she was concerned, conviviality was always a lie. You could fake being nice, she would say, but being a cunt came from the heart.

When Daniel tuned back into the conversation it had turned to politics and failures of government. It never ceased to amaze Daniel that, years after Blair's departure, his shortcomings remained a fixture of dinner-party conversation. If that wasn't a legacy, Daniel didn't know what was.

'I mean,' said Sebastian, 'just *look* at Afhanistan.'

'Oh I know,' said Angelica. 'Afyanistan is a *horror*. To think that man actually took us there.'

It was, Daniel noticed, an unspoken agreement within the group that the names of foreign countries had to be pronounced with a slightly different inflection than was usual, delivered with such confidence that it implied ignorance on the part of anyone oafish and colonialist enough to say Af*ghan*istan.

'You know,' said Sebastian, leaning forward in the manner that always presaged his saying something intense. 'The Native Americans have this really fascinating approach to the whole concept of leadership.'

'Oh I love their outlook on things,' said Angelica. 'Like their system of non-ownership and their whole attitude to the land? It's so awful that we just crush these cultures without learning from them first.'

'It's true,' said Daniel. 'We should learn *then* crush.'

'Oh you know what I mean. Don't be pedantic.'

'What they say,' said Sebastian, quickly heading off any possible sidetracking, 'is OK, you can be our leader, you can be our chief or whatever, but only until you start *behaving* like our leader. You see?'

'Mmmm,' said Plum. 'God, that's so beautiful.'

'Mmmm,' said Angelica.

'Because what they're saying,' said Sebastian, 'is that power corrupts, right? It's like the . . . the inevitability of fascism.' He clapped his hands once, quickly, clearly pleased with the phrase. 'And the second they spot that you're going over to the dark side . . .' He drew a finger across his neck. 'You're finished.'

'So who makes that decision?' said Daniel. 'I mean, is there a sort of matrix of warning signs or something? What are the key indicators? Buying a Porsche?'

'I think that's a very materialist way of looking at what is essentially a spiritual matter.'

'Well I think the whole thing's a very spiritual way of looking at what is essentially a practical matter. Don't you want your leaders to behave like leaders? Don't you want them to take responsibility?'

'Mmhmm,' nodded Sebastian. 'But there's the issue of the common good.'

'Who decides that?'

'Daniel's a bit grumpy today,' said Angelica, rubbing his back and pouting. 'He's had an ickle bit of fwoo.'

'Oh fuck off.'

'You'd be right out of the Native American leadership circle with that sort of behaviour,' said Plum, winking at Daniel. She had a way of somehow joining in with the general conversational trend while at the same time suggesting a degree of sympathy with the underdog, meaning no one could ever justifiably get angry with her, meaning in turn that Daniel quickly became angry with her but had no idea how to express it without looking like an arsehole.

'Illness is such a blessing,' said Sebastian, helping himself to some more of the lentil thing. 'It's so cleansing.'

'I'm full of snot. I don't feel cleansed.'

'Gwumpy wumpy,' said Angelica, reaching down to pick up the cat, groaning a little as she heaved its formless mass onto her lap. 'He's gwumpy, isn't he? Yes he is. Yes he *is*.'

'I remember when I had dysentery in Sri Lanka,' said Plum. 'God, it was like being a new person at the end of it.'

Sebastian put his arm round her and kissed her temple. 'You were so beautiful going through that,' he said.

'Gwumpy man. Gwumpy wumpy daddy man. Yes he is. Yes he is.'

'Do you have to talk to the cat about me in that way? I mean really? Is it really necessary?'

'Animals know our true selves,' said Sebastian. 'If you're comfortable with your true self you have nothing to fear from the cat, regardless of what Angelica says to it.'

'I'm not that concerned about the cat's opinion, actually, it's more the . . .'

'I sometimes feel like he looks right through me,' said Angelica, looking at Daniel but ostensibly referring to the cat. 'Like he can just walk into the room and *know*, you know? Like the other day when I was feeling really negative, you remember, honey, over that whole thing with the phone and the . . . anyway, that's irrelevant, I don't want to go back to that space again, but he just walked into the room, and looked at me, and I just felt he understood, and he came and sat with me, and it was so calming, and I thought, all of this is happening without language, without words.'

'It's true,' said Daniel. 'He knows the pain of being mischarged on your quarterly BT bill.'

'It's not that literal,' said Sebastian.

'I know. I was sort of joking.'

Sebastian nodded as if this confirmed something very important to him. It was one of the things that Daniel had never quite understood about Sebastian and Plum and their ilk. For people who believed in freedom and expression and peace and love, who railed daily against the tyranny of the squares, they were oddly humourless, as if free expression and boundless emotional exploration were such a serious business that they left no room for actual fun.

'Who wants more?' said Angelica, pouring the cat onto the floor as she stood up to attend to the food. 'Honestly, there's loads.'

'I couldn't,' said Plum. 'Really.'

'Not for me,' said Daniel. 'Lovely as it was. I'm stuffed.'

'Looks like it's just you and me, Seb. Go on, have another spoonful.'

'Absolutely don't mind if I do,' said Sebastian, passing his plate over. 'You must give me the recipe.'

'I'm so blessed to have a man who cooks,' said Plum.

'Oh, you are,' said Angelica. 'Daniel's a bloody disaster area in the kitchen.'

'How can you eat something if you don't have a relationship with it?' said Sebastian, dry-swallowing another wad of brownish paste.

'Mmmm,' said Angelica.

Daniel said nothing. The difficulty of these little soirées with Sebastian and Plum was that they had a tendency to cast Daniel as the negative one, the one who blew the vibe all too easily. This meant that he not only had to tolerate them but also had to out-positive them, which of course was difficult when he felt he was about to gag.

He decided to quarantine himself quickly, before all the sewage inside him escaped.

'I'm sorry,' he said. 'I'm not well. I might need to lie down.'

'Really, honey?' said Angelica. 'Are you really feeling rotten and miserable?'

'Yes,' said Daniel. 'Sorry.'

'Maybe we should go,' said Plum.

'No, no,' protested Daniel, noting that Sebastian had remained silent through this exchange. 'Don't mind me. You stay and have a good time. I might even come back down. I just need a bit of a rest, that's all.'

'Feel better soon,' advised Plum.

As he climbed the stairs, already regretting what must have seemed a sudden and rather pathetic exit, he could hear Sebastian taking up the theme.

'You know,' he said, 'the Bhutanese believe that how someone handles illness says a lot about how they handle life . . .'

He lay down on the bed, fully clothed, and closed his eyes. The lentils were repeating. He felt weighed down, awkwardly anchored to the world around him. His brain was somehow racing and limping at the same time.

He was, he thought, slightly self-indulgently but with a certain amount of satisfaction, *troubled*. He recognised this because it wasn't a new phenomenon. Just as spots of blood will point to guilt or illness the scarlet smear on the handkerchief; the pink streamers of sinister matter in the urine), so Daniel's thoughts were increasingly spattered with ugly spots of troubling disturbance. Childhood transgressions bubbled to the surface. Old crimes and embarrassing social stumbles pricked at him from the darker recesses of his memory. At perfectly ordinary moments he found his ears burning, his cheeks flushed, his stomach twisting down towards his bowels at the memory of mistakes gone by. Did he think he was perfect? Did he *wish* he was perfect?

Recently, as if he had unconsciously exhausted his archive of slight yet resilient pains, the memories had begun to be accompanied by sudden, pressing fears. What if Angelica became ill? What if he became ill? What if he lost his job? Perhaps Angelica didn't love him. Perhaps she had met someone else. How would he be able to tell? How could he tell if he loved her? Like the memories, these fears loomed seemingly from nowhere, from the depths or the peripheral distance, like fish nipping at breadcrumbs on the surface of their calm pool. He wondered if it was because, as he had thought before, he was evaporating as he aged. Perhaps as all the fluids of his self drifted skywards, the things he'd long since drowned returned to the surface. He pictured those selfsame fish – beached, gills gaping, scales already losing their luminescence in the suffocating air. Was this what he was? Was this what everyone was, in the end, a collection of buried, ignored, suppressed detritus that remained stubbornly on the tideline after everything else had receded?

Thinking about it now, in bed, with his hand over his eyes and a childish tremble in his upper lip, he realised that this was why Katherine's call had unnerved him so thoroughly. Here, at the sight of a single name scrolling across a screen, was the feeling of everything he'd buried being exhumed without dignity. Yes, he had let Nathan down towards the end, of course he had, they all had. Yes, he had cut Katherine off in a manner unbefitting their five years together, giving her the sense, as she had said in her last letter to him just under a year ago, that none of it had mattered, that it had all been a mistake. And yes, most of all, he had lied to Katherine, had cheated on her in no uncertain terms. This was the crux of it. This was what troubled him, and this, if he was honest, was the main contributing factor in his unease around Angelica: the fact that he had, although he had never discussed it, walked out of the bar the night he'd met her, after all those epic, idealistic conversations, feeling what he knew to be the first stirrings of something he'd long thought lost to him, and gone home, to Katherine, with whom he had not yet parted, and told her, just as he had *this* very evening told Angelica in an uncomfortably similar way, that he had spoken to 'no one' the whole evening. And yes, he had called Angelica when Katherine was at work the next day, and yes, he had in fact fucked Angelica some weeks later, still without having ended things with Katherine, and when Katherine had asked if there was anyone else, that night, when it had all come to an end, he'd told her, with a straight face, that he would never do that to anyone, that he didn't believe in it, and yes, that had been when Katherine had told him, as if she knew (did she know?) never to say never, and had indeed uttered the words that still haunted him now, as he lied and pretended and hid his self-disgust behind disgust at the shortcomings of others: *the higher the horse, the harder the fall.*

The café in which Nathan sat was, to the naked eye, perfectly square. Its lino floor was a black-and-white check, as were, confusingly, the tiled lower halves of its otherwise off-white walls. The tables were square and topped with white Formica, giving a stiflingly uniform appearance against which streaks of ketchup and eggy breakfast remnants stood in garish relief. The chairs were cheap and flimsy and bowed when taking a larger person such as Nathan's full weight. They were also small and made a large person feel larger, a feeling at dissonant odds with the fact that they were low and so made a person of any size feel smaller due to the resulting height of the table. Some tables were placed side by side in order to seat four. One assumed that a party of five or more would need to make their own arrangements. One table had only salt while another had only pepper. The ketchup was dispensed from a fake plastic tomato almost four times the size of an actual tomato. The salt and pepper pots were miniature people with either black or white hats depending on their contents whose blank expressions seemed eerily incongruous given the fact they were stood next to a giant and no doubt slightly threatening tomato. The café was of the cutlery-will-be-dispensed-along-with-food-and-not-before school of hospitality. There were no napkins as these were offered as a scabbard for the cutlery. Nathan's black Nescafé had been served in a black mug. When he leaned over the mug it had the appearance of a dark vacuum into which he might fall or from which something unspeakable might emanate. At least one person in the café was staring at him. The winter sun was level with the roofs of the opposite buildings, allowing its light to stream uninterrupted through the glass door and broad window of the café, backlighting the three other patrons as they sat in relation to Nathan and causing him to squint and then blink rapidly whenever he looked up from the black hole of his coffee, leading in turn to the sensation that reality was a gauzy screen in which some nameless creature had chewed ragged holes.

Nathan's possessions: one holdall containing three complete changes of clothes, two books and basic toiletries; a packet of rolling tobacco that also contained papers, filters and a Zippo lighter; and his wallet. The coat that had once seemed adequate was no longer sufficiently effective despite the body heat generated by the brisk three-mile walk on which Nathan had embarked because he didn't want his parents to collect him directly from The Sanctuary and didn't want any of The Sanctuary's staff to drive him anywhere. He'd thought that walking to the nearest village would make him feel good. He did not feel good.

For much of Nathan's adult life people had stared at him and as a general rule he accepted this, just as he also accepted that it was likely to occur more frequently given certain developments and alterations in his physical presentation. Keeping his coat on had not entirely concealed the tattoos and scars that crept vine-like out of his collar and sleeves. His beard was shaggy and wiry; his hair neck-length and pushed back off his face using some Brylcreem he'd borrowed from another resident. People could have surmised a lot from his eyes, he thought, if they'd been looking at his eyes.

The café was greasily steamed and smelled strongly of damp rag. Nathan had ordered a breakfast the menu described as Olympian. There were four other people there: an elderly couple with mugs of tea, dividing the *Sun* between them according to sections of interest; the woman who ran the place, wearing a blue tabard and a hair net and a smile that looked like she might have to sit under the drier every morning to have it set; and in the opposite corner a stubbly, thick-set man eating a bacon roll and peering at Nathan over the crest of his bap. This wasn't how Nathan had imagined his first meal outside, but when he thought about it he realised this was partly because he hadn't imagined much at all. He felt tired. The conditions were draining. You probably had to wash the walls in a place like this, he thought, but in a place like this that probably didn't happen. He wondered if the café offered brown sauce and if they did what sort of symbolic dispenser it would be served in. Bap-man was chewing ostentatiously, perhaps even aggressively. The woman with the styled smile brought his breakfast and the cutlery that went with it. It was not the first time Nathan had not been trusted with cutlery outside of the circumstantially appropriate setting of a meal. The resonance of this was notable but not particularly upsetting. The newspaper couple were now doing the crossword together. Bap-man asked for another cup of tea. Nathan's eggs were fried just to the point of congealing and no further. The sausages were of the cheap supermarket variety and contained indeterminate pieces of hard matter which he took to be bone. The bacon was not crispy. After asking, he determined that brown sauce was not an option. He'd eaten very healthily for several months and the grease was a shock and the shock was a disappointment because the anticipated emotion was happiness. He was careful to chew his food and to pay attention to what he was eating but the bone in the sausages might have been a reality too far. His coffee was hot and he burned his mouth and then experienced that sandy feeling on his tongue which would last, he expected, about a day.

When Nathan was six years old his mother had discussed with him in detail the *Chambers Concise English Dictionary* definition of *disappointment* and his exact relationship to the word with reference to his relationship to her. During his time away Nathan had at one point redefined the word *sadness* as plural rather than singular and now continued to think about sadness as a sort of extended family of which some members were more approachable than others. His hands had a twisted, tightened look as he ate and after a long period spent abandoning his self-consciousness he realised that he was again self-conscious. It was possible that the man with the bap was not looking at him, just as it was possible that the dimensions of the café were not in themselves unsettling, although the fact that the table and chairs were uncomfortable was certain. It was very strongly possible that he did not want his parents to arrive, although it was also true that he did not want to remain in this particular café or even this village for a moment longer than was strictly necessary. Mustard would have made the sausages more palatable but after failing to secure brown sauce he noted a certain reluctance to ask for mustard.

He finished his breakfast by using a carefully saved slice of fried bread to mop grease and egg yolk and the cooled juice of baked beans from his plate. He finished his coffee although the black void of his mug made this difficult to determine, leading to a sense of exploration when he tipped the mug towards his mouth. The sandy feeling on his tongue remained and in turn caused an itchy sweat across his cheeks. He ordered a can of Pepsi and paid using the money from his wallet which he had not thought to check but which thankfully was sufficient. A cloud moved briefly across the sun and dimmed the extent to which the other patrons were backlit and rendered the face of the man with the bap more focused and less sinister and made it clear he was not necessarily staring. A claret-coloured Rover pulled up to the kerb outside. Nathan drank all of the Pepsi and put the can on the table. He picked up his bag and put his free hand in his pocket and left the café just as his mother, neatly resplendent in a powder-blue skirt suit that sadly accentuated the arterially blown mayhem of her calves, unfolded herself from the passenger seat and opened her arms for a hug with which Nathan was only physically able to engage and so for which he could not really be said to be present.

'Darling,' said his mother. 'We've missed you so much.'

She looked back at the car, where Nathan's father was visible in the driver's seat. 'Roger,' she said. 'Get out of the car.'

Nathan's father, a man who wore a year-round yachting jacket despite never having set foot on a yacht, slid out of the car accompanied by the industrial rustle of chemically complex fabrics.

'Kiddo,' he said. 'How goes it?'

He held out his hand to Nathan, who shook it.

'OK,' said Nathan. 'Fine.'

'Great,' said Nathan's father.

'Well,' said Nathan's mother.

They stood in an approximately equilateral triangle and each somehow angled themselves so as to face the emptiness between the other two. Nathan's father put his hands in the pockets of his yachting jacket. Nathan rubbed his beard. Nathan's mother performed a sort of smile that in order to be complete would have required machinery her face simply did not possess. Nathan debated a cigarette and thought maybe no. Nathan's father slid an iPhone in a protective pleather pouch from his Velcro-sealed pocket and stroked the screen.

'There's a window in the traffic,' he said. 'We should carpe diem.'

He loaded Nathan's bag into the back of the car and popped the rear door so Nathan could get in. Nathan's father drove, his mother sat in the passenger seat looking straight ahead. Nathan stared at the backs of their heads and necks, at his mother's neat grey bob and his father's wide, slightly red neck that always looked as if he were either angry or cooling off from sunburn. Duration of stay had not been discussed.

'Your room's looking lovely,' said his mother without turning round. She tended to direct her conversation to the windscreen when they were in the car. She had, Nathan thought, a child's sense of solipsism. She struggled with the concept of other minds. She thought if she didn't watch the road her husband wouldn't either.

'I see,' said Nathan.

'"I see," he says,' said Nathan's father.

'What do you want me to say?'

'I think your father's just looking for a little bit of gratitude, that's all,' said Nathan's mother. 'Bus, Roger.'

'Noted.'

Nathan's mother unpeeled the pocket-flap of her husband's yachting jacket and located the phone. She prodded and swiped at the screen with an efficiency that Nathan found unsettling.

'Five new mails,' she said shrilly.

Nathan thought his earlier decision re: having a cigarette might not have been the right one.

'Thinking of you as you pass this milestone,' his mother said in a tone of voice that made it clear she was reading out loud.

'Bless,' said Nathan's father.

'Who's that from?' said Nathan.

'Dear MotherCourage. I just wanted to tell you that you are an inspiration to me. I've read everything you've written. I hope so much you get your boy back, love Samantha69.'

'What boy?' said Nathan.

'"What boy?" he says,' said Nathan's father.

'At last count I only had one,' said Nathan's mother.

Nathan's seat belt greatly restricted forward movement and made it difficult to properly converse with his mother. Undoing his seatbelt would have led to an unnecessary conversation with one or other of his parents.

'Are you MotherCourage?'

'Of course I'm MotherCourage,' said Nathan's mother.

'So who's Samantha69?'

'One of my followers.'

'What followers?'

'Now I want you to know,' said Nathan's mother, still caressing the phone and directing her speech to its screen while every second or so checking the road, 'that we are here for you, and we are not seeking confrontation. But at the same time, if there is confrontation, then that is OK. Confrontation is OK, Nathan. It's nothing to be scared of.'

'I'm not being confrontational,' said Nathan.

The angle of the setting sun was such that flipping down the little screens to either side of the rear-view mirror, as Nathan's parents had done, was essentially pointless. The car's dashboard readout showed an external temperature of zero degrees Celsius and an internal temperature of twenty-eight. Nathan had not removed his coat and now felt too restrained to do so. His reluctance to unfasten his seatbelt could not be entirely explained but may have related to a sense of both security and enforced restraint that he found comforting.

'Mothers Who Survive,' said Nathan's mother.

'Who are mothers who survive?'

'Mothers Who Survive *dot com*. The website.' His mother's voice was strategically calm to the point where it aroused the exact opposite sense in Nathan. 'It's for mothers who have, at one time or another, as the name suggests, *survived*.'

'Survived what?'

'"Survived what?" he says,' said Nathan's father.

'Their children,' said Nathan's mother.

A copse of trees split the dwindling sunlight into smithereens and initiated a strobe effect not dissimilar to rapid blinking. The sense of reality-as-gauze-screen was not going anywhere fast. When Nathan clenched his fists the scar tissue stretched across the knuckles in a way that reminded him of Parma ham wrapped round a chicken breast. There was no pain. Use of his fingers, arm, or other bodily parts had not been affected. He said, 'As in what. As in they outlived their children? Or as in their children tried to kill them?'

'Both. Either. All sorts.'

'But I'm not dead.'

'You don't need to be.'

'And I haven't tried to kill you.'

'It's a very inclusive organisation. It's about sharing, not ring-fencing.'

His mother was still talking to the windscreen. Anything to which she didn't pay attention would spiral out of control. Approximately a year ago she had explained to Nathan that failing to think of himself as having a condition was itself a symptom of his condition.

'Sharing what?' said Nathan.

'Our trauma,' said Nathan's mother.

'What trauma?'

'The trauma we've been through.'

'That's not an answer.'

'The trauma,' said Nathan's father bluntly, 'of you.'

Fields rushed by, furrowed, stripped of life. The sense that there had once been crops in fields that were now bare made them appear as places where something had already happened: post-evental; forlorn. Things arrived; departed. The sense of abrasion on his tongue.

The way the sun can seem cold. The way things occurred and were forgotten.

'Nearly there,' said his father.

Nathan's parents' home was a once-beautiful cottage on the Cambridgeshire–Suffolk border that they'd bought cheap and ruined at great expense. Trawling around for their ideal retirement location after celebrating Nathan's departure from what his mother called, without a hint of irony, *the family nest*, they had stumbled on an increasingly frail and not entirely undemented ex-schoolmaster who, due to issues of mobility, sanity and convenience, was looking to sell fast and get the hell out before he was found, as he put it, half-rotted in a pool of his own juices. Struck by his plight, Nathan's parents had immediately and selflessly haggled him down to approximately two-thirds the fair price and had told him, in his best interests, that he really needed to move quickly, and that the best way to move quickly, providing one had the luxury of two such reliable buyers as them, was to cut out the middleman and stay well away from estate agents. As he signed the rudimentary contract he made them promise to stay true to the old place. They'd promised, then gutted it. Beginning the very day he moved out they'd set in motion a process Nathan would later describe as an aesthetic massacre. Never known for their concessions to taste, his parents had, in working on what they quite openly described as their *final abode*, reached the very pinnacle of their ugly aspirations. Leaded windows with wooden frames were replaced by PVC and double glazing which, as Nathan's father put it, kept the heat in and the noise out, although exactly what noise, given the house's location at the far end of an isolated lane on the outer edge of a sleepy village, was never very clear. The Rayburn, which had been in excellent condition due to the fact that the ex-schoolmaster had taken to living entirely off Birds Eye meals for one which he prepared in the microwave, was quickly replaced, to much fanfare by Nathan's mother, by an all-black electric hob with touch-sensitive controls. The original brick floors, which Nathan's father found were cold enough to breach even the luxurious integrity of his slippers, were covered in a thick cream shag. Exposed beams were boxed in ('so much neater'); soft pink Farrow & Ball walls were redone in an infinitely less dated Dulux magnolia; and the iron bath was replaced with something deeper, wider, and entirely more modern from B&Q. In the garden, which, much to Nathan's parents' consternation, turned out to be riddled with things that needed looking after, they ripped up, with the aid of a one-eyed man and his JCB, three apple trees, a greengage tree, a magnolia, and a rather complicated herb garden that was far too untidy to be saved. Appalled at the mess an untamed wisteria had made of the front of the house, Nathan's father set about it with loppers and a hacksaw until all that remained were the stubborn shadowy prints where it had clung to the plaster, which mercifully was going to be redone anyway.

At the end of it all, they were happier than they had ever been, and even invited old Mr Rudge, the ex-schoolmaster, round for high tea so he could see, as Nathan's mother put it, the potential that had been right under his nose all that time, but sadly Mr Rudge was off his food – an early warning as it transpired – and was dead less than a week later.

'At least he lived to see it,' said Nathan's father, nodding sagely.

Such was the work that had gone into the final abode that Nathan's mother was unable to enter it without a degree of show. She swept in, shedding her coat in a single, florid movement, hanging it on the peg Nathan's father had screwed to the wall at a slightly improbable angle and, consciously or unconsciously, trailing her hand alongside her as if running her fingers through the eddies of a refreshing stream.

'Tea,' she said with grandeur, and threw the switch on the kettle.

The dining table, Nathan observed, was fractionally too large for the kitchen, meaning it functioned more as something that needed to be negotiated than something at which one might be inclined to sit. It seated six, despite Nathan's mother's strongly held belief that for an informal gathering four was the optimum. Formal gatherings no doubt went by different rules. The table was pine, but had been varnished with a heat-resistant treatment so thick that it had the appearance of being synthetic. Despite the treatment, cups, plates and most certainly pans were not under any circumstances to be placed directly on the table, even if, as had happened to Nathan, you were foolish enough to have picked up a hot pan and needed to put it down before it burned you.

Nathan's mother didn't know how he took his tea. He noted that he was affronted by this yet not particularly surprised.

'Milk two sugars,' he said.

'I'll give you one,' she said, as if this were the very definition of kindness.

The chairs matched the dining table but, due to concerns about the linoleum (an off-white affair with a very pale yellow mosaic), had been outfitted with felt pads on their feet in such a way as to ensure that not a single chair in the room sat level, leading to a situation where Nathan was unable to stop gently rocking his chair from side to side.

'Stop that,' said his mother.

He stopped it, then started it, then concentrated very hard on stopping it and keeping it stopped.

'You know,' said Nathan's mother, turning from the fridge with a pint of milk aloft. 'You can freeze milk and it comes out just fine. It's worth remembering.'

Nathan nodded.

'And cheese,' she said. 'Cheese freezes ever so well.'

His father entered through the back door and began to struggle gamely with the zip of his coat, first wrenching it, then pausing as if to lull it into a false sense of security, then suddenly attempting to force it downwards with all his strength, as if surprise might have been the vital element missing from the battle.

'Arms up,' said Nathan's mother, motioning with her hands.

Nathan's father raised his arms and frowned as his wife yanked his jacket over his head.

'Now, Nathan,' said Nathan's mother, returning to the kettle and tarrying with a teabag. 'We want you to make yourself at home. I know you haven't been here in quite some time, and that coming home at thirty must come with its own, shall we say, *disappointments*, but I do honestly think you can be very happy here, and I want you to know that we're glad to have you, and that however long you want to . . . PUT THAT DOWN THIS INSTANT, ROGER.'

Nathan turned to the fridge, where his father was upending a flagon of neon-orange fluid into his gaping face.

'Honestly,' said Nathan's mother, marching towards him and snatching the drink from his grip, 'it's just *full* of Agent Orange. Where did you get it?'

'Garage,' said Nathan's father. He pointed lamely at the label. 'It has added vitamin C.'

'Do you want to have a stroke, Roger? Is that what you want?'

'I could go into a home,' said Nathan's father slightly wistfully.

'Oh, darling, don't be silly, you know I'd never allow that.'

Nathan traced a whorl on the tabletop and tried not to look at anything with excessive focus. Colours could be deceiving, he thought. It was possible to bring discomfort with you into a room that wasn't technically uncomfortable, although, that said, he thought the room probably was uncomfortable, one potential cause of which may have been the fact that the floor tilted imperceptibly but slightly tipsily downwards in one corner, creating an angle that opposed the angle of the ceiling's slope and gave the impression of being inside a student maths project completed without the aid of a protractor.

He rolled a cigarette.

'No,' said his mother simply. Then, 'Outside if you must.'

He took his tea with him. He was trying not to do memories, but at times they seemed to do him. He liked the cold. The house was too hot. The Sanctuary had been too hot. There was something immediate about being cold. It was good to stand and think; to breathe deeply. Suffolk skies seemed kind in their expanse; generous somehow; unfurling into scattered occurrences of cloud. His tea wasn't sweet enough and not worth enjoying alongside his cigarette. Most of the plants were gone but his mother was growing beans under teepee'd canes. She'd hung out old compact discs, presumably to keep the birds away. They spun in the gentle breeze. When he was eight he'd planted grape pips because his father had told him he could grow a vine. When the vine failed to appear his mother told him it was probably because he hadn't been good enough. He spent over a week being as good as he thought it possible to be, at the end of which, when there was still no vine, Nathan did not feel he had learned anything particularly positive. He looked at the CDs as they spun. On two of them, in black marker, was written: *Happy Mother's Day, Love Nathan*. He switched off several thoughts and went back to the kitchen. His mother was sitting at the dining table.

'Aha,' she said. 'He returns.'

Sensing an air of upcoming instruction, Nathan sat down opposite her and did four cycles of calming breathing.

'Now,' she said.

She took a deep breath, tapped one index finger against her pursed lips. Someone who knew her less well than Nathan would have assumed she was trying to think of what to say.

'Nathan,' she said.

'Hello there,' said Nathan.

'I need to brief you,' she said. 'Ever so quickly. Won't take long.'

'Brief me?'

'The most important thing,' she said, 'is that no matter who calls or what they offer you redirect them to me, OK?'

'What do you mean, what they offer?'

'No matter how much money, or how big the spread, we absolutely do not accept opening offers. Are we agreed?'

'Opening offers of what?'

'It's rather like when the government says they won't negotiate with terrorists. They do, of course. They have to. But it's important that they say they don't in order to dissuade time-wasters.'

'Are we going to be contacted by terrorists?'

'No. It's a metaphor. For journalists.'

Nathan wondered if four cycles of calming breathing might have been optimistic and considered doing another four.

'Did I not explain this over the phone?' said his mother.

'You said something, but, to be honest, I wasn't really listening.'

His mother blinked three times in an even rhythm.

'I'll reiterate,' she said. 'During your time away, there have been considerable developments. Mothers Who Survive has been very successful. I have nearly four thousand followers on Twitter.'

'What do you tweet about?'

'Well, largely I just link back to my blog, you know. But what with the book coming out I've also been trying to leverage social media as a promotional tool. The response has been excellent.'

Nathan felt slightly unwell in his stomach.

'Now, you can see this two ways,' said his mother. 'And I'm very aware of that. You could see it as selfish, or opportunistic. You could say that I've shown a callous disregard for your dignity and feelings.

And if you did say that, I'd understand.' She shrugged. 'It's nothing that hasn't been said by certain bleeding-heart columnists already. But you could also look at it another way, Nathan. You could look at it as my gift to you. You could look at it as me putting myself on the line, exposing myself, for you, just as I always have. Do you see?'

Nathan did not see and said so. His mother reached across the table and took his hand in hers. He had absolutely no idea how to respond.

'Just give it a chance,' she said.

Nathan's father ambled into the kitchen.

'We can take your stuff up,' said his father.

'Yes, good idea,' said Nathan's mother, releasing his hand. 'We can pick this up later. Just remember: no first offers, that's the main thing. Take his bags, Roger.'

'It's just one bag,' said Nathan.

His father had already picked up the bag and was not to be dissuaded. He was like an ocean liner: a change of mind was painfully slow and required a complex pattern of braking and turning before thrust could be reapplied. The stairs were lined with photos. Nathan watched his parents getting married; watched himself at some family function; watched himself graduate. There was a cavernous distance. Things sparked; faded; failed to echo.

'We can change it, if you want,' said his father, opening the bedroom door.

'No,' said Nathan. 'It's . . .'

He let the ellipsis hang. Somehow he could shape it with his lips. He saw it notated: '. . .' or '–'. Considerable and slightly misguided effort had been made. The duvet and pillows were gunmetal grey. He pictured his mother commenting that it was a good boys' colour. The bookshelves were metal; mildly industrial. His books were alphabet-ised and so were his CDs. On the bed was a toilet bag filled with the brand of men's scented products (Logger: For The Woodsman In You) his mother had bought him every Christmas since he was fifteen. When he swallowed it felt like a small animal had fashioned a nest in his larynx.

'Anyway,' said his father, and left.

There was a book on the pillow: hardback, its title embossed in blue above a picture of his mother inexplicably looking out to sea, wrapped in a scarf, the collar of her Barbour jacket turned up against what Nathan could only assume was a squall of spume-flecked adversity.

Mother Courage: One Woman's Battle Against Maternal Blame

Nathan opened the book to the first page of the first chapter and read:

Looking back, I probably should have known that Harry, as I'm going to call my only son in this book, would be a difficult child. Perhaps it all began with his conception – a lengthy, at times exhausting process made all the more difficult by . . .

He closed the book and lay back on the bed. After a few moments he put the book under the bed. He thought about his mother. She'd aged; found new interests; expanded her vocabulary and social circle; modulated her voice from self-taught social bray to whooping aspirational blare, but had not, as far as anyone who knew her well could see, changed. She still favoured tottering, precarious heels that caused her to tilt aggressively forward at all times and which led to people reactively leaning backwards when they were addressed by her, as one might from a person with particularly toxic breath. She still smiled with a surprisingly limited array of facial muscles.

Nathan's memories of her during his childhood were centred on his schooling. Here she was marching him in by his wrist and pulling up his shirt to show off the bruises he'd received at the hands of Benjamin Hollingdale during a disagreement on the school playing field which Nathan would have been very happy to forget. Here she was at parents' evening, expressing dissatisfaction at certain teaching methods employed by Nathan's middle school which, she said, through their refusal to 'stream' or 'set', disadvantaged the more able students, such as Nathan, by forcing them to learn alongside certain individuals from certain families who in all honesty, without being unkind or passing judgement, were never really going to progress. Here she was at Nathan's upper school explaining to a gathering of three senior teachers why Nathan was 'different' and why, although he didn't need to be treated differently, certain factors did need to be borne in mind when making decisions about group activities and involvement versus individual work and – she didn't want to say special attention but, well – special attention.

In his late teens, twice in his twenties and finally very firmly after the events of what she would only ever refer to as 'That Night', Nathan's mother had attempted to explain to him that because a fairly key characteristic of what she only started referring to as his 'condition' very late on in proceedings was that he didn't actually think he had any sort of condition at all, he couldn't really make what she would later, after much reading and research, call an *informed choice* about what should be done about it. There was, admittedly, a certain difference in approach. When Nathan was ten she might have said something like, *Why don't you at least try and be normal*, whereas by the time he was twenty-five she was becoming more adept in what she saw as the language of understanding, and so would have been at greater pains, if not actually to empathise, then at least to dress her language in the clothes of empathy and continually reiterate how she and Nathan's father were 'there' for him, and how they wanted to 'support' him, but how, if they were going to support him, he would have to take certain things 'on board' and basically stop trying to pretend he was normal, although the word *normal* had by then disappeared from her vocabulary. But these were minor changes and served only to mask what Nathan saw as the basic unchanging nature of the woman who had now taken early retirement in order to devote her life to changing his life.

Just as she was never one to let facts stand in the way of an opinion, Nathan's mother was disinclined to let tragedy stand in the way of potential opportunity. Mere days after That Night, as Nathan was swimming back up from what he regarded as an unnecessarily heavy dose of tranquillisers and attempting to flex his hands and arms under the bandages, his mother had seized the moment of him being at his lowest possible ebb and presented him with a face of such finely crafted tragedy that he was unable to refuse when she near-ordered him to do what she described as *one favour* and submit to a period of experimental residential treatment. At the time, Nathan was beginning to wonder if he *had* inflicted unnecessary misery on those around him, and so had agreed, some small part of him wondering if she might be right: perhaps he did need to change; perhaps it was the least that he owed her.

The spare bedroom had not previously been referred to as his. The change was not one with which he felt comfortable. The effort that had gone into the room's creation was both touching and oppressive. His possessions seemed unfamiliar in a new context. He couldn't be sure he had been the person who had owned these things: incense pots; empty jars; a pair of khukuri knives; a gyroscope. He stood and wandered. The bedside table contained a single drawer in which he found his mobile phone. Turning it on, he was surprised to find that his mother hadn't wiped it. He scrolled through the messages. They asked him where he was. They asked him why he hadn't replied. They dried up. One stood out:

Nathan. Hope you're OK. Call sometime. K x x. PS: Broke up with Dan.

He read it twice. Things rose; sank. He went to the window. The light was too strong. He turned back to the bed and unzipped his bag and then zipped it back up. He'd spent a lot of time being lonely, most of it around other people. He looked at the text again, thumb hovering over the call button. He felt relieved when his father tapped on the door and poked his head in.

'Your mother feels we should have some man time,' he said.

'Oh,' said Nathan.

'Do you like darts?'

'Sure.'

His father led him out to the garage, his yachting jacket squeaking as he pushed open the door and gesticulated towards the changes he'd made to the interior.

'This all came about when she made me get rid of my surfboard,' he said.

'When did you ever have a surfboard?' said Nathan.

'Oh, for a long time. One always thinks,' he sniffed, 'maybe one day I'll get out there, you know, hit the surf. Then she comes along and puts a stop to all that.'

Nathan pictured his father surfing in his yachting jacket.

'Right,' he said.

'Anyway,' said Nathan's father. 'There was something of a compromise. Because OK, maybe the time for surfing has passed. I can see that. But a man needs a retreat, a cave, so to speak.'

He flicked a switch and three strip lights lit the space. It was concrete-floored, chilly and faintly industrial. In the corner was a makeshift bar. On the wall at the far end was a dartboard.

'Let's play darts.'

'OK.'

'But first I need to piss.'

He pottered over to the edge of the garage and tugged at a flimsy-looking plastic door.

'You had a toilet put in?' said Nathan.

'Chemical toilet,' said his father, 'but the absolute best obviously. Very high waste-decomposition factor.'

His father shut himself in the little white cabin. As Nathan wandered about, casting his eye over the small drinks collection and the quiver of Union Jack darts on the edge of the old slab of worktop that served as the surface of the bar, he could hear his father sighing loudly.

'Let's hope that's the last of it,' said his father, still zipping his fly as he emerged. 'Don't seem to be able to tell these days.'

'Right,' said Nathan.

'OK, let's play. Here's your darts.'

He passed Nathan what must have been a spare set, the flights frayed, the tips dulled by countless landings on the concrete floor. 'Round the clock, OK? One to twenty then bull.'

'Right.'

'I'll go first.'

His father took a moment to position himself awkwardly with his toe on a strip of gaffer tape, tugging at his cuffs and waistline in order to throw unimpeded. 'Here we go. Bugger. Bugger again. Bugger. No score. So anyway, your mother says we have to talk about your feelings. Do you want to talk about your feelings?'

'Not really,' said Nathan, placing his toe on the line. 'One. No. Two. Two for me.'

'Thank God for that,' said his father, muscling up to the makeshift oche. 'Frankly I was dreading it. Bugger. Bugger again. So close. No score.'

'To be honest,' said Nathan, 'I'm pretty sick of talking about my feelings. Three. Four. No. Four for me.'

'Well, I suppose that's understandable. Shit. Bugger. FOR CRYING OUT LOUD. No score. Cocktail?'

'Not for me, thanks.'

'Mind if I have one?'

'No.'

While Nathan hit three in a row and took another go, his father moved to the bar and began sloshing a variety of fluids into a cocktail shaker, which he then vigorously agitated before decanting the frothy pink concoction into a highball glass and wedging a busted plum tomato onto the rim as a garnish.

'What's in that?' said Nathan. 'I'm on nine, by the way.'

'Pink lemonade, gin, curaçao and a dash of Disaronno,' said his father, toeing the oche. 'I call it The Quiet Revolt because I'm not really allowed lemonade. One! Whahay! And he's off the mark. Bugger. Whoops, almost. Score one for me. So, what are your plans?'

'Plans?'

'Yeah, your plans. You know, for your life.'

'I have no idea.'

'Fair enough. Early days and all that.'

'Can I have a lemonade?'

Nathan's father narrowed his eyes, a slightly hunted look crossing his face.

'Water will do,' said Nathan.

'Great. Ice and lemon?'

'Yes, please.'

'Or maybe just ice?'

'OK.'

They kept playing until Nathan won, at which point he watched for a further half-hour while his father finished off.

'Anyway,' said his father as they left, brushing invisible lint from the front of his jacket. 'Glad we had this chat.'

Before going to bed, Nathan showered – his first fully hot and undisturbed shower in months – and felt the scalding water ripple through his beard and down over the scars and fragmented tattoos that webbed his arms and chest, feeling cleansed and hollow and tired enough to sleep for days. Had he really slept at The Sanctuary? He'd thought at the time that he had, but looking back now and comparing it with the quiet, warm, well-made bed currently awaiting him, he was forced to wonder.

Stepping out of the bathroom, his lower half wrapped in a towel, he almost collided with his mother. Stripped of her skirt suit and makeup, her legs veined, her face slack and pale and, without its usual layer of makeup, more deeply ridged, more expressive as her eyes swept up his body and traced the patterns of pain he'd caused himself and, by extension, her, she looked, Nathan thought, suddenly older, a little softer, a little sadder. Her gaze roamed his chest. She winced, her eyes filming briefly with tears.

'Oh Nathan,' she said.

She covered her mouth; pinched her nose. Then she started to cry. He hugged her, felt her fingers feeling the ridges of the scars.

'I'm sorry,' he said.

'I know,' she said, nodding into his neck.

She held him at arm's length, taking him in. Then she sniffed, recovering herself.

'Please do something about that beard,' she said. 'You look a fright.'

Back in his room, he lay on his bed. At some point people were going to have to be encountered and dealt with. He was not entirely unprepared but resistant nonetheless. He felt, as always, torn between opposing sensations of loneliness. If there was a word that related specifically to loneliness in the company of others he didn't know it. Calling people would be pre-emptive and would establish a position of control as opposed to sitting around and waiting to see if people called and then being simultaneously relieved and disappointed if they did or didn't. This was the thinking that had led to him organising so many parties attended by so many people he both arrived and left without knowing. Sometimes he had attempted to connect, although mostly not.

He remembered, quite vividly, the evening of That Night, his peripheries hazed with whatever was in the water, the insides of his cheeks gnawed raw, his nerves oddly leaden, sweating behind the mask that was part of his costume, walking through a field of other masks and costumes, the bass heavy in his chest, pressing even at his corneas, at his cheekbones and the base of his skull, and leading a woman, not just any woman but a particular woman, a woman who stood out, with whom he had, on occasion, actually talked and actually come close to being himself, and who he liked because he suspected her of feeling lonely in all the ways he himself felt lonely, off to the side, sitting her on a log away from the din and the press of bodies and the steam of sweat in the cooling air, and taking off his mask and rubbing his eyes, and telling her, quietly and seriously, that he felt alone in what he could only describe as an atomic way; that he felt, sometimes, like a stray molecule in a structure that was always becoming. He could almost feel, he said, the invisible ties that pulled the people around him into a unified mass or whole, the energies and magnetisms that bound them. He could, he said, staring at the leaf-strewn floor and musing briefly that autumn was coming and the gatherings would soon cease for another year, walk through the crowd, and reach out his fingers to glad-hand and flesh-press, and feel nothing bar the enormous and unfathomable forces that rendered them united and him isolated. It howled inside him, he said, and howled all the worse at moments like this, when he felt surrounded and hemmed in and unable just to be alone with his alone-ness, which seemed to be the very thing his alone-ness demanded. He couldn't think, he said; couldn't talk. He looked at people's faces from behind his mask and saw only a flickering cathode blankness; a repulsion where attraction should have been. He was giving it all up, he said. He was turning his back. He was going somewhere where he might have a stab at feeling connected in the way he'd always wanted, connected in the way he felt, as coincidence would have it, to her, this particular woman. He said he thought she might feel the same thing; that she gave off, at times, a sense of isolation and radioactive distance that he understood, and which he believed he could help with, since he felt, as he'd already explained, so very much like her, so very alone like her, and he'd taken her hand and asked her to come away with him and told her everything would change: that they'd be cured; that two people so terminally alone could only ever be good for each other because they'd always need each other in such a vital way.

'Yeah,' she'd said simply, eyeing his costume and then briefly scanning the ululating crowd ahead. 'You're obviously really shy and lonely.'

'You don't believe me.'

She shrugged, exhaling smoke into the night and staring drily at the crush of dancing bodies, their hands stretched skywards in a gesture of celebration, supplication or surrender. 'So you're miserable. So what.'

'I'm saying I think I can be happier. I think we can be happier.'

She laughed grimly. 'Who said I want to be happier?'

'Doesn't everyone want to be happier?'

'Not me,' she said. 'Wanting to be happy just makes you miserable.'

She stubbed her cigarette into the dirt and stood up, shooting another glance in the direction of her boyfriend. 'We're all miserable,' she said. 'Trick is to find a way of doing it without being such a bloody cliché.'

She looked him up and down, quickly, half sneering, half saddened. 'Put your fucking mask back on,' she said.

After that, and after the remaining events of the evening which had led, directly, to his hospital admission and thereby to a lengthy and unhappy Christmas convalescence at his parents' house while he waited for his transfer in the spring to The Sanctuary, he had vowed not only to return to his old routine of silence, exile and cunning, but indeed to strengthen its rigour to the point of such inflexibility that no one would ever in fact be able to know him again. Knowing people, as in really knowing them and, worse, having them know you, was painful, and it was best, he'd decided, watching the woman to whom he'd revealed himself stroll cruelly away to rejoin the throng, simply not to do it, ever, and as if to mark the moment he made the decision, he said her name: *Katherine.*

He tapped the keys of his phone. Her voice, bright yet sharp-edged, bridged the distance.

Hi, it's Katherine. I'm either out or very reluctant to speak to you. Leave a message and find out which.

'It's me,' he said dumbly. 'I mean, it's Nathan. I, um, I'm sorry to hear about, you know, about you and Daniel. I . . . You two really had something, you know? Anyway, I've, ah, I've been away, and now I'm back, and I'd love to see you. Both of you. Do you have Daniel's number? Anyway, give me a call sometime. It'd be great to, ah . . .' He stopped, gears grating in his brain. 'I thought I could do this, but I'm not sure I can.'

He hung up, stabbed with worry. He lay back. He told himself we don't see things as they are; we see them as we are. We name things, sometimes wrongly. The eye plays tricks. We sit in rooms and don't feel well. Our mourning is at times premature; at times too late. The rooms feel external but are not.

His phone buzzed. He reached for it eagerly.

Hi all, he read. *Mother Courage here. I'll be on TV with Dr Dave 1pm Weds talking about my new book. Please watch and tweet! Love to you all. MC x.*

He breathed, and followed his breath inwards, to places where the scale of his thoughts was wrong. He noted; corrected. Long before he found his way back out, he slept.

A typical argument between Daniel and Katherine, during the phase of their relationship in which they'd become adept at disagreement, began with Daniel passing Katherine a book he'd read and urging her to read it, telling her the ending in particular was fantastic. Katherine became angry, saying the book was now ruined. Daniel pointed out that he hadn't told her anything about the ending, he'd just said he liked it. Katherine said she didn't care what actually happened, the simple fact of him saying he liked the ending gave it a certain promise which it would now, almost certainly, fail to live up to. She said she resented the idea that she needed to be told the ending of a book was good in order to encourage her to get all the way through it as this implied she had a tendency not to get all the way through books. Now, she said, the whole book was going to feel like a chore because she'd have to finish it whether she liked it or not just to show him she was capable of finishing it, and when she got to the end it would have Daniel's smug face all over it and reading it would be like eating a chocolate biscuit someone had been holding too long in their hand: it would still probably taste good, but it would be discernibly tainted. To Daniel, this metaphor was suspiciously appropriate, meaning that either Katherine was far more skilled in rhetoric than he was (very likely) or that she sometimes planned out her arguments in advance and then waited for the right moment to set them running (also likely), both of which thoughts made Daniel uncomfortable and gave him a sense of being on the back foot, which he attempted to counter by going on the offensive and asking when the idea of him enjoying or admiring something had become so repellent that it then prevented Katherine from enjoying it herself, as if appreciation were finite and he'd used it up ahead of her. It was more like, he said, someone leaving you a biscuit in the packet, and offering it to you, and you then refusing it because you'd already seen the person enjoying their biscuit too much. He said he felt this whole difficulty Katherine seemed to have with other people's enjoyment went right to the heart of their relationship and constituted a major flaw, since it seemed to prevent them ever enjoying the same thing at the same time. He cited other incidents. He said it seemed like if he told Katherine she'd enjoy something she was bound to hate it, and to practically crucify him for building her expectations to the point where disappointment was the only foreseeable outcome. However, if he calmly, and usually quite reasonably, predicted she'd hate something, she'd shoot him down for being negative. He said he felt pretty much like he was damned if he did and damned if he didn't.

Katherine said that was his whole problem. Why did he have to make a prediction either way? Why did he have to throw his opinion into the ring before she'd asked for it? It was like receiving a running commentary on things that hadn't happened yet. It left her with the feeling that she didn't know if something was happening as it appeared to be happening or if in fact it was only appearing to happen in the way he'd already told her it would happen because he'd filled her head so full of predictions she couldn't tell reality from prophecy anymore. She said she got the feeling that it wasn't about her enjoying or not enjoying anything at all, it was just about Daniel being right, which was so bloody important to him that he had to pre-empt everything just so he could enjoy being seen to be right. Daniel said she was right, this was all about him being right. Naturally, he was being sarcastic. Then he said what it was *really* about was her total inability to accept the times he was right, so she'd cut off her nose to spite her face (Katherine sneered at the cliché) and waste precious time and energy proving him wrong. What was it, he wanted to know, about him being right that was so difficult to take, and didn't she think there was something malignant going on in their relationship if she couldn't bear him enjoying or being right about anything, because what, really, did that leave him with? Then Katherine asked him how *he* felt when *she* enjoyed something and he said he didn't know because he couldn't remember the last time he'd actually seen her enjoying anything, which pretty much immediately upped the hostility level of the whole exchange.

Both Katherine and Daniel argued by continually defining and redefining what they called 'the Real Problem'. Whenever either of them said it they gave it heavy stress. If Katherine said it after Daniel had just said it she waggled her middle and index fingers in the air to indicate quote marks. The Real Problem was never really agreed upon, and so was a mutable term that could be loosely used to stand in for the *real* Real Problem, which was that, just as they couldn't agree on what might constitute the Real Problem, they actually couldn't agree on anything and were making each other miserable.

Daniel deployed the Real Problem Tactic at this point by suggesting that the Real Problem was that Katherine was so hell-bent on being overwhelmingly original and unpredictable that she'd somehow managed to completely divorce the things she genuinely felt from the things she wanted to feel or thought it would be cool or interesting to feel. The end result, as far as he saw it, was that she didn't feel anything at all but just responded in a calculated fashion to given situations and stimuli. If she wanted to be unpredictable, he said, she should try actually feeling things rather than thinking about them and then artificially constructing her feelings as a response to what she thought other people felt.

At this point, Katherine smiled: a pretty strong indicator of upcoming aggression.

Katherine said that she couldn't actually believe that *he, Daniel,* had the audacity to accuse *her, Katherine,* of not having adequate feelings. She said what he couldn't understand was that he regarded her feelings and responses as odd and inappropriate only because he was so bound up in his stupid ideas of what *most people normally did* (here she waggled her fingers with such scorn that Daniel could hear them flapping like little birds) and was so keen to keep his own responses and reactions in line with these broad and basically quite misguided notions of normality and conformity that the minute anyone had any kind of genuine, from-the-gut response he rejected it out of hand. Furthermore, she suggested, Daniel's whole concept of what she should or shouldn't be feeling was itself bound up in his apparently relentless insecurity, meaning that her happiness, or the appearance of her happiness, was of concern to him not because he cared about her happiness but because he cared about the way her happiness reflected on him. He needed her to be happy, was the basic gist, because that way everything, namely *them,* was OK, and this was, she said, a pretty oppressive and dictatorial pressure to live with. Sometimes she couldn't be happy, it was as simple as that, and if he was going to set off down some spiral of concern and doubt every time she appeared to be unhappy or expressed unhappiness in any way then clearly everything was going to fall apart because the very pressure of being happy was itself making her unhappy, just as the very pressure of building towards the ending of a book which was supposed to be great would in itself not only ruin the book because she'd be overly hasty in rushing through it to get to the supposedly great ending but would also utterly ruin the ending because it could only ever be a disappointment. (Katherine was highly skilled at bringing arguments back to their original frame of reference, a tactic that had the double effect of making everything she'd said seem to lead back to some central point, meaning her entire argument was, in terms of its interior logic, bulletproof, while at the same time implying that Daniel had forgotten what they were arguing about and so had unwittingly constructed an argument that was untenable and made no sense.) And anyway, she said, Daniel didn't even care if they were happy, he just cared if people thought they were happy, because happiness, to Daniel, was a way of showing off and feeling successful when in the company of others. So, she said, if Daniel wanted her to be happy and, in turn, wanted them to be happy or at least wanted them to appear to be happy the simplest thing to do would be to just leave her alone and let her be unhappy or happy or whatever the fuck she wanted to be without his needy and emotionally domineering and, when you got right down to it, actually pretty pathetic ongoing attempt to control her every fucking thought and feeling.

Daniel paused before responding in order to shape his face into an expression of combined pain and courage which he felt served the dual purpose of making him look invincible while also implying that Katherine had *really gone too far this time.*

Daniel then said, OK, yes, that was as maybe (which was his way of saying OK, no, that's not as maybe), but what about his happiness? Wasn't it perfectly natural that if you loved someone you wanted them to be happy and that in consequence a big part of your ability to be happy and relaxed was tied up in their happiness? It seemed to him, he said, that this was in fact perfectly normal and not something he had to justify in order to answer her frankly fairly predictable arguments about normality. He used the word *predictable* deliberately because he knew that a great part both of Katherine's self-image and insecurity was founded on the notion that she was different-slash-better-than everybody else, meaning he could very easily pick away at the things that made her feel good while simultaneously inflating the things that made her feel bad – a tactic he almost always felt guilty about afterwards because he knew that making Katherine feel bad could often lead to her feeling very bad indeed, but in the heat of the argument he was somehow never able to resist. Moreover, he said, did she have any idea how selfish her argument sounded? What if he was happy, and enjoying something, and either wanted to share that with her or didn't, whichever, and her non-enjoyment or general unhappiness impeded *his* enjoyment and happiness? Because that was, he said, how he felt, every day, all the time. Like the minute he was happy about anything she'd go and suck the joy right out of it until it was just a dry husk, and it was making him miserable, all the time, every day; and she wanted to talk about him being megalomaniacal about *his* feelings? Please. This coming from the person who whenever she was pissed off had to make sure everyone else was pissed off too, preferably more than she was? And if she wanted to go back to the book and the ending of the bloody book if she really wanted to be pedantic about it, her near-vitriolic dismissal of everything he'd enjoyed about the book and the fact that it had been his very enjoyment of something as simple as a good ending to a book which had started such a sprawling argument in the first place, actually made him think he didn't like the book so much after all, or that he was stupid for liking it. At the very least, his enjoyment of it was now counterbalanced by a lot of very negative feelings and reminders. And honestly, he said, even if you accepted that they were both somehow tyrannical about their emotions and both wanted other people, particularly each other, to feel what they themselves were feeling, wasn't the fact that he wanted her to be happy far more defensible and in many ways more admirable than the fact that she just seemed to want him and everyone else to be as miserable and fucked up as she was?

Then Katherine went quiet, and stared at him coldly, and gave her thin smile and cock of the head and told him in her most cutting and bile-filled yet still oddly calm and polite voice that not everyone was as able, or willing, as he seemed to be, of going through the whole of their lives consistently selecting the appropriate emotion from a fucking drop-down menu.

Unbeknownst to Nathan, it was after exactly one of these episodes (the initial subject shifted, so it could have been about a book or a film or the way Daniel always put sauce on his chips despite knowing full well that Katherine hated sauce on her chips and so wouldn't be able to eat any of his chips, but the routine that followed was usually fairly standard) that Katherine and Daniel decided they needed to get out more and possibly talk to a few people since they were, quite clearly, going stir-crazy within the admittedly rather close confines of their relationship. They had friends, of course, but these had dwindled somewhat over time. Apparently some of their friends found Daniel and Katherine a bit oppressive, and the ones who didn't find them oppressive, or who even seemed actually to be comfortable around them, Katherine and Daniel found a bit weird. It occurred to Daniel and Katherine that they might have been putting too much pressure on themselves; that, possibly, they were each looking to the other to provide a totality of human interaction, despite the fact that, quite obviously, no single person could ever be capable of this.

'Especially,' said Katherine, 'and I don't mean this in an aggressive way, you.'

'Me? What do you mean especially me?'

'Well, it's not like you're some kind of social dynamo, is it? I mean, don't get me wrong, I'm not having a go, but, you know.'

Daniel did know. Daniel knew very well, thank you very much. He found it difficult to socialise in an unpressured manner. This was complicated, and had to do with the fact that whenever he socialised with women he felt as if Katherine's eyes were boring into his vital organs, and whenever he socialised with men all his usual issues with men (their coded language, their constant joshing, the ever-present possibility of violence) got in the way.

'Can't we just go out and talk to some people?' said Katherine, lighting another one of Daniel's cigarettes because she was not, at that time, smoking.

'What people?'

'People people. As in *people*.'

'Where?'

'I don't know. Where people are. In a pub or something.'

'You want to go to the pub and meet people?'

'Not necessarily Meet, as in capital *M*, but small-*M* meet maybe, yeah.'

'People will think we're swingers.'

'So what? We'll meet some swingers then.'

'Why the fuck would I want to meet swingers?'

'This is what you do. You take things and then totally dampen them.'

'Are we going to argue about this?'

'I'm not arguing, I'm just saying.'

'But obviously if you say something like that then I have to say something back and then that's an argument.'

98

She shrugged. 'So don't say anything back,' she said. 'Just get your coat.'

It was easier, at times like this, to go along with what Katherine said. Her attention span and ability to commit were limited; her enthusiasm quickly exhausted. Often it was not so much the execution of the idea itself that mattered so much as Daniel's hypothetical willingness to give the idea a go. Frequently, in Daniel's experience, a notion such as this one would take them as far as the pub for one drink and then, with Katherine satisfied that Daniel was indeed prepared to go with her, they could simply return home refreshed.

On this particular evening, of course, that was not the case, because standing in the corner of the bar, alone and staring oddly, knocking back what was very clearly not his first Guinness of the evening, was the living embodiment both of Daniel's nightmare-man and of Katherine's dream-object of oddness: a hulking, bearded, heavily tattooed bear of a man-boy with a glint in his eye that spoke of, if not actual danger, then at least a pleasing (to Katherine) degree of risk, which presented the perfect opportunity to test the extent of Daniel's love for her through an exploration of the limits of his commitment.

'Go and talk to him,' she instructed Daniel once he'd bought her a drink.

'Fuck that,' offered Daniel.

'We came here to talk to people and that's who I want to talk to.'

'Well go and talk to him then.'

'He'll think I'm trying to chat him up. You go and talk to him.'

'What if he thinks I'm trying to chat him up?'

Katherine laughed.

'It wouldn't be funny,' said Daniel.

'If you loved me,' said Katherine, 'you'd go over there and talk to him.'

'If you loved me,' said Daniel, 'you wouldn't be so keen to see me get my sodding head kicked in.'

'If you loved *me*,' said Katherine, 'you'd do anything to make me happy.'

Of course, throughout these little bartering moments of one-upmanship there was always the question, for Daniel at least, of why precisely he felt the need to go along with them given that they frequently turned on some potential for his humiliation or harm. The answer, which he only ever touched on long after the incident in question was over, when he would lie awake at night and fume both at Katherine and himself for ever going along with her in the first place, was that he wanted to be loved just as much as Katherine and, further, that he wanted to be the kind of man who was capable of loving and being loved, in the kind of relationship where such things were valued, unlike, of course (and he always felt this conclusion needed a sarcastic drum roll, such was the sheer extent of its obviousness), his parents. *There,* he always said to himself just after thinking this: *I've said it.*

On top of all this was the further fact that Daniel looked up to Katherine. He felt lucky to have somehow persuaded her to be with him (despite the fact that he hadn't had to persuade her, a fact that contributed both to his unease and to his willingness to persuade her whenever she asked now, which she did pretty regularly precisely because she was very aware of how little persuading he'd had to do in the early stages); and such was the extent to which Katherine both knew this and reminded him of it, Daniel actually came to believe that he needed to do these things to hang on to a woman he still, despite everything, loved and needed, because as everyone knew a relationship meant work and sacrifice and all the other honourable yet bad-faith traits Daniel associated not just with intimacy but with adulthood in general.

'What shall I say?' said Daniel.

Katherine thought for some time, going over possibilities that might avoid Daniel coming off as creepy or dangerous (although the thought of Daniel coming off as dangerous was so comic as to be faintly tempting in its absurdity). Ultimately, the answer was obvious.

'Go over there,' she said, 'and ask him for some drugs.'

And Daniel, against whatever remained at the time of his better judgement, had gone over there and asked him for some drugs, and in doing so had found himself surprised at how mild-mannered Nathan seemed, and how willing to talk to a stranger, and so had asked Katherine over, and had arranged a time to buy some grass, on which occasion he'd hung around a bit and had a joint with Nathan, after which they felt like they owed him a favour and so offered to take him out for a beer, after which he told them about the parties he sometimes threw in remote and often rural locations, until the day, quite by accident and without any prior thought, they both simultaneously, in conversation, referred to him as a friend and, as much to their surprise as anyone else's, meant it.

I n Katherine's mind, necessity and loss had always been one and the same: what had to be done came always at the expense of what she wanted. Even if whatever it was that needed to be done had, at some time, been exactly what she wanted, the very sense of its shifting from desire to requirement would mean she no longer wanted it. The job she'd spent weeks fretting she wouldn't get became drudgery in practice; the cashmere sweater she'd coveted for months became an annoyance the second she had to hand-wash it. Even Daniel, on whom she'd expended weeks of flirtation and tactical blanking when they'd both briefly temped in the same company and he'd caught her eye by apparently having no interest in catching her eye, became just another source of resentment once the excitement of snaring gave way to the effort of keeping. Disappointment was, disappointingly, something of a habit.

So it was hardly surprising, given this long-standing and, in Katherine's eyes, perfectly reasonable trait, that she experienced the gradual reality of her pregnancy not as an event, or even really as a crisis, but as a loss. Her decisions were no longer her own. She was unfree, and her unfreedom was an ache that woke her in the night and numbed her in the day.

Acceptance was slow. She clung to what she could control. She was smoking heavily, drinking immodestly, eating too modestly by far. Rejection and disavowal were her dance partners. She was holding on, she knew, to all the wrong things. She was in denial about her denial. Daniel hadn't called. Daniel would call, she was sure, but it had been four days and each was harder and colder than the last. Muddy with lack of sleep, she'd passed grainy pre-dawn hours imperviously googling pictures of babies. She thought she might have been born without a cuteness receptor. Where others saw gifts she registered only a ransom demand. A child's needs were occult and various; the knowledge required to meet them arcane and unwelcome. There were patterns of feeding and weaning and putting down and picking up that were near Kabbalistic in their ritual complexity. It was important, she knew, to *support the head*. People kept saying they were a sponge at that age. She feared what the child might absorb. She imagined clasping its ankles and folding it in half and then juggling one-handed the awful array of wipes and creams and wadded packages of shit-filled nappies. People had special bags loaded with equipment. There was a commando element to the whole thing, a sense of technological and biological preparation. People lost their looks when they had kids. They aged; died a little. Katherine had seen it in the office. Zombies: pinched of eye and frayed of nerve; garbed in the rags of defeat. And never mind the psychological issues. That little sponge, sopping up everything you'd sloughed off, then spilling it all to their shrink after half a life of failed relationships and voguishly unfocused life choices. And this if the thing was even born right in the first place. She wondered how people had ever achieved comprehensive worrying before Google, which listed fears you never knew you had in the order other people had them. Global Delay, Down's Syndrome, Cerebral Palsy, Deafness, flippers for hands. Pregnancy post-thirty was something of a fraught business. Worst of all were the unnamed afflictions; the grey non-diagnoses of freakdom. Every parent wanted a label for their kids. At least if you had yourself one of those disabled children you earned a lifetime's free supply of sympathy and respect, like Debbie Boyd on floor three, who was, in the Dances-With-Wolves-style naming system to which the office seemed to adhere, *So Patient*, and who no one ever told off or teased for sleeping at her desk because she was widely regarded as being a saint and a martyr thanks to the fact that her son scoffed foil wrappers while binning the chocolate they contained and had a predilection for whapping his willy against the thighs of his Rainbow Daycentre classmates, whereas having one of those children that was just, as some children can be, *not right*, be it in the head or in the body, meant everyone simply assumed you were a terrible mother who'd ignored some nutritional or pedagogical footnote in the bible of parental perfection. Indeed, now that she thought about it, people were pretty likely to assume she was a terrible mother anyway since there was no father to speak of, and she was, she had to admit, a touch wayward at times, and had probably gone about this whole business with less than the required degree of planning. She'd be blamed for everything. In twenty years' time, when little Whatever-It-Was-Going-to-Be-Called-Presuming-Of-Course-She-Kept-It grew into a fully matured clock-tower sniper and started picking off sales shoppers with some form of coldly efficient semi-automatic weapon, it would be *her fault*.

She wondered if she was becoming manic. Every occurring thought felt like some chubby-thumbed tyke was pawing a pinball machine in her head, with one thing caroming off another and lights and bells going off and then, at the end of all that noise, the thought, whatever it might have been, disappearing down a hole and being replaced by an entirely new thought. Was it her hormones? She wondered how one went about checking one's hormones; wondered if wondering if you were becoming manic was itself a sign of mania.

Eating would have helped, but it seemed to have slipped rather far down her agenda; so far, in fact, that her stomach now prepared itself to vomit on approximately the same schedule as it would ordinarily prepare itself to eat. Now that she was not-eating for two, starvation brought a spangled, almost psychedelic sensation of fizz. It was like pressing her face cheek-deep into a champagne curtain. It pulled at the corners of her eyes and tightened her lips. It was a state of alert, a heightened experience. Even as she felt her insides being eaten, she found herself savouring the buzz. She liked to think of it as a protest. Already, she could feel that little smear of life inside her grasping at scarcely available resources. It wasn't eligible for support, she felt, until certain decisions had been made. The more she fed it, the more it would grow, and anyway, feeding it when she hadn't yet firmly decided for or against exterminating it seemed something of a mixed message.

She wondered how big it would be now. She thought of it as a sort of stain; a thickening puddle or a jellified sac with one unblinking eye.

She made an appointment with the doctor. Her usual GP had left. She picked a woman's name, only to find that Dr Leslie Rubrick was in fact a man. She asked him why he was called Leslie. He asked her why she thought she was pregnant. She told him she'd weed on a stick.

'That's not always an accurate guide,' he said, skim-reading stats on his Mac.

'Nor are names,' she said. 'I also haven't had a period.'

'Have you been taking precautions?'

'Clearly not enough.'

He clicked on a file and nodded.

'It's really important you don't feel judged,' he said.

Initially, there was a mildly pleasing sense of furtiveness and secrecy that, not altogether coincidentally, mirrored the feelings she'd had when she was secretly fucking Keith (yes, past tense for that now). There was something about having a secret, she thought, that brought with it a sense of elevated moral standing or general day-to-day importance. Not telling people removed the burden of explanation, of the need to emote; it allowed her to look at the problems of others as nothing more than the problems of others. How pleasing it was to watch the other women in her office – Jules and Carol and all the rest – go about their daily distractions in blissful ignorance of Katherine's secret martyrdom. Secrecy was an ethos, a point of pride. She wanted it, then of course felt constrained by it and wanted its opposite: attention. People surprised her in their ability not to notice. Not telling them her problems meant she had to listen to theirs. The pains of the supermarket; their Very Repetitive Strain Injuries; the fact that their husbands were too 'closed' emotionally ('I try to ask him why he's angry all the time, but he's so *closed*, you know?'); and the way their neighbours were encroaching on their back garden by shifting their fence six inches over. She started to feel they should know. Not that she should tell them, just that they should know, that they should look up from their trifling, never-to-be-resolved-because-they-didn't-actually-want-to-resolve-them problems and just *notice*, just *see*, that all was not well with another human being and that the things that were not well with her greatly outweighed the things that were not well with them. Problems were competitive in the confines of the office. Sympathy was a contact sport. Even as she felt aloof, the injustice keened away inside her, swelling and fading and dopplering off into her soul. She started to self-sabotage her secrecy, not wanting to tell but desperate to impart. She favoured implication over explanation. When Jules, who, following a hallucinatory spiritual experience caused by an accidental commingling of generic toilet cleaner with branded bleach, *So Compassionate*, caught her coming out of the stalls dabbing bile from her lips and tears from her eyes and asked her what

107

was wrong, Katherine said Nothing while making all the possible facial shapes of someone who should really have said Something. Sadly, Jules would probably have found it difficult to read body language even while being groped, and therefore failed to notice Katherine's shuttling eyes and roving stare and quivering lip as she declared herself to be Fine, really *Fine*, just as Carol failed to notice when Katherine stared at the floor and sucked in her top lip after coming over faint in the staffroom and saying Nothing was wrong, that she was *Fine*.

Her mother was no different. If anyone, Katherine thought, should have been able to recognise her plight without said plight having to be overtly specified, surely it was her mother.

'How are you, darling, are you well?'

'Well . . .'

'How's your love life?'

'I don't want a love life.'

'Now Katherine,' said her mother. 'We've talked about this. That sort of lifestyle is all very well when you're young, but at some point . . .'

'I'm off men,' said Katherine, before shifting into indirect disclosure mode, which meant leaving a lot of pregnant (oh God . . .) pauses in which she took deep and ostentatiously shuddering breaths. 'I've . . . I've got a lot going on.'

'Oh, darling,' said her mother, suddenly and satisfyingly horrified. 'You're not . . . I mean . . . You haven't . . . You haven't *found religion*, have you?'

'No,' said Katherine.

'Oh thank Christ,' said her mother.

'It's just . . .' (deep breath) 'a *really hard time*, you know?'

'Don't tell me about hard times, darling. I've had more hard times than you've had hot dinners. Speaking of which . . .'

'I'm eating fine.'

'Good.'

There was a long pause.

'I think I should come and visit,' said her mother suddenly.

'I'm very busy.'

'No you're not. I'll come on Saturday. I'll be passing anyway.'

Katherine said nothing.

'Aren't you going to ask me why I'll be passing?' said her mother.

'Why will you be passing?' said Katherine flatly.

'Your sister's taking me on a spa weekend. Isn't that lovely? She's been working so hard, bless her, and she feels absolutely awful that she hasn't had time to see me, so we're going to have some good old-fashioned girl time. We can stop in to see you on the way.'

'Wonderful,' said Katherine.

'Oh Katherine,' said her mother. 'Can't you at least *try* to be nice?'

For once, Katherine wasn't lying when she told her mother she was off men. She could feel herself dissolving sexually. Her libido had somehow doubled yet also decentred, as if it were now situated somewhere outside of her and, greedy though it had become, she was unable to sate it simply because she was no longer able to locate it. Pornography and bruising masturbation weren't helping. Images of men seemed fraught and distressing. Her body was unresponsive and blandly dry, yet somehow, somewhere in some part of her with which she was in less than perfect touch, the need for a fuck had never been stronger. Slippery as this urge was, she found it was better to extinguish it than to satisfy it, and nothing did that job better than the thought of children, which could turn lust to revulsion as rapidly as the little buggers seemed to turn pleasure to despair. Just as having problems made her feel suddenly inundated with the problems of others, so it seemed that just when she wanted to avoid not only the presence but even the suggestion of children, here they all were: tottering round town the regulation two paces behind their harried, stringy-haired mothers; getting screamed at outside the supermarket; dangling dead weight from a white-knuckled parent as they were dragged from bus-stop to bus-seat and back again. Sometimes, in passing, they seemed to eye her, and she could never tell if they were seeking her solidarity or, in some eerily psychic way, saying to her: *You're next.*

Where children led, pity unerringly followed. The office was lousy with charity. In a convenient twofer, Dave on floor one was growing a beard for orphaned Malawi babies, then planning to shave it off for domestic violence. Donna on floor three was immersing herself in a bath full of baked beans for the dispossessed street kids of Burkina Faso. Birthdays were heralded with pinkly embossed cards proclaiming that the person in question's gift had been converted into goats and couriered to Kenya. Even her alone-time wasn't safe. *Elle* and *Marie-Claire*, usually such bastions of cheer, were smeared with weepy-eyed close-ups of little Ngugi or Jésus or Kalifa, with their cleft palates and Biafran bellies. *Just two pounds a month can keep little Esmé in clean drinking water*, they blared. *Fifteen pounds buys Fatima a wooden leg.* What, Katherine wondered, about the mothers? Feminism, it seemed, extended only as far as the childless or part-nered. Once you popped a sprog and went it alone, you were little more than the unthinking delivery mechanism for another wasted innocent; the medium by which the misery of the world was multi-plied. Why, she wondered, were people only capable of locating their pity in the most unchallenging of places? They responded to sadness only when it expressed itself as sadness, she thought. Sadness expressed as anger or hostility just turned people off. Why not a picture of her in a glossy magazine, streaked of makeup and ruffled of hair, with a caption that said *Help us to stop Katherine going absolutely bat-shit mental*. She couldn't temper the outer manifestation of her sorrow. She would, she thought, go through all of this alone; the fear and the bitterness and the icy, nauseous starts to grey, lonely days, and at the end of it, whatever happened, all anyone would ever say would be *Oh, that poor child!*

Single mother, she thought. It had a branded ring to it: class-bound, wide open for judgement. No more the offhand excuse of never having met the right man. Now the truth was plain for all to see: fucked a very wrong man indeed. All this time, she thought, spent so carefully maintaining distance from and control over the lesser gender, and now here was this thing inside her that not only served as a continuous reminder of some of the most unsatisfying and ill-judged sex she'd ever had, but also, disgustingly, turned the absence of a man in her life from a secret sadness easily disguised as an ideological stance to a full-on yawning deficit.

She was already assembling a protective veneer of tragedy. The father, she imagined herself saying, had been a wonderful man: masculine and independent; sensitive and attentive, with a job that was both altruistic and admirably dangerous. Nothing military or police related, of course – there was something deeply unfeminist about being an army widow. Perhaps an award-winning photojournalist renowned for documenting the human toll of under-reported wars. Touchingly, with a carefully controlled glisten in her eyes, she would tell the story of how he'd placed his handsome, desert-toughened hand on her belly, his Tag Heuer diving watch glinting in the candlelight, and told her he was giving it all up to be with her and his baby. *Just one more job and I'm through*, he would have said, promising a desk job, an end to the nights of worry when she'd woken in the early hours fearing that some awful yet wonderfully poignant fate had befallen him. There was, he'd have told her, just one more atrocity to document; one more global tragedy to brilliantly yet reductively symbolise in the face of an innocent yet suspiciously well-posed child. She would describe in detail their last night together; the conversation they'd had about names (Leica if it was a girl, Pentax for a boy); about moving to a bigger home; about the values and skills they would instil in little Pentax from the moment he was born; the way she'd woken in the morning to find a rose on her pillow and his watch on the nightstand to remember him by; and the way she'd woken again in the night, two days later, and known, just *known* that something awful had happened, because (deep breath; Pinter pause) . . . *his watch had stopped*. People would admire her. They'd think she was one of those resilient types. She'd be *So Brave, So Strong*.

Something had to be done. She needed, she knew, to take control. Things were getting the better of her. She did not want to be the sort of person of whom things got the better. She decided to begin with the question of income.

'I've switched to soup,' said her manager, wresting the lid off a thermos. 'I just couldn't take that soggy bread anymore.'

'I un-quit,' said Katherine.

'When did you quit?' said her manager.

'The other day. But now I don't want to. I want to rescind my resignation.'

'Oh,' said her manager, looking up from his soup.

'What do you mean, "Oh"?'

'Well, I was just . . . I mean, as I said before, you know, much as we'd be sorry to see you go, I was sort of looking forward to not being your boss anymore so we could . . .'

'Can I not quit, please?'

'Obviously. Not a problem. Can I ask what's changed?'

'No.'

'You're not going to immediately take maternity leave, are you? Because I've had like three people . . .'

'I could take you to court for that question,' she said.

'Right,' said her boss. 'Point taken.'

The television, for so long a friend that had seen her through the gloomiest of times, now held little comfort. Katherine found herself at a loss to find much that might be categorised as entertainment. The news seemed to be infecting everything. Inspired by the economic downturn, the fashion channels were excited about thrift. Tapping into mounting concern about an epidemic, the history channels had shifted focus from Hitler to the Plague. Excited at a rare opportunity to be cutting edge, the nature channels were broadcasting wall-to-wall documentaries about diseases in animals, and the food channels, picking up on the largest swing towards vegetarianism the country had ever seen, strong-armed the zeitgeist with a series of tips towards a meat-free life. She stuck to the news itself, which ran a rolling double narrative of recession and pandemic. The burning of cattle carcasses, initially an experimental measure, now seemed the norm. Talk was shifting to a cull. Men in boiler suits made important pronouncements.

'We've seen Herd Disenfranchisement Syndrome before,' said one, 'and we've seen Herd Disengagement. This is worse. Bovine Idiopathic Entrancement needs to be taken very seriously indeed. *Any* indication that a cow might be staring excessively, ceasing to move, desisting from common bovine behaviours such as cud-chewing and tail-flicking, or indeed simply standing alone for any period of time needs to be reported immediately.'

She began to enjoy the repetition, the sense of predictability that rolling news engendered. The word *news* was, she thought, slightly disingenuous, given that the stations were basically falling over each other to deliver more of the same: heaps of cattle carcasses, splayed legs silhouetted against the winter sky; hooves and heads in smoke and flame.

Whenever the landline rang she would think it was Daniel, who would, she was quite certain, call very soon. She also, however, worried it would be Keith, and so let everything go to voicemail. True to form, her expectant prodding of the playback button did, once, summon up Keith's voice.

'Katie-babes. Long time no see. What's the dilly-deal?'

She hit the delete button, then checked her voicemail again to be sure the message had vanished. She was beginning to realise how few phone calls she actually received.

She thought about Daniel, wondered what he was doing, what he was thinking. She liked to imagine the extent of his pain. She pictured him beset by insomnia; pacing the kitchen in his atrociously baggy boxers; running a hand through his hair and squinting. He'd want to be drawn out of his shell. He'd become sullen and withdrawn around his partner – what was her name? – waiting for her to ask what was wrong. If she didn't ask he'd become angry. If she asked, he'd say *Nothing*. Katherine liked the idea of being someone's secret, and of being Daniel's secret in particular. Not because she wanted him back, but simply because the worst thing anyone could do to you was forget you.

Erasable though Keith might have been from her answerphone, he proved quite the stubborn presence about the office. Katherine clocked him at the water cooler, making eyes at Claire Demoines, who was new and single and wore tights with complicated patterns and said things like 'I get so many offers, you know? But . . . I don't know, maybe I'm just too fussy.' Then Katherine bumped into him on the stairs, which she had only started using through fear that she might encounter him and/or Claire Demoines in the lift. He was smugly calm; greased with a post-something glow and making a grand show of not making a grand show. To Katherine's horror, he looked more attractive now that he was the father of her child, as if she were seeing him through a hormonal filter of potential happiness rather than in the chilly-eyed spotlight of rational thought.

'Hey there,' he said, pausing with one hand on the banister and the other fingering change in his trouser pocket. 'How goes it?'

'Great,' said Katherine, eyeing him icily and feeling no need to slip into her usual routine of drawing attention to her own dishonesty. 'How about you?'

'Making some changes,' said Keith, nodding the nod of a sage and pointing to the red rubber band on his left wrist. 'Learning.'

'Right,' said Katherine. 'That's great. Why are you wearing a rubber band on your wrist?'

'It's for your protection,' said Keith gravely. 'By the way. Were you planning on going halves on that holiday or what?'

'Not really, no.'

'Right.'

'What's the matter? Short of cash to blow on your latest fuck-piece?'

'Wow,' said Keith, nodding seriously. 'Lot of hostility there, duchess.'

'Just asking.'

Keith reached out and put a hand on her shoulder, squinting slightly as though pained.

'You really need to respect yourself more.'

'Keith?' she said earnestly, softening her face and gazing into his eyes, lashes aflutter, sinking swoon-like into his hip.

'Yes, Katherine?' said Keith, tilting his head to one side and nodding gently in a way that said, I'm a Wonderful Person for Listening.

'Do you think, one day soon, just for me, you could die in an auto-erotic accident?'

That same afternoon she saw him talking to Carol by the photo-copier. He looked hangdog and up-to-something. He showed Carol the rubber band on his wrist. Carol touched his shoulder as she listened. He did one of those little smiles and thanked her. When Katherine came closer they parted. When she asked Carol what was happening she said Nothing.

Galvanised by her isolation, and by the slow, creeping dread that Keith might slowly and subtly turn the women of the office even further against her through little more than implication and gentle persuasion, Katherine attempted to make inroads into her iciness. She made sure to say good morning. She stood in the staffroom and listened to Debbie go on about her son. When Jules's close-male-friend-with-whom-there-had-never-been-anything-going-on passed away at the age of fifty after a protracted battle with pancreatic cancer, Katherine rushed straight to the supplies cupboard to upgrade Jules' wrist rest and mouse mat just so that, if nothing else, her carpal tunnel syndrome wouldn't exacerbate her grief. When someone in the office either stole or inadvertently appropriated Janice Johnson's bag for life, which she had very sensibly brought in so as to allow her to transport her macrobiotic stew without it leaking all over her handbag, Katherine sent a global email that resulted, after just thirty minutes, in the bag miraculously reappearing in the staffroom. When Dawn Rickstadt, who Smelled So Good, wafted past Katherine's desk smelling particularly good, Katherine made sure not only to note the name of her perfume (Consensual, by Chanel) but also to check how Dawn might feel if Katherine purchased the same perfume and so also ended up Smelling So Good, to which Dawn had generously replied that she had no problem at all with Katherine buying a bottle of Consensual because it was gorgeous and indeed, since she herself was nearly out, perhaps they could go shopping for it together at lunch.

'This has lovely dirty notes,' said Dawn in Debenham's, misting Katherine's wrist with Reproach, by Comme des Garçons. 'It's sea breeze meets knee-trembler in a Ford Capri.'

'Is that supposed to be nice?'

'It's supposed to be sexy.'

'I don't want to be sexy,' said Katherine. 'I want to be clean.'

'Gotcha,' said Dawn. 'Something more zesty?'

'How about Mace?' said Katherine.

'Oh I know,' said Dawn. 'You'd think with all this research they'd have come up with a reliable twat repellent by now.'

Afterwards they did lunch. After lunch they did coffee. Dawn talked about her relationships, all of which had ended badly, but about which she was still, she said, hypothetically optimistic.

'That must be nice,' said Katherine.

'It has its moments,' said Dawn. 'But anyway. Tell me about you.'

'Ick,' said Katherine.

It was, however, short-lived, just as Katherine's occasional episodes of bad-faith niceness were always rather short-lived, and always left her, like her recent bumptious, bad-faith orgasms, feeling disappointed and faintly dirty after the event. Her suspension of cynicism was brief and incomplete. The more effort she invested in people, the less she seemed able to overlook their flaws. Jules was Too Compassionate. Dawn Smelled Too Much. Debbie's Patience was annoying. They were all annoying. They nibbled their food in naughty little bites because they were watching their weight. They sent global emails listing fifteen things that make you glad to be alive. They thought capital punishment had its uses but only for really bad crimes and only if you could be really sure the person did it. The ones with husbands moaned about their husbands. The ones without husbands wanted husbands. They all definitely wanted more stuff but their houses and flats were very cluttered and they felt they should really get rid of some stuff because the minimalist look was in but then on the other hand it wasn't *homely*, was it, the minimalist look. Many of them wanted to do something worthwhile because they admired people who did things that were worthwhile. They all agreed there was a lot of suffering in the world. Often one of them was coming down with something, and the others would worry that they were about to come down with something, although often they would not and then they would all agree that they were probably just run-down. Yoghurts had a lot more calories than any of them ever really imagined. Somehow, they had all been given computers that were particularly recalcitrant. They liked each other only to the extent that they themselves wanted to be liked. When one stood up to go to the toilet or make a cup of tea the others talked about her, about how she smelled too much or how her patience was wearing them all thin.

For Katherine, a sense of connection with others was no different to the cashmere cardigan; the much-desired boyfriend. She pined for it; drew it towards her; felt herself open ever so slightly outwards, and then recoiled, convinced that the happiness she'd sought was now a responsibility to be managed in much the same way as she managed the height of chairs and the temperature of the air-con: a series of small adjustments which would result, as she made them, in the gradual erosion of her core.

Katherine got caught in the lift with Keith, having wrongly assumed he was now committed to the stairs, and realised with sinking horror that she still wanted him to want to sleep with her.

He said, 'I'm in such a calm place right now. I feel like I'm getting back to the person I've always wanted to be.'

'You look fat,' she said. 'Maybe the person you've always wanted to be is fat.'

'You're angry,' he said. 'Anything I can do?'

'Maybe we could meet up sometime,' she said.

'I don't think so,' said Keith with a smile that was painfully kind. 'I don't think that would help.'

'Don't pity me,' she said. 'Don't you fucking dare.'

'You're right. Better to just stalk around pitying yourself, right, princess?'

'You prick.'

'Right back at you,' he called, as she got off on the wrong floor.

Later, she saw him talking to Claire Demoines, who stood on tiptoe in her fuck-off-red fuck-me heels and gave him a love-me hug. Katherine went round and kicked the safety catches off four of the fire extinguishers so as to have a job to distract her in the afternoon.

119

The cows were endless. They went on and on. She went home every evening and caught up with their lack of movement.

'You join us live and exclusive,' barked Bill Palmer to camera, eyes wide above his protective face mask; rubber-gloved hands gesticulating excitedly towards the motionless cow behind him. 'Behind me is Simone, the first infected cow to be filmed. Beside me here is local vet Bob Chevington. Bob, tell me what we're seeing here.'

Bill Palmer was an ex–war reporter stuck doing domestic reports after valiantly getting himself shot on camera. He was, Katherine thought, clearly relishing this unusual opportunity for drama, and had become something of a ubiquitous presence through what it now seemed de rigueur to refer to as the crisis. His approach was basically sartorial. Outside embassies he wore the foreign correspondent's uniform of blue cotton shirt and pleated chinos. In Afghanistan it was sandy camouflage and a range of helmets. Now, clearly alert to the possibility of both drama and further journalistic recognition, he was in a white boiler suit with the hood pooled insouciantly at his neck, his mane of white hair thrust sideways by a stiff breeze; his generous eyebrows knitted into a frown that spoke of news valiantly borne in the face of heavy peril.

'Well, Bill, what we're seeing here is classic Bovine Idiopathic Entrancement,' said the vet. 'This animal has been staring straight ahead for over twenty-four hours. It remains completely motionless. It is totally unresponsive to stimulus.'

'And what's the prognosis, Bob?'

'Death. Probably by dehydration.'

'Dark times,' said Bill. 'Here's Chastity with the weather.'

The camera lingered on the stricken cow, its glazed, dead eyes seemingly looking straight at Katherine.

All the old patterns were resurfacing. She could see them; name them; but felt powerless to intervene. The feeling was similar to jamming her fingers down her throat and dry-heaving all the food she'd neglected to eat. She was gagging on an emotional nothingness, and in an attempt to circumvent it she returned to the tried-and-tested method of ascribing to Daniel the things she couldn't feel for herself, or perhaps felt but couldn't name. It was all so familiar – her disaffection with kindness at the office so neatly mirroring her disaffection with Daniel. She used to test his commitment by hurting him. She threatened to leave him, or cheat on him, then watched his face and measured the depth of his feelings for her by the extent to which it crumbled. He was insecure; prone to worry. If he ever became confident, she thought, it would mean that he no longer loved her, since to love someone is to worry; to need someone is to fear the inevitability of their absence. Without fear, she thought, without drama, there was only the grey blankness of late-middle-age relationships, where, as far as she could make out, concepts like love and passion were replaced by what she saw as the wretched terminology of codependent ennui: companionship, contentment, compromise; where one person's love for another was no longer stated simply because it was no longer questioned; where the key indicator not only of love but also of solidity would simply be the mere fact of the solidity and love that had gone before. No, no, she thought. Better the sense of odds, of struggle; the ongoing and repeated relief of trauma endured and survived. Without it, there was only the security of the unimaginative: an unspokenly dwindling sex life; roiling resentment; his-and-hers facial hair.

She went back to the charity shop where she'd donated Keith's vibrator. She told them she'd left something in the bag by accident and wanted it back. The woman looked blank yet suspiciously relaxed.

'I haven't seen anything,' she said. 'What was it you left?'

'A vibrator,' said Katherine.

'Oh. Um . . .'

'You can't miss it,' said Katherine. 'It's shaped like an enormous penis and on the side it says THE WIDOWMAKER in Day-Glo letters.'

'I don't think I . . .'

'I know you've got it,' said Katherine.

'I assure you I haven't.'

'Give it back.'

'I would if I could.'

'Whatever,' said Katherine.

Claire Demoines did a lap of Katherine's floor and dropped the news, to which she had, she explained, been privy for some time but which she had promised not to disclose as it was both private and sensitive.

'He really wasn't sure he wanted anyone to know,' Katherine overheard her saying in a low voice to Jules and Debbie and Carol. 'But I mean we've talked about it a lot and I said I thought he'd probably feel better if it was out there and he didn't have to cover it up anymore.'

'Mmmm,' said Jules, being So Compassionate. 'He's being So Brave.'

'There's such a taboo, isn't there?' said Carol.

'It's like you can't even discuss it,' said Debbie. 'But he's really Putting It Out There, which is So Admirable.'

'I just feel really privileged he felt able to open up to me,' said Claire.

'Mmm,' said Debbie, Jules and Carol, all of whom, Katherine knew, now hated Claire for being the person Keith had opened up to more than any of them despite all of their overweening efforts to get Keith to open up. Not that they cared about Keith, of course, or that they really desperately wanted to be involved, but, as Debbie would later put it to Katherine, who exactly *did* Claire Demoines think she was, just flouncing in after, what, a week? and getting Keith, who they'd all known much longer, to totally open up to her.

'What am I missing?' said Katherine brightly, sidling up to Claire Demoines and cocking a glance at the intricacy of her tights. Keith would ladder those in a heartbeat, she thought, with his ghastly fingers.

'Keith's been seeing someone,' said Claire.

'Great,' said Katherine. 'How lovely. Is it serious?'

'No, not like that. He's been *undergoing treatment.*' She invested the term with all the gravity she could muster.

Katherine did a mental checklist of all the things for which Keith might possibly wish to seek treatment. His toxic personality aside, he was quite prone to recurrent urinary tract infections, around which she supposed it was possible to say there was something of a taboo.

'Right,' said Katherine. 'Is it serious?'

'He's a sex addict,' said Debbie, unable to contain herself. 'But now he's getting some treatment.'

'What does the treatment entail?' said Katherine. 'Is it like being a heroin addict? Can you get some sort of sex substitute on prescription?'

'Well, it's a talking cure,' said Claire flatly.

'Like a prostitute, you mean,' said Katherine.

'No, like an analyst.'

'So he's seeing a shrink because he can't stop shagging people.'

'His toxic and addictive attitude to sex has been greatly damaging his relationships,' said Claire.

'Shagging people does that,' said Katherine.

By lunchtime the details were all round the office. Keith was undergoing some sort of aversion therapy. He wore a rubber band round his wrist so he could twang it whenever he felt tempted. This would, apparently, transport him back to certain states of aversion and restraint he'd explored under hypnosis. He told Debbie, in the strictest confidence, that he'd looked back on some of the things his addiction had made him do and, although he didn't want to go into detail for fear of offending Debbie or causing her never to wish to interact with him again, he was not proud of himself. So he had, he explained to Carol in the strictest confidence, taken some of those experiences and had a good hard look at them and then related them to a therapist, who had explained that he had an addiction, and that his addiction was poisoning his life, and that what he needed to do was build meaningful relationships with women without having sex with them. Apparently, he'd explained to Claire in the strictest confidence, his therapist had pointed out that a perfectly natural consequence of building meaningful relationships with women without sleeping with them would be that he would want to sleep with them. This would be partly because he was building a meaningful relationship, which is always arousing, and partly because sex would now feel like something of a taboo, which was, as everyone knew, kind of sexy.

So, Keith quietly explained to Debbie, Carol, Claire and Dawn, who by now had overcome their disappointment at realising they all actually had Keith's confidence and tended to talk to him in a little cluster, the point was that he should not, under any circumstances, reduce his contact with women. Indeed, he should increase his contact with women, since that was how he was going to go about building better relationships with them. So really, what he was saying was that he needed the help of the women of the office. Would they, he wondered, could they possibly, find the time to help him practise some meaningful relationships by, say, going to coffee with him, or perhaps just having a spot of lunch or even, as time went on and Keith's powers of resistance grew stronger, maybe even going to dinner? They could feel perfectly safe, he told them, not only because his days of basically being an absolute *animal* when it came to sex were behind him, but also because his aversion therapy meant he could very easily, if the inclination to sleep with any of them arose (which, he assured them, it very definitely would, because they were all *very* attractive, which was precisely why he was enlisting their support), snap his elastic band, which his therapist had placed there to form an anchor with the images of aversion they'd worked on together which, Keith gravely informed the assembled women, were *so repellent* that a woman would basically have to be the most attractive woman alive to still seem attractive after he'd associated her in his head with what were, he near-whispered, *very unpleasant things indeed*.

'This is horrendous,' said Katherine to Debbie in the staffroom.

'Isn't it?' said Debbie, gazing wistfully after Keith. 'All those awful things he wanted to do . . .'

G od,' said Katherine's mother, dropping by with Katherine's sister Hazel in tow, both of them trailing a flatulent cloud of smugness that Katherine felt would have to be professionally removed after they left. 'This couldn't have come at a better time. Honestly, Hazel, you're a *lifesaver*. Wasn't I just saying to you the other week that I needed to recuperate, Katherine?'

'No,' said Katherine.

'Oh *don't* be like that, Katherine,' said Katherine's mother. 'You can come too, next time.'

'No thank you,' said Katherine.

'And no thank *you*,' said Hazel. 'The whole point is to rid yourself of toxins, not take them along with you.'

'That's enough, Hazel,' said Katherine's mother, then, in a tone of voice that somehow suggested it should make Katherine feel better, 'You look absolutely awful, Katherine.'

'Thanks,' said Katherine.

'No need for sarcasm. It's motherly concern. What are you doing to yourself?'

'I think I'm just run-down.'

'Run-down from what?'

'Life.'

'Spare me. Is there any more coffee?'

'I can make some.'

Katherine's mother looked her up and down.

'Sit still,' she said softly. 'I'll make it.'

It struck Katherine that she might cry: an increasingly common response to unexpected kindness. It was something she had to ready herself for, these days. When it snuck up on her unsolicited, she was thrown.

'What have you been eating?' said her mother, nosing in the fridge. 'God, there's a tumbleweed blowing through here.'

'There's a tumbleweed blowing through a lot of things,' chimed Hazel.

'I eat out a lot,' said Katherine.

'Who with?' said Katherine's mother.

'No one.'

'You eat out alone? God, darling. That sounds depressing.'

'I like it.'

'No you don't. You do it and then kid yourself that you like it. It's how you've always been.'

'How have I always been?'

Katherine felt defensive and edgy, largely because she felt vulnerable and tearful and hated the thought that her mother and, worse, her sister, might see her at a low ebb.

'You've always kidded yourself,' said Hazel.

'Like with what?'

Her family, she thought, had an unwavering desire and ability to gang up on her.

'Like with everything,' said Hazel. 'You don't have the career you want so you always go off on these ridiculous monologues about how glad you are to have avoided the rat race. You don't have a relationship so you go on and on about how glad you are not to be in a relationship because men are such a drag. You miss Daniel, so you take absolutely every opportunity to . . .'

'I do not miss Daniel.'

'Please,' said Hazel. 'Anyone would miss Daniel.'

'What is this?' said Katherine. 'An intervention?'

'Call it sisterly concern,' said Hazel.

'That's enough, you two,' said Katherine's mother, carrying through a cafetière. 'Who wants milk?'

Katherine lit a cigarette. 'Not for me. Two sugars.'

She looked Hazel up and down. *Generic* was the word that sprang to mind. Conservative denim and chunky knits; a makeup routine almost certainly cribbed from a magazine article that used words like *understated* and *confident*.

Her mother sat back down and dealt with the coffee while Hazel, who was sitting opposite Katherine, gave her the appraising eye.

'Mum's right,' she said. 'You do look awful. Do you want the name of my dermatologist?'

'What you need,' said Katherine, 'is a shag.'

Hazel yawned. 'You know what you are?' she said. 'Predictable, that's what.'

'You know what you are?' said Katherine.

'We don't want to know what she is,' said Katherine's mother. 'Katherine. We're worried about you.'

'Well, don't be. I'm fine.'

'There's a job opening up in my company,' said Hazel. 'I could put in a word. Seriously. I mean, all joking aside. You know.'

Katherine lit a second cigarette off the butt of the first. She could, she thought, say yes. She could pack up and leave; start again. She would be good at the job her sister was offering, whatever it was, because she was always good at her job. After work, she and her sister would go to a wine bar or perhaps a restaurant. They would order crisp white wines and light pasta dishes and a salad to share, and when men – half-decent men in crumpled Friday suits with their ties progressively askew – offered to buy them drinks, they would smile and accept, and then afterwards they would laugh and agree that none of the men were good enough, saying *did you SEE what he was wearing?* Perhaps they would share a house. Perhaps for a time they would be happy, at least until one of them met someone and it all fell apart. Wouldn't that, any of that, be better than this?

Except, of course, it wouldn't be like that, because Katherine would be accepting a kindness, and the second she accepted it she would resent it, and her sister would resent her for resenting it, and how long would it take, really, before an argument over food or a night out or something trivial spun on its axis the moment her sister reminded her that *she got her this job* and wasn't she even *grateful* for that?

'No,' she said eventually. 'I'm all right, thank you.'

'I don't even know why we called in,' said Hazel. 'It's an hour out of our way.'

'Why did you?' snapped Katherine. 'I didn't ask you to.'

'We wanted to see you, Katherine,' said her mother, who now sounded hurt in a way that Katherine found enraging.

'Well consider me seen,' said Katherine.

After they left she started to cry, but checked herself. *Won't help*, she told herself repeatedly. *Won't help so don't bother*.

Sometimes, in quieter moments, when her looming fears and preoccupations had, if not exactly receded, then at least temporarily weakened, Katherine would think of Nathan, wondering what he was doing and, more pertinently, what had happened in the past year and a half. Nothing good, she assumed. He was always, she thought, heading towards nothing particularly good, and if their friendship could have been characterised by any sort of arc it would have been that at one stage the knowledge of where Nathan was headed had seemed exciting, even romantic, but later less so. He had always been edgy, of course, and no one would ever have suggested his lifestyle was healthy or that his choices were always the most positive, but in the last months the change had been noticeable. She and Daniel had begun to discuss it – his twitching eyes and sudden non sequiturs; his occasional comments about unhappiness or, as he'd put it to her once, what he saw as an actual inability to be happy – but this had been at a time when she and Daniel weren't discussing anything very much outside themselves, and when they too were not heading for anything particularly good, and when, as is always the case in a relationship that is either decaying or blossoming, events external to them as a couple seemed to require more effort to observe than to ignore. Had they let him down? Had they failed someone at one of those rare critical moments when failure is permanent? Until very recently she would have said, had she been asked by the right person at the right time and in the strictest possible confidence, that they had, but now he had phoned, and he had, quite clearly, asked for help, suggesting that the previous time they'd failed hadn't actually been the irrevocable moment at all, but a precursor, a warning. Of course, that also raised the distinct possibility that this was therefore the big moment, the one they had to get right, which did not make her feel particularly assured, given that it was once again a bad time, and that she was distracted, and that there were things in her life that seemed to preclude the addition of more things to her life.

But of course, there had been that conversation, the last time she'd seen him, which she had not discussed with Daniel, but which she had also not forgotten, and this was, if nothing else, one of those times when being around someone who had a history of finding you attractive would be no bad thing at all.

Claire Demoines had the office in thrall. She'd been to dinner with Keith. Keith had twanged his rubber band. He said he'd never imagined, after the awful techniques of aversion instilled in him by his therapist, that anyone could ever make him think about sex again, but somehow . . .

'His restraint was amazing,' said Claire, running a hand down the herringboned lace of her tights. 'He said he admired me too much to hurt me like he'd hurt all the other women in his life.'

'God,' said Debbie. 'What a man.'

Keen to once again reaffirm her faith in the basic shittiness of humankind, Katherine took herself off to her local strip club and sat sipping a daiquiri amidst the leering, boozed-out stares of AWOL men. Despite using the word *executive* on its membership cards, its posters, even its drinks coasters, L'Après-Vie represented the cheaper end of male entertainment. The girls were foreign and got all the way naked. Private dances took place in clammy rooms that had, as Dawn would have said, dirty notes. Katherine wondered as to the etymology of all this: the precise moment in man's history when the definition of eroticism had been agreed to include a skinny, sad-eyed tween in cheap heels launching herself off a piece of re-purposed scaffolding. She paid twenty quid for a private dance with a girl named Clover, who had pigtails and purple nails and a tattoo of a unicorn just above her groin.

'It's my power animal,' she said.

'I'm pregnant,' said Katherine.

'Congratulations,' said Clover.

Outside, shifty, awkward men queuing for their entertainment eyed her as she left. She felt no vulnerability. She walked home alone through dim-lit streets; crossed the car park under the flyover that she habitually avoided. She wondered idly about rape. It was as if every fuck and kiss, every lingering gaze and hot-breathed whisper, were deserting her, and as she paused in the gloom and spread her hands over the chilly bricks, assuming the stance of someone about to be frisked while she wondered momentarily if she might vomit or sob or both, she felt, rising up from the soles of her feet and leaving through the semi-permeable border of her skin, the evaporation of every intimacy she'd ever known.

She went home and googled porn, only to find she could no longer look at men. She settled for body parts only, happily disembodied and algorithmically collaged. She couldn't come. Afterwards she called three or four men whose numbers she had stored in her mobile, keeping an open line as the call went to voicemail; pacing the room with her phone in her pocket to give the impression of an accidental dial. She wanted to see if anyone called her back, at which point she would explain the mistake and say it was nice to hear from them anyway. She fell asleep holding a silent phone, and in the morning, when it did ring, it was a woman's voice.

'I have Daniel Bryce on the line,' said the voice. 'Please hold one moment.'

Katherine held. He seemed to wait a long time before he came on the line.

'Katherine?'

Her thrill at the sound of his voice was old; almost threadbare. She had, she now realised, spent long stretches of time she would never be able to recoup imagining all the ways he might say hello: the calm; the nervous; the faintly sad; the falsely bright; the careworn; the compassionate; the cocky. She'd imagined all her possible responses: bright and breezy through to nonplussed. She'd wanted this, and now it was here all she could think was that the wanting was a weakness, and all she could feel was the remote and grey-edged disappointment you might experience as you left a party and walked to your car and realised that from outside the music and chatter sounded all the brighter for being muffled, all the more enticing for being far away, leaving you wishing you'd had a better time while you were inside and had the chance.

'Daniel,' she said.

She'd done the wanting, wasted herself on it, and now it was over, and necessity stood in its place. If she spoke to him now, this second, she thought, he would know how weak she could be.

'It's, um . . . It's a bad line,' she said. 'Let me call you back.'

'It seems . . .'

132

She hung up, then sat down on the floor and pressed at the sides of her head with her palms and asked herself why, for once, she couldn't just accept what she wanted and be glad, instead of pushing it away and then waiting for it to return.

It was OK, she told herself. In a couple of minutes she would call him back. Just as soon as she'd been able to convince herself she didn't care.

L ove you darling. Could you pass the milk?'

'Course I can baby. Here you go. Love you.'

'Love you too.'

They had, Daniel thought, crossed all accepted boundaries of decency.

'And the juice?'

'Sorry baby.'

'Thanks sweetie.'

'My pleasure sugar.'

They munched their cereal. Daniel fretted over the headlines; Angelica pored over a paperback called *The Self-Help Habit: How to Put Down the Books and Get On with Your Life*. After a while, she looked up at him and smiled.

'Love you,' she said quietly.

'Love you too,' said Daniel. 'More muesli?'

Asked how it had come to this, Daniel's explanation would, he knew, have differed quite noticeably from Angelica's. Angelica would have called it a breakthrough. She not only *would* say but in fact *had* said, to Sebastian and Plum and one of their sallow-faced right-on friends, that it was like a new relationship. Not that there was anything wrong with the previous relationship, of course, but as everyone knew, a relationship was only as good as its growth, and this was major growth.

Daniel wished this were true. Not in an idle, wouldn't-world-peace-be-a-wonderful-thing sort of way, but in a concrete and decidedly pained way. He wished it were true not just for Angelica's sake but also for his own, because if Angelica's explanation was true, it would mean that his explanation was false, which would mean he really was the brave, generous, emotionally open and fearlessly loving person Angelica thought him to be, and not at all what he knew himself to be: a cynical, scared, duplicitous shit.

It would have been easy to say that things had begun to unravel with Katherine's phone call. Indeed, it would have been so easy to say this that Daniel had, for some time, toyed with the idea of *actually* saying it: of arranging Angelica on the scatter cushions one evening and telling her that Katherine had called and explaining to her in slow, even, unchallenging tones, that this had stirred up a lot of shit for him, and that he needed some time to process it, and that Angelica mustn't worry, because this wasn't about her, it was about him, and he was absolutely certain he would deal with it and all would be well. This would have been the mature response and would, he knew, have been greatly appreciated by Angelica, who would have at least admired its honesty. The problem, though, was that it wouldn't have been honest at all. Up to the part about stirring shit up, it was pretty accurate, but after that it was essentially a patina of falsehood. Daniel wasn't at all confident he could deal with it, and he was twitchingly uncertain that this didn't have anything to do with Angelica. Dishonest as Daniel may have been, even he flinched at the prospect of accruing spiritual and romantic brownie points by pretending to be honest. Lying was one thing, but lying in such a way as to find yourself being praised for your honesty was, he thought, entirely another.

A better approach would have been to say nothing, a technique in which Daniel was well versed, and which had served him quite reliably when coupled with his other favoured strategy of carrying on as normal. Daniel was, or so he liked to believe, very good at carrying on as normal. He knew this because he'd carried on as normal through some distinctly un-normal times, such as the latter stages of his relationship with Katherine; his affair; even Nathan's odd behaviour and eventual disappearance. Why not, he thought, carry on as normal now?

The difficulty, which had become apparent the moment he descended the stairs and used the expression *wrong number* to Angelica, who had believed him so immediately and with such absence of hesitation that he instantly felt staggeringly guilty, was that he could no longer be entirely sure what normal was.

He peered over the top of the paper and studied Angelica as she studied her book. She caught his eye and shot him a little smile, then mouthed something that was indistinct due to having some muesli in her mouth, but which, going out on a limb, he took to be 'I love you.' He mouthed the same back at her and smiled. She smiled back.

'God, this cull,' he said.

'Isn't it awful? Those poor cows.'

Daniel hadn't actually considered the cows. His mind had been on more work-based concerns, such as the potential for a PR apocalypse. But then Angelica was one of those people, the sort who, walking through the city and passing a bedraggled vagabond flanked by neckerchiefed Labradors, would say simply, *Oh, those poor dogs.*

'I know,' he said.

'Do you?' said Angelica, looking up suddenly from her book, her eyes full.

Daniel froze for a moment. Did he? *Did* he know?

'Um . . . Yes,' he said.

'Oh Daniel,' she said, breathing out and beaming. 'I love you so much.'

'Me too,' he said.

He kept experiencing these little freezes: rude sensations of being locked out of his own existence, just for a second. He seemed to come to, though from what he was never sure, to find reality had advanced a beat without him. He was more aware of them now because it was precisely one of these fleeting moments of existential paralysis that had got him into the current thorny predicament with reference to his apparent inability to stop telling Angelica he loved her.

He'd awoken early, the morning after Katherine phoned, and briefly congratulated himself on his handling of the night before. Her call had thrown him, but he felt he'd recovered reasonably well. Angelica hadn't suspected anything; he'd been only moderately offensive in the face of Sebastian's highly offensive presence; his early trudge to bed had surely been successfully masked by his man flu; and he'd acquitted himself more than tolerably in the sack before nodding off. It was while considering these achievements that he became aware that his head had rolled in Angelica's direction and, worse, that she had woken up and was staring back at him with that particular sentimental intensity that always made him feel as if someone had just daubed his skin with tiger balm. When he brought her into focus, he found she was smiling.

'What are you thinking?' she asked.

It was a good question. What *was* he thinking? He realised he needed to think of any random subject in the world – football; the news; work; his dreams – and that would end the conversation, but his brain was suddenly bereft of resources, and when he tried to think he heard only the sort of cavernous echo that might accompany a bucket dropped into an empty well. What *was* he thinking? What was he *thinking*?

'Err ... I love you,' he said, politely ignoring the air-raid siren in his brain.

She beamed. 'Love you too,' she said, throwing her arms around him and hugging him until he perspired.

The damage was done. Now every time he looked at her he felt she was looking at him in anticipation of him telling her he loved her, meaning every time he *didn't* tell her he loved her he felt like exactly the sort of shit he should have felt like every time he *did* tell her he loved her. Somehow, not telling her he loved her had become synonymous with telling her he didn't love her, meaning he had to tell her he loved her just to maintain the status quo.

He glanced again at his newspaper. Some cretin in the op-ed section was going all weak-kneed about animal rights. Daniel imagined him, the columnist, bravely mopping the tears from his keyboard as he typed on. Sebastian would be all over this, he thought grimly. When had normality become so bloody weird?

He gathered his newspaper and stood up.

'Just going to brush my teeth,' he said, tucking the newspaper under his arm. 'Won't be long.'

It was a daily euphemism. Neither of them ever announced they were going for a shit. They were forever cleaning their teeth or washing their faces. For some reason they both always said they wouldn't be long.

He thought about Katherine as he drove to work, or rather, he thought around her, tending as he did to back his way into any reverie in which she might be involved. He'd been turning the telephone message over in his mind for a couple of days, and in between telling Angelica he loved her he'd made a concerted effort to at least begin to diagnose his feelings. Sadly, he'd made little headway, and his sense of how he thought he might be feeling differed depending on his sense of how he thought he might be living, which recently had been fluctuating on a near-daily basis, tied up as it was in Daniel's difficult and shifting relationship to what he thought of as Normality.

His relationship with Katherine had, categorically, not been normal, and now he'd left it and was in a relationship where normal things were very definitely said and done, it was fairly easy for him to think of himself and his life as normal. After all, he thought, here he was: he'd told his girlfriend he loved her; she'd told him she loved him; he'd eaten breakfast; and was now driving to a successful job. That was normal, wasn't it? If it was, then Katherine's phone call had to be regarded as some sort of brutal intrusion of abnormality.

Viewed another way, though, it was also possible for Daniel to reverse the situation. No, his relationship with Katherine had not been normal. It had been jagged and unpleasant. But there was, nonetheless, a creeping and rather disturbing sense of late that although the relationship might not have been as he wished it to be, Daniel had in fact been more himself. After all, he thought, was it really normal to feel so emotionally shifty around your partner? If everything was so sodding normal then why had Katherine's phone call sent him into a state of such disrepair? Worryingly, distastefully, when Daniel looked at things this way he started to view the phone call as a sort of relief, which made him more scared than when he simply regarded it as something scary.

He remembered lying in bed beside Katherine, not just in the later stages but, if he was honest, through much of their relationship, and trying to assess her level of anger by the way that she breathed as she slept, the way she rolled, the sounds she made as she stirred. He tended to wake before her, and found he could tell if she was angry before she even woke up. She was the only person he'd ever met who *slept* angrily. All it would take would be one sniff, one jerk of the shoulders as she rolled, and he'd know, and then he'd be tense, and she'd wake up and see he was tense and get angry. Or so she'd claim. As far as Daniel was concerned the truth was that nothing made Katherine angry. Her anger was organic. It simply *was*.

It was also infectious. Nothing had ever made Daniel angry like Katherine's anger. It flowed straight into his system. Other people had passing flare-ups, but Katherine could sustain the narrative of her rage for alarming periods of time. It would go through discernible shifts in tone. It had plot twists. Sometimes she apologised, even smiled, only to unleash another assault when he weakened. Sometimes she held off for days, edging him this way and that across a range of media: phone calls, emails at work, texts, even notes that she stuck to the fridge. *Don't make any effort*, said one. *I'm really sorry you've taken this so badly*, said another. Once, she'd called him at work and told him in a voice so reasoned it was actually dispassionate that she accepted full responsibility for the argument.

'Really?' he'd said cautiously.

'Yes. It's my fault.'

'Well . . .'

'You're not up to this. It's not your fault. I just forgot it, that's all.'

'Not up to what?'

'It's really not your fault.'

'What's not my fault?'

'Anything.'

He was quiet for several seconds, cogitating. He could hear her waiting.

'Well,' he said. 'OK.'

There was another long pause.

'You cunt,' she said.

'Excuse me?'

'Excuse me? Excuse me?' She mocked his voice. 'You actually think I'd ring you up to apologise? You actually think that *I* think that any of this is my fault?'

'Any of what?'

'Any of ANYTHING, you moron. Of course I don't think it's my fault. You know why? Because it's NOT my fault, it's YOUR fault, and even worse than all of this being your fault, I now know that not only do you NOT think it's your fault, you actually think it's MY fault or why else would you let me take full responsibility for it?'

'I don't even know what I'm supposed to . . .'

Then she'd hung up, and it had been the hang-up that had tipped him, perfectly, into utter impotent rage, shaped and fine-tuned over the rest of the day as he'd called and called, as he'd shouted at her voicemail and kicked his desk in frustration and pictured her calmly watching her phone as it rang, or reading back his abusive texts with that little smile of hers.

Sebastian and four or five of his cronies were installed in the car park. As Daniel pulled into his reserved parking space he found himself briefly flirting with the idea of simply reversing back out; not even going home but absconding, skipping town. What with Angelica, Katherine, work, and now Sebastian and his imbecilic retinue, a fugitive existence seemed increasingly attractive.

They were huddled in a little group, sharing coffee from a thermos and blowing on their hands, which were bound to be cold given what appeared to have been a group decision to wear fingerless gloves.

Daniel locked the car and walked towards them, suddenly self-conscious in his well-shined black Oxfords and charcoal overcoat. He didn't have a briefcase, though, having chosen instead to carry his papers in a battered canvas satchel. He liked the way it undercut both style and status; the way it hinted at an anti-authoritarian seam beneath the suave rock face of aspiration.

'In the old days the generals used to meet on the battlefield,' said Sebastian by way of greeting. Phrases like *the old days* annoyed Daniel. At what precise point in history did the old days end and the new days begin?

'I try not to think of it as a battlefield,' said Daniel, mustering a smile and at least a semblance of cheer. 'It's all a matter of interpretation.'

'Out of the mouths of babes,' said one of Sebastian's leering retinue. No one seemed sure what he meant. His grin hung briefly, like a ball reaching the apex of its flight, then dropped.

'How's the flu?' said Sebastian.

'Not too bad, thank you.'

Daniel's flu had, in fact, almost wholly abated, which, in much the same way as his boiler always sprang miraculously to life the moment he summoned a plumber, was what always happened whenever he went gratuitously public with an illness. So many things in life, it seemed, were cured by simple recognition.

'Do thank Angelica for a lovely meal,' beamed Sebastian.

'I will,' said Daniel, his annoyance operating on several tiers. Sebastian always thanked Angelica, then whenever he saw Daniel he asked him to thank Angelica too. Beyond his irritation that Sebastian pointedly never seemed to thank *him* for having them over for dinner, Daniel also got the sense that it was designed to imply, like much of what Sebastian said, that Daniel was somehow inattentive towards Angelica. On top of all this was the further annoyance that Sebastian only ever made these comments in the present situation, when there were onlookers; when the notion of them having dinner together seemed both odd and faintly inappropriate. He loved it, Daniel thought, this sense of moving between classes and agencies, of having a tentacle-like reach to all the major players. He probably pictured himself as some sort of Scarlet Pimpernel.

Briefly, Daniel entertained a fantasy of kicking him in the balls, or strangling him with his own ponytail. He imagined Sebastian slowly winding down like a broken toy. *You've got a lot of hostility*, he'd croak. *You really need to work on your . . .*

'Busy day ahead?'

'Yes,' Daniel smiled. 'And you?'

'Oh, you know,' said Sebastian, 'same old same old. Not for much longer, though.'

'Really? Are you giving up?'

Sebastian laughed. 'I take it you've been following the news?'

'Mmmhmm.'

'An escalating situation necessitates an escalation in action.'

'Is that Sun Tzu?'

'No, it's Sebastian Freud.'

'Ah. So you're escalating?'

'Onwards and upwards,' said Sebastian.

'When you say "onwards," does that mean . . .'

Sebastian tapped the side of his nose and smiled in what he clearly hoped was a knowing and inscrutable manner. 'There's an ancient Sanskrit expression,' he said.

'Well, work beckons,' said Daniel.

'Back to the grindstone,' said Sebastian.

'I didn't know that was Sanskrit.'

'No, it's not. I was . . . The Sanskrit expression is . . .'

'Don't catch a chill,' said Daniel, walking away.

He felt the casual waft of disdain in the air, heard chuckling behind him, and then, just as the green-tinged glass doors hissed aside at the touch of his swipe card, the sound of Sebastian mimicking his voice, rendering it as a privileged whine. '*Work beckons . . .*'

He was, he thought, angry. Was he angry? It was becoming difficult to tell these days. In a lot of ways, his relationship to anger was rather similar to his relationship with smoking. Having come to the conclusion that neither were good for him, he had given up both. Now, feeling as he did that his life was becoming dull, he pined for both. Yet where he was able to resist the pull of smoking with comparative ease, anger appeared increasingly seductive. At least with fags you could re-steel your resolve with the images of diseased lungs and blackened, crazy-pavement teeth that now adorned the packets. What was offered to people trying daily to tamp down their tempers? Pictures of broken plates? Mug shots of the domestically abused? There seemed to be no real motivating factors in staying calm, particularly, he thought, when so many people around him seemed to become angry so frequently and productively.

It wasn't that he actually *was* angry, of course. That would have been simple. It was more that he missed its release, pined for it at times, and so found himself in the odd position of wishing he could be angry without actually, as he wished it, feeling particularly angry. This had now reached the point where he found himself fantasising about anger. In the lift, his mind sought out possible scenarios in which it would be not only acceptable to be angry but downright admirable. He dreamed of a heroic, righteous rage. *I've never seen him like that*, people would say with awe. *I've never seen him so angry*. Men would be intimidated by him; women would find him attractive. He'd develop the sense of having a whole other side.

Safely ensconced in his office, he sank into his leather armchair, dropped his canvas bag on the floor beside the desk, and turned on his computer. He had fifty-three high-priority emails. Recently, he'd enforced a new three-step priority matrix to help determine which emails needed to be read first. Sadly, everyone now marked their emails as high priority for fear they wouldn't get read.

He looked out of the window at the rag-tag gaggle of proudly dishevelled demonstrators. He had to maintain a certain depth of focus to avoid his own semi-transparent image being overlaid on theirs. He was reluctant to see himself, a sad little man in a nicely furnished box, with nothing really to defend or attack, dreaming, like every sad little middle-class white man in the world, of a good old-fashioned fight that wouldn't make him look bad.

He buzzed Clara, his secretary.

'Morning Clara.'

'Morning.'

'How are you?'

'Can't complain.'

Clara was actually very gifted at complaining, so this statement, with which she started each new day, was something of a falsehood.

'Great,' said Daniel. 'Could you bring me some coffee?'

'Suppose.'

He leaned back in his chair, digging his mobile out of his pocket when it jabbed uncomfortably into his thigh. He scrolled the numbers idly, A through E; F through K. Katherine was the only person in his contacts listed solely by her first name.

'Clara,' he said into the buzzer.

'I'm making it now. Give me a chance.'

'Could you make a call for me?'

'Before I make the coffee?'

'Yes please.'

Clara called Katherine and put Daniel through.

'Katherine?'

As he said it he realised he'd rehearsed this in his head more times than he could comfortably acknowledge. It would all, he knew, stem from his opening sounds. Katherine believed in beginnings, and her interpretation of his greeting would set the tone. He thought he'd done well: not too bright, not too flat; somehow both at ease and respectful of the wider context . . .

'It's um . . . It's a bad line. I'll call you back.'

It wasn't a bad line, of course, meaning that somehow he had blown his opening. In the unnervingly long minutes while he waited for her to call back he examined the way he'd said her name from every possible angle and perspective. Katherine? *Katherine?* Katherine. *Katherine.* How should he have said it, for fuck's sake? Maybe he shouldn't have phrased it as a question. Maybe it came off as tentative. Was it redundant? After all, who else would have answered her phone? *Katherine*, he should have said. Full stop. *It's Daniel. Hi.* No. Too cold. Should have just gone with *Hey. Hey! Long time no speak.* Christ.

His phone rang.

'Hey,' he said.

'Hey yourself,' said Katherine.

There was a difficult pause. Katherine tended not to break pauses, Daniel now remembered, often preferring to revel in the awkwardness of the moment. Comfort was cause for concern, even at a trivial, conversational level.

'How, ah . . .' He decided simply to start sentences in the hope that she would, as was her habit, finish them on his behalf.

'How have I been?'

'Yes.'

'Great. Fantastic. Amazing.'

'Great.'

'You?'

'Great, yeah. Really good.'

'Great.'

'Are you still, um . . .'

'Yup. Same old same old.'

'Mmmm.'

Another pause.

'So God it's been like, what . . .' said Daniel.

'A year? Something like that?'

'Yeah. Must have been. Wow.'

'Crazy.'

'Anyway. It's good to hear from you.'

'Is it?'

He detected, immediately, the shift in tone. He felt like an insect negotiating the tines of a Venus flytrap.

'Yes,' he said quickly. 'Of course it is.'

He could feel her weighing the sincerity of this statement.

'So Nathan,' he said, a little too hurriedly.

'Yeah.'

'How is he?'

'I don't know,' said Katherine. 'He left a message. I haven't called back.'

'Why haven't you called him back?'

'You know.'

'Not really.'

'Why should I take responsibility for this?'

'Because he called you.'

'Only because he doesn't have your number.'

She meant, Daniel knew, that she was reluctant to deal with Nathan on her own and would welcome a degree of support from someone else who knew him. Not that she would say that.

Daniel swivelled gently in his chair so he could again look out the window. Clearly done with the thermos, the merry band outside was unfurling a gaudy new banner that said *You Are What You Eat*. Imaginative, he thought.

He realised he'd had a lingering sense of nameless dread, of something a-stink in the woodshed of his life, for months. Katherine, at least, was a dread he could name. There was something reassuring about that.

'Look,' he said.

A loud crunching came down the phone line.

'Jesus,' he said. 'What are you eating? A car?'

'Rice cake.'

'Do you have to?'

'No,' she said, bearing down on what must have been at least half a rice cake at once. 'Just want to.'

'Right. So. Anyway.'

She sniffed.

'Nathan,' he said. 'What about Nathan?'

'Yup,' she said flatly. 'What about him?'

'What,' said Daniel, with pointed patience and precision, 'shall we do . . . about *Nathan*?'

To his relief, she didn't respond immediately. She seemed to be giving it genuine thought.

'I've got a lot on,' she said eventually.

'Me too.'

'But at the same time . . .'

'Yeah. That's what I think.'

'It's like . . . you know.'

'I know.'

Neither of them said anything for a bit. Daniel had a sudden and slightly bizarre urge to remove one shoe and sock and pick at the sharp corner of his second toenail, which was digging into the flesh of the toe beside it. Wasn't there a school of philosophy that encouraged the excision of that which caused you pain? Wasn't it in the Bible? He rested his foot on the desk, unlaced his shoe, and peeled away his sock. He realised it was the first time the skin of his foot had met the air of his office. Funny, he thought, how certain parts of us never come into contact with things that other parts of us come into contact with every day. He tried to think of other examples, then realised that all the examples involved his feet, and that what he was actually realising was that he wore shoes all day which, now that he thought about it, wasn't exactly a revelation.

'What are you doing?' said Katherine.

'Thinking about my feet.'

'*Riiiiggghhhht.*'

Clara walked in with his coffee.

'Just put it there thank you Clara,' said Daniel, pointing at the free patch of desk next to his foot. She set down the tray with a frown and left. He pressed the plunger on the cafetière and poured himself a cup.

'Just there thank you Clara,' said Katherine. 'That's it. And just tongue my balls while you're there, there's a dear.'

'Touch of jealousy, perhaps?'

'Whatever.'

'So,' he said, taking a sip of his coffee. 'Nathan.'

'I know, I know.'

'What does your gut say?'

'That you or I or we should do something.'

'Agreed. That something being what?'

'Why am I making all the decisions here?'

'OK, OK. Let's think this through.'

'What's to think through? Do you ever do anything without thinking it through?'

This was a fair point, Daniel thought. Maybe he should be a bit more reckless. Maybe it would be good to see Nathan again and get back in touch with that part of himself.

It struck him that the phrase *a bit more reckless* was inherently absurd. He was glad he hadn't said it aloud.

'Well what have you achieved so far?' he said, sounding more petulant than he'd intended. If it was possible to hear someone smile down a phone line, then that was what he experienced as he said it: Katherine's wry, valedictory sneer.

'Tetchy,' she said, pushing another rice cake into her mouth. 'Take it you're not smoking.'

'Take it you still are.'

'Made you give up, did she?'

'No. Who?'

'You know. She.'

He felt a slight lurch at his core; a tectonic shift. He wondered if Katherine knew. If she'd known all along.

'You mean Angelica.'

'If that's her name. What's she like?'

'She's nice.'

'*Nice.*'

'I like nice.'

'Of course you do.'

'Not everyone equates difficulty with passion, you know.'

'Of course not.'

'Anyway, what about you?'

'I'm off men.'

'Were you ever on them?'

'That's one of those statements that initially sounds snappy and witty but which, when you pick around at it, actually turns out not to mean anything.'

'You'd know.'

'Again . . .'

He gave up. She was pushing him around and he couldn't remember how to do anything about it. Perhaps he'd never known. Perhaps he'd never wanted to know.

'Let's go and see him,' said Katherine.

'What?'

'Let's just arrange to go and see him. Or are you not able? Or don't you want to? Or won't she let you?'

'None of the above. Maybe we should go and see him.'

'Great. When?'

He faltered. 'I . . . Um . . . Well, when's he free?'

'How would I know?'

'Can't you call him and ask?'

'Can't you?'

'Jesus. Is that what it's going to take to achieve something?'

'Probably, yeah.'

'What's his number?'

She told him and he took it down.

'When are you free?' he asked.

'Oh,' she said, an odd drift to her voice. 'I'll be free.'

'OK. That's decided then.'

'Yeah.'

There was a flatness to her tone now, as if her energy were fading. She sniffed. Daniel put his sock back on, then his shoe. He tucked the phone under his chin while he tied his laces. He heard a rustling from Katherine's end of the phone, followed by more silence, and gathered that she'd run out of rice cakes. Outside his window, the protestors started an off-key rendition of 'We Shall Not Be Moved', even though no one was attempting to move them. He'd received three more high-priority emails since he'd last looked.

'Good to hear from you,' he said.

'You too.'

'I'll call. It'll be after the weekend.'

'Understood.'

She hung up. He took a deep swig of his coffee and stared a moment at the swirling, lightly oiled surface of the brew. He scrolled blankly through his emails. He checked his schedule. He liked saying that, even to himself. *I'll check my schedule.* Half his life, he thought, he'd longed to be the sort of person who had to check their schedule. He thought about Katherine. He was unable to think about her in her entirety. He had to break her into manageable pieces. He used to think this was because Katherine was Katherine. Now he knew that to be untrue, because he thought of Angelica in the same way. He couldn't, or wouldn't, know someone whole. He would guess at them in pieces and either love the hypothetical sum of their parts or weigh them and find them wanting.

'Clara.' He liked to line up his chin over his extended index finger when he pressed the button and spoke into the intercom, as if taking aim.

'Hello.'

'What's my schedule?'

'You have it there.'

'Come in and tell me my schedule.'

She came in and read him his schedule. It helped.

The day passed in its usual gyroscopic way. He circled his office: a meeting here; a tour of this or that department there; back to the office; an interview; the office; a press release; a walk; the office. It was the circling that kept him upright.

He called it a day at six and switched off the lights behind him. Sebastian and his friends had already vacated the car park. It gave him a sense of satisfaction to think he'd put in more hours. He got in his car and drove slowly home, blinking in the glow of the streetlights across his frosted windows. He felt disassociated, dislocated. He kept thinking of Nathan at that last party: motionless, not even swaying to the music as however many hundred others danced around him. He remembered marvelling at the stillness, yet also feeling a pervasive sense of loss. Nathan had always brought motion; kinesis. It's what Daniel looked to him for. Speed. The pulse of change. Seeing him so still, lost in all the motion he'd created, Daniel had known that something was over. He felt it again now as he drove. That sense of spinning to stand still. He wondered if it was merely a coincidence that, mere months after Nathan had vanished, he'd met Angelica. Without Nathan, it seemed, he and Katherine had unravelled all the more rapidly.

Arriving home, walking in the door, he found Sebastian sitting at the dining table.

'Putting in the hours, eh?' said Sebastian.

'I think most people finish around six, don't they?' said Daniel, easing slightly awkwardly behind Sebastian's chair in order to get to Angelica and kiss her.

'*Most people*,' said Sebastian tartly. 'They do all sorts of things.'

'Hello darling,' said Daniel to Angelica. 'How are you?'

'Sebastian's going national with his protest,' said Angelica. 'Love you my sweet.'

'Love you too,' said Daniel, kissing her again and stealing a glance at Sebastian. He felt a surge of satisfaction. Sebastian could go as national as he liked, so long as he was no longer camped out in the car park.

'Daniel's really been getting in touch with his affectionate side,' said Angelica to Sebastian.

'Great,' said Sebastian, a little thrown. 'Although of course I question the word *affection*.'

'Oh that's just Angelica being euphemistic,' said Daniel, beaming at Sebastian. 'I think it's only natural, sadly natural you might say, the urge to downplay a passion as relentless and thoroughgoing as ours. Don't you think, dear?'

Angelica was looking at him with her mouth slightly open. 'Well, yes,' she said, widening her eyes a little.

'But you must feel the same, Sebastian, no? I mean such is your love for Plum that you must just fall on your knees daily and tell her that you worship her and adore her and that you're basically her slave. Right?'

'Right,' said Sebastian.

'So,' said Daniel, pulling a chair out from the table and sinking back into it with a satisfied sigh. 'The cows.'

'Um, yeah,' said Sebastian, faltering slightly before rallying. 'We're going on the road to defend the cows.'

'This cull has got completely out of hand,' said Angelica. 'Sebastian was just explaining that in Thailand for example they actually nurse their livestock back to health.'

'There hasn't been any BIE in Thailand,' said Daniel flatly. 'It's just the UK.'

'No, but it's the principle,' said Sebastian.

'Not really. They're dealing with different diseases. The difference in response reflects that.'

'You can't just kill a whole race of creatures,' said Sebastian, sucking his lips briefly over his teeth as if to imply barely contained emotion. 'I mean, have we learnt nothing from Auschwitz?'

'Cattle aren't a race,' said Daniel. 'They're a species.'

'Still,' said Sebastian. 'It's an essentially fascist response.'

'So who's Hitler?'

'We're *all* Hitler,' said Sebastian meaningfully.

'Then who are you demonstrating against? Yourself?'

'I think you're using a very limited definition of *protest*.'

'What's your definition?'

'I possibly wouldn't use the word *protest* at all.'

'What word would you use?'

Sebastian thought for several seconds. '*Action*,' he said finally.

'That's a great word,' said Angelica.

'So who are you taking action against?' said Daniel.

'Why does action have to be *against* anyone? Why can't it just . . . *be*?'

'OK. So what's the *nature* of your action, and what is it motivated by?'

'The nature of our action is essentially pacifist and ecological and it's motivated by a deep concern for and . . .' Sebastian raised a finger in the air and leaned forward, punctuating his point, '*empathy with every living creature on this planet*.'

'You empathise with every living creature on this planet?'

'We are *all* one creature.'

'So we're putting *ourselves* into Auschwitz?'

'Yes, but we don't realise it.'

'So, you're taking action against ourselves to stop ourselves putting ourselves into a death camp?'

Sebastian looked at Daniel a very long time.

'Daniel's in one of those moods,' said Angelica. Then, as a sort of PS: 'Love you crumpet.'

'Love you sweetie pie,' said Daniel. 'Do you think you can fit all that on a banner, Sebastian?'

Sebastian was still looking at Daniel with what seemed to be a mixture of disgust and trepidation. After a while he smiled, leaned back, and folded his hands.

'You'll have to ask Angelica,' he said smugly. 'She's coming along to help.'

Daniel did his best not to look shaken, but sensed it was a losing battle from which he almost certainly emerged looking shaken.

'Love you, dear,' said Angelica, with a distinct lack of confidence. 'You don't mind, do you?'

Daniel looked over at Sebastian, who was busying himself retying his ponytail.

'Don't worry, Dan,' he said, sickly sweet. 'I'll take very good care of her.'

'Is Plum going?' said Daniel.

'Sadly not,' said Sebastian. 'She's really tied up with the internet side of things right now.'

'Oh,' said Angelica. 'I thought she was going too.'

There was a long pause. Daniel looked at Sebastian and Angelica in turn. Sebastian and Angelica looked at Daniel. Daniel waited to see if they would look at each other. They didn't. He wondered if he was being lied to. Then he wondered if he was only wondering that because he'd done no small amount of lying himself. It struck him, briefly, that now might be an opportune time, tactically speaking, to announce certain pieces of news of his own.

'Is that something I should have mentioned?' said Sebastian. 'It honestly didn't occur to me at all.'

'Oh,' said Angelica. 'I mean, obviously it's fine, I was just surprised, that's all. She'll be so sorry not to be there.'

'When are you off?' said Daniel, in whom Sebastian's three-second distraction of a statement had caused an almost total reversal of intention.

'Soon as,' said Sebastian. 'Or maybe tomorrow.'

Angelica was looking at Daniel slightly oddly, the way a particularly difficult sudoku puzzle might be regarded by someone who was very good at sudoku: briefly, mildly, happily thrown.

'Are you sure you're OK with this?' she said.

'Absolutely,' said Daniel, meaning absolutely not. 'Love you dear.'

'Ahh,' she said. 'I am *such* a lucky woman.'

'Hey,' said Daniel, winking. 'I'm the lucky one around here.'

'This is, um . . .' said Sebastian.

It was indeed um, thought Daniel. It was as if he'd pushed through some sort of barrier, on the other side of which all polarities of sincerity were reversed. His voice was changing. His very physicality was becoming cheesy. He'd just *winked*, for fuck's sake.

As if sensing the mounting surrealism of the situation, and perhaps keen to lend his dispassionate eye, Giggles came lumbering into the room, his backside nonchalantly swaying; folds of flesh rippling under his fur.

'Look who's here,' said Daniel, by now acting so far out of character that he was actually scared to do anything remotely normal lest doubt should fog the heads of his audience. He bent down, grunting slightly as he seized Giggles around the torso and heaved the animal onto his lap. 'Hey boy,' he said. 'Oooff. Who's a big fella.'

'Are you going to look after Daddy while Mummy's away?' said Angelica. 'Are you going to take extra good care of him?'

'Yes you are,' said Daniel, manipulating Giggles's flab in such a way as to suggest fondness. 'Yes you are, aren't you boy?'

Giggles looked at Daniel with what Daniel would have described, had he been in any way anthropomorphically inclined, as mute scepticism.

'Well I suppose I should be getting on,' said Sebastian.

'Of course,' said Daniel. 'You must have God knows how many banners to furl.'

Sebastian gave him a withering look which by pure free association Daniel then saw transferred to the face of the hulking tabby on his lap.

'There's actually an awful lot to co-ordinate,' said Sebastian.

'How long do you think you'll be away?' said Daniel.

'Just a few days,' said Angelica.

'Very difficult to tell,' said Sebastian.

'I could go and come back,' said Angelica.

'Where will you be based?' said Daniel.

'Not far,' said Angelica. 'Right, Sebastian?'

'Very difficult to tell,' said Sebastian.

Late in the evening Daniel's father called to say he'd died. This was something he was periodically inclined to do.

'I've been counting,' he said. 'My pulse is gone and I haven't taken a breath since lunch.'

He was specific about the symptoms of his death. A whiteness; voices; the presence of other souls.

'Dad,' Daniel said.

'I haven't got a pulse. I'm not breathing. It sounds like I'm breathing but it's not really air. I cut my finger and it didn't bleed and when I went outside nobody could see me.'

'You were outside?'

'But it wasn't outside. It couldn't have been. They couldn't see me.'

'Dad,' Daniel said. 'If you were really dead, how could you call to tell me?'

A pause at the other end of the phone. A deep breath. Daniel could picture him – thin as a sparrow's leg in frayed pyjamas; his skin soapy-pale; slightly hunched, as if he had to lean into the call to achieve maximum connection. His answer took several seconds to arrive, a space of time in which Daniel imagined he could hear his father's thoughts as they ground against each other, as one struggled to beget another.

'They let you,' his father said at last. 'They give you one phone call.'

A t night, in bed, after they had either made love or, as was the case this evening, not, Daniel and Angelica would often pass the time between turning off the lights and falling asleep by talking about other people. There seemed to be an unspoken agreement that discussion of themselves, of their life together, was not to be conducted in such an intimate space.

'Sebastian's funny, isn't he?' said Angelica.

'Funny how?'

'Just funny.'

They were lying side by side in the not-quite-dark of their bedroom, the glow of a nearby streetlight turning their thin blind into an amber screen.

'I suppose,' said Daniel.

'Do you think things are all right between him and Plum?'

'Hard to say,' said Daniel. 'They seemed happy at dinner.'

'He always makes a show, though, doesn't he? Like a big show of what a great couple they are. I suppose sometimes I wonder if he'd need to do that so much if . . .'

'If they were actually happy.'

'Yeah.'

'Hard to say.'

'I mean, do you think Plum really gets him?'

'Gets him how?'

'Well,' she thought for a moment. 'He's . . . I mean there's so much going on with him, isn't there? He's well-read, he's intelligent, he's talented. I just wonder if sometimes he feels frustrated.'

'I think he rather enjoys being with someone he feels superior to,' said Daniel. 'I can't really imagine him being with anyone he found threatening.'

'You don't like him very much, do you?'

'I don't dislike him.'

'You don't have to like him.'

'I know.'

More silence, during which Daniel stared at a thin blade of street-light creeping past the edge of the blind. He felt he knew what Angelica was saying better than she did.

'You're OK with this, aren't you?' she said, reaching for his leg under the covers and gripping him lightly by the thigh.

'Of course,' he said, giving her hand a little squeeze. 'Love you sweetie.'

'Love you Daniel,' she said.

It struck him that she probably did; that he probably did; that Katherine had probably loved him too and that he might at one stage have loved her. He felt the differences between him and Angelica more acutely in bed than anywhere. Angelica's softness; the basic decency of her fears. It made him sad in a way that was difficult to grasp. He was, he thought, rotting from the inside out. He was handling everything badly. He put himself in certain situations because he resented not being put in them by others, but then resented the situations when he was in them. He wanted to be leaned on. He was nothing if not needed; indeed, he was *needy* if not needed, but then . . .

He remembered bedtimes with Katherine, the way he'd tried and failed to fall asleep amidst the hum of tension from her side of the bed. It was like sleeping with a uranium fuel rod: you couldn't see the mutation, the clumsy over-division of cells it set off inside you, but it was there, and it was permanent. And now he was the source, that same malignant glow under the covers. Had any progress been made? Had he learned anything at all? Yes, the register was different, but the basic approach – tactical, self-protecting, reflexively strategic – was essentially the same. He couched his disagreements in Angelica's language of unconditional positive regard just as he had previously battled Katherine in her own language of hostility and aggression. He was kind to Angelica because it was easier than being honest. He had been unkind to Katherine because it was easier than being honest and safer than being kind.

Angelica squeezed his thigh; rolled slightly towards him; kissed him gently on the apex of his cheekbone. Everyone wants to be loved. He wanted to be loved. He wanted, he thought, to make people love him, to need him, and now he had. He'd wanted, from the earliest age he was able to recall, to grow up, to be an adult, and now he had, and now he was, and now he wanted to regress, and climb aboard a bus with blacked-out windows bound for some nameless green-belt field where someone would water-pistol chemicals onto his tongue and steer him into a fog of music so loud that it felt like a shoal of nibbling fish setting to work on the dead skin around his life.

'I love you,' said Angelica.

He thought about Nathan. He'd felt superior to him once. He'd predicted Nathan's slip, had felt vindicated when it happened because it reminded Daniel that there was a reason he wasn't Nathan. Daniel could dabble. He always dabbled. He was hands-clean. He could envy Nathan and watch him fail and then go back to being the man he really was. And he had. And he'd cheated on Katherine because he could, and now Angelica could cheat on him and he could cheat on her, and in a way, he had.

'I love you too,' he said, and he did and he didn't.

He felt Angelica soften into sleep beside him and wondered if she was dreaming of Sebastian. It struck him that, even as he lay awake and dreamed open-eyed about violence and anger and the things he wanted to do but couldn't, he was circling closer towards loving her again, simply because she seemed to be circling away. He reached out and touched her shoulder. He wanted to tell her. By reflex, she rolled and wrapped her arms around him, and he could feel her breath against his cheek and ear, and could smell the hot scent of sleep across her neck and chest as he nestled his face closer, throwing his arm across her hip and squeezing until she exhaled, just slightly. He wouldn't be able to sleep, he thought. Then he did.

Nathan's parents, as became clear to him during the time he spent in their company, never mixed. They co-existed, interacted at times, but consistently fell short of cohesion. His mother was increasingly hot and blustery, moving at speed through the house, revelling in her ability to manage each small crisis. His father, meanwhile, trailed her like a lingering odour. Clearly so accustomed to not being listened to that the entire act of communication had now been reduced to a mere formality that allowed them, after the event, to say in all confidence that yes they certainly *had* told each other about this or that because they remembered it quite vividly, they now conversed almost entirely in the round.

'We need to, ah, we need to have a quick discussion about . . .' Nathan's father would say.

'Roger,' his mother would say, as if her husband had been completely ignoring her and she now needed to get his attention. 'Have we had any news from . . .'

'. . . next Saturday. Because I've got here . . .'

'. . . Jacinta and Gregory re: . . .'

'. . . that we're supposed to be going to . . .'

'. . . next Saturday. Because I've got here that we're supposed to . . .'

'. . . Jacinta and Gregory's for dinner, and I was just wondering . . .'

'. . . go round there for dinner, and I'm not sure we've . . .'

'. . . if that's confirmed or . . .'

'. . . confirmed it. Have we?'

'. . . if we still need to. Do we?'

Each of them felt, and frequently said, that the only way to really get anything done was simply to do it yourself, yet each of them also seemed to find doing anything without alerting the other to what they were doing rather difficult, resulting in a continual barrage of occluding updates. One of them was going shopping and would talk about this when they got back. The other was going to the post and would also talk about this when they got back. The precise nature of 'this' would never quite be defined, yet both would return with the ticklish idea that something would need to be discussed. Later, when it became clear that there had been something they should have discussed, and that problems had arisen as a result of not discussing it, they would debate whether they'd discussed it.

'Oh, Roger,' Nathan's mother would say. 'Do we have to go over this again? I *specifically remember* going over this at the time.'

'Well I don't. I don't remember talking about this at all. When did we talk about this?'

'Last Tuesday.'

'What happened last Tuesday?'

'We went to that thing, and then we came back, and we had this *exact* conversation then.'

'Couldn't have been last Tuesday. I was out last Tuesday.'

'You were out on Monday.'

'No. *You* were out on Monday.'

'For God's sake, Roger. Will you try and concentrate? *You* were

166

out on Monday and we were *both* out on Tuesday, but when we got back . . .'

'There's nothing in the diary.'

'For when?'

'For Monday.'

'That doesn't mean you weren't out. But anyway, look, this is beside the point. The point is . . .'

'We're wasting time by arguing about this, really.'

'We are. That's what I'm saying.'

'I think we should stick to the point at hand.'

'I am. It's you that's straying off to try and find out what you were doing last week.'

'I'm just trying to establish whether we might have discussed this.'

'Roger, I came up to you on Tuesday, and I *specifically* said this was something we needed to discuss, and you agreed, and you said . . .'

'Ah! Yes, I remember. We agreed to discuss it the next day because I was going out. Now, where was I going?'

'That was Monday. Tuesday *was* the next day and that's why we discussed it, because we'd agreed on Monday to discuss it but you were going out.'

'And then we went out on Wednesday and forgot to discuss it.'

'Tuesday.'

'No, Helen, we were *in* on Tuesday.'

Nathan could only assume there was a kind of comfort in the ritual. To him, however, either sitting upstairs reading his mother's book ('Communication,' she noted on page 84, 'is the bedrock of any stable family'), or trying to make a cup of tea in the kitchen without becoming embroiled in what was taking place around him, there was a mounting feeling that, thanks to the circuitous, incantatory conversations around him, time itself was beginning to form loops from which it was difficult to escape. Downstairs, the loops were made of seconds, minutes and hours. He could make a cup of tea, return to his room, drink his tea, and then go back downstairs to find that the previous conversation regarding a previous conversation had started up again exactly where it either had or hadn't left off. Upstairs, the loops were made of years, as he opened his mother's book and encountered episodes from his childhood which, if he remembered them at all, he remembered very differently.

The overall effect was therefore not simply one of dislocation, but of dislocation repeated; an increasingly familiar oddness heightened by the simple fact of Nathan's not having been a part of the wider world for several months, and by his parents' not having been a part of the wider world for several years. Coincidentally, Nathan's reluctant return to society coincided with his mother's not-so-reluctant entry into the public domain, and so both she and he found themselves exposed at the same moment, although the nature of exposure was, for each of them, both different and differently received.

'Nathan,' said his mother, looking up from her laptop. 'Are you on Facebook?'

'No.'

'I don't believe you,' she said. 'How did you get up to all that mischief without being on Facebook?'

'It was different then. There were chat rooms.'

'I see. Well perhaps you could join Facebook?'

'I don't really want to.'

'Right. It would be very helpful if you joined Facebook.'

'Why?'

'Well, my book's coming out, and I've started a Facebook page for it, and obviously I've got everyone from my Twitter feed to like the Facebook page, but it seems to me that if you could get some of your friends to like it too I'd be tapping into a whole new circle.'

'But I'm not on Facebook.'

'What about these chat rooms? Couldn't you start a new thread?'

'They're not really book-related.'

'Right, OK. I can see you're going to be no help with this whatsoever.'

Nathan said nothing. Being no help whatsoever was, of course, pretty central to his approach as far as the whole book issue went.

He spent whole days dedicated to the task of spending his days. He sat in his bedroom and read. He sat downstairs and listened to his parents. He sat in the garden and smoked. Time both passed and lingered. It was empty; fleeting. People stubbornly existed and were absent. He wondered if he should make calls. He'd been told that effort was important.

His mother was a self-described fount of wisdom. A well-planned meal could see you through several days. You could be inventive with leftovers and it never really felt like you were eating the same thing. Home-baked bread was both economical and reassuring in that one had far more control over the ingredients. Laundry was best done on a 'little and often' basis, as were other household tasks, particularly cleaning. Financially, economically, emotionally and nutritionally, staying on top of things was infinitely preferable to allowing them to mount up. The idea seemed to be that you filled time with the simple act of existence. The quotidian was profoundly demanding. Saving time seemed to take a lot of time. He kept checking his phone but nothing ever happened. He lay awake late into the night and sometimes got up and opened the window for a winter rush. He wondered if he'd ever claimed not to like winter, just for convenience or conversation, because people always said they didn't like winter. He felt strongly that he did like winter and was going to say so from now on.

*O*f course, Nathan's mother wrote in her book, *there will always be those dissenting yet misinformed voices who say: But, Helen, this is your fault, you didn't do enough, you could have done more. And to those people I say: What more could I possibly have done?*

His mother said he should set a budget. He told her he had no income. She said that she and his father were going to help until Nathan got back on his feet, which was something she seemed to delight in saying. They were going to give him fifty pounds a week but out of that he had to give them twenty in upkeep. This was to help him develop independence. She handed him fifty quid in clean notes. He folded twenty and handed it back. He walked to the shop and spent ten on tobacco and then went to the pub because there was nothing really worth saving for at this point. The light had that oddly vivid, vibratory quality that seems to arrive at the greying of a winter's day – dimmer than full sunlight, but tuned to a higher contrast, the land looming out in buzzing relief. He could see his breath in front of his face and stepped through the little clouds as he walked. There was no noise aside from the occasional bird. The ground was tough and iced underfoot. Existence seemed very clear, very simple. He felt quite calm, he noticed, when he looked at his feelings as if they were objects.

The pub was called The Rover. Nathan had been in there maybe twice in his life. The barman didn't seem overly friendly.

'Sorry,' he said, distracted by Nathan's hands. 'Are those burns?'

'No, just scars.'

'Oh.'

'Pint of Guinness, please.'

'Right.'

He stuck a pint glass under the tap and let it fill, no pause, no time to settle. Nathan paid and sat at a little round table on a little round stool in the corner, near the door. He looked around for a newspaper. There wasn't one. He wasn't quite sure what to do with himself in the absence of a newspaper and so watched the brown breath of his Guinness as it sought its level. He thought about taking off his coat but he had his shirtsleeves rolled up underneath and he didn't want to upset anyone. Noting that he didn't want to upset anyone made him feel pleased. He thought about phoning Katherine again. She hadn't called, but she would call. If she didn't call there would be a good reason, and that reason wouldn't necessarily have much to do with him.

The door opened, and amidst his usual muted applause of synthetic jacketing, Nathan's father strolled into the pub. When he saw Nathan he looked briefly guilty, then came and stood beside his table.

'Ah,' he said. 'I was um . . .'

Nathan looked at him, smiled.

'Don't come in here often,' said his father, jamming his hands in his jacket pockets and looking around. 'Not a bad place, is it?'

'It's nice enough,' said Nathan.

'Hello Roger,' called the barman. 'Usual, is it?'

Nathan's father did a little double-take, then looked down at Nathan's pint, which was over half full.

'Well, I suppose now I'm here . . .'

'Go ahead,' said Nathan. 'I'm drinking slowly.'

'Righto.'

He ambled off to the bar and returned a minute later with a pint of something red and a packet of dry-roasted peanuts which he spread open on the table as if performing a post-mortem.

'Have some nuts,' he said.

Nathan had a few nuts.

'Nice to get out,' said his father after a while.

'What do you tell her?' said Nathan.

His father looked guilty. 'She just assumes I'm in the garage. She's not there now, though. She's gone to the TV studio.'

'If she never looks for you in the garage, why don't you just go there?'

'Not the same is it? Not really.' He tossed another handful of nuts in his mouth.

'What are you drinking?'

'Bulmer's cider and Red Bull with a dash of crème de menthe. I call it a Mad Cow. Have a sip?'

Nathan raised a hand. 'Might stick to the Guinness,' he said.

'They don't have a pool table here,' said his father.

'Oh.'

'I suppose that's nice though, isn't it, because then you have to talk.'

Nathan nodded.

'I know some people,' said his father. 'See them here sometimes. We don't arrange it, mind. Just leave it to chance. It's nice to have a flexible arrangement, isn't it? I mean, not everything has to be set in stone all the time, does it?'

'No,' said Nathan. 'Not at all.'

His father smacked his lips as he sipped his Mad Cow. 'That hits the spot,' he said.

They looked at their drinks for a bit.

'I prefer dry-roasted peanuts,' said his father. 'They're more interesting in a lot of ways. Helen says they give you cancer, but what doesn't?' He tossed back another handful and then looked at Nathan. 'We get on, don't we?' he said.

'Yes,' said Nathan. 'Of course we do.'

'Good. That's good, isn't it?'

'Yes.'

'I'm supposed to, you know. I'm supposed to say more things.'

'OK.'

'They keep saying that. You know. It's good to talk. Good to say more. But they don't really tell you what to say, you see.'

'Who's "they"?'

Nathan's father waved a hand vaguely. 'You know. All those people.'

Nathan's phone rang.

'Go on,' said his father, looking a little disappointed. 'I'm all right.'

Nathan walked outside as he answered.

'Hello?' he said.

'Buddy,' said a familiar voice. 'It's Daniel.'

'Oh,' he faltered. 'I mean hi.'

'How are you?'

'OK, I think. How, um, how are you?'

'Yeah, OK.'

'I heard about . . . you know.'

'What, me and Katherine? Yeah.'

'Sorry to hear it.'

'Yeah, well. For the best really.'

'Really?'

Daniel seemed to think about this.

'Probably,' he said.

'Right.'

'Anyway,' said Daniel, up-shifting rapidly. 'Never mind all that. How are you? Where have you been?'

Nathan sat down on a wall and breathed.

'I'm OK,' he said. 'I was away for a while.'

'We gathered that,' said Daniel. 'Away where?'

Certain phrases linger in the head so long that we feel as if we've said them already.

'I was a little unwell,' said Nathan. 'I had to have some treatment.'

There was a pause. 'What sort of treatment?'

173

Another pause. Nathan told himself to say it. 'Psychiatric treatment.'

'Oh.'

'I wasn't well. I'm better now.'

'What, uh, I mean, what did you . . .'

'I didn't try to kill myself.'

'Right. Well, I mean, that's something, isn't it?'

'I tried to hurt myself.'

'Ah.'

'The difference is important.'

'Well, yes, absolutely. I mean, obviously, that's a big difference, isn't it? Because you didn't want to, um, you know . . .'

'Die.'

'No.'

'No, I didn't want to die.'

'Good. I mean, that's good, isn't it?'

'I don't know.'

'I see.'

Nathan tucked his phone under his ear and rolled a cigarette without looking too hard at his hands. The cold had numbed the tips of his fingers. He fumbled; recovered; got it rolled.

He said, 'I wanted to change, to be different.'

'I don't know what that means,' said Daniel.

'Neither do I.'

'Oh.'

Nathan lit his cigarette. When he breathed he could feel the cold air pour down his throat like mercury and when he sniffed he felt the hairs in his nose stiffen with frost. In the raw chill, the skin of the world felt transparent and exposed.

Daniel said, 'So what are you up to now?'

'Just sitting outside the pub,' said Nathan. 'Smoking.'

'But generally, I mean.'

'Oh,' Nathan exhaled. 'Little.'

'No plans?'

'I'm sort of waiting for some to emerge.'

'Right.'

'How about you?'

'Oh, you know.' Daniel paused. 'Actually you probably don't really know, do you?'

'Well . . .'

'Ah, Nathan,' said Daniel. 'You old renegade. I guess it's just parties and revolution for now, isn't it?'

'No,' said Nathan. 'That's all over.'

'Right.'

Nathan exhaled; blew into his hands. He did not feel unsettled by the conversation.

'To be honest,' said Nathan, 'I may be in danger of going completely out of my mind.'

'Shit,' said Daniel.

'Although not literally.'

'I see.'

'I'm staying with my parents.'

'Oh. Point taken.'

'When was the last time you lived with your parents?'

'With both parents? About twenty years ago.' He paused. 'And as far as Dad goes, well . . .'

Daniel said it in an easy way that spoke of pain to which he was at least semi-reconciled.

'Sorry,' said Nathan. 'I forgot. How is he?'

'Comes and goes,' said Daniel. 'I don't see him as much as I should, then I feel guilty, then I go and see him and I just sit there wanting to leave.'

There was a pause in which Nathan noticed that the moon was making a daylight appearance.

'Anyway,' said Daniel. 'How did we get onto this?'

'My fault.'

'Whatever. Have you seen anyone? Have you got out much?'

'I'm in a pub with my dad having my first drink in six months.'

'Christ.'

'It's nice.'

'Oh.'

'Surprisingly.'

'Do you need to go?'

Nathan had finished his cigarette.

'Probably.'

'Well, it's . . . It's really good to hear from you, Nathan.'

'Yeah,' said Nathan.

'Look, why don't you come and visit at the weekend? My girl-friend's away, there's plenty of room. We can drink ourselves stupid. It'll sort you right out.'

'I don't know,' said Nathan.

'Think about it.'

'OK.'

'You've got my number now.'

'Yeah.'

They signed off, promised to make contact again soon. Daniel again told Nathan to think about the invitation. Nathan again said he would. After Nathan hung up he thought about calling Katherine, then decided against it. He felt, without quite knowing why, a certain sense of pity for Daniel. His voice struck a certain note; the invitation seemed to carry an excessive heft. In some ways, Nathan thought, he had always felt slightly sorry for Daniel, although this was blunted somewhat by the suspicion that Daniel had always felt slightly sorry for him.

He went back inside and sat down with his father, who was reaching the end of his Mad Cow and jabbing commands into his iPhone with a forefinger so accurate that Nathan wondered if his father's hands had gone through a rapid physical evolution.

'More messages,' said Nathan.

'Oh,' said his father. 'I'm inundated.'

'Are they about me?'

His father shrugged. 'Superficially,' he said.

'I don't really like it, you know,' said Nathan.

'Who does?' said his father with a shrug.

Nathan nodded. 'She always gets her way.'

His father swilled his Mad Cow. Nathan seemed to have pity enough for everybody this evening.

'I might go away at the weekend,' he said.

'You'll have to ask your mother.'

'No,' said Nathan. 'I don't think I will.'

His father nodded.

'You probably think I don't understand,' he said. 'But I do. It's just . . .'

'I know, I know. You have to live with her.'

His father looked at him with a directness that was both unusual and unsettling.

'I don't have to live with her,' he said, 'I want to.' He gave Nathan another glare. 'It's very easy to be judgemental.'

'Or not to be,' said Nathan. 'It's very easy not to be, too.'

The pub was well carpeted; lit by an open fire. The chairs were deeply padded and seemed to exude a warmth of their own. The ceiling was low enough to afford a sense of security yet not so low as to feel oppressive. Nathan did not feel uncomfortable. His father looked a little sweaty. He pinched the zip of his yachting jacket and then clearly thought better of it, as if he didn't have the stomach for that particular battle at this particular moment.

'That's not entirely true,' he said.

'I don't want a semantic argument,' said Nathan.

His father may not have known what that meant, Nathan realised.

'You know your problem?' said his father.

'Everyone seems very keen to tell me,' said Nathan.

'Not just you. All of you. Your generation. The Me generation.'

'I thought you were the Me generation.'

'Whatever,' his father waved his hand. 'Your lot. The perpetual adolescents. You go on and on about your parents, about society, about global this and global that and you don't even understand the most basic fact of life.' He pointed at Nathan. 'You don't understand the world until you have children,' he said. 'You don't stop being a child until you have one.'

'I don't think that's true,' said Nathan, who had very little evidence either way.

'Of course you don't,' said his father, draining the dregs of his Mad Cow. 'Anyway, we should go. Your mother's on the television.'

If Nathan's mother could have been said to have lived by any sort of overarching credo or outlook, it would have been the importance of presentation over content and appearance over actuality. Returning home from another strained and no doubt unacceptably boozy dinner with her alleged friend Rita and Rita's once strikingly confident and now merely boorish husband Tony, Nathan's mother would comment that it was not the disintegration of their marriage that bothered her per se, since this could, after all, happen to the best of us, but rather what she saw as their absolute determination not to conceal it. Why, she would ask, for perhaps the fifth or sixth time, did Rita and Tony feel moved to push their problems in everyone else's faces by getting soused and saying things like, *Well of course that's something Tony's never understood* or *For God's sake, Rita, no one's interested in anything you're saying?* It was, Nathan's mother would say, not on.

Over time, her attitude to Nathan's so-called condition had shifted along very similar lines, and the only way she'd been able to deal with it was to give herself the sense that, even if she was unable to manage it medically, she was at least able to seize control of its public presentation and reshape her mortification into martyrdom. Because, as she'd said so many times, what separated the wheat from the chaff in life wasn't what life threw at you, since life threw all sorts of things at all sorts of people, but the way you carried yourself through it, or, to put it another way: having an afflicted son was no excuse to start letting yourself go.

So it came as little surprise to Nathan to see, as the studio lights went up to reveal the luridly perma-tanned Dr Dave and Nathan's immaculately trouser-suited mother seated side by side on a salmon-pink couch that clashed violently with Dr Dave's skin tone, that his mother had now perfectly completed the transition from frustrated parent to crusading author, and, far from being in any way over-whelmed by the television studio experience, was smiling with the kind of radiance that comes only from the perfect balance of supreme self-confidence and an utter dearth of self-awareness, an expression both absorbed and returned tenfold by Dr Dave, who had, as anyone who watched his show regularly knew, completed a particularly spec-tacular transition of his own by moving, through the medium of emotional televised confession, from disgraced con man to national treasure.

Even before securing his own weekly television programme, Dr Dave was something of a big noise on the Development scene. He'd written two books (*Smile Yourself Thin*, and his breakthrough,

C.H.A.N.G.E: Calling a Halt to All Negative and Gloomy Experiences)
and was a regular fixture on the popular daytime TV show *Sit Down
With Sally*, hosted by the perennially agog Sally Duvall, where he
dispensed well-rehearsed off-the-cuff advice to a 'variety' of callers
whose diversity, in Nathan's opinion, was severely limited by the
daytime TV demographic: housewives, the unemployed, the temporarily sick, the permanently sick, and those in long-term residential
care.

It was on this show that Dr Dave not only developed his theory of
C.H.A.N.G.E. but also demonstrated the notorious level of tactical
disclosure that had turned a C-list TV shrink into an A-list celebrity
in his own right. Dr Dave, it transpired in the gutter press, had not
always gone by the name of Dr Dave. He had, for several years in his
twenties, gone by the name of The Penetrator, and had been a specialist in certain speed-seduction techniques designed to con perfect
strangers into sleeping with him within approximately three minutes.
He'd perfected a slouchy walk, a controlled loucheness of posture.
He'd breezed up to women of all ages, at parties, in bookshops, in the
supermarket, and entered into conversations coldly designed to elicit
the maximum spreadage of leg within the minimum possible elapse-
ment of minutes using complicated matrices of waking hypnosis and
linguistic suggestion. He talked about his 'new direction' so that the
programmable subject heard, unconsciously, 'nude erection'. He
turned to talk of the stars just so he could say 'constellation', on the
basis that what his target probably but unknowingly heard was 'cunt's
dilation'. He was, it transpired, so good at this that he had conned
literally hundreds of 'open' young women, many of whom later
bravely sold their stories for undisclosed sums to drooling dailies, into
bed, and had formed a relationship with not a single one of them.
Somewhere around thirty, however, he had experienced his Moment
of Insight and come to the conclusion that his powers, impressive as

they were, should be used for good as opposed to evil. He had reverted to his given name, enrolled on a distance-learning doctorate in behavioural psychology and, as he was at great pains to point out, taken a vow of chastity that forswore not only sex but all contact with women which might in any way be taken as flirtatious, including warm smiles, charming comments and any even remotely sexual or intimate conversations, unless of course it was within a recognised therapeutic context, in which case all bets were off. As Dr Dave himself put it on a brilliantly conceived crisis-limitation *Sit Down With Sally* special dedicated entirely to his own Personal Struggle that pulled in even more viewers than Sally Duvall's harrowing and award-winning live interview with convicted celebrity rapist Timothy 'The Terror of Television Centre' Turner, former children's TV presenter-turned-social-pariah-slash-cash-machine, the powers of The Penetrator were so . . . (here he struggled for words) . . . *powerful*, that they could not simply be 'switched off' but instead had to be placed in a kind of sexual vacuum so that no more harm could befall any impressionable young ladies, a subject he went on to write about in a much-praised and oft-cited article in *Personal Growth Monthly* entitled 'The Dick in the Jar: Putting Away the Penis for the Sake of Others'. It was, even Nathan had to admit, a publicity masterstroke, and the very next day the same opinion columns that had mocked and denigrated his manipulative tendencies, his shonky credentials, his, dare they say it, hypocrisy, were falling over themselves to praise his honesty, his courage, his sincerity. Within six months, although he continued his *Sit Down With Sally* appearances, he was given his own programme, which ran to a rigid and extremely successful formula of two parts telephone counselling to one part inspirational interview, which latter slot was today occupied by Nathan's mother.

Like Nathan's mother and her new-found penchant for snappy clothes, Dr Dave's mutation carried with it a fashion element. Before his exposure (which he only ever referred to as a confession), he'd favoured pink, slightly formal shirts; brightly coloured ties; chinos. The aim was to give off an air of professionalism. If he dressed like a doctor, went the philosophy, he'd be able to talk like one too. At times, he was even seen with a stethoscope round his neck. Following his decision to share intimate details of his life with his fans, however (which was never referred to as him being forced by the press to fess up to the public), he began to favour jeans and slip-on shoes, T-shirts and, worst of all, extremely low-cut V-neck sweaters worn with nothing underneath, revealing a glowing isosceles of shaved, shined, tanned flesh that Nathan found very difficult to look at but by which Nathan's mother, who was now only a metre or so away from it, seemed happily transfixed.

'Hi,' said Dr Dave to camera, giving a nonchalant wave and an intimate smile. 'Welcome back. Now I for one am very excited about my next guest, because she absolutely exemplifies something I've been giving a lot of time to here on my show over the past few weeks, and something I'm going to go on talking about off and on for the next few months. Why? Because I feel in these difficult times it's a theme we can all relate to, and something which I hope, in its own small way, might be of some help to the country. Because these are dark times.' He nodded, as if he'd been unaware what he'd been about to say but, now that he'd said it, found himself happily in agreement. 'Very dark times.' He nodded again. Still in agreement. 'And during times of difficulty or opposition or tragedy or . . .' he shrugged the shrug of a man whose conclusions have reached such a level of profundity as to render mere words largely moot, '. . . *badness*, we can do one of three things.' He held up his hand, counting them off, clearly coached to begin with the little finger so as to avoid any inadvertent embarrassing gestures that would then appear as screenshots across the web. 'We can give in . . .' Little finger. 'We can battle on and survive . . .' Ring finger. 'Or . . .' Middle finger. '. . . we can do better. We can take that negativity, that tragedy, that badness, and we can grow from it, we can prosper, we can blossom. Yes, it's survival, but it's also something more, something I like to call . . .' he pointed down the barrel of the camera with both index fingers for emphasis, '. . . sur*thrival*.' He nodded; brought his hands together; then gestured towards Nathan's mother. 'And let me tell you people, this woman who I have with me here today is surthrival personified. But hey, don't take it from me, because she's here to tell you all about it herself. Author of the forthcoming book *Mother Courage: One Woman's Battle Against Maternal Blame*, founder of the internet support group Mothers Who Survive, ladies and gentlemen, Helen Coverley.'

The camera cut to Nathan's mother's face in close-up. On cue, she beamed.

'Thank you, Dr Dave,' she said. 'I'm so happy to be here.'

'So happy to have you,' said Dr Dave.

'My pleasure,' said Nathan's mother.

'Keep smiling, that's the way,' said Nathan's father, precariously perched on the very edge of the sofa and slightly obsessively rubbing his thumbs and index fingers together.

Dr Dave's ability to transition between facial expressions was, Nathan noted, remarkably fluid. He was like a human lava lamp. The smile peaked, blossomed, dissipated, and a glowing bubble of sympathy rose up from beneath to replace it.

'So, Helen,' he said, nodding again. 'For those at home who don't know, just share your journey with us briefly.'

'Well, I have to gently correct you there, Dr Dave, and say that I don't actually think of it as my journey at all, but *our* journey, the journey of mothers everywhere.'

Dr Dave nodded.

'That's my girl,' said Nathan's father.

'And really,' said Nathan's mother, folding her legs and resting her hands in her lap, 'it's also our journey in that it's a journey I've shared with my son, Harry, as I call him in the book.'

Nathan had found a stray thread in the hem of the armchair cover and was now gently teasing it out.

'Tell us about Harry,' said Dr Dave.

'Well, I love Harry. I want to say that very clearly. I love him dearly. He's my darling boy. My only child. But the truth is, and I think a lot of mothers out there can relate to this, he has hurt me deeply. And it's taken me years to be able to say that. I mean literally years. Years of asking myself: is this my fault? Years of being *told* it's my fault. You know, at one stage, we had employed four separate counsellors to talk to my son, all at great expense, and all they ever did was listen to my son's side of events. Would you credit it? It was almost as if . . . as if they weren't interested in me at all. And that's the balance I want to redress with my book, because I know for a fact there are hundreds of mothers out there going through the same thing, and feeling all the same feelings of shame and guilt as I felt.'

'Your son had addiction issues,' said Dr Dave, whose nodding by this point seemed to have reached the level of physiological necessity.

'Oh, you name it,' said Nathan's mother. 'Drugs, tattoos. At one point he was living in a squat, selling drugs, organising these . . . *raves* I suppose you would call them. I mean it was. Just. Absolutely. Hor. *Ren*dous.'

The stray thread turned out to be quite long and Nathan now faced a choice between continuing to draw it out and simply snapping it off.

'You know,' said Dr Dave, 'when I work with parents of what I call morally challenged children in my clinic, the thing that comes up for them time and again is just how guilty they feel. Is that something you experienced?'

'Unquestionably,' said Nathan's mother. 'Without question. The guilt is enormous, and very difficult to overcome without being a very strong person indeed. But I think what I really want to stress is the shame. You know, at one point, when he was at his worst, I actually told people I didn't have a son, because it was so much easier than trying to explain.'

Nathan had opted to continue tugging the thread, which was now approximately a foot long.

'We call that emotional disownership,' said Dr Dave. 'A very common response to filial trauma. But then there was a breakthrough, was there not?'

Here Nathan's mother's face clouded expertly with the cumulo-nimbi of grief. She took a long breath.

'There was,' she said valiantly.

'And is that,' said Dr Dave, leaning forward, placing a hand on her knee. 'Is that something you feel able to share?'

Nathan's mother nodded.

'What a surthrivor,' said Dr Dave, awed.

'Thank you,' said Nathan's mother. 'It's . . . it's not something I've really talked about much, although . . . although it is in the book, but . . . Well, after *years*, I mean literally years of all this stuff going on, my son, my boy . . .'

'We hear you,' said Dr Dave.

'I can't even describe what he did to himself,' said Nathan's mother. 'But it was harm. Very serious harm. And when we saw him next he was in the hospital. Covered in bandages. His hands. His arms. His chest. And at first he was on a lot of medication, obviously. But slowly he came round. And me and my husband were there, and . . .'

Nathan remembered his father ambling around the private room they'd somehow secured at the hospital, asking him if he wanted his dinner and then helping him finish it off lest it go to waste.

He gave the thread a sharp yank but only succeeded in exposing more of its length.

'Stop pulling the furniture to bits,' said his father, who had begun jiggling his knees and rubbing his hands.

'Sorry,' said Nathan.

'And I looked at his face,' Nathan's mother was saying.

'That's it, girl,' said Nathan's father. He looked at Nathan shiftily. 'Sorry.'

'And I knew he finally understood. That it had taken this awful moment to . . . to . . .'

'I don't want to watch this anymore,' said Nathan.

His father looked at him.

'OK,' he said. 'But, um . . . There'll be questions afterwards, if you know what I mean, so . . .'

Nathan nodded. 'You go ahead,' he said, standing up.

Upstairs he texted Daniel to say he would be coming. After only a couple of minutes he heard his father emit a long-drawn-out moan. He went back downstairs and found him staring at footage of a transfixed lamb.

'This just in,' said the voice-over. 'The disease previously known as Bovine Idiopathic Entrancement has jumped the species barrier. What you see here is the first recorded case of Ovine Entrancement. Scientists have announced that . . .'

'Jesus,' said Nathan. 'This is . . .'

'You're telling me,' said Nathan's father. 'They cut your mother's money shot for this.'

In Angelica's absence, and in the dead time before the weekend, Daniel fell into the sort of patterns he dimly recalled from his long-ago days of being single. He'd been a student then, of course, and he had to admit that in the intervening years many of the habits he'd once looked back on through a certain rose-coloured haze had, if he was honest, paled. There were, for example, only so many frozen pizzas a man could eat before a definite sense of bodily decay set in; and much as stocking the fridge with beer, chocolate bars and assorted snacks had seemed deliciously sinful when daydreamed about over a fruit smoothie and a bowl of Fairtrade granola, there came a point when the sight of all that badness was no longer exciting and was just, well, bad. Freedom, it seemed, was overrated, particularly if you had no idea what to do with it.

He tried to recall the last time he'd been alone. There'd been the odd evening here and there, perhaps a weekend, but decent stretches of solitude had been rare. Katherine used to threaten to go away a lot but then rarely did, and Angelica rarely even threatened it, leading to those slightly odd conversations when Daniel tried to persuade her to go away while strenuously attempting not to appear to be persuading her to go away.

'I really think you'll enjoy it,' he'd say of some rally or convention or godforsaken gathering of the dreadlocked clans. 'You should go. I mean really. Go.'

'Oh,' she'd say vaguely. 'I might, but you know, we have so little time together as it is.'

'I know, darling, but I'm happy to share you with the world.'

'Oh Daniel.'

'Oh Angelica.'

She wouldn't go, of course, or worse, he'd end up going with her. Either way, he'd spend at least part of the time pining for exactly the sort of alone-time he knew he always squandered when he had it.

The evenings dragged. He called Angelica. She texted a lot but on the phone was distracted and vague. She always said, *Hang on, let me go somewhere quiet*, then went somewhere categorically unquiet. She said it was going well. She said Sebastian was amazing. She felt they were Making a Difference. Daniel started picturing her and Sebastian together. It gave him a little twist in his gut. He imagined Sebastian letting his hair down, giving it a quick toss; slipping out of his knits and mumbling something wanky about worship. For some reason Daniel had a problem admitting he didn't like people. He liked to think he was above it, or that, like anger, it was a response that was unjustly denied to him in his role as a martyr to the rational. But he didn't like Sebastian and Sebastian didn't like him, so perhaps it was time to start accepting things.

He called his father, asked him how's tricks.

'I'm inundated,' said his father. 'Totally inundated.'

Sometimes Daniel tried to be rational, sometimes he didn't. Less and less, if he was honest.

'It's such a busy time, isn't it?'

'Oh God, don't even,' said his father.

'Are you managing to get a break at all?'

'You're kidding, aren't you? They're working me into the ground. Geoff's away; Paul's no good to anyone anymore. I'm carrying the whole team.'

'They'd be lost without you.'

'Don't I know it.'

He thought about going to see the old man, but quickly realised he couldn't face it. It struck him that his procrastination around going to see his father suggested he hadn't actually developed nearly as much as he'd like to think, or at least not in the ways that now seemed important. He was too young for all this ageing, all this *stuff*.

The larger the weekend loomed, the greater Daniel's fears became. He woke twice in the night, tatters of a nameless shame still clinging to his skin. He remembered saying something stupid about how if Nathan needed help he would ask for it; remembered how easy it had been to let Nathan and whatever was going on with him simply vanish. He paced his house and felt embarrassed. He had never, he realised, entertained anyone. Angelica entertained people; Katherine either entertained them or horrified them; and Nathan had a way, if not of entertaining people directly, then at least of leading them towards people and places that would do the job, and procuring the necessary chemicals along the way. Indeed, Daniel and Katherine had always used Nathan for exactly that purpose: for escape; for *fun*; and now, in a development made no less disturbing by its predictability, the tables were horribly turned and Daniel, who had not, if he was honest, really made or maintained any friends at all since moving here, found himself thrust into the role of host and entertainer.

By the time Thursday came around, Daniel knew what he needed to do. He needed, quite urgently, to buy some drugs.

He mulled it over at work, wondering initially about Ecstasy, but then coming to the conclusion that sitting in a room getting off his face on E might not be Nathan's idea of a good time. Indeed, E hadn't been Nathan's idea of a good time for a long time, now that Daniel thought about it. Towards the end (a phrase Daniel realised he needed to stop using, given that it clearly wasn't the end), Nathan had graduated from the largely unalloyed pleasures of Ecstasy and acid, through the more utilitarian amphetamines, to the total vortex of entertainment offered by ketamine and a cocktail of downers, suggesting that a good time, whatever that might have been, was not only no longer Nathan's goal but may actually have been something against which he sought to quarantine himself. Daniel had never understood the impulse. He was down enough day to day; why part with money for the experience? In a way, this both compounded and reflected the widening differences between them: Daniel struggling upwards; Nathan kicking out for the depths.

The obvious option was to get some weed. This was, he thought, the simplest solution to everything. Old friends, getting gently stoned, listening to some classic albums. How could that possibly fail?

The difficulty, of course, was that although Daniel thought of being stoned as a social experience, what he had never really appreciated at the time was that it was a product of social experience too, since, much as getting stoned loosened you up and allowed you to meet people, you still needed to know at least *some* people in order to get hold of the stuff in the first place.

His contacts list was woeful. Everyone in his BlackBerry was either a colleague, one of Angelica's friends, or some professional or other working with his father. He felt a mild sense of panic. The idea had relieved so much of his tension with such rapidity that any consideration of abandoning the plan now seemed impossible. It was vital, he thought, that he get his hands on some weed for the weekend. If he didn't, no one would have a good time, and they would blame him, and the whole thing would be such an unmitigated disaster that he felt slightly breathless just thinking about it.

He put his feet up on his desk and considered his options. He could, he thought, ask around the office. He was fairly sure, for example, that both Jenssen and Meyer would have their sources. Indeed, given their background in organic crop research and the eco-warrior counterculture, they had probably reared their own strain. But still, there was something decidedly unprofessional about asking them, or really anyone with whom he worked.

Another option was to spend the evening in the rougher areas of town and hope for the best. Drive out to some estate somewhere and cruise up to one of those little knots of lads you saw swigging cider at isolated bus stops. *All right, chaps*, he'd say. No, not *chaps*. *Chaps* sounded awful, like something out of *Biggles. Lads,* maybe? *Geezers? All right geezers?* That wasn't bad. He'd breeze up with his hands in his pockets and sort of sniff and look about him, then ask if anyone knew where he might be able to, what was the phrase, score? He was stuck in another decade entirely. How could you get so out of date in so few years?

This was ridiculous. He wasn't going to drive to a rough area. He didn't even know any rough areas. And if he did know one, and did drive to it, he was going to drive right through it and not look back.

He swivelled in his chair. Outside, in the car park, the much-reduced demonstration now consisted entirely, in Sebastian's absence, of three shifty-looking lads in Doc Martens, none of whom Daniel recognised, easing their weight from foot to foot and holding each end of a large banner in rotation so one of them could have a break to blow on his hands. It was a fairly foolish option, Daniel thought, but it was better than no option at all.

Gentlemen,' said Daniel, striding out carrying three cups of fresh coffee. 'You looked cold so I thought I'd furnish you with some refreshments.'

'Furnish us?' said the one not holding the banner, who had a threadbare ginger beard and what appeared to be a piece of copper piping through his earlobe. 'What do you think we are? A room?'

The banner-bearers laughed, but were also eyeing the coffee.

'I don't see why we can't all be friends,' said Daniel. Why, he wondered, *why* did he say such unbelievably stupid things?

'Is that filter coffee?' said one. 'Cos I won't drink instant.'

'And I won't drink anything Nestlé,' said the third, 'or anything that isn't Fairtrade.'

'I'm lactose intolerant actually,' said the first one, distractedly pushing his little finger through his copper piping.

'These are black Fairtrade cafetière coffees,' said Daniel, 'from my very own cafetière.'

'Where do we stand on this, Archie?' said the second banner-bearer, whose end of the banner had dropped somewhat during the exchange.

'We've got our own coffee, thanks,' said Archie, who was clearly the de facto leader.

'No we don't,' said the first banner-bearer, who had now lowered his end of the banner even further than his compatriot.

'Shut up, William,' said Archie. 'We have the means of *production* of coffee, that's what counts.'

'Do we?' said William.

'Well we have the means of procurement,' said Archie.

'Hold on,' said the third member of the group, wedging his pole down the front of his trousers so as to leave his hands free to gesticulate. 'This bloke's offering free coffee.'

'But we don't need his free coffee,' said Archie.

'But where are we going to purchase coffee,' said William. 'Cos, like, the nearest option is a Costa, and they're kind of multinational.'

Archie acknowledged this point with a cock of the head. 'But he's more multinational,' he said, pointing at Daniel.

'I'm not multinational,' said Daniel.

'He's not *profiting* from the coffee,' said the third member, adjusting his banner-pole as if to prevent chafing.

'But we're unclear as to *source*, Henry,' said Archie.

'He just told us the bloody source,' said William.

'That's unconfirmed,' said Archie.

'Look,' said Henry. 'I'm fucking freezing and I don't want to pay three bloody quid in Costa when I can just as easily have a free coffee right now.'

'Plus,' said William, tucking his banner-pole under his arm, 'I find when I'm in Costa it's not just a coffee, is it?'

'It's never just a coffee,' said Henry bitterly. 'You always think it's just a coffee but then actually it's a coffee, an avocado wrap, a detox drink and a date bar.'

'Yeah,' said William. 'And before you know it you're ten quid deep.'

'Those motherfuckers,' said Daniel. 'This coffee's getting cold, by the way.'

'Fuck it,' said Henry, 'I'm having a coffee.'

'Me too,' said William.

'I think we've established that to do so is ethical,' said Archie.

They stood sipping their coffees, the banner momentarily abandoned on the floor.

'So,' said Daniel. 'Missing Sebastian much?'

They looked at him oddly.

'We're not in love with him,' said Archie.

'Yeah,' said Henry. 'We can spend time apart.'

'I meant more in terms of the organisation,' said Daniel.

'We have no fixed centre of power,' said Archie, 'so we're able to adapt to the needs of any given situation.'

'Re-forming like Voltron,' said William, nodding seriously.

'Impressive,' said Daniel. 'How's the coffee?'

'That's good coffee,' said William.

'Good body,' said Archie. 'Do you grind fresh?'

'I buy it freshly ground,' said Daniel.

'Does make a difference,' said Henry.

'I must get a grinder,' said William. 'I mean, don't get me wrong, I make good coffee, but I think grinding's the next step.'

Archie nodded. 'It's another bloody appliance though, isn't it?'

'Don't get me started,' said Henry. 'You should see our fucking worktop. Half the time I can't even carve out the space for a sandwich. I keep saying to Trix: Trix, can we get rid of some of these bloody machines? But she's like, nah.'

There was a reflective silence during which Daniel became increasingly edgy as he weighed the various options for introducing the subject of drugs into the conversation.

'So,' he said finally. 'Has Sebastian got you working the weekend, too?'

'Nah,' said William. 'No point. No one here.'

'If a tree falls in the forest and all that,' said Archie.

'Got much planned?' said Daniel.

'Probably just keep it chilled,' said Henry. 'What about you?'

'Your other half's away, isn't she?' said Archie with a smirk that Daniel chose to ignore.

'Yeah,' said Daniel. 'I was thinking it would be a good opportunity to get the boys round, you know?'

'Oh yeah,' said Archie. 'Good call.'

'Actually,' said Daniel, 'there was something I was going to ask you chaps about.'

'Oh yeah?' said Archie, narrowing his eyes.

'Yeah,' said Daniel, looking from side to side in the universally acknowledged manner of a man about to negotiate a drugs deal. 'It's just, well, my man's fallen through, you know what I'm saying?'

'Not really,' said William.

'Your man?' said Henry. 'What man?'

'You know,' said Daniel. 'As in, *waiting for the man*?'

Blank looks.

'My dealer,' said Daniel.

'Oh,' said Archie with a smirk. 'And you think for some reason, based I'm sure on a whole number of conclusions you've drawn based on your prejudices about our appearance and political persuasions, that we might be able to help.'

'Well, basically,' said Daniel. 'Yes.'

'What are you looking for?' said Henry.

'Henry,' said Archie.

'What?' said Henry.

'What have you got?' said Daniel, before realising that, much as it was wise to conceal his intentions from wider view, concealing them from the person he was trying to communicate them to was going to be somewhat counterproductive.

'No one's got anything,' said Archie.

'But they *might have*,' said Henry, tapping the side of his nose.

'Or they might not,' said Archie.

'Right,' said Henry. 'Absolutely. But equally *they might have*.'

Refreshed by his success, and now reframing the weekend in his mind as a sort of blokey reminiscence session, he called Katherine as soon as he got home.

'Hi,' he said.

'Hi,' said Katherine. She sounded edgy, he thought, as if she were awaiting some sort of verdict. He wondered if he had, again, mis-judged his opening syllable. He told her it was just a quick call, then immediately regretted it.

'Great,' she said. 'I always love it when people open with that.'

'What?' said Daniel, knowing exactly what.

'Just a quick call. Like, don't get comfortable in this conversation because it's not going to last long.'

'I think it's more like, don't worry, this isn't going to take up too much of your time.'

'Why don't you let me be the judge of how much of my time I want to invest in this conversation, and when I've run out of time I'll let you know. How about that?'

Daniel examined his fingernails, then flipped his hand over to look at his palm. Periodically he wondered if one of the lines was his Katherine line.

'Like I said, this doesn't really need to be a whole big thing.'

'OK, right, I give up. You obviously want to converse entirely in bullet points and have me take it down in shorthand or something. Go ahead.'

He could hear her lighting a cigarette: the spark of the lighter followed by the damp lip-smack of her inhalation.

'I was just calling to say I spoke to Nathan.'

'Bravo,' she drawled.

'If you're going to be sarcastic about everything then I may have to just send you an email.'

'Sorry. Go on.'

'Right. So I phoned Nathan and, well, he's not that well.'

'Duh.'

'Right. As I said before . . .'

'Sorry. Couldn't help myself. Please continue.'

Daniel had put some thought into how he was going to phrase this, but in the event all of that thought seemed to dissipate into an insubstantial notion of saying it and backing away.

'I mean, he's sort of better now, is the gist, but at one point he was really very seriously unwell and he, ah, I'm not sure really, if he tried to kill himself, or if he cut himself or something, but anyway, he hurt himself in some way, and he's been away ever since getting some sort of treatment.'

'What sort of treatment?'

'The psychiatric sort.'

There was a long pause.

'Fuck,' said Katherine.

'Yeah.'

'Do we know why he . . . you know?'

'I didn't ask.'

'You didn't ask?'

'No.'

'Well, isn't it sort of an obvious question?'

'That's why I didn't ask it,' said Daniel, sensing a tangent and getting tired in advance. 'I thought it was sort of insensitive or stupid or something. I thought maybe I should just be like, oh yeah, you know, that happens, rather than being ghoulish about it.'

'So basically you just bottled out and avoided the whole issue and talked about the weather or something?'

'No. I invited him to come and visit.'

'Oh,' she sounded slightly deflated.

'You see? And at first he was a bit reluctant.'

'Mmmm*hmmmm*.'

'But then he texted and said OK, he's coming. And I said OK, great.'

'So when's he coming?'

A note of unease had crept in. Daniel wasn't sure if he should try and keep things chipper or take a more business-like, PR approach. He was, after all, supposed to be good at this.

'This weekend.'

'This weekend? God, that's not much notice, is it?'

'Well, I've got a free house.'

'Oh. What's her name's away is she?'

'Angelica. Yes.'

'Everything OK?'

'*Yeeeesss*, thank you. She's, um, she's away on a demonstration.'

This time her pause was for effect. He could imagine her at the other end, drawing her head back, turning away slightly to regard him out of the side of her eye, a smirk of pleasure already beginning to bloom.

'A demonstration? About what?'

'Look, this is kind of a tangent, you know.'

'No, no. I'm interested. What's she demonstrating about?'

'It's a protest against the cattle cull.'

'*Reaaaalllllllyyy*?'

'Are you about to get all judgemental?'

'Not at all. I think that's very admirable. I've always said, not enough people care about the environment and the animals and all that. You know, one earth, one chance, the web of nature and all that. Peace.'

'Shall we move on?'

'I can't believe you're so touchy about this. Aren't you proud of her?'

'Of course I'm proud of her,' he said flatly. 'Anyway, I think we're done here.'

'I think it's lovely that you're embracing your hippy side more. It's always been there. It's like you're coming out.'

'OK, so, take care . . .'

He managed to get the phone from his ear and halfway towards the table before her voice won out.

'Whoa there. What about arrangements?'

'What arrangements?'

'For the *weekend*? I don't even know where you live.'

'Oh. I see.'

'You *see*.'

'Ah . . .'

'I am invited, of course?'

'Well, it's not that you're *not* invited . . .'

'OK. Fuck you too.'

'Hey, hold *on*.'

'No, no, it's fine, whatever. Never mind that he actually called *me* and then *I* called *you*. Never mind that he's *my* friend too, probably actually really more my friend than yours, if we get right down to it. No, you just go right ahead and do whatever the fuck you want to do and fuck everyone else. That's *fine*.'

'Can I speak?'

'Oh don't do the whole thing of asking if you can speak like I'm talking so much you can't get a word in edgeways. Of course you can fucking *speak*. I'd actually be very interested to hear what you have to say.'

'Right.'

Neither of them said anything for several seconds. Daniel wondered if Katherine could hear his brain whirring as the cogs of all his thoughts and motivations and horrid conflicts heaved against each other.

'Well say something then,' she said.

'I'm *about* to say something if you'll give me a chance. *Christ*.'

He heard her chuckle grimly at the other end of the phone, happy at having lured him into anger. He kept forgetting what he'd only just decided to say.

'We haven't seen each other in a year,' he said slowly.

'That's not my fault.'

'I'm not saying it's your fault. I'm not saying it's anyone's fault. But it is a fact.'

'This is going to take forever, isn't it?'

'No. What was I saying?'

'We haven't seen each other for a year.'

'Right. We haven't seen each other for a year, or even actually had any contact. We haven't spoken on the phone . . .'

'I know all this,' she said. 'Although I would point out that you still sent a Christmas card to my mother, which I would ask you not to do again.'

'OK, point taken.' Daniel did a hurrying motion with his free hand despite the fact that Katherine couldn't see him. 'Anyway, we haven't had any contact with each other, and now we are having contact and let's be honest neither of us is enjoying it.'

'I didn't say I wasn't enjoying it.'

'Well you're acting like you're not enjoying it.'

'Me? What about you with all your practicalities? If it's a heart-to-heart you want, try turning your office voice off and being discernibly human for a discernible period of time.'

Katherine was warming up, he thought, finding her rhythm and range. He was warming up too, although in a less metaphorical sense. He ran his palm across his forehead and then wiped it on his leg.

'That's because you're not listening,' he said.

'How can you say I'm not listening when I've responded to absolutely everything you've said? I'm fully alert. I'm catching every word. My ears are open.'

'We haven't been in touch,' he began again, mustering his slowest, calmest tones, which he knew pissed her off but which he always ended up doing anyway. 'Now we are in touch and we're not getting along.'

'Why do you say we're not getting along?'

'Is that a serious question?'

'Yeah. I mean OK, there's a touch of friction . . .'

'A *touch* of friction?'

'Yeah. But that doesn't mean . . .'

'OK, whatever. That's not the point. The point is . . .'

'What's the point?'

'I am TELLING you the point.'

'OK. Don't let me stop you.'

'The point is, do we really want to lay all this on Nathan? That's the point.'

Her silence was pointed. It was her I-can't-believe-the-stupidity-of-what-you-just-said silence.

'OK . . .' she said.

'You see what I'm saying?'

'No.'

'He doesn't need this. He hasn't been well.'

'So he's made of glass now?'

'OK, put it another way: *no one* needs this. I don't need this. You don't need this.'

'Maybe don't start telling me what I do and don't need, yeah?'

'This isn't helping anyone. This isn't making anyone happy.'

'Oh yeah, I forgot, we all have to be happy all the time.'

'Look, the point is . . .'

'Stop *saying* that. Stop telling me what the sodding point is all the time as if I'm too stupid to see what the point is or as if the only point that matters is *your* point. *I'll* tell you what the point is. The point is

Nathan rang *me*, and in trying to be an *adult* I rang *you*, and now you've taken it upon yourself to go all unilateral on the situation, which is what you *always* do because you're obsessed with this idea that there's only ever one way to deal with anything. You've sidelined me without even having a discussion about it because you don't want a discussion because you're a pussy and you know you'd *lose* any discussion we had not only because you're wrong and you know it but also because you're so determined *not* to have an argument or rock the boat or anything that you just end up totally backing down all the time, and you know that, so you just try and do things without discussing them with anyone.'

'How can you *lose* a discussion? Only you, Katherine, would regard a discussion as something that has to be won or lost.'

'Please don't get all Confucius-he-say with me, Daniel, because it's unbelievably pointless and annoying. Of course a discussion can be lost. You of all people should know that because you lose them all the time.'

'Whatever. And I haven't sidelined you. Nathan can still come and see you after he's seen me.'

'How about you just tell me when and where I can come and see you.'

'Jesus Christ.'

'I can find out anyway.'

'Are you threatening me?'

'Are you scared?'

'No, I'm not scared,' said Daniel, who was scared. 'Why should I be scared?'

'Well stop acting like you're scared.'

'Being scared has absolutely nothing to do with it. I just think that Nathan really doesn't need the discomfort of being there when we see each other for the first time in God knows how long, that's all.'

'Ah. Right. Well. The solution's pretty obvious then, isn't it?'

'Is it?'

'Let's meet up before. Then it won't be the first time, will it?'

Daniel considered this, or rather he attempted to consider a response to it that would ensure it didn't happen while also ensuring he didn't come across as a callous shit. He wondered why he was so worried about how he came across all the time, particularly to someone he was fairly sure he didn't like.

'I don't think that's a good idea,' he said.

'You don't.'

'I don't.'

'You don't think it's a good idea.'

Every time she made him say it again his doubt levels crept up another few degrees.

'I really don't think it's a good idea,' he said.

'Why?'

She was, of course, bound to ask that, but the second she asked it it became the one thing he felt incapable of answering. He wondered what the best answer would be, and it struck him that if he could switch off his automatic attempts to find the right answer and just go with whatever his answer actually was then this whole process would be a lot easier.

'I, ah, I think it's too soon,' he said decisively.

'Well, when would be the right time? Tell me, Daniel, what is an *appropriate* amount of time?'

'Well . . .'

'Don't rush your answer.'

'I don't think it can be measured,' he said, pressing on. 'It's more just a feeling. It doesn't feel like a good time.'

She sniffed, lit another cigarette.

'OK,' she said. 'Fine.'

'Really?'

'Of course. If you're really that immature and frightened and pathetic then there's nothing I can do about it.'

All he needed to say, he thought, was: *I am*, and then he would not have to see her.

'Because that's a really mature response,' he said.

She said nothing. She was smoking incredibly loudly.

'I'm just trying to be sensible,' he said weakly.

No answer.

'A lot of people rush into it,' he said. 'And then find it's too soon.'

It sounded like she might be picking her teeth.

'I'm not going to roll over just because you want something.'

'A cup of coffee,' she said. 'One cup of coffee. Say no.'

Daniel seemed to be experiencing some difficulty saying no.

'I mean, I *can*,' he said. 'Of course I *can*, it's just a question of whether it's wise.'

'You're absolutely right,' she said. 'Has to be wise. And hey,' she added, 'don't worry about Nathan, either. He'll totally understand.'

'Understand what?'

'He'll totally understand that we just couldn't get it together for him. You know, he'll appreciate the difficulties.'

Giggles waddled into the room, spasmed briefly, then emptied a stomachful of half-digested cat biscuits onto the floor.

'Fuck,' said Daniel, staring at the mess. 'Fucking cat.'

'You have a cat?' said Katherine quickly.

'Yeah, we have a cat. Look, what are you talking about? I'm seeing Nathan. I'm there for him. You can see him if you want. We're doing everything we can.'

'Don't you think,' she said, 'that after all he's been through, what he'd really want is to catch up with his friends like the old days without having to go through some bizarre system of visitation rights?

Don't you think he'd like to just come and see us and chat and not have to deal with all of *our* problems, which, compared to his, are pretty fucking insignificant? But don't worry. He knows you. He knows you can't set aside your stuff. You're right. Make him do all the running around. Make him feel like he's the inconvenience so you can back away from anything that seems difficult.'

Giggles looked up at Daniel with a slightly sheepish expression, then began tentatively licking the pile of vomit.

'OK,' Daniel said finally. 'You win.'

A pause.

'I win?'

'Yeah, you win.'

'What do I *win*?'

'You just win. We can meet up.'

Another pause.

'Well don't do it if you don't want to.'

'Oh for fuck's sake.'

'No, seriously. I don't want you to do anything you don't want to do. Let's just forget it.'

'No, let's not forget it. Jesus, Katherine will you stop making everything so difficult?'

'*Me?*'

He sank his face into his free hand, defeated.

'Let's have coffee,' he said lifelessly. 'It would be great to see you. Where do you want to meet?'

'Well,' said Katherine. 'Since you ask . . .'

For several minutes, perhaps even an hour after putting the phone down on Daniel, Katherine was seized by an odd sense of disappointment. Perhaps, she thought, it was the old issue of necessity, of the thing she'd wanted evolving into something that was thrust upon her. But it was more than that, too. It was, she thought, a sense of unwanted completion, even repetition, and it was only after an hour of smoking and cupping a cooling mug of coffee between her palms that she realised exactly what the issue was: she had imagined an exit where in reality there was none. Whatever door had opened through her conversation with Daniel, it led only inwards, back to places that were no longer any use. She'd spent days feeling trapped, imagining a release, but when the release arrived, it brought only a further encounter with finitude, with the limits of what she was prepared to be. She wanted, quite suddenly and sadly, to call Daniel back, to ask him things. They were not even, she thought, things in which she was particularly interested, but in the recounting of them something would be achieved. She wanted to ask him about himself; his job; his girlfriend, and she wanted to ask him not because she really wanted to know but because she wanted him to know that she had asked, to feel that she wanted to know. She'd heard amputees say that they still felt an itch where the limb had been. This was how it felt. An irritation of a familiar emptiness. She picked up her phone and tapped his picture to make the call. He didn't answer. She briefly debated a voicemail, then hung up, annoyed that now he would see the missed call on his phone and no doubt misinterpret it as either needy or annoying or both. She let herself cry a little, then sort of angered her way out of the gloom by telling herself she could have asked him those things but he hadn't let her because he was a prick. He *was* a prick. It was true. After all, what had he really asked her? What expression of concern or care, however small, had he really shown? But then, it was difficult to tell. She hadn't given him much of a chance.

It was only after a considerable period of time, during which Katherine continued to hold her hands around the now cold mug of coffee and stare out of the window at the thickening winter gloom, that the realisation solidified inside her that she was actually going to see Daniel. She couldn't quite remember why she'd wanted to see him, and why, specifically, she had wanted to force him into it, but it had seemed desperately important that she did so. Now this was achieved, she was surprised to find herself needled by fear. How exactly *were* they supposed to sit down together and talk? She couldn't determine why or at what point their finely held balance had fallen apart. There was, after all, no definitive transgression. Perhaps, she thought, that was exactly the problem. Without the certainty of the unforgivable, they had been forced to cope with the ambiguity of the irreconcilable. Maybe one of them should have just gone out and fucked someone else, she thought, then at least they could have hated each other properly. But Daniel, of course, would never have done that.

The thought led naturally to thoughts of sex, about which she was still divided. The idea repulsed her, but the repulsion was enticing. At night, in bed, her insides writhed with life and hunger. In her dreams, tiny hands poked at the edges of her face. She was not certain she was in the right condition to meet Daniel. Her desperation was spraying off in multiple directions. She wondered about a safety fuck, then wondered where she might secure one now Keith was supposedly cured. She thought about Claire Demoines in her desperate tights and wanted quite strongly to harm her. The idea of sleeping with Keith was disgusting, and just what she needed.

She lay in wait for him near the stairs at work; grabbed his wrist and snapped his rubber band.

'Ow,' he whined, rubbing his wrist.

'Disabled toilets,' she said. 'Five minutes.'

'You're nuts,' said Keith.

'Five minutes,' she said, reaching for his cock. 'Fuck or flee.'

She sat in the disabled toilet and waited. She gave him fifteen minutes, then fingered herself and started to cry.

Back at her desk she had two new emails, both from Debbie.

Jesus, is it just me or is K like utterly pathetic? said the first one.

Sorry, said the second. *Sent to you by mistake.*

The day they met was cold and sharply bright. Daniel arrived early and, despite the icy air, chose an outside table so Katherine could smoke. They'd agreed on a place about which neither of them was particularly enthusiastic. Neutrality was critical. Neither of them wanted to be anywhere the other seemed too comfortable, or anywhere they had once been comfortable together. Everything, they seemed to agree, should be as mundane as possible. The upshot, agreed upon but never discussed, was that they were going to try and get through a reasonable duration of time without hurting each other.

There was a sense of security in sitting outside. He didn't feel hemmed in. He felt that the notional concept of 'leaving' was something that existed only two footsteps away, with no doors or obstacles between him and it. He wore his black woollen coat and a cashmere scarf and a pale pink shirt he ordinarily reserved for important meetings, but Katherine would not see it because Daniel would not take off his coat.

He was, he realised, flirting with nostalgia the way he usually flirted with illness. There was something nostalgic going around. He liked the idea but didn't want to get all the way stricken, and didn't want it to prove catching. Certain things, though, arose unbidden. Their first date, never actually described as such, had been for coffee. Katherine had devoted two sly weeks to making him uncomfortable, culminating in her breezing up to his desk and saying 'Look, I know you want to ask me out for coffee, so you might as well just get it over with.' He hadn't questioned whether he wanted to ask her out for coffee until long after he'd asked her out for coffee. Such was Katherine's way, he thought. You did things, became things in increments, until eventually you were recognisable only to her.

Exactly ten minutes later than the agreed time he clocked her coming up the street, a strut in her step that spoke of nerves. People gave her space without thinking about it, edging aside as she held her line. She looked different but moved the same. Her face registered not a shred of recognition, even when she'd seen him and was walking towards his table. As was her way, she started talking before actually entering earshot. She had a tendency to fade in and out. People joined her mid-flow, was the impression she gave, and on her terms. She had new hair, he noticed, and a slightly less flamboyant ethos with regards to her makeup, as if concealment, not expression, were now the prime motivating force. He put this down to age. Under the makeup, he thought, she was older, and hence the foundation was that infinitesimal degree thicker, like the concentric rings of an ageing tree.

'Do I look different?' she said, sliding into a chair and placing her hands on the table.

'No,' he lied.

She puffed her hair. 'Really? You're the same as always, of course.'

He was unable to tell if this statement carried an edge. He decided to assume that all statements would carry an edge.

She asked him if he'd ordered anything for her. He told her he had not.

'Do I want a latte?' she said, looking over her shoulder at who knew what.

'I have no idea.'

She leaned back in her chair, lit a cigarette, and told him she would have whatever he was having. He signalled the waitress and told her, with slightly widened eyes for what he hoped was comic effect, that they would have two black coffees. Then the waitress left, and Daniel looked back at Katherine, who was now inhaling deeply on her cigarette and fluttering her eyelashes in an oddly menacing way. He had, he realised, forgotten these details about her. The level of unattractiveness she brought to smoking, for example; the ease with which she could reverse a smile into a threat, a lash-bat into the opening of an argument.

'Why do you do that?' she said.

'Do what?'

'You do this thing with little gestures.'

'What little gestures?'

'Like you widen your eyes or raise your eyebrows or something as if I'm completely mad or difficult and you want to communicate to the waitress or whoever that you're aware that I'm mad or difficult but you're trying to keep me on some sort of level so please just be aware. Or like you say "black coffee" with this expression that sort of implies *we're going to need it*, as if this whole experience is going to be incredibly draining. It's just two old friends meeting for coffee, you know. It's not the start of a long haul at the coal face.'

She stopped, rolled her eyes and held up a hand.

'Sorry,' she said. 'Must try harder.'

Their coffee came. Daniel made a point of not making eye contact with the waitress. Katherine made a point, he noticed, of not looking to see if he made eye contact with the waitress.

'Still on the fags,' he said.

She blew smoke over her shoulder. 'Probably spare me the piety,' she said.

'Right.'

'I like your haircut.'

'Really?' He ran a hand through his hair. 'I'm not sure.'

'Yes you are,' she said. 'It's just that you're always slightly ashamed of loving something you regard as superficial.'

'Got me,' he said.

She squinted, leaned closer, held the position a fraction longer than was comfortable. He experienced her looking at him as a physical sensation, like breath against the downy hairs of his nape.

'I was wrong,' she said flatly. 'You have changed.'

'How so?'

She smiled, sipped her coffee, made him wait.

'You're happy,' she said, like it was a diagnosis.

Daniel thought about this with a degree of paranoia he hoped was not outwardly obvious. He wasn't sure exactly what he was supposed to say and so just smiled and nodded and gave a little shrug like, *Hey, what can you do?* Then he felt his face shift in a way that very definitely was outwardly obvious because he saw her face shift when she saw it.

'What?' she said.

'Nothing,' he said. 'I suppose I am.'

'Happy?'

'Yeah. To an extent.'

She smirked.

'What about you?' he said.

211

She tilted her cup this way and that, frowning. 'This coffee's sort of mediocre, isn't it?' she said. 'Like it's trying to be good coffee but not quite succeeding.'

Daniel wondered again if this was some sort of dig. Everything seemed unnaturally weighted. He felt like she was passing statements to him across the table and asking him to heft them in his hands to see if they held true.

'I think it's a little over-extracted,' he said.

'Do you now?'

'An espresso should take between eighteen and twenty-one seconds to extract. Shorter than that and it's too watery. Longer and it's too bitter.'

'This is filter coffee.'

Daniel looked at his cup.

'So it is,' he said, mortified.

Katherine did her laugh that was an impression of a laugh. Daniel said, 'Anyway.'

'Anyway,' she said, looking sideways and away across the street where a saggy-trousered toddler appeared to be having the tantrum to end all tantrums. 'Bloody hell. Where do they all *come from*?'

'Who?'

'The kids. Who's having all these kids? And why?' She performed the conversational equivalent of heaving on the handbrake. 'Shit, you're not about to have kids, are you?'

'Not as far as I know, no.'

'Do you want them?'

'One day,' he said.

Across the street the toddler's mother was going into the routine where she said she was going home and the toddler could just stay there if that's what he wanted, but she hoped he knew the way home because she was going home and he'd have to find his own way.

'Still in the same job?' said Daniel.

'Yeah. I see you've upgraded.'

'Did you google me?'

'Saw you in the paper.'

He squirmed. 'Yeah. That happens periodically.'

'You seem like you're doing really well.'

Both their coffees were empty but they both kept picking up their cups and sipping at them.

'I keep having these dreams,' Daniel said. 'I wake up thinking I've been found out, that everyone's realised what a fraud I am.'

'What, like you're not actually that good at your job?'

'Like I'm actually terrible at it.'

She nodded; looked at him in a surprisingly level way. 'But you are good at your job, aren't you?'

He was briefly thrown; took another sip of nothing. 'Yes,' he said. 'I'm certainly not bad at it.'

'I'd like to do something else,' she said.

'So do it.'

She rolled her eyes. 'I'm in that place,' she said. 'I go to bed saying tomorrow I'll look for something else, and then I wake up in the morning and it's all I can do to get into work and maintain the status quo.'

'Yeah,' said Daniel, watching the toddler take all of three seconds to go haring after his mother as she walked very slowly down the street. 'We've all been there.' He raised his cup. 'Another?'

'Are you eating?' She was studying the menu, looking somehow keen and not keen at the same time.

'I could definitely nibble at something.'

'Want to split one of these snacky things?'

'Like what?'

'Like one of those platters that has bread and olives and oil and some sort of nameless dip. You know. I fancy one of those but I can't eat a whole one.'

'That sounds fine.'

'Don't just get it because I'm getting it.'

'No. It sounds nice. I'm peckish.'

'Never got that word. Peckish.'

'From the Latin, *peckus*, meaning to allocate a small area of stomach for unnameable dip.'

She deadpanned. It was a point of pride not to laugh at other people's jokes.

'We're going to need a bigger boat, Roy,' she said.

He was ambushed by a laugh. He remembered that finding something in nothing was something at which they had both once, for better or for worse, been adept. It seemed apt, he thought, to laugh at something that had no meaning at all when it was said by someone to whom you'd once attached an excess of meaning.

Katherine summoned the waitress by waving and calling Hello.

'I think she heard you,' said Daniel.

'Good,' said Katherine. 'I hate it when they ignore you.'

The waitress stationed herself slightly diffidently beside their table. Katherine ordered two more coffees and a platter of breads and dips. Daniel felt embarrassed at feeling cold, as if this were somehow an expression of weakness. Across the street an elderly woman in an abundance of padded clothing parked her wheeled shopping device beside a bench and lowered herself cautiously into a sitting position. Daniel realised he was feeling slightly furtive. He kept checking the faces of other patrons as they arrived and departed, fearing being known.

'How's your love life?' he said, for no reason whatsoever.

214

She shot him a death glare in place of an answer.

'That good, eh?'

'Don't get smug,' she said.

'Sorry,' he said. 'I wasn't being.'

'So why say "sorry"?'

'Like, I'm sorry I gave that impression.'

'You've got a black belt in disingenuousness, you know that?'

He chose to assume this didn't require an answer.

'Men,' said Katherine flatly. 'Who gives a fuck.'

'Sometimes I miss being single,' said Daniel. He had no idea if this was an honest statement.

'Of course you do,' she said. 'That's what happens when you're happy.'

Daniel had that paralysis feeling again. He blinked.

'What?' said Katherine.

'It's the way you say it,' he said, not entirely trusting that this wouldn't lead to an argument.

She did the lash-bat again, all ice. Then she did her thin smile that somehow failed to involve the eyes, as if politely inviting him to annoy her.

'How do I say it?'

'I've just never known anyone to invest the word *happy* with such disdain,' he said. 'And I've never been able to decide why that was: if you simply don't believe in the whole concept or if it's more that you hate the idea of other people experiencing something you can't.'

He went quiet while his insides underwent a tectonic lurch.

'I want to say straightaway that that didn't sound nearly as bad in my head,' he added.

'No,' she said, 'it's OK. It's a fair comment.'

He wanted to say, with some incredulity: *It is?* He thought better of it and instead said nothing.

'I mean, I get it, of course,' she said, squinting slightly as if she could see what she wanted to say in the distance and was trying to bring it into focus. 'I get why people want it, but, I don't know. It lacks something for me.'

'Happiness lacks something for you? Is that a serious statement?'

'Have you ever known me to make an unserious statement?'

'Well, admittedly no.'

'Right, so don't ask.'

'OK.'

'Anyway,' she said. 'I've been thinking recently that the whole trying-to-be-happy thing makes people kind of unhappy so I'm experimenting with not trying to be happy at all.'

'And how's that working out?'

She arched an eyebrow. 'It has its moments.' She ran a hand through the air as if to sweep the conversation off the table. 'Whatever,' she said. 'You seem really happy, and that's nice.'

'It is,' he said, after a tactful pause. 'I think it is.'

'Is it the hippy that makes you happy?' said Katherine with a grin that wasn't entirely free of hostility.

'Partly,' he nodded.

'You don't look like a hippy,' she said.

'That's because I'm not one.'

'Is it like a Romeo and Juliet situation? Do her family disapprove of you because you wear a suit?'

'Her parents are very nice.'

Katherine blinked. Daniel wondered if she'd taken his remark to be a dig at her mother. He wondered if he should clarify, but then clarification was chancy because she might not have thought that at all until he sought to clarify, at which point she'd immediately think it. He considered what he thought was a subtle shift.

'How's your mum?' he said.

'Subtle,' said Katherine.

'I didn't mean . . .'

'She's her usual self, let's put it that way.'

'Right.'

'I suppose I sort of worry about her now,' said Katherine. 'I still get annoyed by her and all that, but sometimes I also just find myself feeling sad for her and hoping she's all right.'

Daniel nodded.

'How's your dad, anyway?' said Katherine.

'Comes and goes,' said Daniel.

It was Katherine's turn to nod. They were both, Daniel noted, at great pains to show they understood.

'Does he remember you?' said Katherine.

'Most of the time.'

'Would he remember me, do you think?'

She looked earnest, a little afraid. She had a thing about being forgotten. Everyone, Daniel thought, has a thing about being forgotten. In many ways it was why they were here now, having lunch, swapping inanities.

'No,' he said honestly.

'That's awful.'

He laughed. 'I *know*,' he said, affecting high camp. 'All that fabulous Katherine-ness, lost.'

'That's not what I meant,' she said.

'I know. I was teasing.'

Their food and coffee arrived. They ignored it. In the street, on the other side of the rope that demarcated their eating area, people moved back and forth who were just like them. Daniel imagined the things that worried them as they walked: the phone calls they hadn't made; the phone calls they hadn't received; the micro-disappointments of an average day. A young couple passed a camera to an old couple and asked for a picture. The girl had a blue Mohawk; the old woman had a blue rinse. Momentarily, it looked as if the young couple were handing the camera to their future selves. Daniel looked at Katherine, this woman he knew so well. Too well, really, to talk to now. He wanted to tell her she was lucky, in a way, to be in a position where she could still yearn for more, rather than simply fear the loss of what she already had.

She took a glug of her coffee and watched him over the rim of her cup. For a second he watched her watching him. He felt a nameless tug and wanted to leave.

'So,' he said. 'Nathan.'

'Ah yes. Nathan.'

Saying his name felt like an achievement.

'What's the plan?' said Katherine.

'How should I know?'

'Well you're the planner.'

'What does that mean?'

'You plan. You do plans. You're never knowingly without a plan.'

'Do we even need a plan?'

She held up her hands. 'Hey, you know me. If the plan is that we don't need a plan then I'm absolutely fine with that. The question is: are you?'

'Yes,' said Daniel. It came out sounding like a question.

They went quiet again.

'Fuck,' said Daniel after a while. 'Fuckitty tits.'

'Well,' said Katherine. 'Ain't that the truth.'

'I keep thinking,' said Daniel.

'Naturally.'

'You know.'

'I'm sure there was nothing we could have done.'

Daniel felt stalked again; shadowed. Something nameless and hot licked gently at his nape and slipped a spindly finger through his belly button into his stomach. It was the kind of horror that woke you in the night and sent you pacing downstairs into the dawn. His father was going to forget everything and die.

'That's the statement,' he said. 'That's the statement I keep unpacking. If there was nothing we could have done, then was there something someone else could have done?'

'Why should that worry us? There's always something someone else could have done.'

'But what if all that means is that we should have been someone else?'

'Eh?'

'Never mind,' he said. 'I probably don't want to think about it anyway.'

He made an exploratory start on the foodstuffs. Some were crunchy; some were semi-liquid. Katherine let her fingers hover above the spread, then seemingly thought better of it.

'I know what you mean,' she said.

Daniel nodded. 'I think we had this conversation at the time.'

'Yeah. There's nothing really new to be said, is there?'

'I keep thinking,' said Daniel.

'Look,' said Katherine. 'Maybe he just couldn't be helped, you know? He was in a bad place. He always had the propensity or whatever. Shit. I can't count the number of times he was weird. Right? I mean, don't get me wrong, but I'm not going to go and string myself up with guilt just because Nathan tried to top himself.' She reached for some pitta. 'I'm aware that last statement was in slightly poor taste,' she said, munching.

'He says he didn't try and kill himself,' said Daniel.

'Whatever. Kill yourself. Cut yourself. It's all the same.'

A man at the next table unfolded a newspaper. The headline said: *Daily Exercise Cuts Death Risk.*

'This is bland, isn't it?' said Daniel, meaning the food.

Katherine shrugged.

'So,' Katherine said. 'All this stuff with the cows. Does that affect you?'

'Well, people think it does, so to all intents and purposes it does. That's the joy of PR. It doesn't matter if you've done anything wrong or not. It's what people think that counts.'

'The madness of crowds and all that.'

Daniel nodded. 'Hell of a job to try and keep the crowds sane.'

Katherine rolled her eyes. 'You hero,' she said.

'Just saying. What about you, anyway? Isn't facilities management basically the same? Don't you have to rebalance people's misguided perceptions of risk?'

'Essentially. And listen to them moan.'

The mechanism of their conversation ran down. They nibbled and stared and looked about them until one of them could wind it back up. It was oddly comfortable. Silence had never really been an issue between them. It was all the things they said that were the problem. All those stupid clichés about things going unsaid, Daniel thought. The stiff, buttoned-up English and their repressed ways. Was any of that really true anymore? It seemed to him that there was very little he and Katherine hadn't said to each other at some point, which was why their silences tended to be comfortable. There came a point where it was a relief not to be saying anything.

But then the relief passed, and there was only, once again, the pressure to speak.

'We can just be normal, though, right?' said Daniel.

'Why wouldn't we be?'

'I'm telling myself, really,' said Daniel. 'I don't know why I said it out loud. I'm . . . It's weird. Everything's weird.'

'Is this weird?'

'Slightly.'

'But you did always assume that at some point we'd catch up with each other? Right?'

Daniel shrugged. 'I don't know. I mean . . . Maybe not. You know? Bridges, water, all of that.'

'You weren't curious? You never thought, hey, I wonder how Katherine's doing?'

'I would have emailed.'

'You would have *emailed*?'

'What's wrong with that? Jesus.'

'Nothing,' she said. 'Nothing at all.'

'Don't say "nothing" when it's really something. You know I hate that. If it's something just say what it is.'

'It's nothing.'

'Right, OK, it's nothing.'

Daniel was freezing, and doing a poor job of concealing how freezing he was. He sensed Katherine was enjoying watching him shiver. The whole thing was futile, he thought, utterly futile. It had always been futile and it was going to go on being futile until eventually they both gave up pretending it was anything but. This wasn't a revelation he enjoyed. For some reason he was at a loss to fathom, he wanted this, all of this, to have some sort of point.

'Whatever,' said Katherine. 'We'll just be.'

'Fine,' said Daniel.

Katherine surveyed the platter.

'I think I'm done here,' she said.

'Yeah,' said Daniel, looking at his watch. 'I should probably . . .'

'I need the loo before I go,' said Katherine, standing up. 'I'll say cheerio.' She took out her purse.

'No, no,' said Daniel. 'I'll get it. Honestly.'

'Let me at least pay half.'

'No, seriously. I've got it.'

'Well thank you.'

'Pleasure.'

'Anyway,' she said. 'This has been nice.'

Daniel nodded. 'It has. Good to see you, Katherine.'

'Good to see you, Daniel.'

She leaned forward and kissed his cheek. He held her shoulder briefly, awkwardly. He never knew if he should go for the other cheek as well. It turned out to be a one-cheek kiss.

'See you Saturday,' said Katherine.

Daniel nodded. 'Take care,' he said.

She went into the café and he sat back down, picking distractedly at the almost entirely untouched platter, the world all at once unknowable, unfamiliar; the sense of the nostalgia to which he'd earlier refused to succumb suddenly all too attractive. They could have talked about the old times, he thought. They could have made each other laugh. Even shouting at each other would have been more reassuring.

He took out his mobile and called his father.

'Dad,' he said. 'How are you?'

'Uh . . .' said his father. 'I don't know.'

Daniel chose to ignore this and move on. 'I just called to say, guess who I just saw?'

Daniel's father thought for some time. 'Don't know,' he said.

'Katherine,' said Daniel. 'Remember Katherine? She sends her love.'

'Who's Katherine?' said Daniel's father.

'Katherine,' said Daniel. 'You remember Katherine, don't you? She was my girlfriend but we broke up. You always thought she was fun. She had . . .'

He stopped, wondering now if this was needlessly cruel. Whose benefit was he really calling for, anyway?

'Anyway,' he said. 'She says Hi. I just thought I'd pass that on.'

'Hi,' said Daniel's father.

'Hi,' said Daniel, and hung up.

Here we all are, he thought, forgetting each other.

He saw Katherine leaving the café. He needed a piss before he left but hadn't wanted to run into her again inside.

He left some cash on the table and walked through the café to the toilet. There was only one. He stepped inside and stood for a moment, unnerved at how redolent it was of Katherine's shit. This, he thought, was the smell of a life together; the smell of bodies and time. He locked the door. The more he breathed the less he was able to smell it. He pulled down his trousers and sat on the seat, finding it still warm. There, in a public toilet, drinking in the smell of his ex-partner's shit, he thought quite distinctly of his father; of the things that were failing and fading away; of the things we hope to hold on to even as we can feel ourselves letting them go, and he sobbed, and breathed deeply, and blew his nose and pissed.

Katherine left the café at a trotting pace, lighter for having vomited and shat, but still somehow puffed and weighty. People weren't getting out of her way. She shoulder-bumped two and had a near-miss with another.

She wanted to know how it had felt to see Daniel again. Although she hadn't been able to tell, beforehand, how it would feel, she had naturally assumed that however it felt would become clear afterwards, and that it would, in turn, clarify the things she'd felt since they'd split. In reality, though, all was murk and gloom.

At the office she snagged her coat in the revolving door. By the time she got to her desk she felt like she'd been worked over by goons. She went to the bathroom and adjusted. Her eyes felt fleshy. She leaned on the sink and heaved, got nothing. She and Daniel had, she kept thinking, been happy. She was sure they had. Hadn't they? Hadn't they been happy? If they had, she couldn't remember how, or exactly when.

Back at her desk she decided on a fire drill. She went out into the hallway and slid her key into the alarm system. The siren was pleasing. People berated her as they passed.

'Again with this?'

'It's regulations.'

'We had one last week.'

'Now we're having one this week.'

'It's usually on a Tuesday.'

'It's not a drill if you know when it's happening, is it?'

Outside, workers chatted and smoked in chilly clusters, shifting from foot to foot and checking in with other floors. Katherine left them out there as long as possible while she swept the building. Response time had been poor. Half of them would be dead. There was, she thought, something happily Darwinian about fire drills.

She went outside and told them with great satisfaction that half of them were dead.

Afterwards, she found Keith in the stationery cupboard, selecting a new rubber band.

'Who have you told?' she said.

'Hey,' said Keith. 'Cool it on the hostility, yeah?'

'Who have you told?'

'No one. My therapist. Claire.'

'I'm pregnant,' she said. 'It's yours. I'm going to kill it with my bare hands.'

He stood staring at her dumbly, swaying slightly. Then he laughed. Then he looked at her face and stopped laughing.

'Shit,' he said.

She left him standing there, three sizes of rubber band hanging limp and ignored from his fingers.

The feeling of being out was, to Nathan, at once bizarre, uncomfortable and oddly enticing. He'd been 'out' before of course – wandering the lanes near his parents' house; dropping into The Rover for a Guinness – but arriving in a town centre was a new kind of exposure. He'd forgotten the wildly unpleasant temperament of the average weekend shopper: the steely resolve mixed with constant, bitter compromise. Parents paused outside department stores to scream at their children and partners. Elderly men and women moved with caution through a minefield of charity hustlers, amateur preachers, shabby men selling miniature kites, puppeteers, buskers, motionless women painted silver, beggars, market-stall traders and bored-looking youths handing out flyers for closing-down sales.

Nathan had never seen the value in either goods or the process by which they were acquired. The last time he'd shopped had been under duress, just before he went away for his treatment. His mother had taken him to John Lewis to kit him out. She'd led the charge into the menswear department, hauling cardigans and cords off the racks; preaching the gospel of layering as she pinned sweaters to his chest and squinted. Everything seemed to make him look pale. When they were done they collected Nathan's father from the canteen and began the ceremonial unsheathing of the MasterCard, gathering at the card machine with the grave but dignified reluctance one might expect of two national leaders as they tapped in the nuclear codes. Thinking the chance might not come again, and perhaps already envisioning a time when such information would be useful, Nathan had watched his father as he slowly and with excessive deliberation entered each of the four digits of the card's pin number. Just knowing the code, Nathan remembered now, had brought him a sense of possibility.

He felt he had to pay careful attention to where he was going. He had not been in a crowd since the last of the parties. Faces swelled into view; threatened to collide; then were gone. He remembered walking out into the press of dancers after he'd spoken to Katherine, dimly aware of backslaps and shout-outs, feeling suddenly and profoundly unable to move and so just standing there motionless, feeling everything and everyone move around him and away.

He tried to remember when he had last been here. No single memory stood out. Those visits, and the evenings around which they centred, had always been much of a muchness. Katherine cooked and Daniel skivvied. Often, they were already a glass or two to the good when Nathan arrived. They could be funny, he remembered. They could set each other up and knock each other down. On a good day, they drew on pooled energy. On a bad day, they battled for dwindling air. Sometimes Nathan felt surplus. Frequently, he felt like a much-needed audience. Daniel liked it if Nathan brought drugs. They'd be pissed or stoned before the food even made it out of the oven. Later, Daniel would black out and leave Nathan and Katherine alone, sitting up late into the night, each dealing out profundities in an effort to trump the other. It became a sort of centre of gravity, Nathan remembered. His feelings were shaped over successive visits. She'd sprawl on the sofa and tell it like it was, her head lolling occasionally in his direction, her bare feet tapping gently to whatever was on the stereo. Nathan started taking more control over the evening's outcome. He topped off Daniel's glass without being asked; front-loaded joints so Daniel got the bulk of the hit. He watched for the droop of his eyes, the flop of his head, the loss of blood from his face. It was not something of which he was proud.

The bookshop was just off the central square. Nathan paused outside the window and examined a display of his mother's book. They'd made a poster out of the cover image. Here she was, his mother, inflated to an unnatural scale, gazing out at God knew what with an expression akin to those women in adverts for thrush cream: wounded, slightly pinched, yet relieved of an irritation that had blighted her life.

He went inside, picked up a copy, and took it to the counter.

'How many of these do you have?' he asked the checkout girl.

'How many?'

'How many copies?'

'Er,' she seemed on the verge of asking further questions but Nathan created a facial expression that dissuaded her. She scanned the barcode and scrolled through stock on her till. 'Thirteen copies in store,' she said. 'But they're selling fast. Have you read it?'

'I'll take all thirteen copies please,' said Nathan.

'Excuse me?'

'Please find all thirteen copies that you have in this store and bring them here so I can buy them.'

She did it, then asked him how he wanted to pay.

'Credit card,' he said with extreme satisfaction.

Given their abstemious attitude to credit, he thought, it would be weeks before his parents checked the bureau and noted the card's absence.

He loaded the books into four plastic bags and carried them through the town centre. He had a sense of purpose that was practically holy. He envisioned the feeling of no longer carrying the books and swelled a little inside.

He stopped in Tesco to buy wine. Every single item in the store appeared to be part of some sort of offer. He had, he realised, no idea how to choose a bottle of wine. Whole facets of the world felt locked off and unknowable. People ate as they roamed the shop. When their children started to cry they encouraged them to eat. On every aisle there was at least one child sobbing gutturally through the wilting remains of a Snickers.

He bought one white and one red, then shepherded the bottles through the self-service system, which asked him to wait while someone verified his age. A teenager appeared out of the crowd, looked him up and down and tapped a code into the screen. It struck Nathan with some force that he was no longer young.

He carried the books and the wine and his holdall back into the street and made his way across town to the river, where one by one he took the books from the bags and hurled them into the grey depths. They bobbed briefly amongst drifting fishing tackle and anonymous plastic flagons. After three or four books had hit the water he started ripping out pages before he threw them. He saw paragraphs of his past as they caught the wind and were gone.

He became aware of his phone ringing. He looked at the screen and answered, because of course she would call now, just as he was doing this.

'Nathan,' said his mother.

'Mother,' he said, hurling half a book almost all the way to the other side of the river.

'Nathan. Where are you?'

'I've gone away. I told Dad.'

'Well how long will you be gone?'

'I have no idea.'

'Is this about the television show? Are you upset, Nathan? Because it upsets me to think you're upset. It really does.'

'I'm not upset.'

'I don't want you to be upset.'

'I'm not.'

'I mean it, Nathan. It's really important to me. I hate to think of you being upset.'

'There's no need to think of me being upset.'

'Really, Nathan? Because we worry, your father and I. And I think it's very unfair of you to make us worry in this way.'

'You really shouldn't worry.'

'We're supposed to be looking after you.'

'I know that.'

'How can we look after you if you just keep wandering off and we don't know where you are?'

He tucked the phone under his ear so as to more easily rip the dust jacket off the last book.

'You can't,' he said. 'I don't expect you to.'

'Well with all due respect, Nathan, your expectations are not really the issue.'

He hung up; turned off his phone. He had Daniel's address on a scrap of paper and made his way there.

By the time the appointed hour arrived, Daniel was sitting limply on the sofa having experienced what he could only conceptualise as a crisis of maturity. He had, he realised, no idea how to do this, this having people round thing, and he had found himself, midway through a scorched-earth cleaning policy, wishing quite acutely that Angelica was there. It wasn't as if she'd have known what to do, it was more that she would have done whatever it was that needed to be done without even thinking about it.

Arrangements had not gone according to plan. Cleaning the house, which had entered a state of decay during the few days he had occupied it alone, had taken far longer than intended, and at the end of the process, as he packed away the mop and hoover and considered opening a beer, he'd realised he hadn't made up the spare bed, and having made the spare bed he'd realised he hadn't given any thought whatsoever to drink or, for that matter, food. Were they expecting him to cook? He hadn't specifically mentioned food, but of course, inviting people to your house for the evening, or in Nathan's case the night (God, he thought suddenly, Katherine didn't think she was staying the night, did she? No, he'd be firm. If necessary, he'd call her a taxi), basically implied they would be fed. There was, he thought, no conceivable way he could cook, not merely because his cooking wasn't good, but because the thought of cooking for Katherine and Nathan seemed to carry an intensity and pressure – not to mention an air of surrealism – so overwhelming as to potentially capsize the whole precarious evening.

He'd made it to the supermarket and bought wine and beer and an assortment of finger foods that covered every possible permutation of potato: fried; reconstituted; slathered in mayonnaise. Then he'd returned; changed; unpacked the shopping, and established a position of comparative calm on the sofa just in time to put logistical concerns out of his head and get down to the serious business of worrying about all the other aspects of the evening he'd managed quite successfully not to worry about through strategically worrying about things like making the bathroom smell better and whether, in the modern age, people could truly feel comfortable with a screw-top wine.

Around him, he thought, up and down the street and out in the world, other people, other adults, were doing all of this with a practised, almost cultish ease: lighting votive candles and setting out individual bowls of Japanese rice crackers and finding an appropriate volume for some unobtrusive yet not wholly middle-of-the-road electronica, the very knowledge of which made Daniel feel basically like he had at the virginal age of seventeen, when he routinely walked through town and looked at adults of every shape and size and level of attractiveness and thought, *All of these people, even that enormous old lady with the shopping bags, have at some stage in their lives had sex.*

He was, he had to admit, worried. There was a sense of events and people descending; a flurry of unbidden arrivals. He could, of course, have refused to have anything to do with them, but doing so would have run contra to his sense of doing the right thing, and would have made him feel guilty, and it hadn't seemed worth it. He remembered other times Nathan had visited: always faintly awkward, a little disappointing, but also, in light of Daniel and Katherine's increasing isolation, so needed. Daniel spent most of those evenings trying not to look too out of it while at the same time wanting to get completely out of it, usually leading to an early retreat to the comparative safety of the bedroom in order to focus more closely on the elliptical nature of the ceiling's orbit. Nathan never openly teased, but the judgement was clearly there. Daniel couldn't hold his substances, and where Nathan was concerned, that was something of a barrier to true empathy.

Poor Nathan. Daniel couldn't help thinking it, and wanted to think it a few times before Nathan arrived in the hope that he might be able to get it out of his system. *Poor Nathan.* Daniel supposed that with anyone else there would be the usual questions, the hows and whys and wherefores, but with Nathan such uncertainties seemed somewhat moot. Of course what had happened had happened. It was,

Daniel thought, part of the reason that being around him had been exciting: the sense of borrowed time; of upcoming inevitability. You couldn't live as Nathan lived indefinitely. Everyone knew that. Everyone could see it. More than likely Nathan could see it too. It was probably why he did it. But still. Poor guy.

There would, Daniel thought, be a proper way of handling this. He would have liked very much to know what it was.

Before ringing the doorbell Nathan spent roughly four minutes standing in Daniel's small front garden going through a series of checks not dissimilar to the ritualised switch-throwing of a pilot preparing for takeoff. He smoothed the front of his jacket; tugged his cuffs free of his sleeves; ate a mint; took three deep breaths; rolled his shoulders; straightened his stance and pressed the small round button for the bell with a slow, deliberate motion that he hoped would lead to a strong, confident ring from the doorbell. Sadly, Daniel's doorbell appeared to be playing up and what resulted was more along the lines of a computerised glitch or synthesised approximation of a chime, giving his arrival exactly the sort of hesitancy he'd hoped to avoid and necessitating a further press of the button out of concern that the strangled sound had not been audible, which as it turned out it had, because Daniel opened the door just as Nathan was removing his finger from the second press, catching him standing rather too close to the door with his finger raised and throwing him off guard just enough to lead to his hello being slightly too loud and an uncomfortable failed exchange whereby Daniel and Nathan fell into an awkward and momentarily unbreakable sync.

'Hi,' they both said. 'How are you? Good. I'm good. How are you? Good.'

Then Daniel reached for Nathan's bag, which Nathan misinterpreted as Daniel stepping aside to usher him in, leading to a mutually baffling moment where Nathan advanced towards Daniel, who then appeared to block his passage.

'Sorry,' they chorused. 'No, it's OK.'

'Come in,' said Daniel firmly.

The front room smelled deeply of incense, as if joss sticks were lit so frequently that their scent had impregnated the wooden floors. Judging by the inch or so of visible leather, the two generous sofas were expensive, but both were covered with heavy knitted throws in patchworked rainbow colours, on top of which perched a variety of cushions in a range of sizes and fabrics. A large mirror on the wall was trimmed with intricate beading.

'Very nice,' said Nathan.

'Hi,' said Daniel, spreading his arms. 'Thanks.'

They hugged awkwardly. Daniel seemed reluctant to exert any pressure.

'You look well,' said Daniel as they both stepped back.

'You too,' said Nathan. 'This place suits you.'

'Oh,' said Daniel, with a cursory wave of his hand. 'It's all Angelica.'

Nathan smiled. 'Anyway,' he said.

Daniel pointed at Nathan's bag. 'You're in the spare room,' he said. 'Do you want to take that up? Do you need to freshen up at all? How was your journey? Are you tired? Thirsty? You must need a drink. What are you drinking?'

'It's fine,' said Nathan. 'I'm fine. Maybe a beer?'

'Of course.' Daniel pointed at Nathan as if he'd just given the correct answer in class. 'Sit. I'll get it.'

Nathan ignored the instruction and followed Daniel. He was afraid of sitting, for some reason. He liked the idea of them standing somewhere for a while, perhaps propped against a worktop or leaning on the backs of chairs. He wished Daniel would put some music on.

They wandered through to a dining area. The table, to Nathan's relief, was not set for dinner. The kitchen, half visible through an archway, was long and narrow and brightly lit by a variety of chrome spotlights, all angled in such a fashion as to make their illumination feel inescapable. Daniel reached into a stylish fridge with rounded corners and came out with two bottles of Pilsner.

'Let's get started, eh?' he said.

Nathan smiled. They touched bottles.

'Good to see you,' said Daniel.

'Good to be here,' said Nathan, at which point Daniel's smile went fractionally awry.

A nd then she left me,' said the taxi driver morosely. 'Just like that. Moved in with him next door.'

'Really,' said Katherine, staring determinedly out the window in a way she hoped would make him stop talking.

'I can hear them having sex,' he went on. 'I'm working triple shifts just to avoid being home.'

'Unbelievable.'

'It's so lonely, you know?'

'Mmhmm.'

'What about you? You attached?'

Katherine gave him a long, steady look. 'I get embarrassed when other people embarrass themselves,' she said.

A blank look crossed the driver's face.

'My name's Al,' he said.

'That's lovely, Al.'

'Bit of a one, aren't you?'

Katherine lit a cigarette and rolled down her window. 'You have no idea,' she said.

'You can't smoke in here,' said Al.

'I won't tell if you don't,' said Katherine.

Al looked nervous. Making people nervous made Katherine less nervous. She had entered the stage of spirit-based intoxication that masquerades as absolute sobriety. She met her gaze in the rear-view mirror and knew without question that she was a motherfucking force to be reckoned with.

'How far down do you want?' said Al.

'Probably however far down the number is,' said Katherine, launching her cigarette out the window.

'Yeah,' said Al. 'Course.'

What was going to happen, thought Katherine, was that Daniel was very definitely going to say something to annoy her, and then she would very definitely destroy him. She went through a list of all the possible things he might say and do, and the more she went over them the more likely they looked. She would not get angry, she thought. She would be icy-calm and devastate with precision.

'Do you go out much?' said Al.

Katherine stared at him until he ran the back of his hand across his brow.

'I try and get out,' he said, pressing on.

'Tell me, Al,' said Katherine. 'What would you do if I told you to pull the car over right now and fuck me?'

Al failed to slow for a speedbump. They bounced twice in their seats.

Al said, 'Y . . .'

'This is me,' said Katherine, infinitely revived.

'What?'

'This is where I'm going. The house. The number.'

Al stopped the car.

'What do I owe you?' said Katherine.

'Six,' said Al.

'Call it five,' said Katherine, slinging him a grubby fiver and slamming the door behind her.

D aniel wasn't sure what he should be saying to Nathan and so had been reduced to a series of pre-verbal sounds meant to communicate pleasure, nostalgia, comfort and warmth. He took a swig of beer and said, *Mmmmmmmhhmhmhmhm*. He stretched his arms above his head and said, *Aaaaahhhhhhhhmmmmmmuuuuuhhhhhhhhh*. He nodded, and his nods bore no relation to anything that had occurred or been said, primarily because nothing had been said. He kept trying to sneak a peek at Nathan when Nathan was distracted, but since absolutely nothing was happening to distract him this was proving difficult. Disconcertingly, Nathan still had his coat on, although he had removed his gloves and Daniel had managed neither to turn up his nose nor comment on the state of his hands. They looked burnt, Daniel thought. Had he tried to kill himself with something hot? Was that an accepted suicide method? Christ, was there even any such thing as an accepted suicide method? There were definitely scars on his neck too. Hanging, maybe? But that didn't explain the hands.

'So,' said Daniel. 'How long have you been home?'

'Few weeks,' said Nathan.

'Right. Cool, cool,' said Daniel. 'And, ah, like, how is that?'

'What?'

'Being home.'

'Oh. You know.'

'Yeah.'

They both nodded.

'Sorry about you and Katherine,' said Nathan.

'Oh,' said Daniel. 'For the best.'

'She's coming, right?'

'Yeah.' Daniel looked at his watch. 'Any time now.'

'I hope that's not, like . . .'

'Oh no,' said Daniel. 'It's fine. We're, you know . . .'

Nathan nodded. 'Well, that's good,' he said. 'Because a lot of people just . . .' He shrugged.

'Part of me wonders if maybe we'll actually be able to function much better as friends than we did when we were together,' said Daniel, who appeared, as he often did, to be making pronouncements in which he had absolutely no faith.

'That can happen,' said Nathan, who Daniel already suspected might be losing interest. What a burden it was, Daniel thought, entertaining people. He wondered how he'd ended up being the linchpin of the whole occasion. Probably because he was always the sodding linchpin, he thought, sucking moodily at his beer bottle.

He realised he was desperate for Katherine to arrive. Not for reasons of romance or nostalgia, but simply because there had always been times when her galloping obsession with being the absolute epicentre of existence offered Daniel the welcome opportunity to put his feet up, chug beer after beer, and free himself from all sense of social responsibility. Sometimes, naturally, letting Katherine be Katherine could prove embarrassing in the extreme, but after years of inwardly shrivelling while the woman he was sometimes highly reluctant to describe as his partner held stubbornly forth on such diverse topics as vaginal discharge, child molestation, the benefits of adultery and whatever partially concealed raw nerves she might be able to locate, like a beachcomber stalking the sands with a metal detector, in or among her assembled guests, he had found that it was actually much easier simply to switch off and enjoy the fact that no one gave a shit what he thought or said so long as Katherine was putting on her usual performance. It was, he found, oddly liberating and even, at times, surprisingly beneficial to his ego, as he kept one eye on Katherine and one on the pitying glances of their guests and came to understand that they were going to walk or drive home and, during the usual post-mortem of the evening, describe him as *long-suffering* to the point of heroism. Surveying the post-apocalyptic tundra of silence and awkwardness between him and Nathan now, Daniel felt he could use a bit of heroism, no matter what the source.

'Another beer?' he said, waving his empty bottle at Nathan.

'Still working on this one,' said Nathan. 'But don't let me stop you.'

'No,' said Daniel, creaking out of his chair and making that odd little noise he seemed to have started making whenever he tried to rise from a sitting position. What, he wondered, was happening to him? Was he decaying?

The doorbell rang, then rang again three seconds later. After two more seconds Katherine's voice bellowed at him to open the fucking door. Thank God, Daniel thought, striding through the dining room with his arm outstretched, that she was here to break the silence.

'Katherine,' he said, opening the door wide and affecting a smile he hoped would fill the space. 'Come in.'

The invitation carried a whiff of inadvertent irony, however, as she was already in, turning twice on her heel to take in the room, casting off a glance as she did so.

'Love what you've done with the place,' she sneered. 'You must have spent weeks choosing just the right throw.'

Daniel narrowed his eyes, but was spared the exchange, because Nathan had appeared in the doorless doorway that led through to the rest of the house. He had his hands behind his back and his head tilted to one side. He looked awkward, Daniel thought with a little heart-skip of pity, perhaps even embarrassed: a man still stinging from a fresh slap.

'Hi Katherine,' said Nathan.

She stood and looked at him, semi-quizzical, a little on the back foot. She was smiling, Daniel noted, in a manner that suggested she'd selected the smile quite deliberately from a range of other possible expressions.

'Well,' she said. 'You don't look so bad.'

Nathan nodded. 'I'm not that bad,' he said.

'Liar,' she said, stepping forward to hug him. 'It's good to see you,' she said into his ear.

'It's good to see you too,' said Nathan into hers.

'Fuck me,' she said, drawing back. 'What happened to your neck?'

Nathan's hand shot to the side of his neck to cover the mixture of scar tissue and disfigured crows. Katherine reached forward and grabbed the hand, running her thumb over the ridges of healing skin. She looked back up at him.

'You fucking idiot,' she said.

'Bloody hell, Katherine,' said Daniel. 'Go easy.'

'It's all right,' said Nathan. 'Heard it all before.' He smiled down at Katherine. 'We all have our little moments of madness, I suppose.'

'Be as mad as you like,' said Katherine, 'but no more playing with sharp objects.'

'Understood,' said Nathan.

'Right,' said Katherine. 'Well, some things clearly haven't changed because I've been here over five minutes and this cretin hasn't even offered me a drink.'

'What are you having?' Daniel said, the warmth in his voice surprising him.

'Anything,' she said, strutting through to the dining room, her heels rattling against the wooden floors and no doubt, Daniel thought, leaving some pretty nasty dents in the boards. 'Beer. Whatever you're having. Can I smoke?'

'If you must. But could you maybe take your shoes off?'

She pivoted neatly on one stiletto, as if adding emphasis to the damage, then kicked her shoes one by one into the corner, winking at Nathan as she did so.

'I'm on my best behaviour,' she said with a smile. 'Isn't it fun?'

Nathan's first thought on seeing Katherine was that she looked both wonderful and unwell. Her strut and timing and general flair were all present, but seemingly at some cost. Her smile tugged harshly at the edge of her face. She was pale and thin. Her skin had broken out. It was all, he thought, a little precarious, a little chancy. When he hugged her, she felt delicate, which was not a word one usually associated with Katherine. She was living up to herself, Nathan sensed, to her own aura, and for the first time he experienced a flash of recognition at what a strain that must be.

But he was pleased to see her, and not just because Daniel was proving to be such an awkward host. When she hugged him, when she winked, he felt a familiar sadness, a little stab of regret. She was very much alive, he thought, and where interaction with other people usually caused Nathan to struggle with certain facts of his own existence, as if the very reality of his aliveness was something to which he needed to reconcile himself, Katherine's presence only ever made him wish that he was as alive as she was. He didn't even feel that queasy when she examined his neck, although there was always the question of how much she knew, and how responsible she might feel, which he wanted to address later, when Daniel with any luck would have blacked out.

'So look at you,' Katherine was saying to Daniel. 'You're like a grown-up.'

Daniel was back at the fridge.

'Nathan,' he called. 'Have another.'

'Now, now, boys,' said Katherine, drawing out a chair and folding herself onto it, flashing a clear expanse of thigh before tugging at the hem of her dress. 'I hope you don't have any plans to get me drunk and take advantage of me.'

Daniel stepped back into the dining room in order to narrow his eyes at her.

'Let's keep it clean, shall we? Nathan. A drink.'

'OK,' said Nathan, sitting down opposite Katherine and mustering a smile.

Katherine rolled her eyes at Nathan, smirked, and lit a cigarette.

'Daniel,' she called. 'Ashtray.'

Nathan took out his tobacco and rolled a cigarette while Katherine gawped fairly openly at his fingers. Daniel returned to the table with three beers.

'A toast,' said Daniel, handing out the bottles. 'To Nathan.'

'Oh,' said Nathan, feeling acutely self-conscious. 'Don't, I mean ...'

'Good to see you, dude,' said Daniel, raising his bottle.

'And here's to Daniel not saying "dude" again,' said Katherine. She tilted her bottle towards Nathan. 'Here's to you,' she said.

'To all of us,' said Nathan, fumbling the words a little.

'Anyway,' said Nathan, stepping gingerly into the odd space that follows a toast. 'How are you, Katherine?'

'Oh fantastic,' said Katherine. 'Still stuck in the same job in the same town. Still single.' She dragged on her cigarette and washed it back with a chug of beer. 'How about you? Daniel said you're at your parents'.'

'Yeah.' He wasn't sure what he was supposed to say, not just to this but to anything.

'That must pretty much suck.'

'Yeah.'

'Don't you miss London? Don't you *hate* being in the provinces? In the middle of fucking nowhere?' She leaned back in her chair and grimaced. 'I do.'

'You've been saying that for years,' said Daniel. 'Why don't you just go back?'

'Just go back, he says.' She rolled her eyes at Nathan again. Every moment of conspiracy felt simultaneously astounding and mean. 'Nathan, back me up here. Did I or did I not ask Daniel a million times if we could move back?'

'Oh don't drag him into ancient arguments, for God's sake,' said Daniel. 'And anyway, what's your point? You don't have to ask me now, do you?'

'I didn't have to ask you then,' she said.

'So why did you?'

She turned her attention back to Nathan, who was beginning to wish she'd both stop singling him out but also somehow single him out in a more definitive way. 'Whatever,' she said. 'What about you? How long can you stick it with the folks?'

He shrugged. 'I'm, ah . . .' He slid what scant thumbnail he had under the label on his beer bottle. The corner lifted with surprising ease. 'I don't know. They're pretty determined and I sort of owe them, so . . .'

'What do you owe them?' said Katherine, wearing an expression more suited to a bad smell than anything else.

Nathan could also, he found, draw stripes in the condensation on his beer bottle.

'Well it's . . .' He frowned. 'I mean, I've caused them quite a lot of problems, and they paid for me to go to this place . . .'

'So what?' said Katherine. 'You have to stay with them?'

'Maybe let's not give him the third degree, eh?' said Daniel. He sat down next to Nathan and patted his shoulder in a way that made Nathan want to sob. 'Don't worry about her,' he said.

'Oh fuck off,' snapped Katherine. 'Stop trying to show off. Patronising me doesn't make you Mr Sensitive, you know. All I'm saying is that Nathan is an adult, and he shouldn't feel guilty, or do anything out of some twisted sense of loyalty.'

'I'm sure he feels just great now that you've freed him from the burden of guilt.'

'Well what's your contribution?'

'I do feel guilty, actually,' said Nathan. 'Like, a lot.'

Daniel looked both surprised and slightly put out. Katherine looked smug.

'Of course he feels guilty,' said Katherine.

'Why?' Daniel turned to Nathan, the hand once again on the shoulder and once again causing Nathan distress. 'Why feel guilty, man?'

It seemed the outer edges of the beer label came away more easily than the main body, meaning Nathan now had a tattered mess of a label that wouldn't shift any further. He wondered if he could get away with leaving the room and coming back when they'd moved on to another subject.

'He feels guilty,' said Katherine, 'because of what he tried to do.'

'But that's not something to feel guilty about,' said Daniel, who seemed to be speaking in the abstract rather than addressing anyone directly.

'I'm not saying he *should* feel guilty,' said Katherine. 'I'm just saying that it's inevitable he *does*, that's all. Stop saying really obvious things and trying to pass them off as profound insights.'

'I do feel guilty,' said Nathan. 'I basically did quite a shitty thing and made them worry. They worry a lot and I've made them worry more.'

'But you weren't well, right?' said Daniel. 'I mean, it was a symptom, wasn't it? You weren't yourself. You can't feel guilty if you weren't yourself.'

'I sort of was myself,' said Nathan. 'I'm not really meant to absolve myself by just saying I wasn't myself.'

'What do you mean you're not meant to?' said Katherine.

'It's not part of my treatment,' said Nathan. 'I'm supposed to confront rather than deny.'

Katherine was studying him intently, leaning forward in her chair, blinking in the sting of her own cigarette smoke. Nathan rolled another cigarette so as to have something to look at.

'Did you have ECT?' said Katherine. 'I've heard they still do that.'

'Katherine,' said Daniel. 'For fuck's sake.'

'What?' said Katherine.

'It's fine,' said Nathan. 'It's OK. No, they didn't give me ECT. It was all just pretty much talking.'

W as it, or was it not, sexy and more than a bit thrilling to be fancied by someone who had tried to kill themselves? The question, which Katherine would have been quick to admit was not the most morally on-target she could have come up with, had become one of those stubborn mind-events that resist dismissal until satisfactorily answered. There were other questions too, of course, many of which circled around Daniel, but these were not exactly fun to consider, whereas the whole area of Nathan's attractiveness with reference to his recently very much increased air of unpredictability and the general complexity of risk versus charm and tragedy versus thrill versus pity was exactly, it seemed, where her head wanted to be after a couple of beers and what she saw as an absolutely stellar effort on her part to get this gathering off the ground, because when she'd walked in it had felt like a fucking wake, and she'd had to deploy maximum social weaponry just to correct whatever it was that Daniel had done to the atmosphere.

Nathan looked both well and not-well, a combination that Katherine found quite effective. Just as she liked Keith's weird irises and his gloomy inferences about his smacked-out past, so she found Nathan's scarred physical bulk coupled with his awkward, quiet bashfulness rather appealing. It had all been there before, of course, but a year ago the juxtaposition had felt awkward, whereas now it was fascinating. He seemed, she thought, both broken and fixed, as if he were *on the other side* of something, as people said, yet unsullied by the usual piousness that Katherine found so often accompanied the aftermath of such experiences. She couldn't even begin to tot up all the women in the office capable of the most clichéd of homilies which, thanks to their cheap therapy and off-the-peg religious catharses, they genuinely believed were spiritual and emotional gold. It made her rather queasy, and more than a little offended, all these people, *better now*, cured or enlightened in whatever way happened to suit, tottering round looking down on everyone else just because they hadn't been *fortunate* enough to have their husband cheat on them or become seriously ill or see God through a miasma of toilet products. It was sickening, but there was none of that with Nathan.

She wanted, of course, to know everything. What had happened; what he'd done; why; what treatment he'd had; what he was going to do now; how he felt. But of course Daniel, working as always on the principle that anything difficult was best left unsaid, was in conversation shut-down mode. He really was the boring father of the group at times, Katherine thought, which admittedly might have been quite sexy on a good day with the wind behind him, unless of course you'd actually slept with Daniel, in which case a lot of the oomph went out of the fantasy. Had he always been this tense? Basically, yes. Had Katherine often enjoyed cranking the tension a little higher? Absolutely.

'So what are we eating?' she asked Daniel. She had no desire to eat, of course. The thought of eating in front of them just now seemed oddly approximate to them all getting naked together, but she strongly suspected that Daniel would either not have prepared anything or, if he had, that it would be awful or, even better, that it would have every hope of being good but would then be scuppered by her getting him all flustered.

'Eating?' said Daniel.

'Yeah,' she said. 'As in, you know, food.'

'Right,' said Daniel.

The trick, she thought, was to make Daniel feel horribly guilty and inadequate without pushing him so far that he actually presented them with a meal, because then she'd have to either not eat it (which might, now that she thought about it, be quite funny) or eat it and then schedule a trip to the toilet.

'You have got some food, Daniel?'

'Well, you know. Nibbles.'

'Nibbles?'

'Yes, Katherine. Fucking nibbles.'

'I'm fine with nibbles, actually,' said Nathan.

Katherine held up her index and middle finger, the stub of her cigarette smoking furiously between them. 'Now Nathan,' she said. 'One thing we're going to have to be clear on. You're going to have to stop being so nice to Daniel.'

Daniel tipped some cylindrical shapes of reconstituted potato into a salad bowl, stuffed a handful into his mouth, and then ambled around the kitchen enjoying a brief mental image of twisting a corkscrew into Katherine's head and uncorking her brain, at which point he realised he'd somehow managed to locate a corkscrew and uncork a bottle of red without any conscious engagement whatsoever. This was how murder happened, he thought, looking at the open bottle. There you were, ambling around your kitchen looking for something, and the next thing you knew an hour had vanished from your life and you'd fashioned a necklace from the ears of the dead.

He took a swig of the red. It felt good to mix his drinks. He felt in his pocket for the comforting bulge of foil-wrapped skunk. At what point in the evening was it appropriate to mention it? Now?

'Dude,' he said, ambling back into the dining room and putting the drinks on the table. 'I got you a present.'

'Oh?' said Nathan.

Daniel fished in his pocket and, not without considerable pride, brought out the little foil-wrapped parcel, presenting it to Nathan flat on his palm, the way you might offer a horse an apple. He did a mini mock-operatic song, too, which he felt added both gravitas and amusing self-awareness to the whole slightly complicated moment. He tried not to beam; then, when Nathan made a diagonal with his mouth, tried not to falter.

'Oh,' said Nathan. 'Is that . . .'

'It's really good,' said Daniel. 'I figured it might have been a while.'

'It has,' said Nathan. 'And I'm afraid it's going to be a while longer, too.'

'Oh,' said Daniel. He was still holding his hand out. Already his brain was entering its emergency embarrassment-limitation mode, whereby it instructed him to talk loudly, laugh inappropriately and go slightly floppy as if to demonstrate how literally relaxed he was. 'Well, I mean, that's cool, man, you know? We can crack it out later, or . . .'

'No,' said Nathan, surprisingly firmly. 'I mean it's going to be forever. Like, I can't do that anymore.'

'Right,' said Daniel, nodding. 'Yeah, I mean, of course, like . . .'

'Moron,' said Katherine happily.

'It's just . . .' Nathan looked genuinely uncomfortable, which was making Daniel uncomfortable, which was in turn making the crisis control systems in his head go to ever further lengths to make him look comfortable. By now he'd almost completely lost muscle tone. He draped himself casually over the back of a chair; ran his hand through his hair; slipped off the back of the chair; caught himself; stretched and yawned.

'Totally cool,' he said. 'Totally, totally cool.'

'But you go ahead,' said Nathan. 'It's fine.'

'Yeah, I might do that,' said Daniel, who was beginning to feel distinctly panicked. 'I mean, it's not something I do often, but . . .'

Nathan nodded. Inside Daniel's mind, a vast drug-related difference engine was struggling to compute. His entire coping mechanism for the evening had, quite obviously, been to get wasted. Indeed, his entire coping mechanism for the past week had in many ways centred on this. He looked at his watch. It was early: horribly, terrifyingly early. What in God's name were they supposed to do now? Talk to each other? About what? He was standing, he thought, on the cusp of an existential slurry pit. He sank into his chair and wondered what the best way out of it was. His solution was both predictable and, perhaps as a direct result of its predictability, reassuring: he should carry on as normal.

'Yeah,' he said, unwrapping the little parcel, 'I might just have a quick one, you know. How about you, Katherine?'

'Probably not,' she said. 'But don't let us stop you.'

Having never 'opened up', as the saying went, to anyone before the evening he'd perhaps ill-advisedly opened up to Katherine, Nathan had not only never known how it felt to tell someone something honest and secret about yourself, he had also, perhaps more crucially, never known how it felt to re-encounter the person with whom you'd had that particular conversation in the first place. It was, he thought, rather like the sensation of removing an old plaster from your fingertip. Every time Katherine looked at him it was like touching something afresh with that recently injured finger, always wondering how far it had really healed, for how long the wound might reasonably be expected to hold, yet also marvelling at how real and fragile every touch now was.

He was zoning in and out because sometimes he had to check in with himself to see how things were going. He kept palpating his own more sensitive areas, testing for pain. In the time he'd been absent Daniel had begun rolling a joint using Nathan's tobacco and papers, and Katherine had obviously asked about Daniel's job because Daniel was now explaining it in a way that suggested he was proud of it yet also used to defending it.

'But what are they researching?' Katherine was saying. 'I mean, what do they do?'

'Sustainable food sources, essentially,' said Daniel, gumming together several Rizlas in a way that reminded Nathan of his father trying to undo his jacket: a man embarrassingly outdone by seemingly basic forces. Briefly, Nathan felt a flare-up of shame at exactly how much of an idiot he wanted Daniel to look.

'Meaning what?'

Sometimes, and this was one of those times, Katherine looked Nathan's way when addressing a question or a statement to Daniel, giving a sense of complicity that, like much of what Katherine did, thrilled and discomfited in equal measure.

'Meaning exactly what it says,' Daniel was saying, mashing the papers together with the edge of his fist, then peeling them gently away from the table, to which they had adhered, and finding that, in all their enthusiasm for the surface of the table, they had in fact failed to adhere to each other. 'Food that's sustainable. What papers are these, Nathan?'

'As in what?' said Katherine.

'Rizla,' said Nathan, hurriedly and clumsily unpeeling his gaze from the side of Katherine's face.

'As in it won't run out,' said Daniel, appearing not to notice. 'Must be a bad batch.'

'How can food run out?' said Katherine.

'Well, by us over-eating and over-farming and over-fishing and blah blah blah.'

'Right,' said Katherine. 'And?'

'"And"? What do you mean "*and*"?'

'I mean *and what*. So what? One day all our food will run out and we'll . . . I don't know, eat something else, no? I mean, won't we all be living on some sort of powdered food by then anyway? Or, like, capsules of calories or vitamin injections or apples that fucking self-replicate in the fruit bowl?'

'Well, not really, no,' said Daniel, who had succeeded in joining the rolling papers through sheer force of saliva alone and was now breaking off bits of grass and dropping the crumbs into the crease, an operation somewhat hampered by the stickiness of his fingers. 'The point is . . .'

'Do you want me to . . . ?' said Nathan, pointing towards the mess Daniel was making on the table, his delight in Daniel's inability to perform the task no doubt both obvious and excessive.

'So everyone would *starve*? Is that what you're saying?' said Katherine.

252

'Er, well, worst-case scenario, yes. But it's also about developing food sources and farming techniques that don't harm the ecosystem, and about creating crops that can withstand a period of drought and . . . You know, etcetera etcetera.' Daniel pushed his efforts at construction along the table towards Nathan. 'Lifesaver. No idea what's up with those papers.'

Katherine nodded, apparently thinking this over. 'It's just all so far off,' she said. 'I mean, I *want* to care. I really do, but . . .'

She looked away, shrugged slightly.

'But what?' said Daniel.

Katherine shot Nathan another look which was difficult to decode. Nathan stole a glance at his own fingers as they began rolling a ruinously strong joint, marvelling at his own capacity for guiltlessness.

'I don't know,' said Katherine. 'Forget it.'

'No,' said Daniel. 'What stops you?'

Neither of them was looking at Nathan at this point, although Nathan, out of a combination of politeness and discomfort, was looking at them. He'd also finished rolling the joint, which Daniel took back and lit.

'I stop me,' said Katherine. She shook her head. 'How did we get on to this? It's totally tedious.'

'Well sorry if my job *bores* you, Katherine.' Daniel hauled deeply on the joint. 'I . . . Oh fuck.'

He paused for a moment to cough. Nathan took a deep breath and didn't smile, then shaped his face into exactly the simulation of concern he'd seen, he now realised, so many times on the face of his mother, noting the ease with which it came to him, and how unpleasant that ease made him feel.

'Oh,' said Daniel. 'This . . . this is quite strong actually. Whoof.' He flopped back in his chair and widened his eyes as if the lids were suddenly getting in his way.

Katherine's phone rang. She looked at it, swore, dropped it face down on the table, then clearly thought twice and picked it up.

'Where's your bathroom?' she said.

Daniel pointed and she marched off, answering on the way, leaving Nathan smiling awkwardly at Daniel, trying to forget the muscular flicker he'd seen in Katherine's face as she looked to see who was calling.

What do you want?' said Katherine, sitting on the toilet and speaking into her mobile in a barking whisper. 'I'm busy. I can't talk.'

'Where are you?' said Keith. 'What are you doing?'

'That's none of your business. What do you want?'

'Look, babes. All due respect, OK? But you're carrying our child.'

'Don't say that. Are you drunk?'

'I feel like I'm seeing the world, like, what's the word, *afresh*, you know?' He paused. 'I am a bit drunk, yes.'

'Oh God.'

'You know I feel like sometimes you don't take me seriously.'

'Whatever gave you that impression?'

'Well it's just a sort of niggling feeling that you don't really . . .'

Katherine leaned back and looked at the ceiling a moment.

'What do you want?' she said.

'I've been thinking.'

'That can only be very bad news.'

'I was at home. You know. Up to the usual. Watching a bit of television. And I was watching the news, right? You know, the national stuff, like what's going on and everything.'

'Is that what the news is? I had no idea.'

254

'And I was looking at all the cows, you know, and I was thinking, like, what if we can all catch this? Like they're saying? What if this is, like, it?'

'What if what's it?'

'This. This whatever it is. This thing. What if this is the end of civilisation?'

Katherine rested her forehead on her hand.

'It's just a bunch of cows, Keith,' she said.

'And sheep now,' said Keith with a note of panic. 'It's sheep now too. What if we're next?'

Katherine didn't have a pithy response for this, so she stayed quiet and distracted herself by examining Daniel's bathroom. Either he'd cleaned up his act since they'd lived together, she thought, or Angelica was some sort of domestic powerhouse.

'And then I thought, what am I doing? What am I doing here? What are any of us doing here? What's the point?'

'I don't know,' said Katherine, still taking in the surface glint and atmospheric gloss of a room she was now very tempted to defile in some unspeakable way. 'What is the point?'

'And I was like, look at you, Keith. Look at yourself. There you are on your sofa. Sitting there. Watching the telly. With your feet up. And your shirt undone. Holding a beer. Looking, OK, maybe not so bad considering, but also not great. Because I'm not blind, right? I can see myself. Sitting there. Watching the telly. With my rubber band on my wrist in case, you know, any of the newsreaders happens to be foxy. And I said look at you, Keith. Look at you. Sitting there. Watching telly. What's the point? What do you want? Is this where you want to be in five years? In ten years? Sitting there? Watching telly?'

'That's . . . I can see how that must have been quite a realisation,' Katherine said diplomatically. 'But I have to go now.'

'No. Hear me out, OK? Just hear me out. Because I realised . . . I realised that, no, this is not where I want to be in ten years. I . . . Where I want to be in ten years is sitting there, watching telly, *with my family*. You see?'

Katherine didn't really know where to begin, and so chose not to try.

'I don't want to die alone, baby,' said Keith. 'I don't want to go gently into the whatever with people saying, Oh, look at him, look at Keith, what did he do? Nothing. He just sat there . . .'

'Watching telly.'

'Exactly! Exactly! I knew you'd understand. Oh Katie-babes . . .'

'Katherine.'

'Will you be mine?'

'What?'

'Will you be mine? To have and to hold? Until the end of time, or until we all die of this terrible cow thing, whatever comes first. I've been so stupid. I love you. You're having our baby. I know it seems crazy, bringing a child into a world like this, but you see, this is what I was thinking. What if that's why we're here? What if it's our responsibility to carry on civilisation? What if that's us, Kate?'

'Katherine.'

'What if *this is it*? The big one. The whopper. And it's shit or walk, motherfucker. Shit. Or. Walk. I'm asking you, babes. Are we gonna walk? Are we? Or are we gonna . . .'

'Shit?'

'Exactly. My God, you get me, princess. You really get me. No one gets me like you get me, you know?'

'What about Claire Demoines? She seems to get you.'

'Oh, Claire. Claire. Whatever. She's nothing. Don't you see? All my life, I've . . . I've . . . I don't know what I've done, actually. I really don't know. But I . . . I saw us, you know? I saw us in the future. Sitting right here. With our baby.'

He went quiet, then exhaled at length. Katherine's eyes finished their tour of the room and ended up fixed on the off-white linoleum and the pointless horseshoe of carpet around the toilet. Somewhere, in the midst of everything, Keith had become so irrelevant that she was no longer even interested in hurting him.

'Keith,' she said gently.

'Yes babes.'

'Keith. I'm not going to keep the baby. I'm sorry, but I've decided, and that's the way it is.'

There was a long silence, and then Keith said, 'You don't mean that though, princess. It's just the hormones.'

'No Keith,' said Katherine. 'I mean it. It's not what I want.'

'But . . .' Katherine could practically hear the wobble in Keith's lower lip, the triumph of independent thought now tragically vanquished. 'But . . .'

'Come on Keith,' said Katherine. 'Let's be practical.'

'You could give it to me,' said Keith. 'I'd take care of it, I swear.'

'I know that,' said Katherine. 'But I'd still have to have it, wouldn't I?'

'I know what you think,' said Keith. 'I know what you think of me. I know I haven't done everything right. But I thought about the baby and it made everything different. Doesn't it make everything different?'

'No,' said Katherine. 'It doesn't. Sorry.'

'OK,' he said.

'Bye Keith.'

She hung up; switched off her phone. She sat for a few minutes, not so much thinking as allowing her thoughts to end. Then she stood up and washed her hands and went back outside, where she found that once again Daniel seemed to have steered all interaction into a place of glacial politesse. It was, she thought, more like old times than even the old times had been.

Daniel had left three-quarters of the joint in the ashtray, clearly having reached his limit before even really getting started. She picked it up and lit it, dragging deeply, listening to the satisfying crackle as it burned.

'Right,' she said. 'Let's get this fucking party off the ground. Who's for another drink?'

'I'm fine,' said Nathan.

'No you're not,' said Katherine.

'Yes he is,' said Daniel.

'Oh fuck off,' snapped Katherine. 'Let's make it a rule. No one's fine. None of us are fine. We all need another drink.'

She reached for the wine bottle and sloshed the dregs into her glass.

'Is, er, is everything all right?' said Daniel, smirking slightly, the *er* obviously for sardonic effect.

'Peachy,' said Katherine through her wine glass. She was fucked if she was going to be not–all right in the face of Daniel's juggernaut of all-rightness.

Now Daniel's mobile, which he'd left lying on the table in front of him, started to vibrate. A photo of some piteous little blonde flashed onto the screen, and beneath it her name: Angelica. Daniel pounced but was too late. Katherine had swept up the phone and pressed it to her ear.

'Katherine don't,' said Daniel.

'Hello?' purred Katherine. 'Daniel's phone.'

'I . . . Oh . . . Is that . . . Who's that?'

Katherine could hear the sound of a muffled car engine, the hushed swoosh of motorway traffic. The voice sounded pretty and out of its depth. Katherine thought of the spotless bathroom; the his-and-hers towels. Daniel was out of his seat and standing over her, threatening force he would never actually use. She blinked at him several times, then passed him the phone with ostentatious care.

'It's for you,' she said.

He took it with a withering look to which she could only respond with laughter and then walked quickly upstairs, talking as he went.

'I . . . no, no . . . it's no one. I'll tell you all about it. Where are you?'

Katherine took a long, deep breath and reached up to knead the muscles in her neck. Nathan was eyeing her in a manner that was becoming predictable.

'Well hello there,' she said, re-lighting the joint. 'Come here often?'

Marching up the stairs with his phone, breathless and on the verge of a spin-out that might have been containable were he still seated but which, in light of his body's recalcitrant reaction to the sudden mix of adrenaline and exertion, now seemed as if it would end where so many spin-outs of the past had ended – on the floor, shallow-breathed, seeing nothing but a thick blizzard of white light where once there had been a room – Daniel managed to hold it together despite feeling a very strong sense of excitement and release at the prospect of not holding it together.

'Hello?' Angelica was saying on the other end of the phone. 'Hello? Daniel? Who was that? Are you there?'

'I'm just . . . I'm . . . I'm just going upstairs,' Daniel managed to wheeze as he careened into the bedroom and flopped heavily onto the bed, bunching a corner of pillow into his fist in a hopeless attempt to slow everything down. 'Hold on.'

He was furious, and furiously stoned. How fucking typical of Katherine, he thought, just to *emerge* out of the stratosphere and start fucking up his life for no other reason than the fact that she didn't like her own life and so resented anyone – especially him – who liked theirs. She'd never wanted him to be happy. His unhappiness had always been more important to her than her own happiness. It was *integral* to her happiness, in many ways. Her perspective was the exact opposite of all those couples Daniel loathed who came round and asked how he and Angelica *were*, collectively, as a unit, as if one couldn't possibly experience an emotion not shared by the other. For Katherine, happiness was a finite resource. They could never both be happy. One of them had to selflessly offer their happiness, like a kidney donor, to the other. Now, even though they were apart, she was still leeching away at what he had; still behaving like a four-year-old and embarrassing him in public and determinedly wrecking anything and everything that fell within her reach but wasn't hers. He was going to deal with Angelica, he thought, heaving himself over on the bed and staring upwards at the ceiling, trying and failing to shake the disconcerting sensation that he'd left half his face stuck to the pillow, and then go downstairs and absolutely *unload* on Katherine, and it was going to be fantastic, because this time, perhaps as never before, he had her bang to rights. There could be no moral evasion. Picking up his phone was absolutely wrong, and she was going to have to apologise, and her apology would be glorious and he would milk it dry.

'Daniel?' said Angelica. 'Daniel?'

He was also angry with Angelica. Because where was Angelica? *Where*, he thought loudly, was Angelica? Gadding around the country? With *Sebastian?* Defending a bunch of *cows?* Perhaps, he thought, he should give her a piece of whatever was left of his mind after he'd given Katherine a piece of his mind. Except, of course, that with Angelica there would be so much more to lose. With Katherine, he could now get as angry as he liked and there would essentially be very few consequences. The one thing she'd always held over him – that she'd leave him before he summoned the courage to leave her – was now little more than an uncomfortable memory. It was wonderful, in a way, to see her again, to have this opportunity to vent spleen free from fear of fallout. Indeed, he'd actually imagined just such an opportunity many times, both after he and Katherine had split up and, if he was honest, before.

But that was not the case with Angelica. With Angelica, he thought, there was still much to lose. The situation was unsafe. It would be rash to be entirely himself.

'Hello,' he said.

'Daniel,' said Angelica. 'What's going on? Where are you?'

'Where are you?'

'I'm on my way home. Where are you?'

'I'm . . .' He wondered if he should lie, but it occurred to him that Angelica hadn't actually said how far away she was, meaning she could walk in the front door any minute and catch him in the midst of saying he was out. 'I'm at home.'

'Well who answered your phone then?'

'Katherine,' he said.

There was a moment's silence while Angelica processed this; a moment during which Daniel felt another little swell of excitement. *Take that*, he felt like saying. It lasted approximately a second, however, because as soon as Angelica gathered a breath and spoke, he knew exactly how hurt she was, and how stupid it was to have caused that hurt.

'Oh,' she said. 'I . . .'

Angelica wasn't angry, Daniel thought with a sinking feeling. How could he be angry if she wasn't angry? He felt suddenly deflated and pathetic, and even more angry with Katherine.

'It's not what you think,' said Daniel, slightly hopelessly. 'I mean, Nathan's here too.'

'Who's Nathan?'

'Our friend, you know, from before.'

'You and Katherine's friend.'

'Yeah. An old friend.'

'Who else is there?'

'No one.'

'So, it's the three of you.'

'Yeah.'

'Just sitting around.'

'Pretty much, yeah.'

'You and Katherine. And Nathan.'

'Yeah, but that makes it sound like . . .'

'And was this some sort of spontaneous thing, or has it been arranged for a while?'

'A few days, really,' said Daniel. 'I was going to tell you.'

'You were going to tell me and then something stopped you?'

'No. I was going to tell you and then . . .'

He broke off, unable to determine exactly why he hadn't told her, or more specifically, to what extent his reasons for not telling her would, if expressed, utterly undermine what was left of his standing.

'Is there something going on?' said Angelica, her voice timid. 'Because if there is you should just tell me.'

Daniel sat up on the bed. 'There's nothing going on,' he said, and it was only in saying it that he realised it was true. 'There is really, honestly, nothing going on.'

'Then why would you . . .'

'Nathan tried to kill himself,' said Daniel. He hadn't been intending to say it. He felt cornered. It was said, although he could barely bring himself to admit it, in defence.

'Oh God,' said Angelica. 'I'm so sorry. When? Recently?'

Daniel took a moment to answer. Through the fog of the weed; his anger; his guilt, the dim thought flickered in his mind that he was doing something that it would take a considerable amount of circuitous and dishonest thinking to defend even to himself.

'A while ago,' he said. 'We didn't know at the time. We thought he'd gone off somewhere. He got back in touch and asked to see us.'

'Oh baby,' said Angelica. 'How does he seem now?'

'Well . . .' said Daniel. 'I don't know really.'

'And what about you? How are you? It must be such a difficult thing to try and process.'

'Um . . . Yeah,' said Daniel. 'It's . . .' Was he going to say it? He was, he thought. He actually was. 'It's been kind of hard to take in.'

'I'm so sorry,' said Angelica. 'That's awful. But I think it's really amazing you haven't backed off from it. You know? Like, a lot of people would have tried to distance themselves, but you've got him straight round to the house, and you've obviously set aside so much shit with Katherine so the two of you can help him. I'm so proud of you. I'm really sorry I misunderstood.'

'It's . . . That's OK,' said Daniel. 'I'm sorry I didn't tell you.'

'It's fine,' said Angelica. 'Honestly. I understand. Look, I'll be home soon, OK? But if you guys still need some space . . .'

'No, no,' said Daniel. 'It's fine. Honestly. Are you OK? I love you.'

'I'm fine,' she said. 'I love you too and I've missed you.'

'I've missed you too,' said Daniel, realising as he said it that he had.

'See you in a bit,' said Angelica.

'Yeah,' said Daniel.

He put his phone on the duvet beside him and rubbed his temples. The adrenaline had barged aside most of the effects of the joint, and now he felt only a kind of dull fatigue. He was, he thought, loading himself down. Everything he said, everything he thought, was just another brick in the ever-expanding hod of lies and shortcomings and fears that he carried around daily, minute by minute, and continually tried to pass on to someone else, anyone else, who looked like they might be stupid enough to take it. Or, no, he thought, that wasn't right. Not stupid. Kind. *Kind* enough to take it. Angelica wasn't stupid, she was kind, and the kinder she was, the less he felt he deserved her, and the less he felt he deserved her the more he imposed on her kindness, hoping all the while that it would buckle and fail and prove him right about God alone knew what.

He stood slowly from the bed, suddenly very unwilling to go downstairs and face Nathan, whose suffering he had now mortgaged to offset his own triangulations and mistakes; the thought of sitting next to whom now filled him with exactly the same self-loathing he'd once felt when wriggling out of Katherine's hi-there grip in order to step into the shower and wash away the hour-old guilt of fucking Angelica.

He did not, he thought, deserve kindness.

'That's it,' snapped Katherine. 'Go ahead and stare.'

Nathan felt a sharp lurch somewhere between his heart and his throat. He hadn't been aware of staring, but now that Katherine was staring back he realised his eyes had settled into an idle state pointed directly at her face.

'I . . . Sorry,' he said. 'I was miles away.'

'Were you now?' said Katherine.

'Yeah, just, you know.' He twirled a finger against the side of his head. 'Thoughts.'

Katherine sucked on the joint and studied Nathan through the blue-tinged smoke, narrowing her eyes either because she was affecting some form of expression or because the smoke was irritating them, Nathan couldn't tell.

'I hate them,' she said. 'Don't you?'

'What?'

'Thoughts. Better just not to have them, really, isn't it?'

'They're unavoidable,' said Nathan. 'But you don't have to let them linger.'

She curled her lip. 'Teach you that in therapy, did they?'

He nodded, then looked at the tabletop.

'Did that hurt?' said Katherine, using the exact tone of voice Nathan remembered being used by the doctor who'd first examined him that night, tapping bits of his legs and arms, checking for sensation. *Does that hurt? Can you feel that?* In that situation pain was good, the doctor had explained. It meant there was no nerve damage. His therapist would have said the pain in this situation was a good sign too, but Nathan was unconvinced.

'I'll live,' said Nathan.

'He hates me, doesn't he?' said Katherine, no longer sneering.

'Who?'

'Daniel.'

'No,' said Nathan. 'I don't think so.'

'I know what you're thinking,' said Katherine.

'What am I thinking?' said Nathan.

'You're thinking, What does it matter? What does it matter if he hates me or not?'

Nathan shrugged.

'But it does,' said Katherine. 'It matters.'

'OK,' said Nathan.

There was a catch in her voice, and Nathan felt it reflected in his own face. A little hiccup on the 'a' of *matters*; a little leap in the top of his cheek in response, and then the tiniest of smiles tugging at one corner of Katherine's mouth in response to that. He realised again that she had not called him. She'd listened to his message, and she'd called Daniel. How stupid, he thought, to have come here, making a

265

fool of himself, just so they could interpose him between them like they always had.

'Do you think that was wrong of me?' said Katherine.

'What?'

'Picking up his phone. Do you think that was bad?'

'I honestly don't know,' said Nathan. 'I'm sure it'll be fine.'

'You're sure, are you? You're absolutely sure it will be fine?'

'No.'

She rolled her eyes. *Put your fucking mask back on*, Nathan heard her saying in his head. He felt as if someone had just edged his chair off a cliff.

'I don't know why I'm asking you, anyway,' said Katherine, looking away, apparently addressing herself.

Nathan rolled a cigarette, keeping his eyes on his fingers. Katherine's attention, which as recently as five minutes ago he'd been going out of his way to attract and maintain, now felt like a thick woollen sweater in dense summer heat. He decided not to answer for fear of, if not exactly revealing his discomfort, which must have been obvious, then at least exacerbating its effects. He concentrated on making a perfect cigarette: free from creases and excess spit. He wanted another beer but didn't entirely want the effects of another beer. He bounced his heel gently on the floor, easing the urge to stand up and walk away. When what seemed like several minutes had passed and Katherine hadn't said anything further he decided to risk a glance in her direction. When he raised his head he found his gaze returned, not merely in the sense that Katherine was looking at him at the same moment as he chose to look at her, but also in the sense that the tone of the gaze seemed similar, familiar somehow, sad in the same way, as if expressing a desire to escape to and from all the same places.

'Sorry,' said Katherine.

'That's OK,' said Nathan.

'Do you hate me too, now?' she said. There was no vulnerability in her voice, he noted, just a kind of deadened resolve.

'No,' said Nathan.

Her smile, Nathan thought as he watched her lips shape it, was ghostly: something dead returning to the place it had once lived.

'No,' she said. 'You wouldn't, would you?'

Bludgeoned by her conversation with Keith, and, although she would never admit it, already regretting her interference in Daniel's affairs, Katherine was beginning to wonder if she had, for the entirety of this evening and for many of the days that led up to it, been thinking all the wrong things. Not half an hour ago she'd been sitting in this exact same chair musing on Nathan's attractiveness in the face of the extent to which he was damaged and wondering if she could find a way to be attracted to him since he was so obviously attracted to her. Now it struck her that the real question was in fact one she had asked herself not so very long ago, in Malta, when she'd sat on the promenade and stared out at that odd, crouching city, and considered what a burden it was to be loved, to be offered this small and vulnerable emotion in need of nurture. What she should have been asking herself, she thought, was not whether she was attracted to anyone, or whether they hated her, but whether, at this stage in her life, she wanted anyone to be attracted to her at all. Because nice as it ought to have been to feel that she was wanted, perhaps even loved, it didn't seem to bring her any happiness, and seemed to bring out in her little more than the perverse desire to do damage, which was followed in turn by exactly the kind of regret she delighted in telling people she never felt.

She leaned forward and flicked her fingernail against the rim of her wine glass, sending a single, chiming note out into the room.

'Time, gentlemen,' she said.

Nathan frowned.

'What time is it?' he said.

She looked at her watch and sighed. 'Not nearly as late as it feels.'

'Oh,' said Nathan.

'No offence,' said Katherine. 'But I think I'm sort of realising that I don't want to be here.'

She noted his obvious disappointment, but didn't allow her thoughts about it to linger.

'Were we always like this?' she said.

'Who? You and me?'

'Me and Daniel.'

'Oh.' He leaned back in his chair, pursed his lips and tapped them with his thumb. 'In what way?'

'Christ,' she said. 'You certainly weren't always like this, I'll say that much.'

'Like what?'

'Like captain fucking non-committal, that's what. In all the time I've known you I can't remember you ever asking me what I meant, do you know that? We used to talk for hours. We used to get completely off our faces and talk until we passed out and neither of us would make any fucking sense at all but I don't recall you asking me what I meant. You know what I mean. Stop asking what I mean.'

He nodded. 'Yeah,' he said, his tone ripe with you-asked-for-it. 'You were always like this.'

'I wanted you to say no,' she said.

'I toyed with the idea of saying I didn't really remember,' said Nathan. 'But you wouldn't have let me get away with it.'

If it hadn't been for the certain knowledge that Nathan would have comforted her, and that his comfort would have greatly confused everything, Katherine felt fairly sure she would have cried. Instead she went to the fridge and pulled out two beers, which she uncapped on the lip of Daniel's worktop with a decisive crack, leaving two neat crescents in her wake.

'No,' she said, sitting back down. 'I wouldn't have let you get away with that.' She slid Nathan's beer across the table with enough force to make him scramble to catch it before it dropped into his lap. 'Holy fucking Christ,' she said, pulling out the neighbouring chair and resting her feet on it, pausing for a second to admire her legs with some degree of satisfaction before the thought of swollen ankles and varicose veins forced her to move on. 'Why did you ever come and visit us?'

Nathan laughed. 'It wasn't that bad,' he said.

'Bollocks,' said Katherine.

'If you want to know the truth,' said Nathan, apparently addressing his beer bottle, 'I was grateful to be invited. No one else ever asked me to their house that I can remember, and they certainly never cooked me dinner. They came round to buy or sell drugs; talked shit to me at parties or whatever, but they didn't actually have me round to dinner.'

'Well,' said Katherine. 'If we'd known that, we wouldn't have asked you either.'

Nathan laughed. 'Precisely why I didn't tell you.'

Katherine plugged her smirk with her beer bottle, relieved at being able to express herself through her preferred medium of barbed cynicism and apparent flippancy. God save us, she thought, from the deep and meaningful.

'It's like old times, isn't it?' she said. 'You and me talking shit, you-know-who stoned out of his brain in the bedroom.'

'Is that how you saw it? You and me talking shit?'

Katherine gave him the look she tended to use as the facial equivalent of a shot across the bows.

'Yes,' she said. 'That's how I saw it, and that's how I liked it.'

Nathan raised a hand in acceptance, then was quiet a moment, then seemed to take a breath and summon a degree of resolve that, in suggesting as it did all manner of possible things he might have been about to say, immediately lowered the temperature in Katherine's spine to approximately that of her beer bottle.

'Look . . .' he said. 'I just wanted to say . . .'

She levelled two fingers at him, drawing a bead on the space between his eyes.

'Uh uh,' she said, shaking her head. 'No you don't.'

He stopped. 'Maybe it's a bit early in the evening.'

'It's a lot early in the evening,' she said, allowing herself to breathe again. 'Zip it.'

He nodded. Katherine sat back and let the silence hang. She heard Daniel's footsteps on the stairs and hoped he was angry. Let him come down and insult her, she thought. She was ready. Let him come down and start a fucking fight.

Daniel came down the stairs at a considerably slower pace than he'd gone up them. This was partly because he was tired, partly because he didn't really want to get to the bottom (would it be possible, he wondered, to take the stairs at such a lethargic pace that everyone would have left by the time he got to the ground floor?) and partly because, in the small collection of seconds that had elapsed while he was standing up from the bed and walking to the top of the stairs, he had become confused about his own emotional state and the way he was going to handle whatever conversation or confrontation might be waiting for him in the dining room. He considered, briefly, turning around and going back up to bed, but his feet had already sounded out on the bare wooden steps and he felt certain that

Katherine would have heard him coming and so would immediately know if he'd run into his old friend cowardice on the stairs and turned back, so that when he did finally go downstairs she'd sense blood in the water and go in for the kill. What he needed to do, he thought, was to come down the stairs slowly enough to allow him to rehearse his opening line, which he should really have rehearsed while he was still in the bedroom, but no sense, he thought, crying over spilt milk, yet also loudly enough to give the message that, although he was coming down the stairs slowly, this was in fact nothing to do with feeling tentative and more to do with the fact that he was trying to *hold himself back*, so wild and untamed was his rage.

Which would have been fine, had his rage actually been wild and untamed. As it was, the only thing that could actually have been considered wild and untamed was his deep-seated fear that, by not being sufficiently angry at the fact he had been made a fool of (a shortcoming he attributed to being stoned), he was being disgracefully weak and pathetic, although thankfully the thought of Katherine thinking he was weak and pathetic did make him rather angry, meaning he had to somehow hold on to the sense of his own inadequacy in order to become angry enough to show just how adequate he really was.

Thunk, thunk, thunk. He imagined his tread on the stairs booming out into the dining room below, chilling Katherine's blood as she braced herself for a flaying.

The best thing, he thought, would be to undercut it. That would throw her. She'd hear the anger in his footsteps, brace herself, and then he'd pull the old switcheroo on her by sitting down all calmly and explaining to her in his gentlest tones that what she'd done with the phone was simply not acceptable. *That* way, he thought, he'd have the satisfaction of implied anger as well as the even greater satisfaction of having out-matured Katherine. Because he was, these days, much more mature. Look at what an honest and open conversation he'd just had with Angelica. Look at the fact, he thought, that he even *had* Angelica. What, or who, did Katherine have? Nothing. No one.

Why was he angry with her again? The phone. Of course. Focus, Daniel, focus. Two more steps. *Thunk*. Here comes trouble. *Thunk*.

'Watch out,' said Katherine's voice from the dining room as he rounded the corner. 'Jake the fucking Peg's coming down the stairs.'

She had her back to him: her feet up on the table, a beer in her hand, and what was left of the joint between her fingers. Nathan did not appear to have moved.

Daniel came to a halt just inside the perimeter of the dining room and took two seconds to marshal massive and contradictory forces inside himself.

'Right,' he said, holding up one finger.

'Here he goes,' said Katherine, not even turning round.

'OK,' said Daniel. 'Now . . .'

'Always has to do a lot of throat-clearing,' said Katherine, presumably addressing Nathan. 'He makes, like, sixteen preparatory statements and then forgets what he wanted to say.'

'OK, look,' said Daniel.

'Right,' said Katherine. 'OK. Look. Now. Right. OK. Now. Katherine. Right. This is. OK. Right. Katherine.'

'Right,' said Daniel. 'OK.'

'What?' said Katherine.

'Well if you just . . .'

'Just what?'

'Just SHUT UP for a second,' said Daniel, who was now in the position of having become genuinely angry about entirely the wrong thing, which meant that, through the thickening haze of his anger, he had to try to keep sight of the thing he wanted to be angry about,

272

because the thing he was now actually angry about was, even he could see, a bit pathetic, whereas the thing he wanted to be angry about was perfectly reasonable, so he needed to back the winning horse, so to speak, rather than make an idiot out of himself by getting all worked up about something extremely childish, because this was, Daniel knew, one of Katherine's most successful techniques: she'd get him angry about something serious, then get him more angry about something frivolous, and then, when he got really angry, say she didn't know why he was getting so angry about something so frivolous, to which he'd reply that he *wasn't* getting angry about the frivolous thing, he was getting angry about the *other* thing, at which point she'd invariably interrupt him, and say it *sounded* like he was getting angry, and he'd try and explain that he wasn't denying that he was getting angry, he was denying that he was getting angry about whatever silly little thing she was accusing him of getting angry about because he was *actually* angry about ... And then she'd say that the timing of his anger seemed to coincide more with the latter, frivolous thing than it did with the former, more serious thing, the actual gravity of which, to be frank, she questioned anyway, given the ease with which it had been sidelined by the frivolous thing, and he'd try and interrupt and accuse her of getting off track, to which she'd say, Oh, you get to decide the track now, do you? And so he'd ...

'Right,' he said.

'Right.'

'You're being really childish,' he said.

'Sorry, *Dad*.'

'Right, that's also a very mature response. *Very mature*, Katherine. I see what you've done there. Ha ha ha. Calling me dad. Oh, that's very clever.'

'Sorry, do you prefer to be called Jake the Peg?'

She was absolutely dripping with smirk, Daniel thought.

'Can you stop smirking, please?' he said.

'Yeah, sure,' she snapped. 'I'll just *control my face for you.*'

Tangent, he thought. Shouldn't have got distracted by the smirk. Schoolboy error.

'Right,' he said. 'Now I don't want to have an argument about this, OK? I just want to say . . .'

'Who's having an argument?'

'No one's having an argument, that's the point. I just wanted to say, and like I said, I don't want this to turn into an argument, but I just wanted to say . . .'

'Every time you say that you make me want to have an argument. It's like, Hey, don't think this thought that I just put in your head.'

'Can you stop interrupting me, please?'

'It's a conversation. It goes back and forth.'

'Well, but it's not going back and forth, is it? Because you keep . . .'

'Maybe you should say "Over and out" when you're done.'

'That's very funny. Again. But if we could try and be serious for *one* second . . .'

'Don't tell me when to be serious and when not to be serious. I'll decide when I'm serious, thank you very much, I don't need you to . . .'

'Right, what you've done there is you've interrupted me again.'

'And you've interrupted me.'

'OK, so let's call it quits on the interrupting.'

She hooted with laughter. '*Yes*, Daniel. We're *quits* on the interrupting.'

'This is a tangent.'

'From what?'

Could something still be called a tangent when the central theme of a conversation had not yet been set? Was it possible for an *entire conversation* to be nothing but tangent from beginning to end, or was that like saying a sandwich was all filling, which of course was impossible, because without the element of bread then all you really had was jam on your hands. Or whatever the filling was. Didn't have to be jam. Could be corned beef, for example. Was it possible Daniel was still stoned? It was, he thought. It was very possible. He would have to proceed with caution.

'From the point,' he said decisively.

'And what's the point?'

'The point is . . .'

'Hold on,' said Katherine. 'Drum roll, please. We're about to be told the point.' She drummed her fingers on the table, and continued to drum them while Daniel talked.

'I might just pop to the loo,' said Nathan. Neither Katherine nor Daniel looked at him. He didn't stand up.

'The point is, you shouldn't have done that with my phone,' said Daniel triumphantly. 'You shouldn't just answer my phone like that.'

'OK,' said Katherine, shrugging. 'Sorry.'

Daniel froze. This was, he had to admit, an inspired rhetorical gambit. Of all the things he'd imagined might be said during the course of what he'd hoped would be more of a dignified and lucid lecture than a rambling and semi-coherent spat, a simple apology had not even registered as a possibility. It was brilliant. In the time they'd been apart, he thought, she'd obviously not only honed some of her more notorious techniques of incessant enragement and gradual, sustained torture, but also developed new and nightmarish abilities in the subtler and more arcane arts of deflation and controlled anticlimax.

'OK,' he said slowly. 'That's good.'

'No problem,' said Katherine.

'Great,' said Daniel. 'I'm glad we could . . .'

'Pleasure,' said Katherine.

But then, in this brief caesura, Daniel realised that all Katherine had really done was make him look irrational. By seeming to apologise so easily, she'd implied that what he was angry about was of no consequence. She could apologise for it, she seemed to be saying, without so much as a backward glance, because it was nothing to her, which meant, by extension, that it should also have been nothing to him, which, given it clearly wasn't nothing to him, implied he was getting all worked up about something no one else cared about, which was another way of saying he was mad, which was another way of saying Katherine wasn't mad, which was, ultimately, just another way of her winning.

'But you do see,' he said, 'why I was angry?'

'Yes,' she said. 'Of course.'

'I mean, you agree it was serious.'

'I recognise that it was serious to you, yes.'

'But do you think it was serious?'

'What, my answering your phone?'

'Yes. Answering my phone. Do you think that was serious?'

'Not really, no.'

'Right,' said Daniel. 'This is what I'm talking about.'

Now Katherine did her innocently baffled face, which she always deployed at the exact moment she knew Daniel would be unable to explain himself in order to force him to fail to explain himself.

'What is?' she said.

'You're not taking this seriously.'

'I've apologised.'

'But it's not a proper apology.'

'What would constitute a proper apology?'

'Really meaning it. If you really meant it.'

'I do really mean it.'

'But do you see what I mean? Do you see why I was so angry?'

276

'I didn't think you were that angry,' said Katherine, playing her trump card. 'You seemed quite calm. You weren't shouting or anything.' She looked at him, fluttering her eyelids. 'Were you really angry?'

'Yes, I was really angry.'

'Really really angry.'

'Yes. Really really angry.'

'Why?'

'Because . . .'

'I mean, I just can't understand why you'd be so angry about . . .'

Daniel felt his brain, which up to this point had just about borne up under what was, he had to admit, a fairly ridiculous level of strain, suddenly and irreversibly implode. A red giant of gaseous rage, he leaned down in front of Katherine, his nose a mere quarter of an inch from hers, and went supernova.

'I'M TELLING YOU HOW I FEEL,' he screamed, his muscles clenched and shaking. 'I'M TELLING YOU HOW I FUCKING *FEEL*. I'M FUCKING *TELLING* YOU HOW I FUCKING *FEEL* AND YOU HAVE TO *LISTEN*.'

He leaned back against the wall, not looking at Katherine, running his hand over his face, which he now realised was drenched in sweat. Weakness replaced the anger. There was a moment when he thought he might not be able to breathe. When he removed his hand from his face, Angelica was in the doorway, beaming.

'Oh baby,' she said, lips a-tremble. 'That was amazing. I'm so proud of you.'

Katherine was staring at him with exaggerated, slow-blinking calm, smiling slightly, affecting, as she always affected in the face of other people's rage, a kind of distanced anthropological interest: gently baffled and calmly superior; taking notes on another person's weakness while simultaneously congratulating herself on her ability to have located it. The aim, of course, was to make Daniel more angry, but he was beyond that now, spent and embarrassed and quivering with the exertion. He looked over at Nathan, who was looking at the table, and then back at Angelica, who was still standing on the other side of the room, as if waiting for a safe moment to approach. Everyone, he thought, everyone he knew and had known, seemed suddenly very far away, and known to him only in the shallowest, most cursory sense. He knew people, and they did not know him back. He looked again at Angelica, and she held his gaze and smiled at him. She looked, he thought, awful. Her hair was matted; her jeans and coat were streaked with mud and cow shit. When he crossed the room and hugged her, he caught the deep scent of damp farmyard and days-old sweat.

'I've missed you,' he said.

'Missed you too,' said Angelica. 'What happened? Are you OK?'

'I am,' he said. 'It's nothing. It's stupid. Forget it. What about you? How are you?'

'I'm OK. I'm glad to be home. I'm sorry.'

She squeezed tighter.

'OK,' said Daniel, breaking her grip and returning, as if after hypnosis, to the room. 'I'll start the shower running and get the kettle on. Go and get out of those clothes and I'll get them straight in the machine.'

Angelica nodded, releasing him with a degree of reluctance, then turned to Katherine and Nathan.

'Hello,' she said, giving a little wave. 'I'm Angelica.'

'Hello,' said Nathan, who Daniel was, if he was honest, a little worried about, both in terms of his possible ongoing fragility and also in terms of the fact that he was almost certainly at this point considering leaving, although why that should have mattered now, Daniel couldn't be sure. In many ways, totally humiliating himself had only made Daniel more determined to be a good host. He wanted the evening to be over; wanted everyone to leave, but baulked at being the cause.

Katherine stood up from her chair and, smiling, crossed the room, wrapped her arm around Angelica's shoulders, and kissed her on the cheek.

'Nice to meet you,' she said.

'So nice to meet you too,' said Angelica, before turning slightly, cocking her head to one side, and fixing Nathan with a motherly smile that struck Daniel as at once horribly obvious and therefore possibly incriminating but also genuine and therefore rather endearing.

'And you must be Nathan,' she said, walking over to peck him on the cheek.

'Hello,' said Nathan.

'I want you to know,' said Angelica, resting her hand on Nathan's shoulder and inadvertently causing Daniel's stomach to freefall in the direction of his rectum as she did so, 'that we're really happy you're here.'

Nathan looked at Daniel, who immediately looked away, only to find he was then looking at Katherine, who looked back at him with disconcerting archness, causing him to look at the floor and briefly wish the old feeling of being locked out of his life would return and grant him half a second's respite from reality, but sadly he had no such luck. Everywhere he looked he felt himself looked at, and every time he was looked at he felt compromised.

And then Nathan smiled and, rather oddly, patted Angelica's hand, and said he was glad to be there, and thank you for having him, and it felt, momentarily, to Daniel, as if something, oddly the very same something he'd tried and failed to shake by becoming so pathetically enraged, had fallen away.

Katherine's first impression of Angelica was that she was pretty and therefore threatening. Her second impression was that she was exhausted and off guard and therefore vulnerable.

After the warm and fuzzy introductions, during which Katherine made a conscious decision to appear as normal and friendly as possible in order to cause unease in Angelica, who would then have to be equally friendly and who would hopefully crack under the pressure, Daniel trotted nervously after Angelica and could be heard cooing and fussing from the bathroom as he turned on the shower and encouraged Angelica to take off her clothes. A minute later he strode back through the dining room without paying Katherine and Nathan any attention and disappeared upstairs.

Katherine arched an eyebrow at Nathan, who had spent the last five minutes looking at the grain of the tabletop.

'Psst,' she hissed.

He looked up. His face, which had been blank, seemed slow to take on his features, giving Katherine a fleeting and eerie sense that she was looking at a developing Polaroid.

'Hey,' he said.

'What do you think?' said Katherine.

'About what?'

'About *her*.'

Nathan shrugged. 'Seems nice,' he said.

'Bit bland, though, isn't she?'

Another shrug.

'You're hopeless,' said Katherine, flopping back in her chair with exaggerated exasperation and lighting a cigarette.

Nathan looked at the table again, hunching slightly. Daniel came back downstairs carrying clean clothes.

'Got you well trained, hasn't she?' said Katherine.

Daniel, who had got a little way past her and was nearly at the bathroom door, turned and walked back to stand in front of her. He put the clothes down on the table and held up his index finger.

'Don't,' he said.

'What?' said Katherine.

'Just don't,' he said. 'You know what I mean.' He turned to Nathan. 'Sorry about all this,' he said. 'Back in a minute.'

'No worries,' said Nathan.

Katherine sucked her beer and took a few minutes to try and catalogue the extent of Daniel's kindness to her over the years in relation to the kindness he was now showing Angelica. Had he ever run a shower for Katherine? Had he ever helped her out of her clothes and appeared with a clean outfit for her? Not as far as she could remember, but then, she'd never come home streaked with shit and looking like she'd been gang-raped by cattle so in some ways it was difficult to tell.

She wondered if that was the point, if it had always been the point. She had too rarely (if ever, if she was honest) given Daniel the opportunity to look after her. She had not come over all hopeless in the face of a simple task. She had not phoned him in panic at unsociable hours. She had not, perhaps, let him know that she needed him. Look at this evening, she thought: she'd steered him rage-wards primarily because she knew she could; because it would confirm a connection, a deeper knowledge.

She hauled on her cigarette. Was this what men wanted, in the end? The damsel in distress? The little girl that needed to be protected? It was loathsome, she thought. Of course Daniel thought he loved Angelica: she never gave him any reason to think otherwise. He was happy because he was never threatened, and it was in keeping with Daniel's grossly limited view of life and love that the only way he could imagine someone loving him was to be confronted at every bloody turn with how much they *needed* him, how much they *couldn't live without him*, without ever giving the slightest credence to the possibility that perhaps the very fact Katherine *hadn't* needed him, or at least hadn't needed him in such an obvious way, was the best possible evidence that she loved him. After all, why else would she stay with him? But no, of course Daniel wouldn't see it that way, because it failed to fit with any of the clichés he mistook for truths. He didn't want to be wanted; he needed to be needed, and the only type of need he understood was the most obvious kind, the kind that flopped into his arms with matted hair and a tear-streaked face and said *I love you. Help me.* Christ.

She looked at Nathan, who had clearly just been looking at her. She thought again about the burden of it all; the responsibility. She thought about Daniel and Angelica, and how pointless her pride in making Daniel angry appeared in the face of Angelica's ability to make him care for her, and how nice it looked, actually, being cared for, knowing you could arrive in a state of distress and someone would help you, hold you, patch you up. And she thought of all the mornings she'd woken up sad. She *was* sad, she thought. It was a sad thing to have to admit, but it was true. She was a sad person; a *lonely* person, and, far from drawing anyone near, she'd pushed everyone further away because she couldn't bear the thought of needing anyone to be nearby, and she was going to get sadder, and lonelier, and then she was going to have an abortion, and there'd be no one to tell, so she'd sit at home for however long she needed to sit at home, on her own, in pain, and no one would run a shower for her, or find her some clean clothes, or put the kettle on, because no one would know they had to, no one would feel they needed to, and that would, she thought, be very sad indeed. It would be the life of a sad person, because she was a sad person and that was the life she'd made. So what if Nathan had baggage? It wasn't like she didn't have baggage of her own, for God's sake. And all that stuff about physical attraction, what did that really amount to in the end? Wasn't that for your twenties? Wasn't that something you were supposed to grow out of? He *cared* for her, for God's sake. Take it, she thought. It was so easy. Take it and be glad.

Except, of course, it was too easy. How, she thought, looking over at Nathan and waiting for him to catch her eye, as he surely would, could anything this easy ever be trusted? How would she ever really *know* how dedicated he was? He would enter her life, she thought, untested, with exactly the kind of ease that, while thrilling in the short term, would calcify into mute distrust just months down the line. No, she thought. You had to make people work, make them fight. You had to *know*, and you wouldn't find anything out by just collapsing into someone's arms.

He looked up, then away. Angelica waltzed through wrapped in a towel.

'Is Daniel upstairs?' she chirruped.

'I think so,' said Nathan.

'I'll be down in a minute,' said Angelica. 'Are you both all right for drinks etcetera?'

'Yes,' said Nathan, 'absolutely fine.'

'Fine, thank you,' said Katherine.

She watched Angelica leave, then turned her attention back to Nathan. She might not have been able to break her patterns, she thought, but at least she knew what they were.

'OK,' she said, almost, but not quite, experiencing a tangible click in her core as some old and profoundly integral part of her mechanism locked into its reliable and well-oiled groove. 'You can speak now.'

Nathan looked blank.

'You were going to tell me something earlier,' said Katherine. 'I've decided now's as good a time as any.'

'Oh,' said Nathan. 'It doesn't matter.'

'Yes it does,' said Katherine. 'What was it?'

'No, really,' said Nathan. 'It's nothing.'

'Really,' said Katherine.

'Yeah.'

'So tell me anyway.'

'Why?'

'I'm interested.'

He leaned back in his chair and sighed.

'We don't have to do this,' he said.

'No,' sighed Katherine, putting her feet back up on the neighbouring chair. 'But let's do it anyway.'

Nathan had watched Katherine and Daniel's display with a sense not only of discomfort, but also of fierce, crashing disappointment, which in turn had magnified the discomfort to the point where he was so uncomfortable he was unable even to stand and leave, and so had merely sat rigidly in his chair, willing it all to be over. He was a lot of things, he thought; he'd been a lot of things over the years and he was the first to admit that not all of those things had been positive, but he was not stupid, and he was not so out of touch with humankind as to be unaware that when Katherine had seemed to begin an argument with him but then very clearly thought better of it, she had done so out of pity, and pity, for all it was worth, could never equate to whatever it was that drove her and Daniel to drive each other insane.

So he'd decided to leave. Not while the argument was happening, of course, but immediately after, before Katherine could leave or anyone could apologise or the argument could march even further into territory from which there was ever less hope of return. He shouldn't have come, he thought. He should have suggested coffee with Katherine, or not called her in the first place, or, even better, not had that stupid conversation with her a year and a half ago which had, and he could admit this now because he felt done with it all, led him into all this in the first place.

But then Angelica had arrived, and although she couldn't possibly have known (despite the fact that Daniel had, very obviously, said something to her), she had in fact said the only thing Nathan had wanted to hear since the day he'd left his treatment and come home: *We're so glad you're here*, and that had made it rather more difficult to leave, and there was something about the fact that he had, in that simplest of everyday moments, *decided* to stay a little longer, that meant he was no longer trapped, and which meant in turn that, as he now found himself at the centre of exactly the attention he'd spent all evening trying to get but which, now that he had it, he was no longer sure he really wanted, the sense of being pinned to his seat left him, and he felt opened up and oddly calm.

'Well,' he said. 'I was . . .' He paused, thinking. 'I was just going to talk about the last time we saw each other, really, and ask you how you felt about that now.'

'Felt about what?' said Katherine.

'About what I said, then. That night.'

'Which bit of what you said, specifically?'

Nathan took a breath, allowing himself a moment to reflect. There was not, now, any need to do this, as he'd said, but there was perhaps some sense in doing it, in seeing it all through and being done.

'Well I can't remember exactly how I put it,' he said, 'but I think the basic message was that I was in love with you.'

Katherine arched an eyebrow. 'Was it now,' she said.

It was, Nathan thought, fairly foolish of him to have thought Katherine would help him in any way, or reveal any of her feelings before he did, or indeed do anything to make this experience anything other than the ordeal she seemed to want it to be.

'Yes,' he said. 'I think that was the gist of it.'

'Funny,' she said. 'That bit was lost on me. All I heard was a load of stuff about you. About how you were lonely. About how you thought I was lonely, and how together we might be less lonely, or something.'

Nathan remembered trying to tell her how he felt, and the grim, dawning realisation that what he felt was indescribable, and the disappointment he'd felt at realising the one person he'd hoped would understand was not going to understand – not because she couldn't, he realised, but because she didn't want to, just as she didn't want to understand now, either.

'I probably didn't express myself very well,' he said.

'You can say that again,' she said.

'I had a lot on my mind,' he said.

She stubbed her cigarette out in the ashtray, holding his gaze.

'Why don't you try again?' she said.

'How do you mean?'

'You know what I mean. Stop asking what I mean. *Christ.*'

Nathan nodded. He looked down at his hands, turning them over, holding them up in front of his face. After the dressings came off, he'd worked hard to help them heal. There were ointments and oils; stretching exercises to make sure his skin still fit his knuckles. After months of pain, there were now patches where he had no sensation at all. He stood up and took off his jacket, then rolled up his shirtsleeves, revealing the vines and creepers of scar tissue and tattoos that crept over his forearms. Katherine did her best not to appear shocked. He sat back down and crossed his legs. He felt a great sense of clarity and calm. He'd come here, he now saw, for all the wrong reasons. He'd wished, for over a year, that Katherine had understood him, and that had been for the wrong reasons too. And now here she was asking to understand, again, for all the wrong reasons.

'After we'd talked,' he said, his hands now folded neatly in his lap, 'I walked out into the woods.'

'This isn't what I asked,' said Katherine.

'Tough,' said Nathan.

D ear God,' said Daniel. He was sitting on the edge of the bed, squeezing his cranium between his palms while Angelica wriggled her way into a pair of jeans. 'Dear holy fucking Jesus fucking God make this evening be over.' He made a grab for the waistband of her jeans and pulled her sharply towards him, then wrapped his arms around her waist and pressed his cheek to her stomach. 'I'm so glad you're back.'

'I'm glad I'm back,' she said, rubbing his hair. 'And I'm glad I came back when I did.' She laughed.

'Sorry about that,' said Daniel. 'I must have looked ridiculous.'

'Nooooo,' she said, ruffling his fringe and settling into the kind of voice a loving owner might use for their ageing English Shepherd. 'You looked very brave. I was proud of you.'

'Hmmm,' he said, enjoying the feeling of her fingers against his scalp.

'That was something you've wanted to say for years,' said Angelica. 'And now you've said it. It's out. It's gone.'

'Silly,' said Daniel.

'Nooooo,' said Angelica.

He hugged her a little tighter. He would, he saw now, always be able to settle back into this: this sense of comfort and ease; of reassurance and reliability. Much as it might have been what he feared – the unbending known-ness of the day-to-day – it was also what he wanted, what he needed. Much as he might have wanted to be someone else, he thought, there was no one else he knew how to be.

'Tell me about you,' he said, releasing her and patting the bed beside him. 'What happened?'

She shook her head. 'To be honest, I just thought, *What's the point?* We made our banners, did a bit of shouting. Sebastian went on the news. He got more and more puffed up. More and more cocky. He started saying we needed to make some kind of statement; do something shocking. I just thought, About what?' She laughed. 'Don't get me wrong, Sebastian's an old friend, but he doesn't give a fuck about cows.'

'Probably not,' Daniel said.

'Anyway, I was glad I left when I did.'

'Why?'

She looked at him. 'Oh of course,' she said. 'You wouldn't have seen the news. They're not letting them leave. The protestors. I've had about ten texts. Some sort of quarantine or something. So now they're stuck there till God knows when.'

'Quarantine for what?'

'It's just a way of containing the demonstration. They'll wait till it's all died down and then send them home.'

'So Sebastian's with them?'

'I don't know. He threw a wobbly and went off on his own.'

'Hm.' He gave her another hug. 'Well I'm glad you're home,' he said.

'Me too,' she said.

He stood up. 'Right. Better face the music.'

She gave his hand a squeeze. 'Don't worry,' she said. 'I'll be right down. It'll be fine.'

Her phone rang. She picked it up off the bed and answered it.

'Hello?' She covered the mouthpiece with one hand and mouthed to Daniel: *Sebastian*. Daniel sat back down on the bed. 'Hello?' Angelica said again. 'Hello, Sebastian? I can't . . . It's hard to . . .'

Daniel gestured at her to hang up, but she held up a finger, making a sorry face as she did so.

'What? No, I don't . . . Well . . . No I don't think . . .' She covered the mouthpiece again. 'He says he's on his way here,' she said. 'He needs help apparently.'

'No,' said Daniel, then, when he saw Angelica's face drop a little with disappointment, 'All right, all right. Whatever.'

Thank you, Angelica mouthed.

Everything, Daniel thought, was going back to the way it had been. Sebastian would come round. He'd be annoying. Perhaps they'd argue. Angelica would keep the peace. He'd feel frustrated and annoyed but not, he thought, anything beyond that. He would be able to handle it. In many ways, he thought, it would be reassuring.

Of course, Nathan said, he was disappointed after they'd talked that night. Not that it was Katherine's fault, but he'd built up a certain vision of the future that was hard to let go. He'd felt, for a short time, like something inside him had opened up, *blossomed*, if you wanted to be clichéd about it, and then suddenly it was like he had to close it all back up again and he didn't know how. People always said that things were better when you talked about them, when you shared them, and although now after his experiences in treatment and everything he could see that that was certainly true sometimes, in the right circumstances, at that particular time it wasn't true at all, and everything was very much worse for having been brought out into the open. He remembered, he said, cutting his finger when he was a kid, and staring at it, watching the blood bead up along the edge of his knuckle, and feeling nothing, and being unbelievably excited by the thought that he didn't feel pain anymore, that perhaps he'd grown out of it, and running to his dad and holding up his finger and telling him it didn't even hurt, and his dad saying it was because the air hadn't got to it yet, and then right as his father said that he could feel the air get to it and his finger started hurting and he started to cry. Well it was just like that, he said. The air got to everything, and he could feel all the areas where he was exposed, as if someone had folded his skin back and he was just bare muscle and nerves.

By this time, he said, he was just standing there, right in the middle of the crowd, and everyone was dancing around him, and he felt overwhelmed, and all this, this *stuff* was roiling away in there, and he didn't know how to put his skin back on, as it were, or his mask, like Katherine had said, and he got it into his head that somehow, somewhere along the line, he'd become the wrong person, a person he'd never intended to be, and it was like he saw himself for the first time, and he looked ridiculous, and he was in pain, and it was all so stupid, and he'd left the crowd and walked off into the woods and sat there a while, spinning out, everything warping and floating, his hands leaving smeared contrails when he moved, the air very thick when he tried to breathe, and all of him straining outwards and trying to expand but held in check by what he'd become.

Anyway, he said, shaking his head. The point was he'd stripped off most of his clothes and taken hold of his camping knife and started hacking away at his tattoos, beginning with his calf, then moving on to his arms and chest, and then even having a go at his neck, and he'd felt very clear and calm, even when he was holding a tatter of his own skin in his hand, and he remembered thinking that it didn't hurt because the air hadn't got to it.

Here, Katherine, who had managed to get through everything up to this point without saying anything, and indeed without even making any especially communicative facial gestures, which just half an hour ago would have unnerved Nathan, but about which he now no longer cared, interjected in a voice she had very obviously run through several pre-speech checks to ensure it was bleached of all inflection.

'Who found you?' she said.

'No one found me,' said Nathan, who didn't see why this was particularly relevant. 'I was out in the woods and no one knew where I'd gone.'

Ultimately, he said, the knife had got pretty bloody, and therefore pretty slippery, and so luckily he'd had to give up on his project, and as soon as he stopped he started to panic, like really freak out, and started to cry and call for help, but then the shame found its way in, and he realised that he didn't want anyone to see him, so he called an ambulance on his phone and walked through the woods to the main road, and when it came he held up his hand like he was hailing a taxi and blacked out, and woke up in the hospital covered in bandages with his mother sitting over him looking like he'd ripped her heart in half.

When Nathan finished, he spread his hands as if to show they were empty. He had imagined this conversation, rehearsed it, more times than he would ever be able to enumerate, but in the end, in reality, it was a sort of negative image of everything he'd pictured. The outline was the same, but all the colours were reversed, and now that he saw the change, he felt all the events between then and now neatly reverse themselves along similar lines. He wasn't in love, he realised. He was angry. He'd phoned Katherine because he was angry with her. He was here because he was angry with her. He'd hurt himself not because he was upset, but because he was angry. He'd told her everything not because he wanted to explain, but because he wanted her to have to know. If she hadn't needled him, he thought, it might have been different. It could have gone on being different for a very long time.

She was looking at him coldly; breathing slowly but determinedly.

'And what the fuck,' she said, 'am I supposed to do with that?'

Nathan shrugged.

'Nothing,' he said. 'You don't need to do anything with it.'

Her upper lip was quivering almost imperceptibly. She seemed at pains to slow her every physiological function – her breathing, her blinking – to near inertia, creating an oddly sympathetic sensation in Nathan: time not so much stopping as becoming impossible to parse.

'Do you want me to *help you*?' she said. 'Is that it?'

'No,' said Nathan.

'Because I can't,' she said. 'And I'm not going to apologise for that. I'm not going to feel guilty.'

'I don't want to be helped,' said Nathan. 'I'm tired of people helping me.'

'Why didn't you just say what I wanted you to say?' she said. 'You knew what I wanted you to say. You said it before. Why couldn't you just say it again? Why did you have to go and give me all this *stuff*? I don't want your fucking *stuff*. I . . . I have *stuff of my own*. Can't you *see* that? I was giving you a *chance*. I was giving you what you wanted.'

'I'm sorry,' said Nathan. 'But I don't think that's true.'

She seemed to draw herself inward and upwards, straightening and steeling herself. She looked at him coldly. 'So you hate me too, is that it?'

'No,' said Nathan. 'That's not it.'

'Liar,' she said.

He sat forward in his seat. He had very definitely had enough. He rolled his sleeves back down and slipped on his jacket.

'That's it,' said Katherine. 'Fuck off. Just like last time.' She shook her head. 'Nothing changes, does it?'

She started to cry. 'Oh fuck,' she said. 'Nathan, I'm sorry. I'm so sorry. I . . . I keep saying these things to people and . . .' She took a long, shuddering breath. 'Please don't go,' she said. 'I don't want you to go. I didn't mean it. I *never* mean it. You of all people know that.'

Nathan picked up his bag, which he'd left under the table.

'Take care,' he said gently. 'Give Daniel my apologies.'

In later months, and even more so in later years, it would be clear to Katherine that she had made a mistake. She thought about it now, slumped in her chair, alone, holding the flame of her cigarette lighter to the burnished edge of Daniel's dining table and watching the wood as it blackened. The regret, she felt, was looming at her as if from some far-off place: distant, but edging in. What she felt now was merely the recognition of what she would feel, one day, when she let herself, at which point it would, of course, be too late. She tried, as she always tried, to recalibrate. She tried to picture Nathan, increasingly paralysed by remorse, calling her up at an ungodly hour and trying to pour his guts out. He'd be back, she told herself. They always came back. She'd tested him; he'd failed. It was disappointing, but at least now she knew.

If only she was more stupid, she thought. If only she was more blind. Then she'd be able to believe all that and be happy. But she wasn't; she couldn't; and she wouldn't be. Clarity was cruel that way. It eased nothing; spared her nothing. If people knew her as well as she knew herself, she thought, as well as she knew others, they would forgive her. But to do so they would have to know her, and that was something she simply couldn't allow, because what they

293

saw, though forgivable, would not be something or someone they could love.

Her lighter became too hot to hold. She let the flame go out and watched a seedling of smoke push its way up from the wood before dwindling. She thought about Daniel's face as he screamed at her. At least she had that, she thought. We all, at some stage of our lives, need someone we can control.

She wasn't quite sure why she was still here, and then she realised it was because she had, over the course of the evening, felt the dark tickle of a growing certainty at the base of her brain, as if it were being licked by the little wisp of smoke that had risen from the edge of the table, that she was not going to see Daniel again after tonight, and once that certainty solidified, she felt unexpectedly unable to leave. She had not, despite all the things she'd said and thought up to this point, wanted to leave in quite this way. Arguably, she had not wanted to leave at all, just as she had not wanted Nathan to leave her.

She was very tired, she now realised. Not just from the strains of the evening but from the strains of her life to date. She took out her phone, wrote *SOS, K*, and sent it, along with Daniel's address, to Keith's number. It was hit and hope.

This time, Daniel took a very different approach to descending the stairs. Where previously he had wanted to convey simmering rage and carefully marshalled argumentative force, he now wanted to communicate a sense of carefree lightness, almost frivolity, as if to make it very clear that he had either completely moved on from the evening's distressing events or, even better, that those events had failed even to register sufficiently to necessitate him now putting them behind him. If he'd put less thought into it he would have near-skipped down the stairs, but he didn't want to overdo it, and so trotted lightly from step to step and emerged into the dining room with what he hoped was a perky energy, only to be confronted by an energy that was very much the antithesis of perky.

'Where's Nathan?' he asked Katherine, who was slouched moodily at one end of the dining table flicking her cigarette lighter on and off. 'And what's burning?'

'Nathan's gone,' she said flatly. 'Nothing's burning.'

'Gone where?' Daniel felt a quick, hot wave of panic as he realised it was all over, followed by what would have been relief had it not been tempered by the niggling sense that he had, in some adult and therefore critical way, failed.

Katherine shrugged. 'Just gone. Had enough. Said to tell you he was sorry, thanks and everything, but he had to go.'

Daniel sat down at the opposite end of the table and pulled Nathan's half-finished beer towards him. 'Well,' he said. 'Shit.'

'Yeah,' said Katherine.

'Maybe I should call him,' said Daniel, patting his pockets for his phone.

'I'd maybe give that a few days,' said Katherine.

'Right,' said Daniel. 'Yes, of course.'

They sat in silence, Daniel continuing the work Nathan had begun on the label of the beer bottle, Katherine continuing to click her lighter on and off. Now that the evening was essentially over, Daniel found he just wanted it to be completely over.

'That'll be Angelica,' he said pointlessly as footsteps sounded on the stairs.

'Really?' said Katherine.

'Oh,' said Angelica, perching herself on Daniel's lap and looking around. 'Where's Nathan?'

'Gone, apparently,' said Daniel.

'That's such a shame.' Angelica sighed, giving the statement an appropriate moment of concern, then deliberately brightened with a show-must-go-on smile. 'Katherine. What can we get you to drink?'

'I'm OK – I'm waiting for a lift,' said Katherine. She mustered what might have passed for a smile, but seemed to give up on it the moment it arose, letting her face drop back in defeat.

'OK,' said Angelica gently. 'Well, I'm going to have another cup of tea. So I'll put the kettle on, and if your friend hasn't arrived then . . .' She made a vague gesture and wandered into the kitchen.

Katherine stared at Daniel.

'What?' he said.

'Nothing,' she said.

'Do, er, do you need any help with that tea, dear?' Daniel called through to the kitchen.

'No, no,' said Angelica.

'Right,' said Daniel.

'You two chat,' said Angelica.

'Yes Daniel,' said Katherine. 'Let's chat.'

The doorbell rang. Daniel was out of his seat before the chime had even faded. Angelica came out from the kitchen.

'That'll be Sebastian,' she said. 'I'll . . .'

'No,' said Daniel, already half-running for the door. 'You make the tea. I'll, er . . . I'll just . . .'

He opened the front door. He had never in his life greeted Sebastian with anything even approaching the relief he felt now. All he had to do, he thought, was set Sebastian going. Lead him through, introduce him to Katherine, ask him about the protest, and he'd be off. Katherine's lift would arrive before Sebastian had even made it through his central ideological precepts.

Opening the door, however, Daniel quickly felt his plan turn to tatters. Sebastian looked wild-eyed and filmed with sweat. He was shifting from foot to foot in a manner that was more than a little unnerving.

'Sebastian,' said Daniel. 'Come in.'

'No time for that,' said Sebastian. 'Come out here.'

'Why?'

'I need to show you something. You're cool, right?'

'Well, ah, I think so but . . . Are you sure you don't want to . . .' He was about to suggest that Sebastian show whatever it was to Angelica, but then he remembered the vertigo-inducing silence and general bad energies of the room behind him.

'Right,' he said. 'Yes, of course. Which way?'

'So,' said Angelica brightly. 'This is funny, isn't it?'

Katherine, who had drifted into the kitchen, eyed Angelica as she made the tea, watching her facility with everything. Her manner, Katherine thought, was irritating. She almost certainly subscribed to the philosophy that being kind to others led to them being kind to you – the exact antithesis of Katherine's philosophy. This is what you turned into if you bought into all that stuff, Katherine thought. All that crap about love and kindness and vegetarianism.

'Hilarious,' said Katherine.

Angelica blinked but didn't respond.

'Daniel's told me a lot about you,' said Angelica.

'Oh?' said Katherine near-automatically. 'He hasn't mentioned you much.'

'No,' said Angelica, apparently unfazed. 'He's not really like that. Do you take sugar? Since your lift hasn't arrived yet I thought I'd do you a tea.'

'Like what?' said Katherine, lighting a cigarette. 'Two please.'

'Forthcoming,' said Angelica with a smile, spooning sugar into Katherine's tea and taking it back through to the dining table. 'Here you go.'

'Thanks,' said Katherine, sitting down opposite her.

'I think it's great you two can get along like this,' said Angelica.

Katherine laughed despite herself. 'Get along like what?'

Angelica smiled. 'Oh, I think you get along,' she said. 'In your own way.'

Katherine wasn't sure what this meant but found it annoying nonetheless. The thought of someone else knowing Daniel, as in knowing him well, was surprisingly upsetting. After all, one of the things they'd clung to through their time together had been the notion that each knew the other better than it would ever be possible for anyone else to know them. She realised that she'd always assumed, after they'd broken up, that Daniel would simply stop existing, not just as far as she or even others were concerned, but as far as *he* was concerned, that he would no longer leave a tangible trace in the world. She thought of those twins, separated at birth, reunited in later life to find themselves with matching jobs and houses and partners. There was an element of that in meeting Angelica, she thought. In knowing the same person, they somehow *were* the same person, and it wasn't a person Katherine wanted to be.

She wondered what, specifically, Daniel saw in this pretty little void, and then wondered if any of the things he saw in Angelica were things he'd also seen in her, Katherine. Because people had types, did they not? Men, in particular, were unimaginative; fixed of border. There had to be similarities.

'So how did you two meet?' said Katherine.

'In a bar,' said Angelica, rolling her eyes. 'Predictable or what?'

Katherine managed a smile. She tried to picture Daniel chatting someone up. When she'd met him she'd had to do everything:

approach him, seduce him, ensure he didn't startle. *I know you want to ask me out for coffee.* She'd felt like Dian Fossey, camped out in the jungle with her hand extended while Daniel roamed the thicket and cast her the occasional cautious glance. Whatever he'd seen in Angelica, it had clearly been something he wanted, unlike whatever it was he'd seen in Katherine. Or had he just evolved? If he had, Katherine thought, then it was surely as a result of being with her. Christ, she'd been the fucking making of him. She'd made something of him and then he'd left her, and he had, quite clearly, ended up better off, too. How was that possible? She used to *pity* him, for Christ's sake. And now look. What did she have? Who did she have? *Keith?*

'I guess it's all worked out, hasn't it?' said Katherine.

Angelica nodded. 'Touch and go for a while, though, wasn't it?'

Katherine smirked. 'When isn't it?'

'Are you always so cynical?' said Angelica.

'No,' said Katherine. 'Sometimes I'm asleep.'

Angelica laughed.

'He must have changed,' said Katherine. 'When I knew him he'd never have chatted anyone up in a bar.'

'Oh,' said Angelica. 'We'd both had a few by then.' She made a queasy face. 'Christmas spirit and all that.'

Katherine felt a kind of distant nausea; a far-off rumbling that spoke of storms to come.

'Oh,' she said, 'so you haven't been together long at all, then?'

'Over a year,' said Angelica. Before she even got to the word *year* her face seemed to falter under the pressure of what she'd said. Her mouth flapped for a moment, her eyes suddenly panicked. 'Oh God,' she said.

Katherine put her mug of tea back down on the table and dropped what was left of her fag into the dregs, where it hissed quickly and was gone. She felt cold; imagined herself in tattered clothes.

'We were still together that Christmas,' she said.

'I know,' said Angelica.

Katherine lit another cigarette.

'You're right,' she said. 'That is very predictable.'

'Katherine,' said Angelica.

Katherine felt as if the person hearing this news was not the person who'd once imagined hearing this news. She wanted very desperately to be angry, because that would obscure the hurt, but it seemed beyond her, edged out by pain. Already, her mind was at work with history, struggling to reshape it. She told herself she'd always suspected. She told herself there had been signs. But she hadn't; there hadn't. Lying, it turned out, had come surprisingly easy to Daniel. Or at least, lying to Katherine had. Perhaps with everyone else he'd been honest. Perhaps he'd saved all his duplicity for her.

'Look at you,' said Katherine, looking at Angelica.

Angelica's eyes were filling up, but nothing was overflowing. 'He would have left you anyway,' she said.

'That's right,' said Katherine. 'He would. He'd have met some other sucker and run off with them. How lucky you must feel that timing was on your side and you got to be that sucker.' She sneered. 'You probably think he loves you. He probably tells you he loves you. He probably tells *himself* he loves you. Because Daniel would never do anything so immoral, right? There'll be a reason. There'll be a way he can still come out of this looking like the patron fucking saint of self-regard.' She hauled deep enough on her cigarette to feel sick. 'I bet you sit up at night,' she said, 'telling yourselves it was *fate*, that the *planets conspired* to bring you together. I bet you've got this whole narrative about how you overcame the odds and the *universe*, through its magnificent fucking beneficence, *smiled on you* and made it all cosmically OK, so now you can spend the rest of your lives just . . .'

She hadn't meant to cry, but now she was crying she felt she might be able to overcome it through the sheer toxic force of what she felt.

'Burn all the fucking joss sticks you like,' she said. 'You'll still stink.'

Angelica leaned back in her seat and looked at Katherine. She sniffed; knuckled the tears out of her eyes.

'Poor you,' she said coldly.

'There you go,' said Katherine, collecting her shoes from the corner and wrestling with the straps. 'That's the real you shining through.'

I liberated it,' said Sebastian proudly.

Daniel ignored him, and took a moment instead to contemplate the 'it' to which Sebastian referred: a cramped horsebox, containing a rather nonplussed cow. Strung from its neck, draping over its back and flank, was a large banner which read, in day-glo pink paint, *What passing bells for these who die as cattle?*

The cow looked dimly at Daniel. Daniel looked back at the cow, then at Sebastian, who was nodding slowly.

'Yeah,' Sebastian said. 'Like, *oh* yeah.'

'Sebastian.'

'I always say, Daniel, as you know, that there's talk, and then there's action, and this is action. This is the ANC. This is Subcommandante Marcos. This is PETA on steroids. This is . . .' He mimed a firework taking off, its rise, apex, slow descent and ultimate explosion. '*Brrrccchhhhhhowwwww*. You know?'

'Sebastian.'

'It's like R. D. Laing throwing open the asylum. It's the doors of perception. It's Timothy Leary turning on in triplicate. It's like, maybe you weren't taking me seriously, you know? But now you are. *Now* you are. Because I've got a *cow*, motherfucker.'

'Sebastian.'

'Evolve and adapt. Change it up. Take it to the next level. Go *bovine* on the bastards.'

'Sebastian.'

'What?'

'Stand still.'

'Yeah.'

'How did you get that cow, and what are you going to do with it, and why have you brought it here? And why for God's sake has it got that ridiculous banner tied round its neck?'

Sebastian nodded, taking a moment to gather his thoughts, then held up the fingers of his left hand and counted off his answers in turn.

'One, I was able to coax it into a horsebox by virtue of the fact that it understood me spiritually and sensed my desire to bring it to safety. Two, I'm going to liberate it. Three, I brought it here because I need a hand. Four, that's our protest slogan. Where's Angelica?'

'Never you mind where Angelica is. You need to take your cow and get out of here.'

'Right,' said Sebastian, nodding seriously and taking a moment to cinch his ponytail a fraction tighter. 'I get it. I get it. You're threatened.'

'I'm not threatened.'

'You're threatened by the fact that you've always . . . no, let me finish . . . you've always looked down on me. Let me finish. You've always looked down on me, and . . . Don't try and deny it, OK? I know. I know how it is. You're all Mr Superior. I've seen you. Looking out your window at us. Having a good old laugh. But now the boot's on the other foot. You look at me and you think, hold on, he's got a *cow*.'

The cow was chewing the cud, blinking gently, apparently unconcerned by her graceless arrival in an urban environment. Sebastian reached up and offered her his fist, which she sniffed, licked briefly, and then ignored.

'Should you be doing that?' said Daniel.

'What?' said Sebastian, wiping his hand on his jumper.

'What if that cow's infected?'

'It's a government conspiracy. Propaganda. There's no infection.'

Daniel took a long breath. 'Sebastian,' he said. 'You need to get that cow out of here.'

At this point, perhaps sensing that the conversation was likely to continue for some time, or perhaps simply wishing to stretch her legs, the cow stepped surprisingly gracefully from the horsebox and ambled out into the road to urinate.

'For fuck's sake,' said Daniel. 'Get that fucking cow out of the street.'

'How?' said Sebastian.

'However you got it in there in the first place,' said Daniel. 'Do that again.'

'Might be a bit of a problem there,' said Sebastian.

'Why?'

'Well, I might have lied a bit about coaxing her in.'

'I thought you had a bond.'

'Oh, we do, but if I'm being really honest it was mainly forged during the drive up here.'

'So how did you get this cow?'

'Found it.'

'You *found it*? Where did you *find it*?'

'Well, I infiltrated the farm, and there she was, so I just hot-wired the car, and . . .'

'Right, whatever. You need to get the cow back in the box.'

'Yeah,' said Sebastian vaguely. 'Natch.'

Daniel stared at him. Sebastian sighed and held out his hand in a limp gesture towards the animal.

'Here Mavis,' he said. 'Here girl.'

'Mavis?'

'After Mavis Staples. Here Mavis. Here girl.'

'Look,' said Daniel, mustering epic levels of patience. 'It's not a trained cow. You can't just say "Come here" and expect it to come here.'

'So what are you proposing, Mr Omniscient Knowledge? That I pick her up and carry her over?'

'You need to flick her gently in order to encourage her back into the box.'

'Flick her? What do you mean, flick her?'

'Tap her on the flank.'

'I don't think I can do that.'

'Why can't you do that?'

'Seems cruel.'

'Whereas leaving a cow in the middle of a suburban street is the height of kindness?'

They were both quiet a moment. Mavis lowed softly, and began to move off up the road.

'I can't be involved in this,' said Daniel. 'I'm going inside. All the best.'

'Hey,' said Sebastian.

Daniel ignored him.

'Oh there he is,' came a familiar and oddly cheerful voice from the doorway. 'Hello cunt.'

'Katherine,' said Daniel. 'Hello.'

'Don't come near me, you cheating piece of shit,' she snarled.

Daniel looked at her face, at her streaked makeup, at the bubble of snot from her nostril. For some time, he had not believed it would have been possible to dislike himself any more than he already did. He now saw he was wrong. It was possible. There were whole continents of self-hatred and shame waiting to be explored.

Fond though she was of confrontation, and better though she always felt after the first sting of anger had been transmogrified into the happy relief of open hostility, Katherine had not, on this particular occasion, been looking for a fight. Instead, perhaps slightly envious of Nathan's exit, which seemed to neatly excuse him from any discomfort or recrimination, she had hoped simply to slip away. She found the fantasy of Daniel living with his guilt far more appealing than the reality of having to dilute it by screaming at him, which would, she thought, only reinforce all those buried, passive-aggressive ideas he had about her and which had, she suspected, basically caused him to cheat on her in the first place, because heaven forfend that Daniel would ever actually try and discuss anything difficult. No, for Daniel, it was always the slinking exit; the barb buried in a platitude. The only thing aggression would achieve now would be for Daniel to be left with a memory of a final outburst – the word he used to describe any moment she became angry, regardless of the reasons or justifications for her anger. For Daniel, she thought as she left the house, head high, hoping in a considerably less head-high way that Keith might be outside, *life* was an outburst. He drifted from here to there, seeking calm, and when he failed to find it, he railed against whatever he thought might have taken it or prevented it.

But now here he was, doing the guilt-face. If there was one thing she hated in a man it was the shrivelling, the soul-coddling, the blub-bery indignation, that seemed to arise whenever they felt they had been misunderstood, and they always felt they'd been misunderstood, it seemed, right after they'd fucked someone behind your back.

'Katherine,' Daniel said.

'Don't speak to me,' she said. 'Don't speak to me ever again.'

'I . . . I'm so sorry, Katherine. I never meant . . .'

She wanted to push past him and keep walking. She wanted to be very far from him indeed. She didn't want to have to look at him or feel him looking at her. It was only as she began to muscle past, however, that she became properly aware of the fact that a lone cow was standing in the middle of the road, eyeing her oddly, while what looked like a mad hippy gestured awkwardly at its back end.

'Just tap it on the flank, you say?' said the hippy.

'Fuck off, Sebastian,' said Daniel, trying to reach for Katherine's arm. 'Katherine, I . . .'

'I think she's feeling kind of un-chill about this,' called Sebastian. 'I mean, she's kind of giving me evils.'

As Katherine hesitated, feeling suddenly vulnerable in the face of such a large and uncannily out-of-place animal, a car came round the corner, turning into the street. She winced in the undipped head-lights, bringing her hand briefly to her eyes and trying to blink away the spangled swatch of reds that now stained her vision.

'Shit,' Daniel said. 'Sebastian. Get that cow out of the road.'

Springing into action, the man apparently named Sebastian skipped forward and thwacked the cow across the buttocks with the palm of his hand, causing it to leap surprisingly far into the air, yelp in a distinctly unbovine manner and charge directly towards Katherine.

The whole life-flashing-before-your-eyes thing turned out to be a load of crap. A life certainly appeared in the foreground of Katherine's mind, but it was not her own, and it was not a life that yet had any recognisable past. The only thing she thought of that even indirectly involved her was, as she had imagined so many times, her own funeral, her hysterical mother hurling herself on the coffin and then seeking solace in the arms of a swarthy mourner. Other than that, everything that glittered in Katherine's adrenalised brain was something that hadn't yet happened, concerning someone who didn't yet exist.

As the cow drew near, Katherine swallowed a great lungful of air and began charging towards it, screaming at the top of her lungs. She saw the cow's eyes widen in alarm, saw it halt, skid slightly, then turn on a sixpence and, blinded by panic, barrel headlong into the approaching car, which swerved just enough to take the impact to the driver's side. The door crumpled; the window shattered. The cow lost its footing on the asphalt, sprawled, recovered, turned again, and thundered past Daniel and Katherine up the road, its hooves ringing out on the quiet street, an absurd banner a-flap in its wake.

'Katherine,' said Daniel again, valiantly dashing forward and pulling her aside now that there was absolutely no danger whatsoever. She ignored him. She felt shot through with delirium and awe.

From inside the by now horribly familiar car a cry went up, followed by the sound of someone kicking against the hopelessly warped door for all they were worth.

'*Babes*,' came the well-known wail. 'I'm coming, Katherine. Don't worry. If I could just . . . I'm going to . . . Somebody help me. This is an emergency. We've got a . . . She's carrying my baby. This is . . . I'm going to get out the passenger side, actually, because it's . . . I'm coming, baby.'

The passenger door flew open, and a crumpled, wild-eyed Keith emerged, wearing saggy jogging bottoms and a T-shirt that read *I Am the #1 Source of Greenhouse Gases*.

'Oh,' said Katherine. 'For fuck's . . .'

'I'm here, baby,' he said breathlessly, limping forward. 'Everybody out of my way.'

He surged forward a heroic six inches, then, putting his hand to his chest, sat on the bonnet of his car to catch his breath, his other hand raised as if signalling to the onlookers that he'd be with them in just a moment.

'That'll be my ride,' said Katherine.

'Baby?' said Daniel. 'What baby?'

The night air was damp and cold. It edged its way in through Nathan's clothes and laid itself against his skin. His scars ached. His stomach heaved with hunger. The streets already had a morning-after feel, the abandoned kebabs and puddles of beery vomit beginning to congeal; a hard frost across car windows.

He would not, he thought, be seeing Daniel or Katherine for a very long time, if ever. If he did see them, it would be years hence, and would be more out of mutual curiosity than any real sense of goodwill. He would not call them. They would not call him. It was a comforting thought.

He found an all-night café on the edge of the city centre. It was quiet and warm. The walls were a soft yellow. The chairs were comfortable. The tables had everything a customer might need. He ordered a cup of tea and some chips. He was, he realised, starving, and in no particular rush to be anywhere at all. When he had finished, he paid and left, feeling awake and calm and happily lost. It was good to be lost, he thought. He had nothing, really, that might be endangered by staying lost a little longer.

His mobile vibrated with a text. It was from Daniel. *Sorry about tonight. Just checking you're OK.*

Don't worry, he texted back. *I'm fine.* Then he dropped his phone into a bin.

It was not yet light. The streets were empty, and they were his to walk.

'Well,' said Daniel.

Katherine nodded. They were sitting in the front room, on separate sofas. Daniel had ushered her there after the business with the cow, and in her momentarily dazed state Katherine hadn't thought to refuse. Angelica had made the excuse of going to feed the cat.

'Is there any value at all in saying I'm sorry?' said Daniel.

'Depends if you're sorry.'

'I am. Of course I am.'

Katherine thought about it for a moment, weighing the statement as if it were an unusually shaped stone she'd found on the beach, deciding whether to keep it or toss it back to the waves.

'No,' she said finally. 'There's no value in it.'

'Why did you make me say it then?'

'I was just wondering if you would.'

'If you could make me, you mean.'

'Did I make you?'

'No. I really am sorry.'

'Well whoop de doo.'

'Still,' said Daniel.

'Yeah,' she said. 'Still.'

They looked ahead of them for an indeterminate amount of time. Sitting perpendicular to each other as they were, it was possible to imagine a point in space at which their gazes might intersect.

'Maybe one day,' said Daniel. 'We can . . .'

'Yeah,' said Katherine. 'We could be friends, couldn't we? Because, you know, we get along so well.'

'Point taken.' He paused, his mouth still open with a word stuck somewhere inside.

'Go ahead,' she said. 'Ask the obvious.'

'What are you going to do about the baby?'

'I think I'll keep it,' she said. 'Why not.'

Daniel nodded, then cocked his head towards the window, through which Keith could be seen, engaged in a titanic battle to straighten his car door with his knee. 'He, ah, he seems like a decent chap.'

Katherine snorted. 'Please,' she said. 'I'll just tell the kid I reintroduced Daddy to the wild.'

She followed Daniel's gaze, taking a minute to study Keith's straining form with dispassion. She thought of the baby, hoping that, just this once if never again, nurture would win out over nature, despite the fact that there was, patently, a hell of a lot of nature for nurture to overcome.

'Well, anyway,' she said, standing up.

Daniel stood up. She looked at him. He sat back down.

'Take care of yourself,' he said as she reached the door.

'Don't I always?' she said, stepping out into the street.

Acknowledgements

First, and most important, love and thanks to my family – Sue, Richard, Mollie, Graham and everyone else – for offering every possible type of support in every possible type of emotional, professional and financial circumstance.

Tom Rowson provided inspiration, blunt criticism, unwavering positivity, healthy cynicism, a roof over my head, and the very best of friendships.

Kevin Cuffe brought highbrow chat to lowbrow bars; Dawn Marrow set me on the right road; Giles Foden found a shape amidst the mess; Anjali Joseph believed before anyone else; Philip Langeskov offered spiritual first aid; Mark Richards, Peter Straus and Mitzi Angel took a gamble and guided me through; Phil Craggs and Blank Pages indulged my InDesign obsession; Siddharth Dhanvant Shanghvi braved the early pages and sent the email to beat all emails; everyone at *Granta* gave me the happiest and least terrifying first publishing experience possible; Jonathan Gibbs made me say hello; my work colleagues put up with my ways; Jeanette West helped me find the time; Owen Carroll and John Everson entertained, embraced, and lent me a bag for life; and Lola Byers mainly just kept an eye.

A NOTE ABOUT THE AUTHOR

Sam Byers is a graduate of the M.A. program in creative writing at the University of East Anglia. His fiction has appeared in *Granta* and *Tank*, and he regularly reviews books for the *Times Literary Supplement*. He was born in 1979, and *Idiopathy* is his first novel.

Printed in the USA
CPSIA information can be obtained
at www.ICGtesting.com
LVHW090803150724
785511LV00004B/359